INFAMOUS

A KINGS OF CAPITAL NOVEL

IVY WILD

Cover Design: Betty Lankovits
Photographer: @reelmaxphotos
Cover Model: Francis Barbery

For dream chasers

All that glitters is not gold;
Often have you heard that told:
Many a man his life hath sold
But my outside to behold:
Gilded tombs do worms enfold.
Had you been as wise as bold,
Young in limbs, in judgment old,
Your answer had not been inscroll'd:
Fare you well; your suit is cold.

— WILLIAM SHAKESPEARE

Theme Song

Tennessee by Kiiara

ONE

Sophie Strong

"I THINK IT'S REALLY IMPORTANT THAT YOU DO THIS, SOPHIE," THE guidance counselor said in a sugary sweet voice that made me feel slightly nauseous. "I know things didn't go completely as anticipated for you, but perhaps this will give you something you can be proud of."

"That's the understatement of the century," I muttered, as I twirled a piece of my bleached blonde hair around my finger and fixed my clear green eyes on the woman in front of me. I'd been around people like this for the past five years. Everyone tried to claim that they were there to help me but really, they were just there to claim a piece of my fame. And ultimately that had been my downfall.

It was no surprise to those closest to me that I'd been "discovered." A lot of people had expected it to happen sooner than it did. But the right person had finally seen my strong singing voice and previously upbeat attitude during my senior year of college.

My rise to fame had been swift—and so had my fall. I shook my head slightly, berating myself for falling back into the trap of reliving everything that had happened to me in the past year. I very much wanted to keep that behind me.

But it was my past that led me back to this office. At twenty-seven years old, I was a washed-up pop star with one semester of college left to obtain my degree. How fabulous.

"Well, I believe in you," the counselor said, trying to regain my attention.

I rolled my eyes at the rather plain-looking woman. Her somewhat messy brown hair and equally brown dress annoyed me. I didn't believe what she said for a second. I wasn't worth believing in, anymore. "Great," I said in a bored tone. "Let's just get this over with. How do I get signed up for classes?"

The counselor's face brightened and I internally groaned at my current situation.

Two hours later and I left the stifling little office with a complete schedule of classes and an accompanying headache. I squinted my eyes against the setting winter sun, before pulling my coat up and around my shoulders. I shivered at the crisp air, feeling slightly annoyed that I was back in Washington D.C. after living in Los Angeles weather for the past five years.

I pulled out my phone to check the time and sighed. It was only the early afternoon and I had absolutely nothing planned for the rest of the day. Having unstructured time was a huge change and I didn't know quite what to do with it.

I looked out across the campus square and my eyes landed on a tall figure. He was just as I remembered him, only with a good deal more muscle and a more mature look. His black hair ruffled in the wind slightly as he spoke with the person in front of him. I blushed when his blue eyes locked with my own. I had been caught staring. Besides, I hadn't spoken to him since I'd left school. My heart beat fast in my chest and I turned around, quickly walking in the opposite direction with absolutely no plan.

I just wanted to avoid him.

I couldn't face him right now.

"So I JUST WASN'T POSITIVE that I was thinking about the problem in the right context. Did you have any thoughts, professor?"

A flash of blonde hair caught my eye, momentarily distracting me from the conversation I was having with a student.

"Yes, that sounds like a good idea," I responded absently, not paying attention to what the girl in front of me was saying.

"Huh?" she huffed in a bit of annoyance.

"Please excuse me," I said, dismissing myself from the conversation when I saw a ghost from my past begin walking away at a fast clip.

"But, professor!" the younger woman called out to me as I left her standing there by herself.

I began to pick up my pace as my intended target turned a corner and disappeared from view. It had been several years since I'd seen Sophie but even still, I thought for sure that it had been her. Even after all these years, I'd like to think that I'd recognize her anywhere.

Sophie and I had been close before she left for the west coast. And her departure had been so sudden we hadn't even had the opportunity to say our proper farewells. Not that I'd ever be able to properly say goodbye to Sophie. Attempts to call her had gone unanswered until finally, her number had been disconnected. I had tried to avoid reading about her on the pop culture columns, but for those years, her face was on almost every magazine and her voice was on almost every radio station. Avoiding the hurt had been near impossible.

But all of that fell by the wayside when I caught a glimpse of her from across the square and I gave chase without a second thought.

SHIT. Connor was following me despite my best efforts to lose him. I was desperate not to talk to him right now and I just needed to get away. I turned to enter a random building to my right and walked through the empty corridor, my boots clicking against the tile. I heard the door to the building open further back down the hall and I ducked into a room to my right, hoping there was an additional exit.

Bright lights caused me to blink as I looked around at what appeared to be a nurse's office. "Just be sure to get some good rest this weekend," a kind voice said from the corner of the room. "I'll be with you in just a minute," it called out to me and all I could do was nod my response.

Looking around the room I realized that there was no second exit. The irony of my life continued.

A few cots were set up with curtains that could be drawn around them and I walked towards one to try and shield myself from view. But before I had the opportunity to pull the material around me, a younger male approached me.

"Oh my gosh, you're Sophie Strong, aren't you?" he exclaimed. He was young-looking, likely no older than nineteen and his dirty brown hair was a mess atop his head.

"I don't really—" I began to respond, but he cut me off.

"Oh man, so did you really do what everyone says you did?" he asked, his voice beginning to get whiny and I sighed at the inevitable question.

Before I had a chance to respond, a deep voice echoed in the room. "Are you done with your visit to the nurse?" It was Connor and he was directing his question to the younger man.

"Well yeah, but—"

"Then I suggest you respect the privacy of others and leave this woman alone," he said with a bit of an edge to his voice. It had been the first time in five years that I had heard that deep baritone of his and it gave me the shivers.

The younger man rolled his eyes. "Fine," he said, as he stormed out of the office.

Connor turned to give me a brief smile before directing his attention to the nurse. "Do you think we could have a moment alone?"

The woman in the white coat stood and grabbed her computer, switching off her desk light in the process. "As long as you don't need anything else from me, I was actually about to head home for the day." She looked at me and I shook my head. "Great! Just lock up for me when you leave, Connor," she called out to him, as she exited with a wave.

Connor nodded his head in agreement before turning back to direct his attention to me. I looked at the man with whom I'd had been so close for so many years and my heart ached for him. More than anything during my years away, I'd missed Connor. I'd never been able to get over how things had ended between us, no matter how hard I tried.

His look had changed but he also looked very much the same. He'd always been fit, having run track all through college as a sprinter and his body filled out the dark blue suit he was wearing perfectly. The white button-up contrasted with his almost black hair as his ice-blue eyes fixated on me.

"I guess you—" I began to say but I suddenly found myself unable to speak as Connor closed the gap between us and pressed his lips against mine suddenly.

A strong arm wrapped around my body to pull me in closer. As I felt the heat from Connor, my own strength all but gave. It was the first time in our entire history that he'd kissed me and I melted into the feeling of him. I gasped as I felt myself being lowered before I realized he was pressing me down against the makeshift hospital bed.

His arms caged me as he pulled back, his blue eyes looking into mine. One hand cupped my face delicately. "I've missed you," he said, his voice dripping with need.

"I—" I hesitated. I didn't know exactly what to say in this situation.

The Connor I had left years earlier had been my best friend, yes, but he had been a bit shy and unsure of himself. This entire situation really knocked me off my feet.

His hand moved down to rest against my hip and I suddenly felt like my coat was suffocating me. I gasped as his strong fingers brushed against me, almost as if he was testing my limits. I looked up at him uncertainly and suddenly the warmth that had felt so good was gone. He sat up abruptly and ran a hand through his black locks.

It took a moment for me to realize what had happened and I cleared my throat before asking, "Is everything okay?"

"Fine," he said in a rather flat tone. I sat up and brushed my hair back, feeling extremely confused by the entire situation. "What are you doing back here?" Connor asked, his voice still emotionless.

"I, um," I started, trying to make my brain turn back on. "Finishing my degree," I managed to respond. We sat in silence, neither of us saying anything to the other before finally, I decided to break the awkward space. "What are you still doing here?"

"I'm a professor," Connor responded.

"What? Really?" I exclaimed, momentarily forgetting the rift that had formed between us. Connor hadn't been particularly known for his academic prowess while we were in school together. He was a dedicated student, but never the top of the class.

"Well, adjunct professor. I run my own business now, but I teach a seminar course as a favor over at the business school," he explained.

"Oh," I replied, not knowing what to say. It was so obvious that I didn't know anything about the man that had once been my closest friend, and that pained me. It also seemed like in the years we had been apart, he had really made something of himself, whereas I was still back where I had started.

"I'm sorry for—" I began to say, but he cut me off.

"Don't," he replied a bit sharply. My eyes followed his form as he stood and adjusted his tie. "I've got a meeting to catch. I guess I'll see you around, Sophie," he said, without turning back to look at me.

"Yeah," I mumbled, still in a bit of shock. Before I had the chance to say anything more, Connor was closing the door to the nurse's office behind him on his way out.

I touched my fingers to my lips, which were still tingling from our earlier kiss. I sighed, not knowing how to make sense of what had just happened. Had something like this occurred even just a year ago I would have cried, but those reserves were all dried up now.

Shoving the lid back down on my emotions, I stood up and exited the space, hoping I could leave everything that had happened there behind.

TWO

"Fuck!" I cursed as I slammed the door to my office. The entire afternoon played out in my mind over and over again on my drive there and I regretted everything. The way I had lost control over my emotions when I finally saw her to the way I realized I'd gotten too close too quickly and pulled back suddenly. I was furious at myself.

I took a heavy seat at my desk and placed my head in my hands as I sighed. Here I was, thinking I'd gotten over Sophie but within one minute of seeing her, I was chasing her skirt like a teenage boy.

My phone buzzed from somewhere next to me and I growled as I grabbed it and looked at the screen.

"Hey," I said in a flat tone.

"Well, that's no way to speak to your girlfriend, is it?" the voice on the other end responded with attitude. I rolled my eyes. Aubrey and I had been on a few dates and the woman seemed so caught up with labels. I'd made it clear to her that our arrangement was just casual, but she seemed intent on making it more serious. But now, with Sophie potentially back in the picture, I knew I needed to be firmer.

"I've just got a lot on my mind." I said, trying to hold back my frustration.

"Just wanted to make sure we were still on for dinner this evening?" Aubrey asked hopefully.

I grit my teeth. "I never agreed to dinner tonight."

"Yes, you did," she replied instantly, giving me no leeway.

"I've got a few things to handle here at the office," I started to say but she cut me off.

"That's fine! I'll meet you there! Be ready around six-thirty! Bye!" The phone clicked, leaving me slightly shell shocked on the other end. I really should have expected this behavior by now; it's not as if this was any new pattern.

I had met Aubrey at the beginning of the Fall semester. She was a graduate student in her last year and she'd signed up for one of my classes. She'd ended up dropping the class due to a scheduling conflict with a prerequisite but she had kept in touch via the occasional email. She'd been the one to propose dinner and I'd accepted, perhaps too quickly. I thought back on what made me think it was a good idea and sighed. Her hair had been dyed red at the time and it had reminded me of Sophie's.

I played with the phone in my hand out of nervous habit. My contact list pulled up and I scrolled up and down through the names absent-mindedly. My thumb hovered over the name "Soph." I sighed. For almost a year after she'd left, I'd pressed her name every few days in the hopes that she might answer, only to be told the number had been disconnected.

I smiled, realizing it had been quite some time since I'd even thought about Sophie. I really had thought I was over her. My thumb pressed down and I put the phone to my ear, ready to hear the disconnection tri-tone I knew so well.

"Hello?" a woman's voice answered on the other end.

I stood immediately, my eyes wide at the sound of the voice. "Sophie?" I asked in disbelief.

"Who is this?" her voice replied, a bit defensively.

I deflated a bit, realizing that she hadn't kept my number. "It's Connor," I admitted, beginning to pace back and forth in my office.

"Oh," she responded, a bit of surprise coating her voice. There was a drawn-out pause before she finally added. "Sorry. I got a new phone."

I didn't have the full story behind what had happened to Sophie. I knew as much as the rest of the world did, but that didn't mean I knew anything at all. And I could tell from her voice there was more there.

"So, why are you calling?" she asked. I picked up a bit of hesitation in her voice, which wasn't like the Sophie I had known. She had always been headstrong and confident, almost to a fault.

I stopped my pacing as I looked out at the view over the city from my office. "I guess I was wondering if you needed help getting settled in," I said quickly, trying to recover the botched dial.

There was a pause on the other end of the line before she responded. "I guess so," she said finally.

"You guess you need help or you guess you're settled in?" I tried to clarify, my worry for my previous best friend increasing as I realized she was not acting like herself.

I heard her sigh on the other end. "I guess I need help," she admitted.

Truthfully, I hadn't expected her to say that and once again, I found myself searching for how to respond. "Did you," I hesitated, not sure how far I should go. "Did you want me to come over?" I asked, almost wincing.

Another sigh and a murmur on the other end was all I got back.

"What?" I asked, honestly unable to hear her response.

"I said yes, Connor! Jeez!"

My eyes widened; this was the Sophie I knew. "Well, that's what happens when you mumble," I retorted, the two of us falling back into a familiar routine.

"I NEED YOUR HELP CONNOR DRISCOLL. Loud enough for you?" she said with agitation.

"Plenty," I said, having had to pull the phone away from my ear in the process. "Just a little heavy on the sass."

There was silence on the line before we both started to laugh. Another silence followed when we had calmed down and I decided to break it with a bit of honesty. "I miss your red hair."

"Yeah, well," Sophie huffed. "A lot of stuff has changed."

"Clearly," I scoffed and I just knew Sophie was giving me the middle finger through the phone. "I can sense that, you know," I said.

"You've got a middle-finger sixth sense?" Sophie mocked in a joking tone.

"Connor! Baby!" The door to my office burst open and I whipped around to find Aubrey walking through my door. I pointed at my phone and made a gesture to try and tell her to keep her voice low. Aubrey scrunched her face and pounded her foot a bit. "You promised you'd be ready!" she pouted at equal volume.

"Um, sounds like you've got to go," Sophie said, slipping back into her previous, more-timid voice.

Of course, I was the victim of shit timing. "I'll call you back later?" I said, the line halfway between a question and a statement.

"I guess," Sophie replied before hanging up the phone.

"Hey, are you there?" I asked, hearing the beep but not wanting to believe she had just hung up the phone on me. I pulled the phone down from my ear to see that the call had indeed ended.

"Great!" Aubrey exclaimed, wrapping her arm around me. "Now that that's done, we can go get dinner," she said, starting to tug me towards the door.

"Bee, please," I began in a stern voice. "I've asked you before—" but she cut me off.

"Can you not ruin the dinner, please," she said, her face turning sour as she shifted the blame onto me like she always did.

I sighed. There was no use fighting with her and this arrangement wasn't going to last; I'd known that for a while now. I disentangled myself from her grasp and gestured to the chair in front of my desk. "Have a seat," I instructed, but Aubrey just narrowed her eyes at me.

"Why? We have dinner reservations."

"We're not going to dinner," I replied calmly, walking around to the other side of my desk where I took a seat.

"You said you would be done with work by now," Aubrey snipped at me.

I kept my features cool but stern. "I never actually said that. But even still, this isn't about work. Please have a seat."

"Whatever you want to say to me you can say to me now. I don't have to follow your rules," Aubrey all but sneered.

"Bee," I began, but she cut me off, again.

"Don't call me that!"

This time I couldn't help the groan that escaped my lips. "Fine. Aubrey, I'm not interested in continuing this relationship."

"Who is she?" Aubrey immediately responded.

"What?" I replied as I furrowed my brow.

Aubrey put her hand on her hip dramatically. "Oh come on, don't play dumb with me. Our relationship has been perfect and then all of the sudden you want to break up? Clearly, there's another woman in the picture. And I want to know who."

I pinched the bridge of my nose. "Okay, our relationship, if that's what you want to call a few dates, hasn't been perfect and there's no other woman."

Aubrey gave me a smug look before flipping her now light auburn hair over her shoulder. "Okay, fine. I'll find out myself," she spat as she turned on her heel and left the office, all but slamming the door behind her.

I winced as the glass shook and sent up a silent prayer that none of my employees were present to see that clusterfuck of a situation. I knew Aubrey meant what she said—she would try and find out if there was another woman.

I thought about Sophie and sighed. I really didn't want to bring her into all of this and my decision to split with Aubrey yes, may have been accelerated by her reappearance, but it was by no means the cause. I leaned back in my chair and covered my eyes. Today couldn't have been any more fucked up.

I reached back out for my phone and clicked the screen back on. Did

I dare redial her so quickly? She said she needed help. Logically it made sense since I didn't know where she lived. I let out an audible growl. It had been so long since I felt this level of frustration about a woman; I thought I was past this sort of thing.

"Damn it," I said as I touched her name to redial her number.

"Hello?" her voice sounded a little agitated on the other side of the line.

"It's me," I responded.

"And?"

"And nothing. I don't know where you live," I snapped back.

"Don't be a creep," she said, clearly trying to push my buttons.

"I'm not being a creep, Sophie! I told you I would help you get settled."

"Oh. Right." Her voice sounded a bit sheepish on the other side. "I'm at the loft again."

"Just like old times, I guess."

"I guess," she responded in a smaller voice.

Silence passed between us on the phone before a thought popped into my head. "Hungry?"

"A little," she admitted.

"Meet me at the Friendly Pancake?" I could almost hear her smile on the other side of the line.

"Yeah," she finally responded. "Be there in fifteen." She hung up the phone again before I had a chance to respond. I'd have to talk to her about that habit she'd picked up while she was gone. Grabbing my coat off the back of my chair, I switched the light off to my office and headed towards the elevator.

THREE

Sophie

I LOOKED AROUND AT WHAT USED TO BE MY FAVORITE RESTAURANT AND couldn't help but smile. It was still the same old run down pancake house it had been when I'd left, staffed by extremely eccentric college students and I absolutely loved it. I was glad that at least one thing in my life had remained a constant over all these years.

I'd purposefully gotten here a bit early, wanting to beat Connor to the place. I asked for my favorite booth in the back and the hostess just smiled and said "Right on," before letting me walk there myself. I looked left and right at all of the worn photos of people smiling over massive stacks of pancakes. I slid myself into the booth all the way in the back and touched my finger to the frame that hung on the booth's wall.

It was an old photo of me and Connor, several years younger, sharing a massive plate of pancakes. Connor looked so carefree back then. He wore his hair different than the power fade he had now and his arm was swung around the back of the booth, hugging a younger and happier looking version of me gently. I sighed, I wasn't sure I ever remembered being as happy as I looked there.

"I see some things haven't changed," a deep voice said, startling me out of my reverie.

I looked away from the younger Connor to see the older and more polished version before me. I had to admit, he did look pretty sexy in his dark blue suit and his hair looked way better styled than it did a mess.

"Yeah, I guess it wasn't in the budget for this place to remodel," I responded sarcastically.

Connor chuckled and slid into the booth across from me. "No, I meant you sitting at your favorite booth."

"*Our* favorite booth," I corrected, pointing to the picture. "After all these years, it's still here."

I watched Connor's expression sadden as he looked at the photo and I hated thinking I had something to do with it. "You're different than you were back then," I said, twirling a piece of my damaged hair around my finger.

Connor looked back at me. "Some things change people, Sophie. You're far from your old self."

We stayed quiet for a minute before a small smile cracked my lips. "At least we can count on the Friendly Pancake to not practice self-growth."

Connor chuckled. "I suppose that's true."

The waitress came over at that point to take our orders.

"I'll have the egg white omelet with a side of fruit instead of pota-toes," he said to the waitress. She scribbled his order down on a Lisa Frank notepad that she must have had since the nineties. I made a face at him as he ordered and Connor looked at me. "What's that for?"

"I don't even know you," I said, my nose still scrunched up.

Connor just rolled his eyes. "I'm not some college kid anymore, Sophie. I can't just go around eating stacks of pancakes like we used to."

This time it was my turn to look exasperated. "I'll have the blueberry pancakes *and* the chocolate chip pancakes." I paused and looked at him, "Just so I can test someone's willpower."

"Cool," was the waitress' response before walking off. I watched her walk away, totally mesmerized by her bright silver hair and pale complexion before turning back to Connor.

I shook my head. "An egg white omelet."

Connor chuckled. We were quickly falling back into our teasing routine with one another and in some ways, I was glad for it. I was glad that we weren't so far gone, even if I knew there was little chance at getting back to where we'd started.

"So, tell me all about you. Seems like you've been busy," I said as I leaned back with my arms crossed.

Connor furrowed his brow. "Between the two of us, I'd say that you've got more to share."

"Yeah, well, I'm not up for sharing right now, so you go."

Connor raised an eyebrow. "That hardly seems fair."

"Fine, I guess we'll just sit here awkwardly then," I replied, turning my head so that I wasn't looking at him. I tried to keep a straight face but couldn't and we started laughing.

"You win, as always," Connor said with a wink as I turned to look at him, a satisfied smile on my face. "Not much to say that you don't know. I own my own company and teach a seminar once a semester at the business school now. More as a favor for one of our professors than anything else."

The food came quickly and I smiled at the waitress as she set the plates down. I went on automatic, pouring a river of syrup over my pancakes before diving in. It'd been so long since I'd been allowed to eat what I wanted. "What sort of business? Which professor?" I asked with my mouth full.

Connor shook his head. "Sophie, slow down before you choke," he said as he watched me push the fluffy cakes into my mouth.

I suddenly became extremely self-conscious of myself and my eating. I swallowed my food before saying, "Don't do that."

"Do what?" We had always teased one another about our eating habits and I knew Connor was just falling into our old routine, but still.

"Just, my eating and stuff. Don't."

Connor looked at me and reached his hand over the table and I withdrew slightly. The next moments happened in slow motion as I watched him grab my fork and shove a bite of pancakes into his own mouth. I looked at him with wide eyes before I started to smile.

"I was just trying to distract you so I could steal your food, that's all," he said, finishing my bite.

I shook my head, my damaged hair moving from side to side. I looked down and whispered, "dumbass," with a smile.

"It's a development company. We specialize in renovating older buildings throughout the city with green technology. We also do some ground-up construction," Connor said, clearly trying to distract me from what had just happened.

It worked and I started eating again, but slower this time. I nodded my head. "That's cool. If weird."

Connor chuckled. "What's weird about it?"

"Just never saw you as the real estate mogul," I teased.

Connor just rolled his eyes. "Yeah, well things change."

"Clearly," I said.

"So what about you?" Connor ventured to ask.

"Which professor?" I replied, sidestepping.

"What?"

"Which professor? What was the favor?" I repeated.

"Remember Professor Philips?" I shook my head. "Well, he and I connected my senior year."

"Well, that's cool I guess." My tone was sad as I thought about Connor going through the last semester of college alone.

Connor nodded and was clearly about to open his mouth to try and get information from me about my life, but I stopped him. "I'm not ready to talk about it, okay?" I said with a bit of my old attitude.

Connor put up his hands. "I get it. Whenever you're ready, I'm here."

He pushed his plate aside, leaving a bit of leftovers and I did the same, leaving significantly more uneaten. The waitress stopped over and insisted she pack up the pancakes to go and we relented. Within a few minutes, she returned with the to-go box, complete with a sketch of a unicorn on the lid. Connor picked up the bill despite my protestations and we walked out of our old hangout.

As we took a few steps outside into the cold night air, I thought it was sad that the waitress never noticed we were the same couple in the picture. In just a few years, we'd become almost entirely different people.

"So, you're back at the loft?" Connor asked as we started making our way down the street.

I nodded my head. "Yeah, it was just the easiest thing to do, ya know?"

"I didn't realize you still owned it." My mom had owned the loft and I'd lived there all during college. While Connor had his own place, he barely stayed there given how much he slept over at my place. When I left our senior year, my mother had the place rented to someone else, but when things started to go downhill with my career, I'd offered to buy it from her, more as an insurance policy than anything else.

"Yeah, well I bought it off my mom like a year ago or something."

Connor furrowed his brow. "Why?"

"Don't worry about it," I said, running a few steps forward to the ground level door that led up to the top. I turned the key and disappeared behind the door, leaving Connor alone on the street. I could hear his sigh as he stood outside the weathered blue door and I threw my head back and closed my eyes shut. He was so different than he had been when I'd left him. I didn't like it. And it was my fault.

But I didn't know how to process those feelings, so I pushed them down

"Come on!" I finally yelled at him as I started making my way up the stairs.

18

I LOOKED around the loft and rubbed the back of my neck. All of Sophie's belongings were still in boxes and all of the boxes were completely strewn across the apartment. As much as I wanted to be around her right now, I was suddenly regretting the offer to help her unpack. It looked like the time away did little to improve her organizational skills.

"So where do you think we should start?" I asked tentatively.

Sophie looked around and twisted her lips. "I really don't feel like doing any of this right now."

I sighed. "Classes start in three days, Sophie. You really should be up and running by then."

Sophie took her coat off and let it fall on the floor before dramatically crashing onto the couch, knocking over a small box in the process. She cracked an eye open at me and smiled. "When did you get so responsible?"

I turned to give her a stern look, something I'd never done with her before. "I told you, Soph. Things are different now."

Sophie smiled. "It's nice to hear you call me that." I furrowed my brow, not catching on to what she meant. "You called me Soph. No one's called me that in ages. It's nice."

I stared at her. I hadn't caught my own slip-up. I was falling back into my pattern with this girl so fast that I felt like I couldn't stop. It felt like I was on a slide covered in oil. All I could hope was that I didn't break something on my crash landing.

"Don't do that," she said, still looking at me in a way that made it hard to look away.

"Do what?" I asked.

"Be upset with me."

I shook my head. "I'm not upset with you."

"Yeah, you are. And you should be," Sophie said, covering her eyes with her arm. "But please, don't be."

I watched as Sophie's demeanor turned from carefree to unsettled and I couldn't stop myself from moving towards her. I kneeled next to her on the couch and pulled her arm away from her face. "Hey. What's this all about?"

I could see the tears start to well in her eyes and it surprised me. I'd never seen Sophie cry before. "I thought I'd have more time to put myself together before I saw you," she said, not really answering my question.

"Is that why you ran?" I asked with a small smile.

"Yeah," she admitted. "Stupid, right?"

I shook my head and I sighed.

"I owe you an explanation for everything. Just not yet. So please don't be mad at me."

"I'm not mad at you, Soph," I said, wrapping my arms around her. Sophie turned those clear green eyes on me and I forced myself to pull away. If I didn't, I knew there was no way I'd make it out of the loft this evening without doing something I'd regret. Besides, if anything the tabloids had reported about Sophie was true, then there was no way she was ready to jump into my bed.

But Sophie was intent on making things difficult for me, because as I moved back, she followed, grasping my shoulders before pushing her lips against mine. I gave myself a moment to revel in the feeling of her before forcing us apart.

"Sophie, no."

She shook her head, looking suddenly agitated. "What's with you?"

"What's with me?" I repeated, suddenly feeling off-balance.

"Yeah. You chase me across the school and attack me in the nurse's office and then just walk away. Then call me not an hour later asking me to dinner and now you won't even kiss me back? God, Con! You're so frustrating!" Sophie huffed. I knew she was just getting angry to try and cover the hurt she felt at my rejection. But, after all this time, and after everything that happened, I wasn't thinking straight.

"Like you're one to talk," I said, standing to my full height and moving away from her. I started to pace the floor, an old bad habit of mine returning. "You disappear from my life and just when I think I'm starting to pull it back together, you reappear. And then you run away from me before trying to kiss me when I'm only trying to do right by you," I responded, my thoughts a jumbled mess.

"That isn't fair, Connor!" she shouted back at me, standing up herself.

"No, what's not fair was you running out on your best friend. You knew I loved you, Sophie!" I yelled back, the words leaving my mouth before I had a chance to stop them.

Sophie stopped and just looked at me.

"You know what?" I said, turning towards the door to leave. "This was a mistake."

"Connor wait," she said. "Please, don't leave."

I turned back around, my blue eyes fixating on her. "What could you possibly have to say that could make this better, Sophie?"

"Nothing," she admitted and I turned to leave again. Sophie ran towards me, grabbing my hand. I stopped at the gesture, my hard stare softening slightly. "I can't say anything to make it better," she admitted. "Because it was a shitty thing to do to you. I know that now."

I turned and looked at Sophie. She was different than she had been all those years ago, and yet, at moments like these, I wondered if she had really changed at all. I kicked myself for letting my temper get the better of me. I had every right to be angry at Sophie, but this wasn't how I wanted things to start or end between us.

A sad smile lifted the corner of Sophie's lips. "I'll figure out just how to explain it to you. And I'll tell you what everyone doesn't know. But right now, I just really need my best friend back." A tear slipped down her cheek and I sighed.

Sophie was my drug. I knew she was bad, but no matter how hard I tried, I was unable to give her up. "I'm not sure I know how to be friends with someone anymore, Soph," I admitted. It was the truth. Ever since she'd left, I never let myself be vulnerable in the way I had with Sophie. It had hurt too much when she'd disappeared from my life. I couldn't risk that again.

"Well, maybe you and I could both learn?" I could tell Sophie was toying with her next move.

"I'm not sure there's any hope left for me," I mumbled, mostly to myself.

"Me either," Sophie said sadly. "But I'm willing to give it a try if you are."

I couldn't stop myself. I pulled Sophie into my arms, invading her space and she gasped as I wrapped my arms around her. "You realize that I never wanted to be friends with you, don't you? You have to know that."

"I know," Sophie said as I rested my forehead against hers.

"And that I still don't want to be your friend, right?"

She stayed quiet, not responding to my admission and it made my heart clench. This was why I'd avoided places like the Friendly Pancake when Sophie left. It held memories of a younger me that had been so naïve. A me that thought everything would eventually work out and I'd work up the courage to confess to Sophie everything I felt and that we'd end up together or some shit. Her silence hurt, but it also gave me the strength to do what I needed to do.

"When you figure out what you want from me, Sophie, then call me. But until that time, I can't be around you."

A tear slipped from her cheek and I brushed it aside. I lifted her chin with my finger and pushed my lips against hers. The kiss was soft and gentle and I didn't try and deepen it.

I pulled back and she took a deep breath. "I'm sorry, Connor."

My eyes met her clear green gaze. "I know. Goodnight, Sophie." And with that, I turned and left, leaving Sophie alone in our old loft.

FOR THE SECOND time that day, I found my anger flaring up, an emotion I wasn't used to experiencing much anymore. Of course I'd felt it when Sophie had left all those years ago, but I thought I had worked through that pain. And then, in less than twelve hours, she had managed to completely undo everything.

I started the walk home through the cold, dead streets of the city. I could have gone back for my car, but I needed the walk and the still of the night. My breath formed a cloud in front of me as I walked, giving physical forms to my sighs.

I hated making her cry. Even though she had done that and worse to me, I still hated to see that tear slip down her cheek. And what was more, I hated myself for still caring. In my industry, I dealt with men who had too much power and too much money. I saw the way they treated women and for a brief moment in my younger days, I thought I could be like them. I thought maybe their attitudes held the answers for not getting hurt and always having a warm pussy available when my dick got hard.

But the endless stream of nameless faces felt empty after the high of sex. And pretty soon, that emptiness started to seep into the act itself. It was much easier to just throw myself into my work and my business had profited from that sacrifice. My company was the number one green developer in the city and I was starting to field requests to expand into other areas.

As the blocks passed under my feet, I started to feel better about the decision I'd made. I wasn't going to allow Sophie to dictate my life like I had when we were in college together. I was a different man and I wouldn't allow myself to slip back under her spell, no matter how sweet she sang her siren song. I'd fallen in love with Sophia Stronglen, but unrequited love is like the sweetest fruit. You can only leave it sitting there for so long before it starts to rot.

And that fruit had rotted into nothingness by now.

At least that's what I told myself as I entered my building and pushed the "PH" button to ride up to my floor.

FOUR

Sophie

I watched as the last person in the world I thought I could rely on closed the door to my loft, locking me inside. I stood there, tears streaming down my face as the emptiness of the place started to seep into me. The quiet pressed against my ears, broken only by the sound of my sniffling.

Which only made me angry.

How dare he? How dare he walk out on me like he hadn't started this entire evening? He was the one who had chased me across the college square. He was the one who had kissed me in the nurse's office. And he was the one who had invited me to dinner. What sort of game did this man think he was playing? And just where the hell was the Connor Driscoll I remembered from college?

The Connor I knew had been the classic nice guy. A bit shy, always reliable and—

—I gulped. And always just a friend. Of course, I knew how he'd felt about me even before he told me. Anyone that came within a mile of us could instantly sense it. And, if I was being honest, I was always too afraid to let our relationship morph into something else. Connor's friendship was a safe harbor and I was too frightened to let us venture out into the storm, even though staying put was a slow death for both of us.

I blanched and was forced to sit down on the couch. I pulled my face into my hands as I let out a heavy breath. I was just as bad as the people who had betrayed me in the industry. They were selfish people who used my trusting nature to extort me and I was just like them. The only difference was that my relationship with Connor hadn't been made public.

Tears began to slip down my face again as my anger melted into anguish. Maybe all the tabloids had been correct about me. Maybe I was just some scheming slut after all and no one should look up to me, no matter how catchy my songs were.

I grabbed my phone and swiped it open. I needed to talk to someone, anyone, who might be able to help me make sense of all this. I just needed a friend who would tell me how to make this right. Tapping the phone icon, the list of recent calls displayed, and Connor's name was right at the top. My thumb danced over it. I wanted to press it. I wanted to tell him I was sorry for all I'd done. But I couldn't do that to him. I *wouldn't* do that to him. He'd built a life for himself without me and I wasn't going to mess that up.

I knew what I wanted.

It was him.

But I knew I didn't deserve him.

I chucked the phone down against the cushions and grabbed a pillow, pulling it into my chest so I could have something to hold while I cried myself to sleep.

"I DON'T UNDERSTAND. I thought I was all done with class sign-ups?" I asked in an irritated tone to the counselor on the other end of the line.

"Unfortunately, when reviewing your record, it appears that one of the classes you took in the fall semester before you departed was marked incomplete."

"I don't understand. What are you trying to say? That I have to take an entirely new course on top of a full course load in order to graduate on time?" I knew my attitude was getting the better of me but I couldn't bring myself to care. After the day I had yesterday, it was inevitable that someone was going to end up as collateral damage. Too bad it was the sweet guidance counselor.

"I realized that might be too heavy of a load for you. So, I've come up with a solution that I think could be a great workaround."

I waited for the woman to continue, who was clearly waiting for me to express some enthusiasm. Too bad being a part of Hollywood for the past five years numbed me out to pretty much every emotion known to man, most of all enthusiasm.

"And?" I said, giving the woman the opposite of encouragement.

"Right, well, the school has an internship program that you can participate in. It will give you the extra credits that you need without requiring you to take an entirely separate course. The only requirement is that you work two full days per week, most students do Tuesdays and Fridays, and you'll need to submit journal entries for each week of the internship."

I rolled my eyes. "Seriously?"

"Is there something wrong, Ms. Stronglen?" the counselor asked, my attitude clearly starting to affect her sunny disposition.

"No. Everything is perfect. This is exactly what I want to be doing with my life right now. I couldn't have written the script of my existence any better. Great work, God," I said, my voice dripping with sarcasm.

"Great," the counselor responded, choosing to ignore my minor tantrum. "I'll go ahead and email you a list of the available companies so you can choose."

"Don't bother," I said, interrupting the woman. "Just put me down for the first one on the list. I really couldn't care less."

"That would be Phoenix Development," the counselor said.

"Like I said, I really don't care." And with that, I hung up the phone and allowed myself to fall backward on the couch. I looked around at the loft. Things were starting to feel a bit better now that the movers had come to unpack all of my belongings.

I hadn't actually needed any help unpacking. I may have been a disgraced pop star, but that didn't mean that all of my money had disappeared—only most of it. I still had enough reserves left to avoid manual labor.

I shouldn't have lied to Connor. Another thing I'd also fucked up regarding our reunion. But when he'd asked whether I needed help, I couldn't help but say yes. In the last five years, no one had ever done anything for me out of the goodness of their own heart. There was always some ulterior motive to their actions.

My phone buzzed against my hand and I flipped it over to see three letters that always made me grimace. "Mom."

"Yeah," I said, immediately regretting my decision to answer the call.

"That's really no way to speak to your mother, Sophie," my mother chided.

"Did you prefer I speak to my mother in no way, instead? I've read about that whole 'being estranged' thing and maybe we should try it?"

"Don't be a brat." My mother's tone was cutting before it switched to sugar. "Have you been doing any songwriting lately, dear?"

I rolled my eyes. There were few things I hated more than when my mother tried to be sweet to me to get something she wanted. This tactic was only second to the guilt, which was sure to come next. "No," I responded simply.

"I really think you should just get back out there!" That sweet voice had me ready to hurl.

"No one wants anything to do with me right now, Mom. It would just be wasted effort."

"You don't know that until you try."

"Look, I know that you're worried about your income stream drying up and your lavish lifestyle coming to an abrupt halt, but if you only take one river cruise this year instead of five, I'm sure you'll survive. Or are your extra vacations worth the pride and dignity of your only daughter?"

"Go ahead and crucify me for caring. I'm used to it by now, Sophia." There it was. My mother's world-famous dish of guilt. Hot, steaming, and full of shit.

"I guess you'll just have to find another sugar daddy, Mom. Since my bank account is all dried up and I'm not picking up a pencil to write a song anytime soon, if ever."

"You're throwing away a perfectly good career." My mother's voice returned to its normal hostile tone, which made me feel a bit more at ease. It was at least what I was used to.

"No, mom. Unfortunately, the label executives did that for me. And I didn't even have to pay them for their services."

A beep of my phone told me that my mother had ended the call. I threw the stupid device down on the couch and let out a heavy sigh. Talking with my mother always raised my blood pressure.

"So you really are Sophie Strong. Damn, I told you it was her!" one of the movers said to the other, with a punch to his shoulder.

I looked at the duo with a death glare. "I'm sorry. You're mistaken."

"No way. You're definitely Sophie Strong. Dude, I can't believe that you tried to—"

I cut him off with a raise of my hand. "Say one more word and not only will I not tip you for the job, but I also won't pay the company at all. And when your supervisor calls to collect, I'll be happy to tell him about the harassing behavior of his employees."

The men rolled their eyes but kept their mouths shut. Within the balance of an hour, they'd finished unpacking everything and I did tip them, but not as much as I had originally intended.

I was so sick of everyone asking about me, about the scandal, about my songwriting. Those days were done and the sooner I could get away from pop star Sophie Strong and start living my old life again, the better.

I walked over to the bathroom to wash the dust from the move off my hands. I looked at myself in the mirror and at the bleached blonde hair that I'd been forced to wear these past five years. It'd been so long since I'd gone to the salon. Of course, Jeff, my hairstylist back in LA had said that he would still cut my hair but I wouldn't intentionally bring bad press on his business. He was hands down the best hairstylist I'd ever had and I wouldn't do that to someone so talented.

My red roots were peeking through, a bit of my old self trying to push through the lies and bullshit painted onto me. I smiled as I made up my mind on what I was going to do. Jeff would kill me for using box hair dye over his art, but I'd likely never see him again so, oh well.

FIVE

Connor

"THAT'LL BE JUST FINE, THANKS FOR LETTING ME KNOW," I SAID AS I hung up the phone with the university's counselor. I really did owe so much to my school, it was the least I could do to teach a one-credit course and offer an internship at my company's city headquarters.

I leaned back in my chair and looked out at D.C. from my vantage point. I could see the lights begin to flicker on as people began to make their way home and to their families. That familiar feeling of emptiness started to creep in again, but I pushed it aside as I thought about what I needed to do to prepare for the week.

The school hadn't expected an intern this semester, but apparently, the university indicated that someone had signed up at the last moment. Originally, I had been a bit relieved that no one had signed up. My company's internships somehow attracted the worst types of students, but

I put up with it because for one, it was a chance to put the little shits in their place and two, I owed the university a lot.

For some reason, an internship with Phoenix Development brought out the little boys that thought they were going to become big-time real estate or energy moguls. As I knew quite intimately, these aren't the types of industries you can sweet-talk your way into. It took a lot of hard work and a lot more luck to land me in the position I was in today.

But these kids didn't get it. As much as I loved my *alma mater*, I had to admit that the vast majority of the students there were from wealthy D.C. families. I'd been lucky enough to receive a full scholarship for running track otherwise I'd never have been able to afford it. But I'd been surrounded by spoiled rich kids who assumed that everything was just going to be handed to them, probably because everything always was. Maybe that's why Sophie and I had bonded so well.

I shook my head. I'd been fairly successful in keeping Sophie out of my thoughts during the weekend and I wasn't going to let Monday be any different.

"Hey Kris," I called out to my executive assistant who poked his head through my office door.

"What's up boss?"

I looked at the young man. His messy brown hair was combed back and he was a little heavy set. Kris had been one of the different ones that had passed through my internship program and had really made an impression. It had been right around the time where the company was starting to take off and I had my eye on other investments around the city. Kris's time here had made things run so smoothly that when he'd graduated from college, I had a job already lined up for him if he wanted it.

"School called. Apparently, someone signed up last minute for the internship program. Have it ready by tomorrow."

"You got it," Kris responded and I nodded. "Do you have any info on who it is?"

I shook my head. "I got nothing."

"No problem," Kris said before he closed the door behind him.

I loved working with Kris. It was just easy. I didn't have to ask if it was okay for him to do things. I just told him what needed to be done and Kris would do it. And if something went wrong, Kris always made sure I was the first to know. There was a mutual respect between the two of us that made the gears turn smoothly.

I looked back out the window at the street below as I tried to think about what project I could throw myself into next. A flash of red hair caught my eye on the street and I stood and quickly made my way to the window. I looked down and for an instant and could have sworn the woman was Sophie until I remembered she was currently sporting bleached blonde hair, which I hated.

Actually no, I had no opinion about her hair, I had to remind myself.

I turned to look at the Rolex on my wrist. It had been a gift from a client but it never did feel quite right on my wrist. But, I wore it as a reminder. The day it started to look like it belonged was the day I needed to check myself.

Four-thirty. Maybe I could squeeze two more meetings in before the end of the day to keep my mind occupied.

And by tomorrow, the new intern would arrive and I'd have my hands full, trying to knock some sense into yet another entitled rich kid.

I'd have my hands full.

There'd be no time to think about Sophie.

And how much I missed her.

Sophie

"Shit," I cursed under my breath as I made my way up the city blocks back towards the university. I'd been so set on walking into the city and eating my lunch on my favorite park bench overlooking the national mall that I'd completely lost track of time and the fact that I had a five o'clock evening class that I needed to be on time for.

The counselor had completely lied to me. In order to be available two full days of the week, I had to swap out one class for an evening class, and of course, it had to be on a Monday. I had thought I might be in charge of my life when I finally went back to school, but that was looking to be a pipe dream now.

The only good news that came from my extended lunch had been that I was able to successfully test out my new—or old, depending on your perspective—hair color. And up to this point, no one had asked me whether I was Sophie Strong, whether I had done all the things the tabloids had said I'd done, or any other weird and perverted questions people inevitably asked me.

When I'd been "discovered," I thought that I would have adoring fans who loved me and for some reason I pictured all these fans being young girls in school or super hot guys that wanted to love me right. While the fangirl estimation was pretty much correct, the hot guys were a long shot. More accurately it was a lot of middle-aged men with twisted fantasies about young pop stars. I shuddered and pulled my scarf tighter around myself as I continued to make my way back to the school.

In my morning classes I'd been successful in getting to the professors ahead of time and requesting that they not use my full or real name. I'd gotten a few raised eyebrows but they'd all complied. I was really hoping I'd make it on time to maintain my anonymity otherwise all the red dye stains on my bathroom counter (and my shower wall and floor) would be for nothing.

I absolutely loathed running, but the dash for the bus before it departed the station was worth it because the bus driver held the door for me with an exasperated look on his face. I muttered a "thank you" as I boarded and tried to keep my head down at the annoyed faces of the timely people I'd made wait. I walked to the back of the bus, holding onto the railings to make sure I didn't go tumbling into someone as the bus driver made a right turn onto Massachusetts Avenue that would take me back up to the school.

As I sat down, I fished my phone out of my pocket and breathed a sigh of relief as I realized that, while I'd have to rush to chat with the professor before the class started, I'd hopefully make it on time. When the ten minutes that felt like ten years had finally passed and the doors opened to offload the bus, I dashed in front of everyone and ran across the college square to the newest building in the university's ever-growing collection.

As much as I complained to the counselor about the schedule change, I was actually pretty excited to take this class. It was a class through the business school and it was all about marketing. I knew I shouldn't care. There was no undoing the damage that had already been done to my reputation and I wasn't going to be putting myself out there in the world of music again. But at the same time, I did secretly want to learn the world I'd been forced to participate in or at least some component of it.

I rushed down the hallway, my freshly dyed red hair flying behind me as I rounded the corner and breathed a sigh of relief as the classroom came into view with people still milling around outside.

I slowed to a normal pace as I walked into the classroom and looked up at the front of the room. A pretty chestnut-haired woman was sifting through papers on the podium and the clock behind her told me I still had five minutes before the class was scheduled to begin. I walked to the back of the classroom and placed my belongings on the furthest chair from the front and all the way in the corner before bending down to adjust the leg warmers I had on overtop of my leggings. Washington D.C.'s winters were no joke compared to LA weather.

When I finally felt put back together, I made my way to the front of the classroom, trying to keep my head down as much as possible.

"Can I help you?" the instructor asked, her tone a bit sharp.

I narrowed my eyes slightly. I wasn't sure what I had done to piss her off, but maybe she was just a pissy person in general. I could sympathize with that on a very personal level.

"Yeah. I just wanted to touch base with you on the roster before the start of class. I don't go by my given name so I just need it updated on the roster."

The instructor looked at me and furrowed her brow as if she was trying to make sense of what I was saying. "That's fine. When we call out the roll call, just let me know then and I'll mark it down."

I shook my head. "You're not getting me. I can't have it called out in class. I need to update it now."

She gave me an irritated look. "What's your name then?"

"Can I just see the roster? I'll go ahead and scratch it out myself if you don't mind." I really didn't understand why this woman was being so difficult about it. All my other professors had said it was not a problem but of course, the last class of the day had to be giving me issues.

I knew it was sort of my fault. I should have updated my counselor about it so that the roster wouldn't be sent out with my actual name, but it was too late now. I'd have to email her about that tomorrow when thankfully, I didn't have any classes, only the stupid internship to go to.

"I'm sorry. For privacy reasons, I can't give you the roster," the brunette replied, meeting my gaze.

"Fine," I muttered before internally calling this girl a bitch. I was only thankful that my real name was not exactly the same as my stage name. That was my one saving grace in all of this. Some people were dumb enough not to notice and this girl really seemed like she might be one of those people. "Sophia Stronglen," I said as quietly as I could.

The instructor looked down at the roster and put a line through my name before looking back up at me.

"And what would you like to be called instead?" she asked, her feelings about the entire situation clearly showing.

"Sara Len is fine," I responded. I hadn't had much time to think about it before my morning class and it was the first thing that had come to my mind. Sara was close enough to Sophie that the name still sort of got my attention, although I had totally blanked out on responding a few times.

"Fine," the instructor said as she scribbled the new name next to the old. "Now that this idiocy is over with, you can go ahead and take your seat so we can get the class started."

I turned around to see that the entire class was looking at us. I blushed before I cursed under my breath. This was exactly the situation I was hoping to avoid by sitting in the back. I ducked my head quickly and headed towards the back of the room, making sure not to make eye contact with anyone.

"Alright, let's get started, shall we?" the instructor started to say before I had a chance to take my seat. "My name is Aubrey Knight and I'm the teaching assistant assigned to this class. Unfortunately, Professor Peterson was unavailable for today's class so I'll be covering for him as we work through all the administrative materials."

I opened my laptop but kept my head down. The woman at the front of the class was droning on about grades and attendance and I pulled up my email to read through the slew of messages I'd received. Of course, I'd completely deleted all the social media accounts of Sophie Strong and had reverted to using an email account from before I'd become famous, but my addiction to checking for messages was a hard habit to break.

I clicked on the bolded email from my course counselor entitled "Information about your Internship." I cast my gaze forward to see what the teaching assistant was talking about now but quickly realized none of it really mattered. I double-clicked the email to read its contents since there was nothing better to do in the meantime.

"Congratulations on selecting Phoenix Development for your internship. We hope the experience is both challenging and rewarding. Attached you will find a PDF with information about the company, along with your journal requirements in order to receive credit. If you have any questions, please do not hesitate to contact me."

Gross. Everyone was so formal on the east coast. I had totally forgotten about the "please do not hesitate to contact me" culture that existed here.

I double-clicked the attachment and a flame logo lit up on my screen next to the company's letterhead. I read through the bullshit information that always filled these company bios.

"Phoenix Development is the leader in utilizing alternative energy options in residential and commercial development and bridges the gap between consumers and green investors."

It continued this way, talking about the company's major accomplishments and I rolled my eyes. "One of the most successful public offerings in the last decade," "a leader in their field," "unparalleled commitment to their products and the consumers that use them."

More gross.

I scrolled down to the "About Us" section and the face that stared back at me had my mouth falling open.

"Sara," Aubrey's voice called out over the room. "Sara, is there a problem?"

I realized the instructor was talking to me and I looked up sheepishly and shook my head. "No problem."

"Well, then will you kindly introduce yourself to the class?" the woman asked, clearly annoyed.

"Right," I stumbled to try and think of what to say. "I'm Sara Len. Senior and mother of three. Just trying to finish up my degree so I can get a better job," I lied. In my world, lying had become a mundane experience and I did it so easily that I wasn't sure where the truth stopped and where my lies began. Of course, I didn't have any kids, but setting Sara's situation as far away from Sophie's as possible would hopefully stop people from making the connection.

Aubrey narrowed her eyes at me but didn't say anything and moved on to the next victim.

As soon as the looks from my classmates turned away, I clicked back into the attachment to look into those striking blue eyes I knew too well. I bit my lower lip as I looked at the picture of Connor Driscoll, a bit of that sexy crooked smile on my lips as he sat on the conference table in the photo.

Wait, did I just say sexy?

No. This was Connor.

Sure, I'd tried to kiss him yesterday. But that was just because I'd gotten wrapped up in the moment, right?

I didn't actually find him sexy.

But my body betrayed me and my mind knew I was lying anyways. And that smirk Connor was wearing in his photo said that he knew it too.

I sighed. Tomorrow was sure to be a special kind of fucked up.

SIX

Sophie

I SPENT FAR TOO LONG TRYING TO PICK MY OUTFIT OUT THAT MORNING. I'd ultimately settled on a black pencil skirt and white chiffon blouse with tasteful gold jewelry and a pair of pumps. I wasn't entirely sure why I had spent so much time getting myself ready. Connor had made it clear that nothing was going to happen between us.

Well, that wasn't exactly what he had said. But there was no way I was going to throw myself back at Connor when he had so clearly rejected me. No matter how sexy he was.

As I finished curling the last bit of bright red hair around the curling iron, I hastily unplugged the device, sprayed my hair with a bit of hairspray, and spritzed a bit of my favorite perfume onto my neck. As I looked in the mirror, I tried to convince myself that this was all about me and that I wasn't going to all this extra effort on the off chance that I might see Connor today.

My heels clicked in the hallway as I pushed the button for the elevator. Turning my smartwatch over on my wrist, I was glad I'd decided to just order a car rather than try and catch a bus and risk being late. Climbing into the back seat of the black sedan that was waiting for me, I confirmed that the driver knew where to go before sitting back and trying to take a deep breath.

I watched as we made our way down Massachusetts Avenue. There was something about the city that I had missed, even if I hated to admit it. I could see the embassies dotting our journey through the car's tinted windows and couldn't help the smile that formed on my lips as we passed the naval observatory and the master clock that told the world precisely what time it was. It was nostalgic and had me reflecting on better times.

I turned my head left as we made our way around DuPont Circle, idly wondering whether my favorite coffee shop was still there before realizing I hadn't eaten anything for breakfast. It was probably for the best. I had very little breathing room in this skirt. Those all-day dance practices had clearly helped maintain my figure. Plus, I hated to admit it, but I was downright nervous about the possibility of seeing Connor.

Would he think that I was trying to toy with him by selecting his company? I didn't want to hurt him. I would leave him alone if that's what he wanted, even if the thought of never speaking to him again made tears well in my eyes.

I shoved the thought out of my mind. I'd gone without him for these past five years. Of course, my schedule had been meticulously managed and I was all but prevented from making contact with anyone from my "old life" for fear that I might ruin the carefully constructed reputation that had been created for me. How fucking ironic.

"We're here, ma'am," the driver said, startling me out of my woolgathering.

"Thanks," I mumbled as I opened the door and climbed out of the car. I looked up at the building in front of me. I felt so small compared to it as it towered over me, its tinted windows hiding its inhabitants' movements from the world. I shook my head. I'd walked into an infinite number of buildings like this during my short-lived fame and this was no different.

Head held high, I stepped forward, intent on making the best of my situation.

Connor

"NEW INTERN SHOULD BE HERE in about ten minutes," Kris said from the doorway and I nodded my head before my assistant closed the door. I turned back around, surveying the city in front of me. I knew I spent far too long looking out this window, but this was the one spot where I was able to completely calm my mind. I'd solved some of my most complex problems by just staring out this pane of glass.

A flash of red on the street directly below me caught my eye and I looked down to see a beautiful woman exiting a black sedan. My thoughts immediately went back to Sophie and how she used to look so incredible with her red hair. A small smile threatened to creep up on my lips but I pushed it down. I'd been clear with Sophie; the door was still wide open, but she needed to be honest about whether she was willing to walk through it. No more of this hanging out in the threshold nonsense.

But over the course of the entire weekend, my phone had remained silent. Well, except for Aubrey's incessant calls, which were finally starting to subside. It pained me to think that Sophie had to take time to think about whether she wanted to be with me and I tried to push the thought out of my mind that perhaps she'd decided that she didn't want anything to do with me at all.

I watched as the woman disappeared into the building I was currently standing in and I crossed my arms as I readjusted my gaze to the cityscape. I had an extremely important meeting with the local housing authority this afternoon about securing grants for a few new developments and I needed to maintain my focus. I'd been able to put the thought of Sophie out of my mind for five years before. I needed to do it again.

Muffled conversation from outside my door filtered into my office and I figured the new intern had finally arrived. Kris had made it so that my initial meeting with the intern would happen first thing this morning and then I'd have the entire day to prepare for my afternoon meeting without being disturbed.

"I'll go ahead and introduce you to Mr. Driscoll and then we can get you set up with the orientation materials," Kris said, his voice getting louder as he opened the door.

"Actually, we've met." That was Sophie's voice.

I turned around and there she was.

Her hair as fiery as her attitude.

Looking exactly like the day we'd first met.

And the day she'd left me behind.

"Great, well then I'll let you two get reacquainted," Kris said, completely oblivious to the situation, before closing us into the privacy of my office.

I stood there, my eyes raking over her form, and by the way Sophie was shivering, I knew she could feel it. My eyes traveled up and down her body and I knew I shouldn't be staring at her like this, but I couldn't help myself. She reached up and began to twirl a piece of her bright red curls around her finger, an old bad habit of hers, and I sucked in a breath.

"I didn't know," she started to mutter but I cut her off.

"Your hair," I said simply, not elaborating.

"Yeah. I thought it was more me. Do you like it?"

"I do," I responded before I could stop myself. Every logical thought had left my brain the moment she'd stepped into the room, with that red hair and in that outfit. She looked stunning and I couldn't stop my eyes from moving down the curves of her body, only to flick back up to her bright red hair and green eyes when she started to loop those beautiful curls around her finger.

All I wanted to do was wipe my desk clean and bend her over it and run my hands through that flaming hair of hers while I pounded into her from behind.

"Connor, if this is going to be a problem," she said, a bit of her impatient attitude showing through and I cut her off again.

"No problem. Go ahead and have a seat," I said, regaining my senses. I stayed where I was standing and watched as Sophie strode over to one of the two chairs in front of my desk. She looked amazing just standing there, but the way the swell of her hips moved from left to right as she took each step in those come fuck me heels of hers had my cock hardening at the sight. I definitely liked Sophie's body better when she wasn't starving herself for the spotlight.

Normally I would have sat across from the intern and given them my standard speech about the experience, their involvement in the company and the company's core values, but I found myself unable to sit across from Sophie and look at that stunning red hair of hers. I turned around and looked out the window, surveying the city like it was my domain. I needed to regain some of the footing here, otherwise I was going to renege on what I'd said to her just a few days ago and I wouldn't allow that to happen. My word meant something and it always would.

Phoenix Development was something that I'd built out of the ashes of my previous self. I couldn't allow her fire to burn me once again. I needed to regain control of the situation.

CONNOR'S deep voice was booming in the small room and I hated to admit how aroused he was making me. When I'd entered the office, the way he looked at me made me feel like I was

Sophie

on display for him as if he was some buyer, deciding whether to make a big purchase. I couldn't figure out exactly how it made me feel, but I wasn't very good at processing emotions these days.

He looked stunning in a thin tie and black suit that matched his hair perfectly. Connor started rattling off about the company, its values and other nonsense as he stared out the window like he was some mob boss. At first, it was incredibly sexy. The confidence he was showing was something unlike I'd ever seen before. Sure, he'd been intense when he'd taken me in the nurse's office and told that stupid frat boy to beat it, but seeing him here, in his own office, of the company that he'd built from the ground up in less than five years, it was a Connor I'd had never experienced. He kept surprising me.

But then he didn't turn around. He continued to voice his clearly practiced monologue, the same one that he likely gave every stupid intern that came into his office, as if I was no different than any of the others that sat in this chair. And it was pissing me off.

How dare he just stand there and not look at me, like it didn't matter whether I was listening or not. Like I didn't deserve the respect of his eye contact.

"What the hell, Connor?" I said, my voice dripping with agitation.

My words forced Connor to turn around and he fixed me with his intense blue gaze. I instantly regretted saying anything because the way he was looking at me was downright scary. But I was never one to back down in the face of a fight.

"Is there a problem, Ms. Stronglen?"

Now he wasn't even calling me by my name? What the hell kind of game was he playing?

"Yeah, there's a problem, *Connor*," I said, emphasizing his name. "How about you look at someone when you're speaking to them? I can't imagine you built this entire company without looking people in the eye. How about you show me some respect? Pretty sure you said that was one of your company's core values," I said with ire in my voice.

A small smile tugged at the corner of Connor's lips. I watched him look like he was ready to gloat and I nearly got up out of my chair.

"Ms. Stronglen. Perhaps you don't realize the situation you've found yourself in here. You are an intern, working for my company. I am well aware of our history but this is a place of business and if you wish to remain working here for the balance of the semester, then you'll need to govern yourself accordingly. There's no way I can give you special treatment just because we were friends."

My eyes widened as my rage increased. I thought to say something but immediately thought better of it. I needed the credit from this internship in order to graduate and I wasn't going to give Connor the satisfaction of messing this up for me. Nor was I going to let him know that he got to me.

He was playing a game. I could see that now.

Well, he better get ready, because two could play.

"My apologies," I said, my tone much sweeter. I placed a hand on my breast and began to toy with the necklace resting there, catching Connor off guard so his gaze drifted down. A smirk was on my lips as I said, "Please continue."

In that moment, he seemed to realize that I'd pushed all my chips forward. I only hoped the cards I was holding would be enough to get me through what was turning into a very high stakes game.

SEVEN

Sophie

"Hey, were you at the Friendly Pancake the other day?" I turned to look at the girl sitting next to me in class and realized she looked familiar. I tried to keep my head down during class; the less I talked, the less attention I would draw to myself. So I always got here early so that people didn't watch me walk to the back of the classroom, but the last two classes, the same girl had just happened to sit next to me.

"Uh, yeah," I responded as I looked at the woman. I finally realized she had been Connor's and my waitress when we had visited last week. She was dressed in tattered black jeans and a red crop top and her pale arms were both covered in intricate tattoo sleeves. Her hair was dyed something between silver and purple and she had most of it stacked on top of her head in a messy bun.

"You were there with that crazy hot but intensely uptight suit, right?" the waitress asked, picking a bit of dirt from her fingernail before turning her intense wing-tipped lavender eyes on me. They must have been contacts, I figured.

I couldn't help but giggle at the woman's description of Connor. It was even more accurate after my experience with him yesterday. "Yeah. That's right. Sorry, what was your name again?" I asked, breaking my rule of getting too close to people. I knew I should just brush the woman off and keep my head down, but a small part of myself was yearning for someone to call a friend, especially since I couldn't say that about Connor anymore.

"Skyler Jackson. But my friends call me Sky," she responded simply.

I nodded my head. "Sara Len."

"Cool fake name," Skyler said and my eyes widened.

"Uh, what do you mean?" I asked, trying to act like I was confused.

"You're that pop star aren't you? The one that basically disappeared after—"

I cut her off. "I get that a lot," I said, trying to divert Skyler's attention.

Skyler shrugged. "I'm not gonna say anything. I get it."

I couldn't believe what I was hearing. Most people would be clambering to take their phones out so they could sell pictures or a story to paying tabloids. "Really?" The word was out of my mouth before I could stop myself, given how much of a confession it was.

"Really," Skyler said, confirming what I thought was impossible. "I've done my fair share of hiding in life. When you're ready to come out, that's your decision. And if you wanna start over, that's your decision too."

For the first time in a long time, I felt like I could actually trust the person sitting in front of me. It felt weird, if a little refreshing.

"So what's up with the suit? He your boy toy or something in the city?" she asked, continuing the conversation.

"Ugh, no," I said, putting my head down on my desk. "He's an old friend and things are . . . complicated."

"Too bad. He's crazy hot."

"Tell me about it," I sighed and Skyler stopped looking at her nails to fix me with an interesting stare.

"Oh, I know that look. By complicated, you mean things are fucked up, huh?"

This woman must have superpowers for reading situations with very little facts or something. I scrunched up my face. "Beyond fucked up."

"Wanna talk about it after classes?"

"Really?" I found myself asking again, totally dumbfounded that someone wanted to just hang out with me.

"Yeah. You look like you could really use a friend right now," Sky said.

I nodded my head. "You have no idea how true that is."

Sky smiled. "I was a stray once so I know how that feels. Still am, really."

I smiled as our conversation was cut short when the professor dimmed the lights and started the lecture.

♪

"So TELL me what the story is between you two," Sky said as she cut up a lime into two wedges and shoved them into the tops of the Coronas she had already opened. She rounded the leather sectional where I was sitting comfortably and handed me a bottle before taking a seat herself.

It turned out that Sky was living in the building just next to my loft so I hadn't even bothered changing out of my pajamas for the walk over. Sky's apartment was just as interesting as its owner. Most of the walls were exposed brick, just like at my loft and the furnishings were a mismatch of colors and patterns that somehow all worked together. A Persian rug was in the center of the great room but no television, just large bookcases full of everything imaginable.

I took a swig of my beer, letting the alcohol run down my throat and sighed at the sensation before diving into the history that was me and Connor. "Connor and I were really close during college. But when a record label approached me during my senior year, I sort of disappeared and pretty suddenly."

"Well, didn't you guys keep in touch at all?" Sky asked, taking her own swig before pulling a knitted blanket over her inked legs.

"No." I made a face, which Sky returned. "Plus, they didn't really let me have outside friends."

"You make it sound like you were in prison."

I pursed my lips. "Honestly, it sort of felt like that sometimes. Everything in my life was completely planned out. Where I'd be, on what tour, what interview, what I was wearing."

"That sounds horrible."

"It was," I said, trying not to think about how depressed I actually was during those times.

"The only upside to being that famous is having all that money. And the only upside to having tons of money is being able to go on crazy trips and buy stupid stuff. But it doesn't sound like you were able to do any of that."

"Bingo," I sighed as more alcohol made its way down my throat.

"That's depressing. Looks like the rat race is a total lie."

"Yeah, unless you're someone like Connor Driscoll and you run a crazy successful company. I bet he takes fancy vacations and buys stupid stuff."

"So he runs a company now?" Sky asked.

"Yeah. And you wanna know what's even more fucked up?"

Sky nodded her head, her silver hair swaying with the movement.

"I'm his intern for the entire semester. Well, not his intern personally," I tried to explain. "The company's intern."

A sly smile took up residence on Sky's face as she looked at me. "But you'd definitely rather be his intern, huh Sophie?"

"What? No!" I tried to deny it but I knew I was doing a horrible job.

Sky threw a pillow at me and I laughed. "Just admit that you want him. If you don't, there's something wrong with you. Cause he's dark and handsome and now you're telling me he's also rich and powerful?"

"I *do* want him, but it's not that simple."

"Why not?"

I looked out the window at the city lights and tried to organize my thoughts. I slid down on the sofa more and threw a hand over my face. "I sort of tried to get with him the first night I saw him. And he sort of rejected me."

"What do you mean, sort of?" I stayed quiet and Sky pushed me. "Come on girl, spill."

"He told me that he loved me and when I figured out what I wanted, I should let him know." The words confused me even as I said them. How was I supposed to figure out what I wanted? What did that even mean? I wanted him. I wanted things to go back to the way they had been. But I didn't want to hurt him, which I so clearly had. I was at a total loss.

"And then when I showed up yesterday, one minute I thought he was about to fuck me and the next he was speaking to me as if I was just another one of his new employees."

"That's a total power move right there," Sky said and I sat up and cocked my head to the side.

"What do you mean?"

"He one-upped you. Look, if I know anything about men, which is debatable," she said with a wink, "then you clearly got to him and he had to figure out a way to take back control."

"He did say that he missed my red hair when we were together and then I showed up with it." Sky just nodded as I talked. "And I'm not gonna lie, that outfit hugged my curves just right," I said with a laugh as I shimmied my hands down my sides.

"Get it girl!" Sky said with a giggle.

"Okay, so he power moved me. Now what do I do? Because, honestly I don't know how to handle this situation. He's so different than the Connor I knew."

"How so?"

"The Connor I knew was such a nice guy. He was just always there. Dependable, reliable—"

Skyler cut me off. "And totally unfuckable, right?"

I scrunched my face. "Yeah."

"And you leave and come back and find out that while you were gone, your strictly friend zone man has now become Mr. Fuckable of the Year."

"Double yeah."

"Well, then what's stopping you?"

I slumped back down. "I don't want to hurt him. He's so clearly still in love with me. He said so. And with my reputation right now, I could destroy everything he built. I don't want to do that. Plus, I'm just not in a place right now to be with someone after everything that happened. And he wants a yes or no answer."

Skyler snorted. "Men always do. They're the black and white in this world and women are the force that creates the gray."

"Yeah, so what am I supposed to do?" I sighed, feeling defeated.

"Didn't you hear me, girl? she said. "Women are the force that creates the gray."

"So you're saying . . ."

"Go ahead, smudge his hard lines a little. It'd probably do him some good," Sky said.

"I dunno," I replied, scrunching my face. "I don't want to mess things up for him."

Skyler downed the rest of her beer before she fixed me with an intense lavender stare. "Look, if that man is as successful as you say he is, you flirting with him a little bit while he's at the office isn't gonna suddenly tear down the company. And if he's as uptight as he seemed when I saw him last week, it would do him a hell of a lot of good. You feel me?"

The corner of my lips lifted as I thought about Sky's advice. "Yeah, I think so. So it's a take back the power thing then?"

Skyler shrugged as she laid back down on the sofa and stretched her legs out. "Or a fun game that the two of you so clearly need to play."

I smiled, feeling a lot better about my situation with Connor. "So what made you so wise in the way of men?" I asked my new friend as I got up to grab myself another beer.

Skyler snorted at the comment. "I would not say I am wise in the way of men."

I laughed. "That gives me a lot of confidence about taking your advice then."

Skyler shrugged. "Can't help you there."

I rounded the sofa and handed Skyler another beer before sitting down and curling my legs up. "So, you know my story—"

"Sort of. I know there's more and I know you'll tell me when you're ready."

I smiled at Skyler's thoughtfulness. "Thanks. If I keep drinking, that may be sooner rather than later. But what's your story? You don't seem like the normal rich snob that attends this school."

"First of all, that's probably one of the nicest things anyone has ever said to me," Sky said with a laugh. "So thanks for that."

I tipped my beer in Skyler's direction before taking a drink and Sky continued. "I'm nothing special. I was engaged to a total prick of a man. Dropped out of school for a variety of reasons." She said it, but her previously upbeat attitude shifted when she did, making me think something was up.

"Anyways, I bounced around a bit after that and finally decided to come back and finish up my final year. So, sort of like you. Except you were engaged to the *actual* man."

"Thanks for sharing, Sky," I said. "I didn't mean to pry."

"Fuck that noise, I'm an open book girl. And you don't need to apologize to me. If one less woman says 'sorry' in this world, I'd be happy. All we do is go around apologizing for . . . nothing. Stepping down from my soapbox now."

I smiled. "Yeah, I can totally relate to that. I can't tell you how many times I've said sorry for things that had nothing to do with me."

"My point exactly," Sky responded, taking another swig from her beer and crossing her legs.

I looked at the intricate tattoos on the woman's legs. "Those are really beautiful. Your tattoos, I mean."

Sky held up a lean leg and turned it this way and that before putting it down. "Thanks, babe. It was sort of my last 'fuck you' after I broke off the engagement. I'll never forget when he saw me not a month after. I think he almost had a heart attack. Maybe the fucker did, 'cause I just turned around and walked the other way."

"What, he never like tattoos?"

"Uh, no," Sky said very matter of fact. "He had pretty crazy ideas about how women should and shouldn't look. I think he read somewhere in the bible that tattoos meant you went to hell."

"Pretty sure that's not in the bible."

"Good. Cause I'd hate to be stuck down there with him for eternity after we sort out all this shit up here."

I couldn't help my burst of laughter and Sky joined in. "Thanks for this, Sky. I can't tell you how much I needed it."

"I told you, girl. I'm a stray myself. We protect our own kind." Sky blew me a kiss and I smiled.

I watched as my new friend downed the rest of her second beer and jumped up before saying, "Let's go check out that closet of yours and see what you're gonna wear to throw Mr. Straight and Narrow off his game tomorrow."

I smirked. "Yeah, let's do it."

EIGHT

"I GUESS I'M NOT UNDERSTANDING THE REASON FOR THE DELAY," I SAID
to the voice on the other side of my phone, trying hard to keep my cool. I
reached forward and pulled the door open to my building. "Yeah . . . yep
. . . still falling short on an adequate reason."

I waited for the elevator, keeping my head down so I could hear the
lame excuses I was being fed from the local housing authority on the
other side. The elevator car arrived and I stepped inside. "Alright, yeah.
We'll just have to readjust the budget to factor in the delay. Yeah, I'll get
with the accountants today."

Hanging up the phone I let out a deep sigh as the doors began to
close. Changing the entire budget on such a large development was going
to be a pain. Not to mention working out the delay with all the contractors. I really didn't understand why people couldn't just get things done
by their given deadlines.

I heard the sound of heels clicking against the tile lobby before a voice called out to hold the elevator. I groaned but pushed the door open button out of force of habit.

"Thanks," a breathless Sophie said, my eyes widening upon seeing her.

I immediately cursed being late this morning. It had never happened before, but I was feeling a little off my game lately and waking up at my usual 5 a.m. had been difficult the last two days.

"No problem," I said as I watched Sophie walk forward. Her perfume immediately filled the small space and I instantly regretted my act of politeness. That brilliant red hair of hers was up in a tight bun, with a sweep of bangs tucked gently behind her ear and I couldn't help but look at her.

The car climbed the floors, uninterrupted by our awkward silence. Finally, the chime at the top floor sounded, signaling an end to my torture and Sophie stepped out of the car, but not before saying, "I hope you have a great day, Mr. Driscoll."

My name dripped off her lips like honey and I swallowed hard as I watched her walk into the lobby, bits of red peeking out from the bottom of her shoes with every step she took. I stepped forward myself, narrowly missing the closing doors and did my best not to watch Sophie as I made my way into the main office space. Somehow, it didn't feel like she was the intern and I was the CEO.

Sophie thankfully split off down the first hallway and I finally felt like I could think again. I made my way to the corner of the floor where my office was located and rounded Kris's desk. "Got a call from the folks at the housing authority. New projects on hold until City Council can get the budget approved."

"I'll let the accountants know they need to run us a 30/60/90-day delay chart to see what we're dealing with," Kris said, springing out of his chair and heading towards accounting.

"Thanks," I said as I made my way into my office. I threw my coat off and sat down heavily in my chair, trying to make sense of what had just happened this morning.

Sophie was a distraction, that was for sure. And thankfully, I hadn't completely lost my head this morning. I'd still been able to fill Kris in on what needed to be done. But the idea of her being in the office twice a week for the next four months had me running my hands down my face.

I could still smell her perfume. It had been the same scent she'd worn back in the day and it drove me crazy. She had to be doing this on purpose. Was it her goal to tease me until I caved on what I'd said to her that first night in the loft? She had to understand that I still wanted her, right? So why bother trying to seduce me? What sort of game was she playing?

I growled. I just couldn't figure her out.

For a split second I thought about taking my laptop back to my apartment and working from home. But that was something the old Connor would have done. I hadn't been a pussy like that in years.

I steeled my nerves. If Sophie wanted to play her little cat and mouse game, then I'd bite. There was no way I was going to let this woman completely control my life the way she had all those years ago.

I reached into my desk drawer and pulled out my preferred cologne and dabbed a bit behind my ears. Closing the drawer, I stood to my full height and buttoned my suit jacket. I schooled my features, letting the corner of my mouth drift up slightly into a confident yet sexy smirk.

I strode forward, my steps intense even against the rugs in my office and opened the door. Kris was sitting at the desk just outside and of course, Sophie was looking comfortable, leaning against the surface of his desk in an outfit that had me almost losing my nerve.

"Ms. Stronglen, I'm glad you're here. Step into my office. I have an assignment for you."

"Of course, Mr. Driscoll," she said in a smooth voice before standing up and running her hands slowly down her thighs to smooth her skirt.

My eyes followed her movements and I stopped the groan that threatened to crawl up my throat, opting instead to just close my office door and give myself a moment to breathe.

Sophie opened the frosted glass door to my office and walked inside. I was standing behind my desk, my head down as I looked over a document. I lifted my eyes as Sophie approached and was thankful I'd readied my features, otherwise that outfit would surely have broken me.

An emerald green wrap dress that cinched her curves at the waist and flared slightly around her hips hugged her body and a long gold pendant disappeared into her cleavage which was slightly on display given the dress's low neck. I gestured to the chair in front of me and she gracefully took a seat. I cleared my throat before saying, "I was informed this morning that the City Council has to approve a new budget before one of our development grants can be funded. Kris has spoken with accounting and they're going to prepare us new balance sheets. What I'd like you to do is some research on the City's current budget proposal and the likelihood that it will pass and when."

Sophie rolled her eyes. "That sounds incredibly boring." She looked up at me and I met her green gaze without hesitation.

"Successful business deals often are," I said, my voice deep and commanding. I watched Sophie shiver and smirked. "If you've been caught by surprise, it means you weren't prepared."

"Alright, fine," she said with a huff. She looked at me, meeting my gaze and added, "Anything else?"

I narrowed my eyes. "I expect your analysis by the end of the day."

"Ohhkay," Sophie said. "Anything else . . . Mr. Driscoll?" she asked, rolling her tongue.

I let my lips curve into the barest of smiles. "That'll be all, Ms. Stronglen," before I sat down at my desk and turned my attention away from her.

Sophie sat still for a moment, waiting for me to say something else but I didn't. I busied myself on my laptop and she bristled before she finally exited the office.

The moment the door clicked shut I leaned my head back and took a deep breath. I seriously wondered if I knew what I was getting myself into.

FIVE O'CLOCK CAME and went and Sophie still hadn't shown back up to my office to deliver her report. It wasn't the nicest thing I had ever done to an intern on their second day, but it also wasn't the meanest. I generally let Kris handle assignments for the interns so that I wasn't bothered, but for the especially bratty cases, I liked to take an interest and try and show them what it really meant to work for someone. The brattier the attitude, the worse the assignment. So far, Sophie was landing somewhere in the middle, edging towards brat.

I pinched the bridge of my nose as I watched the clock tick past five-thirty and wondered if she had just decided to leave without completing my assignment.

The door to my office opened and I lifted my gaze. "I'm going to head home, if that works for you," Kris said.

I sighed and nodded.

"Have a good weekend," my assistant said as he started to close the door.

"Kris, hold up a minute. Did the intern leave already?"

Kris shook his head. "She's been working on that assignment you gave her all day. I see we're not taking it easy," Kris said with a wink.

I stood. "I'll go check on her. Have a good weekend, Kris."

Kris gave me a friendly salute before heading out. I turned to look out at the city lights. The days were still so short around this time of year so the sun had long since set. I sighed as I realized I really did not want to be sending Sophie home alone in the dark. Another problem Sophie caused that I was going to have to deal with.

The building was quiet as I exited my office. I always encouraged people to leave early on Fridays if all their work was done. They appreciated it and often came in ready to tackle the week on Mondays. But a single light in one of the interior cubicles was still on and I made my way there.

But when I leaned over the edge of the cubicle, the desk was empty except for a neat report left atop the keyboard. I looked around but the only evidence that Sophie had ever been here was the lingering smell of her perfume. I shook my head and grabbed the papers with a bit of a growl before walking them back to my office.

I threw the papers down on my desk and began to read through her memo. With every page turn, my eyes widened a bit more at how thorough and accurate it was. She'd actually managed to uncover a few things I wasn't aware of and her analysis about the suspected outcome was just about on point with where I thought things might end up.

I sat back in a bit of stunned silence before flipping to the final page. A handwritten note was there, in Sophie's pretty script.

Hi Mr. Driscoll,

   I had to leave at five to attend to a personal matter, but I hope you find my report to your liking. I will give you the oral Tuesday.

I did a double-take at the wording and realized she had inserted a carrot with the word "report" between "oral" and "Tuesday." She'd signed it *Ms. Stronglen* and had placed a giant kiss next to her name in her bright red lipstick.

Now I knew she was testing me.

And I knew I was fucked.

NINE

Sophie

"I CAN'T BELIEVE YOU SNUCK OUT OF THERE TO AVOID GIVING HIM THE report," Sky said with a laugh as she lounged on my couch.

I stifled a giggle. "I don't know what came over me. But it was such a ridiculous assignment. I wasn't going to give him the satisfaction of me obeying all his orders."

"They're called tasks when you're working for someone. Technically, he is your boss, you know."

"Yeah, I know. But even still," I said with a shrug. I didn't have a good defense for my actions and I knew that they could definitely get me in trouble but it was also sort of exciting. This whole situation was definitely risky business, which only made it that much more fun.

"You're crazy," Skyler said. "But that's why I love you."

"You're the one that said I needed to take the power back!"

"And you're certainly doing that and more. I'd give him another day before he breaks, max. I bet if you'd stayed, he would have taken you on his desk as soon as the office cleared out," Sky said with a laugh.

"I dunno," I said. "He's always just so calm and composed when I see him. I sort of wonder if I'll be able to break him at all. He's just so different than how he used to be."

"First, he's in love with you and second, you wear come fuck me heels every day you walk into that office," Sky said, referring to the pair of Louboutins I had lifted from my famous days. "The fact that he's made it two days already says how strong he is. But he'll cave. All men do." Skyler said it with a sly smile that made it seem like she knew what she was talking about.

"I hope you're right," I said with a quirk to my lips. "Cause if he thinks that I'm just going to throw myself at him after he walked out on me like that, he's got another thing coming."

"Get it girl!" Sky took a sip of her beer before turning onto her stomach and fixing me with those lavender eyes of her. "So, whatcha wanna do tonight?"

I shrugged. "I dunno. I can't really go out to bars and stuff yet . . . for obvious reasons."

"I know where we could go if you're up for it?"

"Oh yeah?"

"Yeah. Come on," Sky said and before I even had a chance to gather myself together, my friend was pulling me towards the door and outside to the parking lot. I crawled into the passenger seat of Sky's old Prius. I looked around me at the car's many contents. Some sort of peace charm hung from the rearview mirror and the dashboard had been decorated with some intricate henna-like art. It fit Sky perfectly.

"Where are we going?" I asked, suddenly feeling a bit nervous about going out in public.

"Don't worry. I wouldn't take you anywhere you wouldn't be safe," my friend responded, adjusting the rearview mirror while she puckered her lips before turning the car on.

"Okay," I said, feeling a bit more assured.

Within ten minutes, Sky had driven us north and further out of the city until we landed at a tiny strip mall. Sky pulled her little car into the back parking lot and said, "we're here."

I looked around in confusion. "And just where might that be?"

"Oh, come on," Sky said. "I want to introduce you to everyone."

I followed Sky to one of the doors that lined the back of the run-down building before we entered. Walking through the door, I realized Sky had taken me to a tattoo shop. The place had a really cool vibe. The back wall was painted an intense red and was covered in sketches of everything imaginable.

Sky led me to the front of the shop where a pair of people were chatting to their left and another was working on someone in the chair to their right.

"Sky, baby!"

"Hi Trev!" Skyler said with a bit of excitement to her voice. The man ran forward and wrapped her in a complete bear hug, picking her up in the process. Skyler laughed and batted at his back before telling him to put her down.

I couldn't help but smile at the pair. Trevor was tall and had brightly bleached blond hair, so I couldn't tell what color it had originally been. The amount of tattoos he had easily exceeded Skyler's and they were all done in an old fashioned style, most of them depicting nautical related things that I didn't quite understand.

"Trev, I wanna introduce you to someone," Skyler said, leading him over to me. "Sophie, this is Trevor."

"Nice to meet you, Sophie," Trevor said as he shook my hand before wrapping an arm back around Skyler. "Glad to know that someone finally managed to become friends with this train wreck."

I smiled. "It's probably fairer to say I'm the train wreck and that she made friends with me."

Trevor pressed a kiss to Skyler's silver locks before saying, "My little girl is finally growing up."

Skyler pushed against his chest and I laughed as the pair separated. "Lay off, Trev," but I could tell my friend loved the attention.

"Anyways," Skyler said, righting herself. "That over there is Britney," she said, pointing to the brunette Trevor had been talking to that was currently texting on her phone.

"Hey!" Britney said with a wave before immediately turning back to her phone and I waved back.

"And the guy doing some kick-ass art is Little John," Skyler said, referring to one of the largest and burliest men I had ever seen. Little John was easily over six feet, heavyset and had intense ginger colored hair.

Little John just grunted. "Nice to meet you guys," I said a bit sheepishly. I trusted Skyler, but I still felt nervous about being out in public.

Skyler clearly picked up on my nerves because she wrapped an arm around me and leaned in to whisper. "You're safe here, I promise."

I nodded, feeling a bit more at ease. "So, are these the folks responsible for your awesome ink?"

"That would be me," Trevor said, sliding back over to take credit for the compliment. "When I met Skyler, she was just a kitten with virgin skin. I like to think my needle popped that cherry."

"Weird, Trev," Skyler said with a look on her face. "Have you ever thought about getting any ink, Soph?"

I shrugged my shoulders. Of course I had thought about it, at one point I'd even brought it up to my manager but the answer had been a resounding no. There was a chance that the tattoo could interfere with the revealing stage costumes I was instructed to wear and they couldn't have that. But now that I was free of that and trying to stay under the radar, getting a tattoo might actually be helpful in completely changing my image.

"No, but to be honest, I've always thought about it."

"Another virgin. Yes, please," Trevor said as he wrapped his arm around my shoulders. "Come here, baby. Let me show you everything you've been missing." I let Trevor lead me over to the counter where even more designs were displayed underneath the glass.

"Point to which ones you like and then tell me what design or objects you were thinking of including."

I looked down at the images beneath me. Some looked exactly like photographs but I really wasn't into those. Others had more of a cartoon feel whereas others were somewhere in between. "This and this," I said, pointing to the middle ground drawings.

"Got it. Ideas? Something important to you? Something you don't want to forget?"

I thought about my situation and all I'd been through in the last year. The way that my music and my life had been extorted by greedy people for money and how they'd yet to face any true consequences for it. A small smile curved on my lips as I realized what I wanted.

I described the design to Trevor who listened quietly. He nodded his head and drew me a sketch, the design coming to life as I described it to him and handed me the paper. "What do you think? Ready to pop that cherry?"

I looked over at Skyler who rounded the counter to look at the design. "Soph, it's totally rad."

"It's perfect. Let's do it," I said, my green eyes full of conviction as I looked at Trevor.

"God, I love a willing virgin," Trevor said with a wink and I couldn't help but laugh.

TEN

Aubrey

I BRISTLED. AN ENTIRE WEEK HAD GONE BY AND CONNOR HAD REFUSED to return my calls. I thought I might give him the silent treatment at the end of the week but that hadn't worked either. He hadn't called, texted or responded to any of my messages.

"Aubrey, dear, you seem distracted," my mother said to me across the dinner table. The woman was the quintessential old school congressional wife. Her brown hair had been cut short and curled at the ends and even at a simple family dinner, she was still wearing a couture skirt suit with elegant gold jewelry.

I plastered a fake smile on my face and shook my head. "No mother. Not distracted at all."

"Well, then were you planning on answering your mother's question?" my father asked, the mirror image of my mother. Although unlike my mother, my father had decided to let his thick hair go gray. But he was also wearing khakis and a sports coat to the dinner table as well.

"I'm sorry, mother. What was your question?" I hated these dinners, but my parents required them of me in order to continue receiving my weekly stipend.

"I was wondering how things were going between you and that big-time CEO. Connor Driscoll was it?"

My father grunted and chimed in before I could even respond. "Owner of Phoenix Development, fastest-growing developer in the city currently. A great catch, truly."

I tried to hide my disgust at my father's words. I knew that he was only interested in who I dated if it meant that he might garner additional campaign contributions. "I think things are going well," I lied.

"You think or you know, dear?" my mother asked, pushing food around on her plate that I knew she wasn't going to eat for fear of not fitting into her size 2 suit.

"What difference does it make, mother?" I asked, my tone exasperated.

"It makes a great deal of difference. It sounds to me like something might be wrong. Is that true? Did you two break up?"

"That would be a true shame, Aubrey. You should see if you can get back together. That man is going places," my father added, taking a bite of steak. He didn't have the same reservations about eating as my mother did.

"We haven't broken up and there's no cause for concern," I said. "I'd really rather not discuss my personal relationships, if you don't mind. I am a grown woman."

"We just want to make sure you end up with someone suitable, dear," my mother said with a smile.

"Yeah, I know," I responded. "Thanks."

I excused myself from dinner and told my parents I would see them next week. As I waited in the lobby for the car to arrive that would take me home, I sifted through my messages, hoping that maybe there was something from Connor that I had missed.

Of course there wasn't. I let my head fall back and scrunched my eyes closed. This entire situation was a nightmare. I didn't know what had gone wrong. I'd been attentive, caring, but still Connor was cold and distant. I really did not want my parents to try and start setting me up with men again. That was always a disaster. Their choice was always way too old for me, usually divorced with kids but had "good connections." For once in my life I thought that I had actually found someone that me and my parents liked.

I was resolved to figuring out what had gotten in the way of our relationship. Connor could try and hide it but he had dropped me like a sack of bricks and the only explanation for that was that he was seeing another woman. I was smart and had a knack for getting to the bottom of things. I would figure out exactly what happened and then I would know how to make him come running back to me.

"Your car is here, Miss," the doorman said and I stood and exited the house. I climbed into the backseat of the black Escalade and the driver pulled forward. I swiped left on my phone to read my news flash during the drive home and something caught my eye.

Sophie Strong, where are you now?

Disgraced pop idol Sophie Strong is still staying away from the spotlight six months after news of the latest in a string of scandals broke to the media. Her former manager and publicist were reached for comment and they assured the press that the star was just taking some time for herself and that she would be back in the spotlight in no time. But we're not so sure. Sightings of her have been made across the country, including the most recent reports from the east coast, but unfortunately, nothing has been verified yet.

Wherever she's gone, one thing is for certain, the world loves to hate Sophie right now.

A picture of the idol in sunglasses with bleached blonde hair showed her walking in the LAX airport in leggings and a leather jacket. I pinched my fingers on the photo to make it bigger and the realization hit me.

"Sophie Strong . . . Sophia Stronglen . . . Sara Len. Holy fuck," I breathed out.

"Something wrong, miss?" the driver asked at hearing my expletive.

"No, nothing," I said dismissively as I turned back to my phone.

I wasn't completely convinced that the two were the same person, but it did seem highly likely. I laughed to myself, wondering why I cared. Honestly, Sophie was completely washed up. The entire world hated her and if it really was her, she was just trying to finish her last semester of college under the radar. I tried to think of a way I could benefit from knowing her true identity but was coming up short.

I had bigger things to worry about. Uncovering the current whereabouts of a washed-up pop star was not something I should be concentrating on. I needed to refocus my efforts on how to get back with Connor. That would definitely be more worthwhile.

"We're here, miss," the driver said and I clicked my phone screen off before exiting the car without saying a word.

ELEVEN

Sophie

It had taken a few days, but Trevor had finally finished the design.

"Do you like it?" I asked Skyler and my friend nodded.

"I do, but that doesn't matter. Do *you* like it?"

I nodded my head enthusiastically as I turned this way and that, looking at the new art on my upper arm in the mirror. "It's perfect. Thank you, Trevor," I said.

"I take my thanks in the form of hugs and . . . other things," he said, casting a wink to Skyler who rolled her eyes at him.

"I'll choose the hugs as currency then," I said as I watched the exchange between the pair. "Cause I don't want to know what the other thing is."

"Come here then," Trevor said, wrapping his muscled arms around me and I laughed as he picked me up the way he had when he'd seen Skyler that first night at the shop.

As he put me down, I righted my clothes and then said, "But seriously, I am still going to pay you with actual money."

Trevor smiled at me. "Only if you insist."

"Is he always like this?" I asked, turning to Skyler.

"He's usually worse," my friend responded. Trevor gave Sky a feigned wounded look and she blew him a kiss. "Alright, you ready to head to our evening class?"

"Yeah," I said, before pushing three hundred dollars at Trevor who nodded his thanks. "I wonder how much of a pissy attitude Aubrey is going to be in tonight. Man, that woman is just not fun."

"Who's Aubrey?" Trevor asked, folding the money into his back pocket.

"Our bitch of a graduate teaching assistant for this course we're taking on business marketing."

Skyler had transferred into the class during the first week after I had shared my schedule. It turned out that we had a lot of the same interests so it made sense to try and coordinate our schedules.

"What's so bad about her?"

"She just has a completely sour attitude about everything and it seems like she delights in making people feel stupid."

"Sounds like she's not getting enough sex," Trevor said.

Skyler sighed. "That's your explanation any time a woman is upset, Trev."

"And I'm usually always right."

I shook my head with a laugh. "Yeah, well I hope she figures it out soon because she makes the class totally miserable."

"Agreed," said Skyler. "But we still gotta go. Come on."

We said our goodbyes and I thanked Trevor for my amazing work on my arm again before we piled into Skyler's car and made our way back to the college for our evening class.

THE CLASS WAS JUST about what I had expected. The professor's portion was really interesting and I was learning a ton about the industry and marketing strategies, but Aubrey's Q&A portion was horrible. Anytime anyone asked her a question, she might as well have said it was a stupid question and that they were stupid for asking it, given her tone.

"I really wish we could just skip her portion of the class," I said to my friend quietly as we gathered our books.

"Yeah, but she takes attendance cause, you know, we're children," Skyler replied with a roll of her eyes.

"So have you thought about how you're going to handle Mr. Hot and Serious tomorrow?" Skyler asked as we walked back to her car.

I scrunched my face up. "No. Aside from having wet dreams about him, I've tried to put him out of my mind."

"Boo," Skyler said with a smile.

"You're just loving the drama."

"Of course! It's nice to not be the one caught up in nonsense for a change."

"Yeah, I'm sad to admit it, but my entire situation is nonsense," I sighed.

"Good thing it's the fun kind," Skyler said with a wink. Skyler pulled into her parking spot at the back of the building. We exited the car and Skyler rounded the hood to give me a hug. "Don't worry about it babe. I know we kid around about it, but just be yourself and do whatever feels right. Everything will sort itself out with Connor."

I hugged my friend back. In less than a week, I'd gone from having no friends to two friends, both of whom were excellent huggers. I hadn't realized how much I'd missed the feeling. "Thanks babe."

"Now go get some beauty sleep," Skyler said as we parted ways, each to our respective buildings.

I dragged myself up the stairs to my door and kicked my shoes off before crashing down on my bed. I looked at my closet and thought about what I might wear tomorrow to see Connor before having a pang of guilt for trying to play games.

The truth was, I didn't want to play games with him. But I also didn't want to just throw myself at someone who had so clearly rejected me a week before. I'd been through too much to let that happen. So while I really *really* wanted to be with Connor, I also knew that I couldn't give him the answer he was looking for. At least not right now. There was no way that I was ready to be in any sort of committed and serious relationship with my life completely in shambles. That just wouldn't be fair to him.

I groaned in frustration as I kicked off my clothes and pulled the covers over me. Why did Connor have to make everything so difficult? All I wanted was to come back and restart the friendship we used to have and he had to go and get all successful and hot and dreamy and make me want him, again. And then he had to complicate everything by confessing how much he still loved me while simultaneously trying to force me into some exclusive and serious relationship. The whole thing just wasn't fair.

I wanted him. And it was pretty fucking obvious that he wanted me too. So why couldn't we just hook up? Why did Connor have to go and complicate everything?

I thought back to my conversation with Skyler. Maybe this was what my friend meant. That Connor was overly complicating everything and it would be good for the both of us if we just got together. Maybe I wasn't actually playing games with him, maybe I was doing him a huge favor.

I didn't know. I couldn't figure it out and I was frustrated beyond belief.

I rolled myself over and reached for the small bottle of melatonin on my nightstand. I needed sleep and I needed to just not think about this man anymore. Tomorrow would come and whatever happened between us wasn't in my control.

TWELVE

IT WASN'T EVEN LUNCHTIME AND ALREADY, MY DAY HAD BEEN A SHIT show. Between a public hearing for one of the new developments being pushed up to tomorrow's agenda and getting word that one of the contractors hadn't been paying his subcontractors, I was about ready to punch a wall.

But it had been a long time since I'd let my anger get the better of me and I wasn't going to start now. I'd gone down to the work site myself in the morning and made it very clear that if payments weren't made by the end of the week, I would call the loan my company had given to the contractor and considering the confession of judgment clause it contained, those wages, plus attorneys' fees and costs, would be paid one way or another.

I looked at my Rolex as I walked into the office and groaned at how late in the day it already was. I needed to prepare for tomorrow night's public hearing on the G Street refurbishment and I wasn't entirely certain I had enough time to get all of the exhibits together and over to their office before their deadline.

"Kris, the G Street hearing—"

"—has been pushed forward by a week, I know. I've already started working on pulling together the substantive information and Sophie has been a big help in pulling together the exhibit component."

I raised my eyebrows at that. Sophie had certainly proven herself competent from her last report, but I was surprised that she was so willing to help, given last week's attitude.

"That's great. I'm going to start my round of calls to the Board members and see if they have any questions ahead of the meeting. Once all the materials are pulled together, can you let me know?"

"Absolutely."

Feeling a lot better about the situation, I entered my office and sat down before pulling up a list of the Board members and their contact information. The rest of the day would be spent with the phone pressed to my ear, unfortunately.

"THAT'S CORRECT. The building once belonged to the Salvation Army but it's been vacant for several years now. . . . I'd say it's been on the market just under the four-year mark. . . . Yes, four units in the old church and ground-up construction in the next lot over." I listened as the Board member thanked me for my call and indicated he didn't see any reason why he would vote down the measure.

"I appreciate your candor. If something comes up, please let me know and I look forward to seeing you tomorrow evening."

With that, I hung up the phone on the last phone call for the day. These phone call marathons were grueling and I usually locked myself in my office when I had to do them, lest people see me without a jacket and tie and my sleeves rolled up. I looked at the clock above my door and grimaced as I realized it was past five.

"Kris," I said, calling my assistant in.

"Finally done with the calls?" Kris asked, opening the office door and standing in the threshold.

"Thankfully yes. And it seems like we'll have the votes. Were you able to get all the documents in before the city's deadline?"

"Done and done. I hope you don't mind that I made an executive decision to go ahead and submit before you had a chance to review given you were still on the phone."

I shook my head. "Not at all. I appreciate you making things happen."

"I've gone ahead and emailed you the substantive portion of the presentation so that you can review that at your leisure and here is a print out of the exhibits that Sophie put together."

I reached out and accepted the papers from my assistant's hand. "Thanks, Kris. Why don't you head on home? I'm all set here, I'm just going to review all this."

"Thanks. If you need anything, let me know."

I nodded as Kris closed the door behind him. I took a second to stand and to stretch my arms over my head. I looked out at the darkened city, dotted with lights and finally allowed my mind to drift to Sophie for the first time all day. It seemed like she had really come through in a pinch to help out with this. Kris normally prepared the exhibits but with everything needing to be turned around so quickly, if she hadn't been here, I wasn't sure we would have made the deadline.

Looking at the stack of papers left for me on my desk, I decided to get myself a cup of coffee to help fuel the reviewing process. Of course I had tomorrow before the meeting to review, but if I could knock this out now while I was still focused on it, I'd feel a bit more caught up on the day.

I pushed open my office door into the silence. The place was quiet and mostly dark except for one light just down the hallway. I furrowed my brow, wondering who it could be that decided to stay late and made my way there.

Sophie

I HAD CHECKED in with Kris when I'd arrived in the morning about any work he or Connor needed done. I was a little disappointed when Connor's office lights were off and Kris said that he was dealing with a matter offsite. However, there was some big emergency that required someone with marginal media talent and I had volunteered to lend a hand.

It wasn't until around noon that I had heard the intense footsteps that could only belong to Connor come down the hallway before I heard his deep voice conversing with his assistant about the status of the day.

I couldn't help but lean out of my cubicle to see if I could catch a view of Connor, but as soon as I did, I regretted it. I could tell that he was upset. While his calm demeanor might have fooled others, I knew him too well and saw the telltale signs that he was seriously stressed out. He'd run his fingers through his black hair twice and looped a finger into the neck of his shirt collar all within the span of a five-minute conversation.

I looked back at the exhibits I was preparing. Kris had told me that a new proposed development in an up and coming area of the city required a rezoning approval by the Board of Supervisors and that the meeting had been unexpectedly pushed up to tomorrow. Well—they'd given them the opportunity to postpone until the next meeting, but that would mean delaying a full month and all parties involved really wanted to get this project going.

For the first time in a long time, I actually felt connected to a project and I really wanted to see it succeed. If I could help Connor in some small way to pull something together, I wanted to do it.

So thoughts of trying to break Connor's willpower and the game we were playing flew right out of my mind and I worked intently on the project I'd been given until I'd completely lost track of time.

I HEARD someone making their way down the hallway and I looked up from my desk, surprised to see that everyone had already left.

I startled as Connor draped an arm over the side of my cubicle. His jacket was off and his sleeves had been rolled up and he was no longer sporting a sleek tie, but instead the first few buttons of his shirt were undone, letting a bit of the tattoos I knew didn't match his current image peek through.

"Looks like someone's taking their job seriously after all," Connor said in that deep voice of his.

I looked up at him, fixing him with my emerald eyes. "Yeah, well I can't have you giving me a bad review and messing up my ability to graduate on time."

"Well, I appreciate the effort, Soph, truly." We stayed quiet for a moment. I didn't know what to say. Even more, I wasn't sure why I'd decided to stay so late. But a part of me knew it was because I missed seeing Connor and I'd been hoping for a moment like this.

"Well, I hope everything goes okay tomorrow," I said. It sounded lame and I knew it. "I like seeing the looser side of Connor Driscoll," I said, reaching out for his rolled up sleeve.

My finger brushed against his arm and I saw goosebumps form on his skin at my touch. Connor fixed me with those ice blue eyes of his as they looked me up and down. Fuck, I was in way over my head. Being alone with him again was a bad idea.

I'd worn something a bit more conservative today. A sleeveless pinstripe pencil dress with a square neckline and a cardigan to cover up my new ink for the office. Unfortunately, I'd been hot all day because of it and was dying to take it off.

"You know you don't have to stay past hours," Connor said, his deep voice echoing through the emptied space.

I bit my bottom lip. How was I supposed to explain to him that I had stayed late so I might get the chance to be around him? It was totally pathetic and I knew it. The exhibits had already been turned in an hour ago. But I'd pretended to continue looking at them as people around me started to leave.

"I thought maybe you wanted to go over that budget report. I told you I would give it to you Tuesday," I finally said. It was the only reasonable sounding excuse I had.

"Alright, well how about we go over it now?"

I looked at him incredulously. "Isn't it a little late?"

Connor furrowed his brow and his demeanor shifted. "But isn't that the reason you stayed this late?" His voice was low and I hated how much it made me shiver.

"Yeah, right," I said, trying to recover from my mistake as I grabbed a printed version and my notes.

"Follow me," Connor said and I complied, falling into line behind him. I watched his form as I walked and couldn't help but appreciate how much larger his shoulders were and how well they filled out that pressed white shirt of his.

I tried to shove thoughts like that out of my mind. I needed to focus on giving Connor the best report he'd ever had from an intern. For some reason, I really wanted to prove to him that I was more than just some washed up pop star.

He opened the door to his office and I walked through, my head held high despite the fact that being in my pumps all day was absolutely killing my feet. I hadn't had a chance to appreciate how nice of an office it truly was yet. A lacquered wood and glass desk stood in the corner with two leather chairs opposite it. To my left was a large photo of a finished development hung above a sleek leather sofa and the entire office had floor to ceiling windows overlooking the city.

I walked forward and the scent of sandalwood and spice met my nose and I did my best not to close my eyes at how good it smelled. I strode into his office like I owned the place and took a seat at the front of his desk without his invitation.

I could hear Connor take a deep breath before closing the door behind us. Walking over to the desk, he pulled out my first report and began to move the PowerPoint and exhibits to the side but a smile unexpectedly lit up my face as I saw the exhibits I had recently been working on.

"Oh, did you get a chance to review these?" I asked, my voice edging with excitement.

Connor looked at me. I'm sure my attitude shift surprised him, but it made me feel good knowing that something I'd done might actually help him. "Not yet. I was actually going to stay late to review them," he said.

"I dunno if Kris told you, but I put them together," I said.

Connor smiled and my heart swelled. "He did, and thank you," he added. "He said you worked really hard on them."

With just a few words, Connor had completely disarmed me once again. I felt powerless against his draw, much like the last time I was in his office, but in a completely different way this time. He made me feel valued, capable and like a member of the team. If this was the Connor Driscoll the other employees saw, it was no question why he'd been able to build such a successful company in such a short amount of time.

"Well, if you want, I could walk you through them?" I hesitated. "Unless you'd prefer going over the budget report, that's fine too." I grimaced as I thought about the last page of the report. It had seemed like such a good idea at the time, but I was completely regretting it now. I wondered if maybe Connor hadn't had a chance to look at it yet. It was on its own separate page. If I could just get my hands on it, I might be able to discreetly remove it.

"Great idea, Soph. I'll grab us some coffee. Make yourself comfortable."

I watched Connor rise from his chair, his height and complete composure making me shiver. I turned and watched as he walked out of the office and let the door close behind him before I stood up and rounded his desk intent on snagging my old report. I flipped to the back page and blinked in surprise to find my note completely missing.

"No, no, no, where did it go?" I whispered frantically to myself as I leafed through the pages roughly. It didn't make sense. What could have happened to it?

Connor returned with two cups of coffee much too soon, catching me standing behind his desk, completely off-guard. "I, uh, just wanted to make sure you had the most recent copy of the exhibits," I said, stumbling over my words.

Connor strode forward, still completely calm and placed the cups on a side table. "You're holding the budget report," he said, pointing at the papers in my hands.

"Am I?" I asked, looking down with a fake laugh. "My mistake."

Connor came around to where I was standing and faced me. His woodsy scent coupled with how close he was standing to me was making me feel weak in the knees. He pulled open a desk drawer without breaking eye contact with me and grabbed a piece of paper from the top. "Were you looking for this, Soph?"

He held up the piece of paper, complete with a comment about giving him oral (a report, that is) and a giant imprint of my lips in bright red. "I, uh—" I did not know what to say. What could I say? That I'd been mad at his belittling and I was trying to give it back? It sounded petty and childish now.

"Why'd you write it, Soph?" he asked.

I tried to take a step back from him but he wrapped a strong arm around me, preventing me from moving. His fingers curled into the cinch of my waist and I gasped. "I—I don't know. It seemed like a good idea at the time," I admitted.

I tried to drop my gaze but his other hand reached down and grabbed my chin, lifting my head so I had to meet his piercing blue eyes. "And what about now?"

I felt like I'd fallen completely under his spell. The way he was looking at me was sending shivers up and down my spine and all I wanted was for Connor to lean forward and kiss me. "Yeah, I still think so."

His thumb pressed against my lips and I opened my mouth slightly to run my tongue against the pad of his finger. Connor's gaze intensified on me. "And what makes you think that?"

I smirked. "Because of the way you're holding me right now," I breathed out.

"Are you playing games with me, Soph?" Connor asked, his grip on my waist tightening. I shook my head but Connor pulled me tighter against his body and I gasped. "I think you are. I think you're testing me. I think you want to see when I'll break. Is that it, Soph?"

His scent was completely overwhelming my senses and was actively short-circuiting my brain. Had this been any other situation, I would have told the guy to fuck off and have meant it. But this was Connor and I couldn't help what I felt. "I can't help that I want you, Connor."

Connor sucked in a breath as I said those words as he ran his finger along my lips again. I closed my eyes and leaned into his touch. "You always were such a pain," he said with a smile before he wrapped his hand around the back of my neck and pressed his lips against mine.

I didn't wait for Connor to reconsider his actions. I didn't want to give him a reason to reject me again. I responded by opening my mouth and sighed as he pushed in his tongue. His hands started to roam my body and I moaned at his touch.

Connor pulled my bottom lip into his mouth, swiping his tongue left and right against the skin before releasing it. We separated, breathing hard but neither of us could fight what was about to happen.

"I fucking missed you, Soph," Connor said as he squeezed me tight against his body.

"Connor, I need you so bad," I said, my voice breathy.

He pressed his lips to mine again as he pushed my sweater off my shoulders. My breathing hitched as he ran his fingertips against my skin before moving to press kisses into my neck. I arched my head back, giving Connor a greater canvas and shivered as he started to glide his lips over my collarbone.

Connor pulled back when he saw the ink on my shoulder that I hadn't been there before. I smiled as his hands moved gently over my newly inked tattoo. "Do you like it?" I asked him, a twinkle of mischief in my eye.

I watched Connor look at it with bated breath. It was the Greek goddess Themis, blinded but dressed in one of my more famous stage outfits, a sword in one hand and a scale in the other, one side showing a pile of coins and the other a pile of music notes. The scales were tipped towards the music notes.

"I do," Connor said honestly. He dove back in, pressing his lips against my neck and I sighed. His hands ghosted over my body before reaching up to search out the zipper on my dress. Pulling it down, he pushed the fabric off my shoulders and over the swell of my hips, his fingertips ghosting against my skin causing arousal to pool low in my belly.

I stepped out of the dress, kicking it to the side and sat down on his desk, spreading my legs to accommodate his large frame. Connor shuddered with need as his eyes raked over my body. I was wearing a bright red lace bra set, the exact same color as my hair and I could tell by the way he was looking at me that he liked it.

I reached out and fisted my hands into his collared shirt as I pulled him forward. I separated the shirt, buttons flying off as I pushed it off his muscled shoulders. "Fuck I missed you," he said as his bulging biceps were revealed. Connor reached up and fisted his hands into the white tee, pulling it over his head, revealing rows of sculpted abs and a large chest, marked with his own ink.

I ran my fingers over the intricate designs. He'd gotten the first one while we were in college but there was another large design that stretched from his left shoulder over his chest of a phoenix bursting forth from the flames. My hand danced across it and I smiled before Connor moved back in to kiss me.

I moaned into his embrace as I wrapped my legs around him sighing at the feeling of his manhood pressing against me through his trousers. Connor's hand moved down my body, making me shiver in anticipation before his fingers gripped my thighs. "Wet for me already, huh Soph?" he asked, feeling the slickness near my junction.

"Fuck yes," I said as he teased me, touching everywhere but the one place I needed him. "Connor, please," I moaned.

"That's it, beg for it Soph." His lips moved down to my neck before he unclasped my bra and threw it somewhere in the room. As his lips sealed over one nipple, his fingers finally touched my core, rubbing me atop the lace.

"God yes," I said as I ran my fingers through his dark locks. Connor moved to the other breast while he palmed its pair and I moaned at the feeling.

His hands dropped to cup my ass as he pulled me down from his desk and flipped me around. He pressed a hand to the back of my neck and I moaned as he pushed me down onto his desk, my breasts pressing against the glass.

Connor looped a thumb in my panties and slowly began to pull the material off my body. I groaned as the fabric left me, the feel of it and his fingers against my skin causing me to shiver even more. His hand trailed up the inside of my thigh to my exposed sex before I felt the slightest of touches. My hips bucked and Connor stood, pressing his hand into the small of my back to hold me down.

I felt his large frame leaning over me as he continued to tease me, but I was unable to do anything but wait to receive what he wanted to give me. "Tell me, Soph, just how long have you been wet for my cock?"

His words made me shudder and all I could do was moan in response. His finger flicked my clit and I gasped. "I can't wait to give you the fucking of your life, but first I need you to come." His voice was deep and I moaned in response.

"Please touch me, Connor," I whimpered.

His fingers moved against the outside of my lips at my words. "What was that, Soph?"

"Please," I begged.

He leaned over me on the desk, his breath hot against my ear as he whispered, "I want your come dripping off my desk, Soph."

"Fuck," I breathed out before his fingers plunged into my core. I keened and tried to move but Connor's strong hand against my back left me unable to do anything but grip the front edge of the desk as he pumped his fingers into my core. His thumb moved up to press against my clit and I could feel the end just out of reach.

"Oh fuck, Con," I breathed out as he refused to let up on his rhythm.

"That's it, Soph. I want your juices dripping down my fingers by the time I'm done with you."

His filthy words coupled with his intense movements had me at a complete loss. I felt the orgasm build and before I knew it, I was crashing completely over the edge with a scream of his name.

He pulled his fingers from my core and walked around his desk. I watched him, his muscles gleaming in the low light of the dark office, as he kneeled in front of my prone figure. He held his fingers up, my juices glistening. "Look at the mess you made, Soph. I need you to clean this up," he said before pushing his fingers into my mouth one by one.

I shuddered at how filthy he was being. This was not the Connor I'd expected but I was absolute putty in his hands. I wrapped my tongue around each digit in turn as Connor fixed me with that intense stare of his. When he was satisfied, Connor reached forward and pressed his lips against mine before pulling back. His fingers were grasping my chin, making me look at him. "I'm going to fuck you now, Sophia Stronglen and by the time we're done, you're not going to think of ever running away from me again."

I gasped at his words as Connor rolled a condom onto himself, but I didn't have time to think about what he'd said because within seconds, I could feel his manhood pressing against my core. This encounter had been almost a decade behind schedule and there was no more waiting.

He pressed into me as I gasped, my slick heat taking his thick cock inch by inch. I could feel that he was large and he pressed into me slowly, inch by inch.

"Fuck, Soph," he said as he was finally completely joined with me.

"Oh, fuck me Con," I said and that was all the encouragement he needed before he began to move. He wasn't gentle. His movements were fast as his hips snapped forward, my ass cheeks bouncing against him with each of his thrusts.

I could feel my body heating up again as his cock hit that special spot inside of me over and over again. All I could do was grasp the edge of the desk as he continued to pound into me, but I loved every second of it. "Yes, Connor. I'm gonna come," I let slip from my lips and Connor increased his speed.

"Fucking come for me, Soph. I want to feel your pussy clench against my cock."

I closed my eyes, the movement of Connor the only thing that was grounding me at this point until finally, a wave of heat crashed through my body and I screamed his name for the second time that night.

My walls clenched against his cock hard and Connor followed me over the edge, pushing hard into me as he came.

It took us several moments of heavy breathing before either of us moved. Connor slowly pulled out of my heat and I gasped as I felt him leave me. He ripped the used condom off himself and tied it off before throwing it into the waste bin below his desk.

I continued to lay atop the desk, my body feeling completely spent and unable to move. Connor's features softened and he pulled his trousers back up and tucked himself into his briefs. "Come on," he said as he helped me right myself.

He leaned down and grabbed his dress shirt and draped it over my naked shoulders before he lifted me up and walked me to the couch. He sat down and placed me on his lap, his fingers idly tracing patterns into my exposed skin causing me to shiver.

I looked up into his intense blue gaze and gave him a lazy smile. "That was amazing."

Connor looked at me and leaned forward, pressing a gentle kiss to my lips. "I knew you always would be."

"Connor, I—" I started to say, wanting to solve everything between us but also not knowing what to say.

But Connor shook his head. "Don't worry about anything right now."

"But you said—"

"I know what I said. But we're here now. So just relax and we'll figure it all out. Right now, I just want to be here with you."

I closed my eyes as Connor curled around me, pulling me into a tight embrace. After five years of being without him, after just one night, I knew I'd never be able to be apart from him again. I just hoped being around me didn't ruin everything he'd built while I'd been gone.

CONNOR PARKED the car behind my building and cut off the engine. We sat in silence before I turned to look at him with a smile. "I'm sorry we didn't get around to reviewing those exhibits," I said a bit sheepishly. "I hope your presentation goes well tomorrow."

Connor leaned forward, wrapping his fingers around the back of my neck before pulling me in for a gentle kiss. "Thanks. I'm sure it'll go great, thanks to your help."

I couldn't help but feel a swell of pride at his words. "Okay well, I guess I'll see you on Friday?"

"Yeah," Connor said, his thumb caressing my cheek gently. "See you Friday."

He pulled me in one last time to place a kiss against my lips before letting me go. I felt his eyes follow me up the stairs to the top floor before I disappeared behind the door.

Upstairs, I peeked my head out my back window to watch Connor put his head to the steering wheel. I shook my head. He used to do that when we were young, when he couldn't figure something out. But within seconds, he was back to the Connor I knew before tonight, features schooled and calm as he pulled his silver Lexus out of the parking lot and zoomed off.

I stood there in the silence of my apartment. I wasn't sure what tonight meant and where we went from here. All I knew was that I didn't regret what happened and I really hoped Connor didn't either.

THIRTEEN

FINAL REMINDER to submit your journal entries no later than tonight at midnight. Any journal entries submitted after the deadline will be considered untimely and will require a letter of explanation in order to be accepted.

I GROANED AS I READ THE EMAIL ON MY PHONE JUST BEFORE I WAS about to collapse in bed. I was exhausted—and completely sated—and all I wanted to do was go to bed and relive the way Connor had fucked me on his desk.

Did I really just think that? It sounded so dirty but that is what had actually happened. I'd seen porn that was less cliché than what happened between us this evening.

I turned to look at the clock. It was nearing nine in the evening and I sighed as I grabbed my computer and made my way to the sofa. Opening up a blank word document, I began to type my journal entry.

Internship Day 3

This evening I fucked the company's CEO. I let him bend me over his desk and finger my tight cunt until I came. Then he made me lick my own cum off my fingers and beg for his cock before finally giving it to me. He showed me how important leadership skills and taking control of a situation can be.

I laughed as I typed out the words to my recent porno before sighing and burying my head in a pillow.

And now I have no idea how I'm going to make it through another day at my internship without bringing at least three spare pairs of panties. Consequently, I may need to apply for additional student aid in order to fund my panty purchases.

A knock drew me away from my computer and I shuffled my way to the door. There was only one person that would be knocking at this hour of the night.

"I saw the car!" Skyler said, pushing inside and past me before heading to the refrigerator to grab a bottle of white wine.

She uncorked the thing and grabbed two coffee mugs (despite the fact that the wine glasses were located on the shelf just above the mugs), pouring ample amounts into each. She shoved a cup at me and I took it with an amused look.

Skyler took a swig from her own mug before making her way to the sofa and sitting down. "So, what happened?"

I hesitated. Skyler was fast becoming an incredibly trusted friend, but should I really admit that I had just slept with Connor? It was one thing to joke about it, but it was an entirely other thing to do it. If it got out, it could cause issues for Connor too. Or at least I was pretty sure it might.

"Oh my gawd, Soph, is this true? Did you really?" She paused. "Damn girl, he sounds like he knows what he's doing."

I looked on with horror as Skyler read my fake journal entry on my computer and I rushed forward to snatch the machine out of her hands. Skyler chuckled and took another sip of wine. "Come on, babe. You know you can trust me."

I internally berated myself for doubting my friend. "Sorry. The past still haunts me sometimes. I know I can."

Skyler gave me a kind look before inching forward. "So spill."

"Yeah, it's true," I said with a bit of a small smile and a grin broke out across Skyler's lips.

"So what now? Where'd you guys leave it?"

I shook my head and took a swig of wine myself. "Fuck if I know. We didn't really talk about ever-after."

Skyler shrugged. "I guess that's not so bad. That's sort of what you wanted right? Just to take things as they come . . . and come and come," she said with a wink.

I rolled my eyes but couldn't help but laugh.

"But seriously, what's your plan?"

"Right now? To finish this stupid journal entry and go to bed. I'm beat."

"I bet you are," Skyler said, grinning like a Cheshire cat.

I got up off the couch and pulled Skyler up. "Good night, Sky," I said, pushing her towards the door.

"Okay, okay. Goodnight for now, but I want more details later."

"Fine," I said before closing the door on my friend with a wave before turning back to my sofa, intent on actually writing the stupid journal entry so that I could get to bed.

"HEY," I said as I walked into the office on a Friday morning to see Sophie chatting with the receptionist in the lobby.

"Hey yourself," she said a bit sheepishly, turning around to look at me with those beautiful emerald eyes of hers.

"Thanks for your help Tuesday. Those exhibits were really helpful," I said honestly.

Sophie brightened and I couldn't help but feel my heart swell a little at seeing her smile. "That's right! How did the hearing go?" she asked.

I knew I was treading in dangerous waters, but once you've already jumped in the shark tank, you might as well swim around a bit. "Good. Come to my office and I can fill you in on the details?"

Sophie smiled and nodded. She stood, removing her coat and I took in what she was wearing and instantly regretted my decision to be alone with the woman. Her bright red chiffon blouse was just sheer enough to entice your gaze and that gray pencil skirt hugged her in all the right places. I tried not to groan as I turned around and bent over to pick up my notebook from my bag. This woman was going to destroy me.

Sophie must have caught me looking, because the blush that dusted her cheeks was beautiful.

"Shall we?" I asked and Sophie nodded, following me as I turned towards my office down the corridor.

I closed the door after Sophie walked through and watched as she looked at the desk with a bit of hesitation and a bit of—could it be longing? "I will say that since you've gotten here, my desk has been absolutely filthy." My voice was gravelly and Sophie shivered.

"Is that a problem?" she asked as she took a seat.

I rounded the desk and sat. "On the contrary. I prefer it this way." I kept my blue eyes on her as I said the words and Sophie finally had to shy away from my gaze.

"You were going to tell me about the hearing?" Sophie reminded me.

I could sense that Sophie was trying to deflect and decided I would allow it. In all honesty, if I kept our conversation on this track, I'd end up fucking her on my desk again and I'd rather keep that to a strictly after-hours situation.

"The measure passed."

"That's great!" Sophie said with genuine excitement and a breath of relief.

"But it was a rather interesting evening."

"Oh?"

"Apparently, there's a coalition of residents located on Redbud Landing Road that aren't happy with the entrance to the development connecting to their street," I said.

Sophie shook her head. "Um, how is that even a complaint?"

"When you deal with this kind of work, everything is a complaint," I said with a chuckle.

"So what happened?"

"Practically every single resident attended and got up to speak out against the development for their allotted five minutes. We were there until after nine."

"That's crazy."

"What's crazier is that the guy that organized the whole thing followed me into the bathroom during one of the recesses to tell me that he didn't actually think there would be an issue with the road."

Sophie laughed at the absurdity of the whole thing.

The door to my office opened and I looked up to see the woman that had been causing me a serious headache over the last two weeks. Kris was following close behind her and he looked frantic about the entire thing.

"I'm sorry, Connor. I told her you were in a meeting, but she insisted on coming in to see you."

I clenched my jaw as I looked at Aubrey. "It's fine, Kris. I'll handle it," I said through gritted teeth.

Kris left the office with a hasty apology and Sophie stood, thinking she might do the same. "It's fine, Soph, stay here," I said.

"I think she should leave, Connor. This is a private conversation," Aubrey said in a haughty voice.

Sophie inched out of her chair, desperately wanting to get away, but I fixed her with a piercing look. "Stay there. This won't take long at all."

Sophie sat back down in stunned silence and put her head down.

"So is this how it is? You kick me to the curb so that you can hook up with the infamous Sophie Strong?" Aubrey asked with a hand on her hip.

"Whom I choose to spend my own time with is none of your concern, Aubrey. It never was and it never will be. You will *not* barge into my office and you will *not* interrupt my meetings. We went on three dates over the course of several months. I'm not sure what you think happened, but I can assure you, there was never going to be a fourth." Aubrey tried to speak but I held up my hand and even she didn't dare interject. "If you continue to try and contact me or the office, I'll instruct my attorneys to file the paperwork for a restraining order and you will have to explain to a judge why you've felt the need to call me and my business upwards of ten times a day. Now, you will kindly take yourself out of my office, otherwise I will call security to have you escorted. Your choice."

"You'll regret this, Connor," was all Aubrey said before she turned on her heel and left.

Sophie turned back to me and I was almost certain she could see the rage seething underneath my features.

"Are you okay?" she asked.

I turned my gaze on Sophie and I could see the concern for me reflecting in her emerald eyes. The anger I was feeling started to melt away and I nodded. "Fine."

"Connor—if I somehow—" Sophie started to say but I cut her off.

"You did nothing wrong, Soph." I sat down with a heavy sigh. "Did you know she knew who you were?"

Sophie grimaced. "I suspected. Like an idiot I forgot to have the registrar change my name before the student rosters went out. She's actually an instructor for one of my classes. I'm quite sure I'll fail now."

"If that becomes a problem, I'll take care of it for you," I said.

"Do you think she was serious about what she said?"

I shrugged. "I'm not worried about it."

"Yeah," Sophie said with a bit of a sigh.

We sat silently for a bit, both coming down from the adrenaline of the situation. I looked at Sophie and I could tell that she was distraught. I hated that I had something to do with that and wanted to fix it. I turned my watch over to check the time. "What do you say we go grab some lunch? My treat."

Sophie looked at me and her eyes lit up. "Only if it's pancakes."

"Deal."

♪

I HAD SET rules for myself when Sophie left. Those rules were simple and they'd gotten me to where I was now.

Work hard.

Trust myself.

Don't get distracted.

Unfortunately, the girl sitting in the car next to me had shattered through that last rule of mine when she'd come waltzing back into my life. The way her pretty red hair fell against her shoulders and those matching red lips puckered and stretched as she talked had me about to break my second rule.

Because I absolutely did not trust myself around this woman.

So when I should have turned right to head to our old spot, I blazed right through the intersection, the engine of my car running nearly as hot as I was.

"Connor, where are we going?" Sophie asked, pointing to the road that would have taken us to the Friendly Pancake.

"Your place."

"Why?"

I turned to meet her eyes momentarily before looking back at the road. "Did you think I was just going to have you once and be done with you?" Sophie's eyes widened at my words as my gaze fixed on the car in front of us.

I parked behind the building before Sophie had a chance to respond. My fingers brushed against the nape of her neck had her shivering and she turned to look at me as I fixed her with an intense stare.

"I told you that first night that I couldn't be around you because I knew that as soon as I got a taste of you, I'd never be able to stop myself. You're like the sweetest nectar, Soph. I've wanted you for close to a decade and now we're about to make up for some seriously lost time."

I pulled her in for a kiss and she let it happen. I deepened the kiss and she moaned, opening her mouth and I took advantage, pushing my tongue in to tangle with her own.

I forced myself to pull back. If I wasn't careful, I'd end up fucking her in the backseat of my car and while that was certainly something I intended to do at some point, right now I wanted to see her laid out, body on display and framed by that gorgeous red hair of hers as I explored every inch of her.

Sophie sucked in a breath and I gave her an intense look. "Get out of the car, Soph and go inside. Strip those clothes off and wait for me on your bed."

Sophie's mouth fell open in surprise at my words and my tone. She put her hand on the door handle but I touched her arm and she stopped to look at me.

"And don't you dare touch yourself. That sweet little cunt is all mine."

"Fuck, Connor," she breathed out and I felt my cock twitch.

"Now go."

My words were erotic and my tone was dark. There was no room for argument in my voice. But I didn't think Sophie would argue this time. Her body betrayed her. She wanted this just as much as I clearly did.

So she did what I said and exited the car and I watched her climb the steps to her apartment slowly before she disappeared behind the door. The image of Sophie draped across my desk from earlier that week flashed before my eyes. Her panties pushed down to her ankles while I finger-fucked her to orgasm was something I would never forget. And while I'd always imagined my first time with Sophie would have been something softer, more romantic and sweet, taking her that way gave me a deep sense of satisfaction. And today I was going to push that even further.

My tastes had changed when Sophie left. The entire situation, every-thing that we'd said to one another, and the way things had ended felt so terribly out of control. It left me needing to fill that control another way. I'd had a few partners over the course of our years apart that indulged my fantasies. But, there was no replacement for Sophie. There never would be. And fuck, the fact that she was submitting to me now was enough to bring a man like me to his knees.

I grabbed my phone and dialed Kris' number before I pressed it to my ear.

"Go ahead and cancel the rest of my meetings for the day. Something's come up that I need to take care of. Thanks, Kris."

Hanging up the call, I looked at my watch. It'd been about five minutes since I'd given Sophie my instructions. Another few minutes and she'd be more than ready for me, which was just how I wanted her. If she was going to so easily threaten the carefully constructed control I had, I was going to do what I could to even the playing field. And making her wait to receive my cock was about the best I could do on short notice.

When ten minutes had finally passed, I adjusted myself through my pants and calmly exited the car. As I walked up the stairs, I wondered if Sophie had done what I told her to. It wouldn't surprise me in the slightest if she was standing there fully clothed, nowhere near the bed. And while I wanted her submission, the thought of punishing her disobedience was making me rock hard. But as I stepped into her apartment, I looked down in front of me to see a trail of clothing that led to her bedroom.

The heel of my dress shoes clicked against the wood floors as I made my way slowly towards her. I followed the trail of clothing with increasing approval as I looked at each piece that had been dropped to the ground. One shoe, then the other, red blouse, gray skirt, red lacey bra and finally those sinful red panties. I almost regretted telling her to take those off. I loved the feeling of dragging them down her arousal drenched thighs.

She was laying on the bed, but not the way I wanted her. That was fine. I could move her when I was ready. But for right now, I was enjoying the way her peach of an ass was on display, hiding the heat that I knew was already slick for me.

"Eyes forward, legs down," I said, my tone dark.

"Fuck," she breathed out but she complied.

I moved my hand against her asscheek, ghosting my fingers against the soft skin as lightly as possible.

"Connor," she tried to say, her voice dripping with need. But she wasn't in control of this situation. I was. And begging me to take her wasn't going to change that. I'd barely touched her but my grip on her was absolute.

My finger slipped down over the swell of her ass and I knelt down next to her, my finger brushing against the crease at the bottom of her cheek.

"I'm very pleased with you, Sophie," I said, my voice deep and Sophie shuddered. "But, I have to know. Did you touch yourself while I was gone? If you lie, I'll find out and all this will stop."

"I may have." The words were shaky on her breath and I knew I had her.

"You may have or you did?"

She squeezed her eyes shut and nodded her head. "I did."

My fingers made their way up her body to play against her chin. "I told you not to."

"I know, but—"

"But nothing. Come here," I said, sitting on the bed and moving her so that she was draped over my knees. I leaned down close to her ear and whispered, "Yellow to slow, red to stop." Pulling back, my voice returned to its demanding tone. "Tell me you understand."

"I understand," Sophie replied.

My palm moved against the curve of her ass and she shivered. "How long?"

"What?" Sophie asked, clearly caught up in the scene.

"How long did you touch yourself without my permission?"

My fingers continued to move across her ass and her arousal began to drip down her thighs. I wondered how Sophie would respond to all this and my cock was pressing against the front of my trousers with how fucking hot she was.

"I don't know, maybe five seconds?" she mumbled out but I wasn't satisfied.

"How long, Sophie?"

She gulped. "Five seconds."

"Then count to five with me," I said.

A SMACK CAME DOWN on my asscheek harshly and I gasped as a shock wave of pleasure spread through my system. I'd never been spanked before but . . . I liked it. I hadn't known what was about to happen. I just knew that I felt totally and utterly exposed to Connor, bent naked across his knee. And I also knew that I loved it.

When he'd instructed me to go upstairs, I had no idea what he had planned for me. Submitting to him was thrilling and also, something I'd longed for. The only thing I'd learned during my time away was that the one person in this world I could trust was Connor. Even after I'd so clearly hurt him, even after he told me he couldn't be around me, he went back on his word, for *me*. No one had ever done that for Sophie Strong. No one.

So, when he asked me to submit. When I looked into his eyes and saw that he so desperately needed me to, I did it without hesitation.

Connor immediately moved his hand to soothe the pink spot that had formed in the shape of his hand on my ass cheek.

"One," I said in a breathy tone.

He moved his hand up my cheek to the small of my back and I shuddered. He lifted and tapped it gently and I gasped just the same.

"Two," I said. He was playing games with my mind and I knew I was falling completely under his spell.

A single finger circled the pucker at the top of my ass before gliding down between my cheeks. It passed over my asshole with the faintest of touches and my entire sex clenched. The finger teased my folds gently, touching the skin there as if it was a delicate flower and he didn't want to bruise a single pedal.

Another light tap to my backside had me gasping and saying, "Three."

A fourth smack came down almost immediately and I screamed out at the shock and pleasure, all mixed into one. When I had finally caught my breath, I let out a shaky "Four," as he continued his torturous game.

A finger danced around my wet heat, moving my folds this way and that. I moaned and tried to push against his fingers but his strong grip came down on the small of my back. "Naughty girl. You'll take what I give you when I give it to you," he said and I groaned.

A single finger slipped inside me pumping me gently. I knew I shouldn't allow Connor to distract me. I knew he was trying to make me forget that I still had one pat left but thoughts flew out of my mind as his thumb passed over my clit and I cursed under my breath.

"Oh fuck me." The words fell from my mouth and Connor smirked.

A second finger speared into me as his thumb continued to move against my clit. I could feel myself climbing that familiar cliff. Connor seemed to be able to get me to heights I could never reach on my own and I bit my lip in anticipation. I could feel how wet I was from his ministrations. His fingers moved in and out of me with ease and I knew I was close.

Smack. Just as I thought I might come, his fingers left me, feeling utterly empty and both hands came up to smack across my ass, hard.

I screamed. Not from the pain. His hands stung but it didn't hurt. But from the shock and the immense pleasure I felt as my sex clenched with need. My clit pulsed and my breathing was labored. "Five," I said weakly.

Connor smoothed his hands over the swell of my ass which was now pink from his attention. He moved me so that I was sitting next to him. I looked down at the lap I had just been draped across and sucked in a

98

breath. A small wet spot had formed on the leg of his trousers where I'd just been. Connor followed my gaze down and smirked.

"Did you cream on my suit, Sophie?" he asked before looking back at me and taking my chin in his strong grip.

"I—" I hesitated. I wasn't sure how I felt. Was I embarrassed? Should I be?

"Say what you did, 'cause I think it's hot as fuck." His blue eyes didn't flicker from my green ones for even a second.

"I came on your trousers."

Connor lifted an eyebrow and shook his head. "No, but your about to."

I gasped as I felt myself being lifted in the air before I was once again straddling him. But this time, I was upright, facing away from him, my thighs spread on either side of one knee while my sex pressed into the wet spot on his trousers.

A hand snaked around the front of my body, caressing my midriff before moving to the apex of my thighs. I sighed as Connor started pressing kisses into the back of my shoulder, nipping and sucking at the skin as he pleased. His other hand came up the front of my body, cupping my breast and I nearly came from the touch of his fingers finally on me.

He moaned and pulled back from me slightly. "I'd have been playing with these a lot sooner if you hadn't decided to hide them from me." His tone was dark and full of promise. "I don't ever want you hiding your beautiful body from me again, Sophie."

I nodded as his fingers moved closer to my clit but refused to give me the release I needed.

"I require an answer, Sophie."

"Yes."

"Yes, what?"

"I won't hide my body?"

"Your beautiful body. Say it."

"I won't hide my beautiful body."

"Good girl," he whispered against my skin, his words gentle and comforting. His thumb pressed against my clit and I gasped as I quickly returned to the high I almost flew off of earlier.

My hips began to move against him, grinding on his leg and he let me this time, not restricting my movements, but letting me experience the sensations coursing through my body.

I knew that I was drenching Connor's pant leg beneath my sex, but I couldn't stop myself. The way he kissed the back of my neck, tugged at my hardened nipples and played his thumb on my clit had me completely slave to the pleasure that was coursing through me.

"Fuck, Connor!" I screamed as I came, my high overtaking me as pleasure coursed through my body. As soon as I climaxed, he was pressing hard against my clit before circling it gently, making the waves that were crashing through me last that much longer.

I slumped forward and Connor caught me with strong arms around my waist. "I'm not done with you, yet, gorgeous," he said as he moved me so that I was sprawled out on the bed.

I looked up at him as he began to undress, first removing his jacket and then that sinfully sexy vest before moving to unbutton his dress shirt. I looked at the fabric as it fell off his shoulders and instantly decided I was going to steal that shirt from him somehow.

Connor watched my eyes and my fixation on his movements and smirked. He tugged his tee off underneath and stepped forward, holding his dress shirt in his hands. "I'll let you have this, on one condition."

"What's that?" I asked, looking up at him with lust-filled eyes.

Connor sucked in a breath but continued. "Anytime you even think about touching yourself, you wear it. The only time you'll be allowed to come without me here is if you're wearing this. Yes?"

I couldn't believe the shivers that his words caused in my body, especially considering I had just come so hard I was quite positive I couldn't have walked if I wanted to. I nodded my head before adding, "Yes."

"Good girl," he said, draping the shirt over the side of my headboard. He reached for his belt and I held my breath as he pushed his trousers down and off his body. The last time he'd fucked me, I hadn't gotten the chance to look at his equipment. I knew he had to be large. I had felt it. But there was nothing quite like looking a cock in the eye before sucking on it for all you were worth.

Tight black boxer briefs stretched out across thickly muscled legs and

I groaned at how amazing he looked. It was no wonder his thrusts had been so powerful. He certainly wasn't the skinny track kid I had met back in college. This was an entirely different Connor.

"Come here, gorgeous," he said and I sighed at his words as I allowed him to pull me where he wanted me, which was face up with my head slightly off the edge of the bed. "Ever sucked a man's cock like this before, Sophie?"

I shook my head. "No." I was slightly nervous but also really excited. I wasn't experienced by any stretch of the word, but Connor was showing me things that had never even crossed my mind before.

A small smile tugged at the corner of his mouth. "Grab my hand if it's too much, okay?"

"Okay," I responded and Connor pulled himself out of his briefs. He was big, but from this angle, he seemed larger than life. A thick vein traveled down the front of his shaft, leading to his crown, which was exposed given how incredibly rock hard he was for me.

I reached up to pump him in my hand and Connor sighed at the sensation.

He moved, pushing his cock forward and I opened my mouth to let him inside. "Good girl," he said as I wrapped my lips around him. He looked down and groaned. "I knew those bright red lips of yours would look amazing around my cock," he said. He kept his movements slow at first, so I could keep up.

His hands came down to toy with my breasts and I moaned, sending vibrations up his length that had him gritting his teeth.

"Feel that, Sophie. This is how I'm going to fuck you. Slow and smooth, until you're begging me to go faster."

I moaned again and Connor pulled out of my wet mouth. I watched him as he reached back into the pocket of his trousers and pulled out a condom. Rolling it over himself, he walked his way to the other side of the bed before getting on, straddling me as he pumped his cock over me a few times.

I pushed my feet up, bending my knees, and reached my hands towards him. "I need to feel you inside of me again, Connor."

He lowered himself to me, rubbing his solid cock against my weeping flower several times before finally entering me.

I LOOKED DOWN, wanting to memorize everything about how beautiful Sophie looked, spread out and waiting for me to fuck her into ecstasy. Her red hair was fanned out around her and she looked like a goddess on fire. Because she was.

I was slow and took my time, but her slick heat was trying to suck me in and I grit my teeth to try and slow the encounter down. If I wasn't careful, he'd be ramming into her with abandon. When I was finally seated in her warm heat, Sophie threw her head back and moaned. "Fuck, Connor. You feel so good."

I began to move and she was moaning a mingle of curses and my name with every thrust. My hips snapped forward and her sex held onto me like a vice. "Sophie, your tight little cunt feels so good," I said, my head falling into the crook of her neck.

I never lost control during sex. I never lost my presence when I was buried inside a partner and I certainly never lost command over my body. But Sophie was different. Sophie had me thrusting into her tight pussy with a speed and a need that I'd never experienced before. It was just like the other night in my office. I'd planned to do so much more with Sophie, but before I knew it, I was thrusting into her from behind as her name tumbled from my lips.

"Fuck, Sophie," I said through gritted teeth.

"Yes, Connor," she breathed out as I continued to thrust into her. I grunted and adjusted our positions so that I was on my knees and she was draped over my lap. My hands were firm on her hips as I used them to push inside her body.

"Oh, fuck," she breathed out as her breath stuttered.

I could feel that Sophie was about to come. Her walls were clenching my cock like a vice and I knew it would only take a few more thrusts and she would crash. "Fucking come for me, Sophie. Scream who fucked you into ecstasy," I said as I brought one hand up to press against her clit.

Sophie's mouth fell open and her breath hitched as her sex clamped hard on my cock. "Fuck, Connor!" she moaned.

It was the moment I'd had been waiting for. My hips thrust forward and I let myself crash over that edge with her, her tight channel still milking my cock long after I'd come down from my high.

I fell forward, careful not to crush her and pulled her tight against my body. Our skin was slick with sweat but I didn't care. All I wanted to do right now was hug her tight to my form with my cock still buried inside of her.

She turned to look at me with a lazy smile and I moved forward and pressed my lips to hers. "You're amazing," I said as I pulled back from her lips.

"Connor, I—" she started to say but I pressed my lips to hers again.

"Shh, just rest," I said as I tucked her head under me and pulled her tighter against me. Right now, I just wanted to hold her in this moment.

FOURTEEN

Connor

I WATCHED THE FAN BLADES AS THEY MADE THEIR SLOW, CIRCULAR PATH above my head. I turned and my gaze fell on Sophie, sleeping peacefully beside me. I couldn't help but draw a metaphor. Our relationship had been following its own circular path these last few weeks.

There was clearly something on Sophie's mind. I knew her too well. Even after all these years, she was still an easy read for me. So every time she started to say my name with that particular tone in her voice, I knew she wanted to talk about something serious.

Like last night, she had said my name with that look in her eyes that told me she was about to spill . . . something. My heart ached as I looked at her. More than anything, I wanted to feel close to her the way we had all those years ago, but I was still unsure about opening myself up to her that way. And while I didn't know what it was she wanted to say, I figured it had something to do with us.

So, I stopped her. Because, if she was going to try and tell me anything other than "I love you," I wasn't sure what I would do. Being the CEO of a successful company had worn away at my patience. I was used to getting things when I wanted them and up to my standards. If she were to deny me—I shuddered at the thought of how much it would mess me up again.

But I also knew that Sophie's emotions weren't some business deal. Things were more complicated than that. I guessed that's why I had said what I'd said that first night. Perhaps that had been my way to try and transform this situation into something I understood and could therefore control.

I was leaving for a business trip on Monday and I knew that would give me the time I needed to sort this out. But as Sophie turned and flashed me a sleepy smile, I found myself completely caught in her web once more.

"Spend the weekend with me?" I asked her.

"Don't you have work?" she replied, rubbing her eyes slightly.

I smirked. "It's Saturday. Besides, what's the use of being the boss if I can't take a weekend off?"

Sophie smiled and allowed me to pull her on top of my body. I raised my knees, caging her form between them. Sophie raised an eyebrow as my manhood began to harden and I pushed myself into her.

I raised my hand and caressed the side of her face and she sighed and leaned into my touch.

"Do I have to ask again?"

She shook her head and met my blue stare. "You know I can't say no to you."

A smile tugged at the corner of my lips at her words and I flipped us over so that Sophie was trapped beneath me. She looked up at me, my fierce eyes looking down at her and I felt my body heat up, despite how many times I had come less than twelve hours ago.

"Are you protected?" I asked, referring to birth control.

Sophie nodded her head. "And clean, if you were wondering."

I leaned in to kiss her neck and she gasped before I pulled back and whispered, "I never believed a word those fuckers said."

I could tell my words had gotten to her. The slightest bit of moisture collected in the corner of her eyes, as if she couldn't believe what I'd just said. But I meant it. I didn't care what the tabloids said about her. And I didn't care how she was acting at the moment. I knew Sophie. I might be the only person who *truly* knew her. And I knew she was nothing like they said.

She was a kind, beautiful, free spirited soul. She was the sort of girl that stopped to buy a homeless man a sandwich or just listen to someone in need, even if it meant missing her bus. She was everything right with the world. Which was why she'd been so taken advantage of.

It was why, more than anything, I wanted to make her mine.

"Yesterday I fucked you rough. But today I want to take it slow and explore your amazing curves," I husked against her ear, trying to distract her from herself.

Sophie shuddered at my words as my lips pressed against hers. I moved my legs so that she was completely beneath me and she gasped as I rocked my body against hers, letting her feel my hardened cock against her core. I seized on the opportunity, pushing my tongue into her mouth to swirl my muscle against hers and she groaned.

Her hands lifted to circle around my neck and I pulled back with a bit of a smirk. "Needy this morning, are we?"

"You've completely ruined me for any other man, Connor," she breathed out as I moved back in to press kisses against her neck.

I sucked in a breath at her words and my heart clenched. She must have sensed my response because she was looking up at me, trying to make me meet her gaze. "Connor—"

There was that tone again. I shook my head. "Later, Sophie. Right now, I just need to fuck you slow until you're screaming my name." My head dipped back down to her neck and my tongue traced patterns against her skin.

My cock ached to be buried inside her warm heat, but more than that, I wanted to take it slow with her, explore every curve of her body and find every spot that made her shiver, curse and scream. And so I held myself at bay, memorizing every line, arc and curve of her form before I finally couldn't take it anymore.

Sophie's thighs were completely drenched with the evidence of orgasm my fingers had just given her, so when I moved forward and entered her, I slid into her heat easily. She gasped as my cock stretched her walls. She felt amazing raw and as much as she claimed I'd ruined her for other men, she'd completely decimated me for anybody else. I'd never known a love like Sophie's.

I knew I was large and I pressed a kiss against her lips before I started to move. My rhythm was smooth and Sophie fell under the spell of my movements, her walls still pulsing each time I pushed into her. She kept her eyes closed as I rocked against her, taking everything I gave her.

I could feel her walls convulse against my cock and I grit my teeth as my balls drew up sooner than I would have preferred. But I couldn't stop it from happening. Sophie's cunt felt amazing and I knew I'd never tire of it. I came hard, pressing into her before the words, "I love you," spilled from my lips.

We laid there, trying to catch our breaths. I knew what I'd said, and I hoped Sophie might just let it go, but of course, she wouldn't be Sophie if she did. She rolled over, placing a hand and then her chin on my chest and smiled at me. I let myself caress her beautiful red hair, even tangled from lovemaking and a night's sleep as it was.

"Can we talk?"

Those crystal green eyes of hers turned on me and she bit her bottom lip.

"About what?" I said, hesitantly.

"About us."

"What's there to talk about?"

Sophie stayed quiet and I jumped in on the silence.

"Look, right now, I'm just happy being with you, in whatever way possible. Let's just enjoy this moment right now. We can figure things out later."

Sophie nodded and my heart relaxed. I smiled and moved my hand against her temple again, caressing her lightly. "Hungry?"

"Starving," she replied. "Someone still owes me lunch from yesterday," she said with a smile.

I pulled her close so that I was holding her tight against my body.

Sophie rested her head on my chest and sighed into my touch. "Pancakes it is then," I said with a laugh. "But we're going to have to stop at my place first."

Sophie's eyes widened.

"I can pick you up in an hour?" I asked. Sophie deflated slightly and I instantly picked up on it. "Or you can come with if you want to."

Her emerald eyes perked up and my heart clenched at the thought of her wanting to see my place. My cock also twitched at the subsequent thought of her spread out on my bed, that beautiful red hair of hers framing her face as it twisted in the throes of ecstasy.

"Can I make a suggestion?" she asked.

"Of course. You are the intern after all. You're supposed to bring fresh new ideas to the old stagnant company."

Sophie snorted and covered her mouth with a giggle at the noise that came out. My chest rose and fell slightly beneath her with my own laugh. "I'm starving. You're starving. Why not just let me run in and grab our pancakes to go?"

"Are you going to order me chocolate chip pancakes again?"

"Of course!"

I shook my head with a chuckle. "Okay."

FIFTEEN

Sophie

I SPUN MYSELF AROUND IN THE CHAIR WITH A SIGH AS SKYLER WATCHED Trevor add some color to someone in the seat in front of him.

"What's got you so pouty?" Skyler asked.

"She hasn't been laid recently," Trevor piped up and my eyes widened.

"That's your answer for everything, Trev," Skyler said with a roll of her eyes.

"And I'm *never* wrong. Go ahead, Soph, tell her. Prove me right."

I twisted my lips and looked at Skyler. "Connor left on a business trip Monday."

Trevor chuckled and I blushed.

"I thought you two spent the weekend in ecstasy?" Skyler asked.

I sighed, thinking back to how incredible the weekend had been. I hadn't gotten done any of the reading assignments I'd intended to and this week's classes had been a bit of a shit show, but it'd been worth it. Connor had taken me back to his penthouse apartment and the place was incredible. From the fourteenth floor, he had a view of the Washington monument and the Capitol. I had never particularly liked D.C., but I had to admit that Connor's set up was very nice.

We had spent the entire weekend at his place and he'd only relented to dropping me back to the loft on Sunday evening because he had to get to the airport early in order to catch a flight to California to meet with a group of potential investors. But the entire week had gone by and I'd heard nothing from him.

"Guys are single-track minds, babe," Trevor said, wiping a bit of blood and ink from his customer's arm. "If he's working on some deal or whatever, that's all he's thinking about. Don't take it personally."

"Would it kill the guy to shoot me a text message?" I huffed. I really didn't recognize this side of myself. I felt like I was being needy and clingy, but I couldn't help it.

Trevor shrugged. "He's just focused right now, that's all."

Skyler came over to my side and gave me a hug. She pulled back and smiled. "Did you ever think of contacting him?"

"I don't want to bother him."

"He's a big boy," Trevor chimed in. "If I can't answer the phone for you, he won't."

"How long is he out there?"

"Another week," I said with a sigh. "Apparently, he scheduled a bunch of other meetings when the first group agreed to meet with him."

Truth be told, Connor had asked me to go with him. But I'd refused. He was headed to Los Angeles and I couldn't be seen there. Besides, I wasn't going to risk failing any of my classes by taking an impromptu week off just to hang out in a hotel room.

"He's got to be back to teach our weekend seminar next week," I said. "So at least I know there's an end in sight."

Skyler sat in the chair across from me and fixed me with a lavender stare. "Are you in love with this man, Soph?"

My eyes widened in surprise at how direct her question was. "I don't . . . maybe? . . . why did you ask me that?" I finally ended with a huff.

"I've just never seen you like this before. When we first met, it was all about reconnecting with an old friend and maybe getting some good sex out of it. But this, hating being away from him, looking forward to when he's back. I dunno, it just feels different."

"Maybe he's just that good at sex," I said immediately and even Trevor laughed.

"That's not really how that works, babe," Skyler said. "It's one thing to miss a man's cock, it's another to miss the *man*."

I made a face at my friend.

"Take her word for it, Soph," Trevor said, still working on his customer. "Skyler misses my cock all the time."

"Trev!" Skyler exclaimed and I laughed.

"Well, maybe if *the man* would let me talk to him about our feelings, I could figure it all out."

"Whatchya mean?" Skyler asked, pulling a granola bar out of her purse.

"I mean, that every time I try and bring up the subject, he finds some way to avoid it. The entire weekend I tried to have the "us" conversation and we just ended up fucking instead. It's so frustrating!"

"Sounds horrible," Skyler said with an exaggerated roll of her eyes.

"You know what I mean," I huffed. I threw my head back in the chair and closed my eyes. "I just want to figure all this out before things go any further. I don't want to hurt him . . . again," I had to add.

"Then stop sleeping with him," Skyler said with a wink.

"Easier said than done," I muttered.

"Sounds like it's easier done than said," Trevor smirked, washing his hands at the sink, having finished the design.

"Finally," Skyler said, throwing the rest of her granola bar at him with a laugh.

THE WEEKEND with Sophie had been everything I had wanted and more. I had made sure of that. I'd taken her on my bed, on my counter, in the shower, the list was exhaustive. And even still, I hadn't had enough of her. But I knew this was how it would be with Sophie, I'd always known.

I knew Sophie wouldn't agree to accompany me on my trip and as much as it pained me, it was probably for the best. Sophie had a way of short-circuiting my higher faculties when I was around her and I did not want to lose the shot at a partnership with the company representatives currently sitting across from me.

"I've got to say, Connor, I think the agreement could do a lot to enhance both businesses," the man to the left said. Steve was your classic investor; a successful transactional lawyer who had too much money and had started funding other side projects, only to make more money. He looked like a younger Mitt Romney, with salt and pepper hair combed just right and an expensive suit.

His business partner was the complete opposite. An older gentleman whom I had heard had been involved with the Navy Special Warfare forces when he was younger. Mike was your classic no shit, salty sailor.

"I'm glad you think so, Steve," I said, leaning forward to take a sip of my whiskey. "Solar panels are an integral part of our development designs and I think this exclusivity agreement could be very profitable for both sides."

Steve smiled. "Making money together. That's always the goal.

Mike?" he said, turning to his business partner. "You on board with this?"

I could feel Mike's eyes looking me up and down and I didn't flinch from his gaze. "I'm good."

I smiled internally. This deal was huge for Phoenix Development. It meant guaranteed panels for all of the developments at a fixed price. Integrated panels were still a relatively new technology and as such, pricing was fairly volatile. Knowing how much such a large line item would cost would do a lot to help balance budgets for all of our future projects.

We stood and shook hands. "Should I have legal go ahead and send you a proposed draft of the contract?" I asked, but Steve shook his head.

"No need. We've got a preferred form."

I nodded. We said our goodbyes and I made my way out of the restaurant towards my hotel. I was only a block from here so I decided to walk. I'd forgotten how nice the weather here was compared to D.C.

When I landed back in my room I threw my jacket down on the chair and made my way towards the bathroom, intent on showering off. The hot water streamed down on me from the rain shower and I heaved a heavy sigh. With my mind clear of this round of negotiations, I had a little space to think of other things.

Of course my brain immediately shifted to Sophie. I wondered what she was doing right now and also wondered if I should try and call her. Things between us were simultaneously simple and complicated. We were sleeping together without any strings attached. But at the same time, I knew that both of us wanted more.

I leaned my head against the side of the shower and let the water stream down my face. Sophie had tried several times over the course of the weekend to talk with me, but each time I'd stopped her. Hence all of the places I'd fucked her across my apartment. I was being selfish and I knew it, but I didn't want to have that conversation because I feared how things might change between us.

My entire attitude towards this problem was foolish. I would never approach an issue for Phoenix this way, by putting it off and refusing to deal with it. Turning off the water, I committed to having that conversation with Sophie as soon as I was back in town.

I grabbed my phone, intent on checking the news and taking care of any lingering emails before heading off to bed. Sitting on the bed, I swiped the screen open and pulled down on my notifications banner.

"Hey."

The three little letters sat there next to "Soph" sent over an hour ago. I felt a small smile tug at the corner of my lips. I hadn't meant not to contact Sophie for the week, but with the time difference and my crazy schedule trying to woo Mike and Steve plus still manage things remotely from the office, I'd barely had any time to even sleep, let alone have a proper conversation.

I looked at the time and winced, realizing it was nearing midnight by her.

"Hey. Been stuck in meetings. You still up?"

I wondered if she would respond, but the three dots popped up pretty quickly.

"Did you forget I existed?" was her response. I chuckled. I knew Sophie was teasing me. This was just her way.

"That'd be impossible."

The dots appeared and disappeared several times, as if she was trying to decide what to say before finally her response came through.

"Well, good."

"What are you wearing?"

"Are you trying to sext with me?"

I laughed. *"Yes. Answer the question."*

"Wouldn't phone sex be easier?"

"Soph—"

"Fine, nothing. I'm wearing nothing. Happy?"

"Extremely. Have you touched yourself this week?"

"Yes," she answered honestly.

"Did you behave yourself?"

"I can still smell the cologne from your shirt on my skin, if that's what you mean."

"Good girl. Get me off."

"*What?*"

"*My cock is so hard for you, Soph. I'm going to stroke it while you tell me all the filthy things you want me to do with your body when I'm back from my trip.*"

I watched the dots appear and disappear again for several long seconds. I wondered how far I could push her, but she was driving me insane with lust and being away from her for an entire week had been almost unbearable. I knew Sophie wasn't all that experienced. If I couldn't tell from the past weekend, I knew that she lost her virginity her senior year of high school and had only one other partner from college before we met. It seems I'd outpaced her during our time away, which was fine. I may have missed out on some of her firsts, but pushing her boundaries open and watching her react was becoming a new favorite hobby.

Finally, her text appeared.

"*The feel of your hand caressing the curve of my ass before plunging your fingers in my dripping cunt was what I thought about when I climaxed earlier.*"

Fuck, yes.

"*Tell me what you want me to do with you next, Sophie. Not what I've already done.*"

I knew her too well. I knew she was slightly embarrassed. But I wanted to know what made my Sophie tick. I would fulfill every last one of her fantasies. And then I would *own* her.

The dots started and stopped again before finally a large message came through. I stroked my cock up and down as I read her words.

"*I loved being laid out on that big poster bed of yours. I can't wait until I'm back at your place and you strip me down, peeling off the layers of my clothing until nothing but my panties remain.*

"*You'd tie my hands first. One wrist attached to each post before you kissed your way down my body, licking my cunt until I begged for release. But you wouldn't let me have it. Not yet.*

"*I'd feel the soft leather around each ankle before you forced my thighs open.*

"*I'd be completely helpless. Unable to stop you even if I wanted to.*

But I wouldn't want you to stop. All I'd want is for you to fuck me. As hard and as deep as you wanted until I came and you doused me in your come."

"Fuck," I cursed as I read the last lines, my seed bursting from the tip of my cock to spill on my stomach. My breathing was ragged and I rolled off the bed to head to the bathroom and wash off quickly.

When I returned to the bed, a new message from Sophie was waiting for me.

"Connor?"

"Good girl," was my response.

"Did you . . ."

"Come? Yes. And I can't wait to do just that to you when I'm back. I've got a set of cuffs I think you'll really enjoy."

"Can't wait. Night, Con."

SIXTEEN

Aubrey

"I HAVE NO INTEREST IN JUST SELLING HER WHEREABOUTS TO A TABLOID for a quick buck," I said to the voice on the other side of the line. "Perhaps you're not aware, but money really isn't a concern for me."

"What is your concern then, Ms. Knight?" Lennie Webb said. This guy seriously owed me one. I knew Sophie was one of his biggest clients and it was obvious she had up and disappeared on him.

"It's a means to an end for me, that's all," I said, not feeling like I owed him any sort of explanation.

I could hear him sigh through the phone. "Again, how can we make this work, Ms. Knight? We'll arrange it in a way that suits both of us."

"I want it to be big. And I want it to catch her off guard." Now that I knew the little hussy was an intern for Connor's company on Fridays, I could have her bombarded when she left the office. If things went my way, the paparazzi might also catch her leaving with Connor.

After the way Connor had treated me last week, there was no way I would ever take him back, even if he begged. But there was also no way I would ever let someone get away with embarrassing me that way. He clearly didn't know just who he was messing with. I was committed to finding out a way to mess up his perfect life. If I didn't get to have him, then I'd make sure he wasn't worth having.

The fact that the disgraced pop star was working for Phoenix would do enough to bring negative publicity to Connor's company. But if the two were caught together, it couldn't be more perfect.

"I'll need the details to get it all set up," Lennie said.

I shook my head. "No. I'm not just handing this information over to you. Take a few weeks to get everything set up and have your people prepared to head into the business district on a Friday afternoon. I'll tell you the exact location the week of."

Lennie scoffed. "Ma'am, we can get things arranged much sooner than that."

"No." I wanted this as close to the end of the semester as possible. At the very least, Sophie might be so distracted that she might fail an exam. In the best situation, she might not show up for final exams at all. I would take out Connor, his company and his little skank in one blow.

"In the meantime you can build up things in the press. Get them interested in the girl's whereabouts again. Or spread some more lies. You're good at that."

Lennie gasped. "I certainly did not spread any lies about my own client, Ms. Knight."

"I'm not a child, Mr. Webb and this isn't my first rodeo. I don't care how you make your money. Let's just make this arrangement work for us. I'll be in touch in a few weeks' time."

I heard a sigh on the other side of the line before he finally said. "Until then, Ms. Knight."

 IT'D BEEN several weeks since Connor had returned from his business trip and he'd delivered on his promise to fulfill that specific fantasy of mine and so much more. It seemed like that first text of mine had broken the ice because the last few days of Connor's trip had been full of some of the hottest sexting, phone sex and facetime sex I had ever experienced.

I'd gotten more of a sense of the things that turned Connor on over the last week and a little voice inside my head encouraged me on. Apparently, my dirty-side had murdered my more prudish-side with me totally unaware.

I was currently lounging on the curved recliner that doubled as the most amazing sex couch in his bedroom wearing nothing but one of Connor's dress shirts. The shirt laid open, giving him a fantastic view of my perky breasts as I sat there, reading a book. For the first time in a long time I felt comfortable, confident and sexy.

"Soph," he said, bringing me a cup of coffee.

I took it and smiled up at him. "What's up?"

Things had been better than ever since Connor had come back from his trip. I spent increasing amounts of time at his place, especially on either side of my internship days. We were careful to leave and enter separately, but ending up back at Connor's penthouse apartment had become a regular thing for me.

I laughed to myself as I thought about how everything in our relationship this time was completely reversed compared to the last time. For starters, we were sleeping together . . . a lot. I spent almost all of my time at his apartment, whereas before he'd always been at my loft. And this time, Connor was completely in control.

"I know you've been trying to talk to me about something on your mind for a while now. I just wanted to give you the chance."

"Oh," I said as Connor lifted my legs before sitting and draping them over his lap. My feelings for Connor since that first night and every time we'd gotten together afterwards had changed so drastically. If he had let me talk to him the first time I'd wanted to, I might have tried to tell him that I wasn't looking for anything more than a friends-with-benefits situation, but I knew that just wasn't true anymore.

I took a sip of the coffee and placed it on the side table next to me. The morning light filtered in through the windows, reflecting off his blue eyes, making them look somehow brighter than usual. He looked at me so intensely, I could tell that this was a big deal for him.

"I guess I just wanted to clear the air about us," I said as he caressed my legs gently with his fingertips. "Especially how everything happened that first night."

"Sophie, I don't think I've hid the fact that I'm in love with you," he said, his deep voice making me shiver.

I nodded my head. "You're right. But I have." Connor stayed quiet. "I've had so much bad shit happen to me over the past year, Con. When I landed here, you were the last thing in my life that I felt like was still good. But I hated myself. In some ways, I still do. And I didn't feel like I deserved you . . . don't deserve you. You deserve better. I'm toxic and you really shouldn't be in love with me."

Tears started welling up in my eyes and Connor watched quietly as my words turned more and more against myself. He reached forward, pulling me into a strong embrace. I sighed as his musky scent filled my space, feeling somehow instantly calmer.

"Soph, you don't get to decide who I do and don't love." He pulled back and looked into my eyes.

I shuddered at his words. "I know. But, you've done so much since I've been out of your life. Everyone hates me right now, Con. I don't want to be responsible for tearing down everything you've worked so hard for."

"Why don't you let me worry about my own business? All I want to know from you is how you feel about me. I'll take care of the rest."

"I love you, Connor. I always have. I'm just an idiot—"

His lips pressing against mine cut me off. He pulled back and pressed a finger to my lips. "You don't get to say things like that about yourself anymore, understand?"

I nodded my head at his commanding tone.

"I'll not have my woman saying such nonsense."

"Your woman?"

Connor pressed another kiss against my lips. "Did you think I was going to let you run from me again?"

I shook my head as he wiped a stray tear from my eyes. "Soph, you have been through some real shit the past few years, I don't deny that. But you showed a strength few others could even contemplate. You picked yourself up and did what you needed to do to better yourself. I know plenty of people that would have just crumbled in your situation."

"I ran away," I said, shaking my head and denying all the things he was saying.

"No. You didn't run away. You ran from toxic people. There's a difference. So don't ever call yourself an idiot. And I don't want to hear you saying you or anyone else hates you." He pressed a kiss to my cheek before adding, "and if you ever start to doubt yourself, just remember that I love you. And Connor Driscoll doesn't make mistakes."

I giggled through the tears that started to fall from my eyes, but Connor wiped each of them away. "Come on, don't cry."

"I'm just happy," I admitted, letting Connor wrap his arms around me. He picked me up and carried me to the bed, laying me out before climbing on top. He moved his lips against mine and if it was even possible, he tasted better than he had before.

He ghosted kisses down my face before latching onto my earlobe. "You're *mine* now, Sophie. You understand."

I shuddered beneath him and nodded my head.

"I require an answer. Tell me, Sophie. To whom do you belong?"

"You, Connor. I belong to you," I replied in a heated whisper.

Connor smiled against my skin. Just as he was about to lick the skin on my neck, an alarm sounded from somewhere to the right of us.

I groaned as Connor rolled off of me to shut off the device. "Sorry, Soph. But we both gotta get going."

I pursed my lips. "Class on a Saturday should be a crime."

Connor chuckled. "You're the one that signed up for the course."

"My mistake."

Truth be told, I had been looking forward to the one-credit seminar that Connor was scheduled to teach for most of the semester. Skyler had swapped it for another course in her schedule so the two of us had planned to study together. And besides, an entire weekend of watching Connor stand in front of the class and command a room wasn't anything to complain about. I just would have preferred to finish what we had started instead of heading to the campus.

"Come on," Connor said, climbing off the bed before pulling me up to his side. He pressed a kiss against my temple as he wrapped an arm around me. "We can get ready together. You have to shower, yes?"

"Check out that CEO-level efficiency," I teased as he led me into what might have been my favorite bathroom to date.

"Strip," he said, and I shivered.

I dropped the dress shirt and thong I'd been wearing to the floor. The gray veined marble felt cool against my feet as Connor moved beside me to turn on the shower.

With my past life, I had stayed at some of the fanciest hotel suites in the world, but Connor's bathroom rivaled the best. The shower was encased in glass with beautiful, smooth river stones that felt amazing to stand on and a jetted Jacuzzi tub sat in the corner with a large roman faucet hanging over the side.

"Can't we just stay here forever?" I whined but Connor just pointed to the shower.

"Get wet for me."

I bit my lip but walked myself into the spray, letting the hot water douse my hair. When I had finished washing my red locks, Connor entered the space, not wasting any time before he crushed me into the wall. I gasped as the cold tile pressed against my back but my body was quickly overheating as Connor's hands began to roam.

"Unfortunately, we have to be quick about this, so I'm going to fuck you hard, fast and rough. I'll lavish more attention on this sweet little cunt later," he said before spearing two fingers into my heat.

I keened as he moved his digits inside of me, stretching me out quickly so that I was ready to take his thick length. Within seconds, he was turning me over, pushing on the small of my back and directing me to grab onto the stone bench that sat in the corner of the shower.

"Pop that peach of an ass up for me, Soph," he commanded.

Connor pressed his cock into me as I moaned at the feeling of him stretching me. "Fuck, Connor," I cursed under my breath as he started moving. His hips snapped against me with an intensity I'd only felt that first time we'd been in his office. Connor reached around to thumb my clit and I could feel myself climbing a high I hadn't thought I'd be able to reach so quickly. But as his cock moved in and out of me at a knee-weakening pace, I could feel my walls drawing upward with each thrust.

My breath hitched and I screamed his name before pleasure bloomed throughout my entire body. "Fuck yes, baby," Connor said through gritted teeth as he grabbed back onto my hips and pressed into my body quickly, letting his own release rip through him.

When I had finally regained my bearings, I felt Connor pull me up so I was standing straight. He pressed a gentle kiss to my lips and smiled. "I'll never tire of the feeling of your beautiful cunt wrapped around my cock."

"That's just about the sweetest thing anyone's ever said to me."

Connor smirked and smacked my ass before saying, "Rinse off. We gotta get going."

Thirty minutes later found us in the car, driving up Massachusetts Avenue towards the school.

"Oh, drop me at the loft," I said.

"You sure?" Connor asked.

"Yeah. Sky's taking the class too. She'll give me a ride up."

Connor looked at me and nodded, pulling into the little lot behind my building. "Don't be late. Otherwise I *will* punish you."

I shivered but nodded my head.

He reached behind my neck and pulled me in for a searing kiss. "All mine."

"All yours," I giggled back.

"Alright, get going," he said, releasing his hold on me. I opened the door and blew him a kiss before running upstairs to grab my books quickly.

"You ready?" Sky said as she pushed the slightly ajar door open to see me running around the room frantically gathering my school belongings. "Oh, you are not ready."

"Almost," I said with an apologetic smile.

"Busy morning?" Skyler twirled a lock of silver hair while biting her lower lip.

I giggled. "Something like that."

"You've been spending an awful lot of time at that big city penthouse of his."

I grabbed the last book I needed and turned to my friend. "I'm ready."

"And you avoided my question."

"Come on, I want coffee before we go. I didn't have a chance to finish mine."

"I can only imagine why," Skyler said with a wink as we made our way down to her car.

♪

I HEARD Connor sigh as Skyler and I tried to sneak into the back of the classroom five minutes late.

"Ladies." His voice boomed over us as the rest of the room filled out their initial paperwork. "Class started at ten, in case you were unaware."

Skyler giggled and nudged me in the ribs as we took the last remaining seats in the back of the small classroom. "Sorry, Professor," I responded immediately and he raised an eyebrow at me.

"Explanation?"

"We got lost, Professor," I said, knowing I was teasing him with my choice of words.

"Of course you did." He seemed slightly exasperated, but there was also a hint of excitement there, as well. "I expect you to be on time moving forward."

Me and Sky both nodded our heads, trying to suppress our giggles.

"Come here and get the handouts," he directed and I stood, walking around the class to the front where he was standing.

He handed me two packets of course materials and I looked up at him. "Thank you, Professor," I drawled before heading back to my seat.

Connor cleared his throat and I thought for a moment, I'd had a small victory over him.

"Alright, let's get started."

"AFTER LUNCH, we'll dive into what happens when the fund closes," Connor said, leaning against the large desk in the front of the room. "Does anyone have any questions before we break?"

I looked at him in his blue three-piece suit. His command over the class had been absolute, which was saying something. Because as I looked around the room, I recognized most of the faces that were attending this Private Equity seminar and a majority of them were talkers. The fact that Connor had managed to keep the entire class entertained and engaged throughout the first half of the day was truly amazing.

I found myself needing to concentrate on the lessons more than normal since I kept getting distracted. Connor knew I was trying to keep a low profile, so other than pointing out the fact that Skyler and I had been late to class, he hadn't called on me during class. But there were a few times that his blue eyes caught mine and I'd blush and instantly look down at the handouts in front of me.

A girl up at the front asked a question about placement agents and he answered her question quickly and surveyed the room confidently. "Anything else?" The class stayed silent and he clapped his hands together. "Be back in an hour." He fixed his gaze on me momentarily before everyone stood and shuffled out of the classroom.

"Ms. Len," Connor said as I started to follow Skyler out of the room.

"A word," he said as he looked down at the papers on the desk in front of him.

Skyler threw me a shit-eating grin and whispered, "Go on. I'll catch you later."

"You sure?" I asked and Skyler nodded her head.

"Go see what the sexy professor wants and tell me about it later."

I rolled my eyes but told my friend thanks nonetheless.

The last of the students cleared the classroom quickly, glad to be taking a break after a solid three hours of lecture, leaving me and Connor alone. The heavy door closed behind the last student out of the room and I drew in a breath as Connor looked up at me.

"Naughty girl," he said in a hushed voice. "Showing up late for class. Are you trying to test me?"

I bit my bottom lip and shuffled my feet slightly. "No." I looked up at him briefly. He looked like he wanted to devour me and I couldn't believe how much he was turning me on with just a look. "But it was just five minutes," I said with a huff.

Connor raised an eyebrow. He fixed me with that blue stare of his and I shuddered. "In five minutes I want you to go up the stairs and enter the first office on your right. I'll be waiting for you there."

I thought I might pout and ask about lunch, but the intensity of Connor's gaze told me that wasn't a good idea. Instead, I just nodded and Connor pressed his thumb against my lips gently, enough to make me shiver before he swept out of the room.

I rolled my eyes back before closing them. Being with Connor was unlike any experience I had ever had—and I'd been a world-famous pop star for Christ's sake. How this man did these things to me I just didn't understand.

I pulled out my phone and texted Skyler.

"Grab me a skim latte? I'll pay you back, promise!"

I could see Skyler typing her response.

"I got you, girl. Enjoy your extra lessons."

I just knew Skyler was smirking on the other side. Clicking my phone off, I made my way to the stairs. As I climbed each step, I had some time to reflect on just how much I had changed. I had always been a good girl in the worst ways. I never took risks and I never spoke my mind.

People had taken advantage of it during my few years of fame and the lack of control I had over my life had probably led me straight into the depression that I was finally coming out of. Every one of my relationships while I was on tour, whether it was romantic or not, was the polar opposite of mine with Connor. True, Connor was certainly calling the shots on a number of decisions, but I knew that if I had a real problem with anything, he would listen to me. I also knew that everything he did was for my benefit.

When I was Sophie Strong, decisions were made for the benefit of others. And if I ever objected to anything, my opinion was always cast aside. I was too "naïve" or too "young" to understand these things. Looking back, I couldn't believe I gave those people such control over my life.

Reaching the top step, I looked to my right to find a Visiting Professor's office. The door was slightly ajar and I opened it slowly, to find Connor sitting on the loveseat opposite the door. The office and its furnishings were simple. An old aerial of the university was hanging above the sofa and a large bookcase leaned against the right wall. A desk was on the left wall and there were no windows.

I shivered as Connor looked at me. "I see we can be on time if we want to be, Ms. Stronglen," he said in that deep voice of his.

I smiled, realizing just what Connor had planned. The thought of it had me squeezing my thighs, it was just so filthy. I stayed quiet and Connor stood. He walked right up to me and his woodsy scented cologne began to cloud my senses. The door closed behind me and I looked up into his eyes.

"Now," he said, sitting back down on the sofa. "I wonder how I should punish your tardiness."

I just looked at him with lust-filled eyes but didn't dare speak. With how aroused I felt right now, I wasn't sure I'd be able to form complete sentences anyways.

"Come here," he said, patting the inside of his thigh and I stepped forward.

"Connor I—" I started to say with a bit of a smile but he cut me off with a shake of his head.

"I'm in charge here, Ms. Stronglen. Go ahead and get on your knees. I know how to deal with insubordinate students."

I dropped down to my knees and leaned forward, my hands ghosting the inside of Connor's trousers. He raised an eyebrow at me. "Could it be that someone is craving their punishment?"

"Maybe," I said with a bite to my lower lip.

"Well, if you enjoy it, I'll just have to punish you again, in a way that you won't forget." I shuddered and my sex clenched at his words. "Go ahead, Ms. Stronglen. Show me how sorry you are for being late to class."

I grinned and leaned forward, unlooping Connor's belt and then the fastenings of his trousers before finally reaching in and freeing his cock. He was already so hard for me and I moaned at the feeling of his thick length in my hand.

I gasped as a strong hand gripped my chin. "I know you're craving it, but you have to keep quiet. Understand?"

I nodded my head with excitement and suppressed a moan before I began to pump his hardened cock in my hand. Connor sighed and let his head fall back briefly at the feeling of me working him.

He sucked in a breath as I let my tongue dart out and lick around the crown of his cock. He cracked an eye open to watch me work before I was once again trying to push back a moan as my lips closed around his member. His hands thread through my bright red hair and he sighed as I moved up and down his shaft.

In one swift movement, he pulled me off his cock, suddenly.

"Come here," he said quickly under his breath, pulling me up and making me straddle him. I was wearing a flippy skirt with a pair of tights and he reached down the front of them, tearing them just enough so he could push the lacey thong I had on over and push his cock inside me.

I gasped as I watched what Connor was doing, but I was so turned on, I didn't have the ability to stop him. I moaned as he seated himself inside of me but he brought a hand up to my mouth.

"Don't make a noise, understand?" he said, fixing me with those blue eyes of his.

I bit my lower lip and nodded, not sure if I'd be able to do what he asked. He started to move and I fell against his shoulders.

"It'd be a shame if someone decided to walk in on us like this because you made a noise, wouldn't it Ms. Stronglen?"

My eyes widened and I looked at him, holding onto his shoulders as he continued to thrust his hardened cock inside of me. "You didn't lock the door?" I whispered urgently.

Connor smirked. "More fun this way, isn't it?"

I gasped but Connor shook his head, reminding me to stay quiet. I fell forward again, trying my best to stop any noises crawling up my throat but Connor was making it incredibly difficult as he kissed and licked my neck.

"Connor," I whispered as I could feel my body begin to twitch as my walls tightened.

"That's it, baby. Come for me," he whispered back as he continued to bounce me on his cock.

I threw my head back as his cock began hitting the deepest parts of me and I felt the pleasure crash through me. I bit down on my lip hard to stop the moan as my release moved through me. Within a few seconds, he was following me over that edge, releasing his seed into me as he held my limp form against him.

When I had finally regained my breath, I looked at Connor as I climbed off him, moving quickly to grab a few tissues from the nearby box and wiping his essence off my skin as best as I could under the circumstances. I moved my panties back in place and sighed as I looked at my ruined tights. At least they hadn't ripped all the way down my legs, so I could still wear them to class.

I shot Connor a narrowed glance and he just smiled back at me with a satisfied grin. "I can't believe you didn't lock the door," I huffed turning around to look. But my words died on my tongue as I saw the deadbolt well in place.

I turned back around and Connor was grinning like a Cheshire cat.

"Admit it. It turned you on thinking that someone could just walk in on us like that."

I hung my head back and looked up at the ceiling but I couldn't help the smile on my lips. "I can't believe you," I said before he reached forward and pulled me down onto the couch with him.

"You were incredible, as always. I can't wait to get you home so I can punish you properly," he said before pressing a kiss to my neck.

I giggled and tried to push him away but he was insistent. He finally relented, placing a gentle kiss to my hand before getting up and opening the desk drawer. "Hungry?" he asked, pulling two catering lunch boxes out.

"Where did you get these?" I asked, opening my own box with anticipation.

Connor shrugged. "There was a reason I wanted a five-minute lead. I had them delivered to the staff lounge earlier. I take care of my own," he said with a wink before we both dug into our respective lunches.

SEVENTEEN

Sophie

"HAVE YOU SEEN THE TABLOIDS LATELY?" MY MOTHER ASKED ME through the phone.

"No, mother. I haven't."

"Sophie, darling. How are you expecting to improve your image if you don't even know what they're saying about you?"

"I'm not trying to improve my image. I could care less about my image. I'm trying to improve *myself* and do things for *myself*. Can't you understand that?" I bit back.

"I just know how important your music is to you," my mother said, clearly trying to garner sympathy.

"Yeah, but this isn't music, mom. This is something else entirely."

"Fine," my mother said, her curt tone finally breaking through. "If you want to be some poor nobody for the rest of your life, who am I to stop you?"

"Thanks, mom. I can always count on you for your support," I said in a sarcastic tone before my mother simply hung up the phone.

I let out a mangled groan as I collapsed on the sofa. Skyler tapped the pen that she'd been using as she worked on our assignments for the seminar. Connor had asked me to come back with him to his place but I'd refused. I knew if I did, I wouldn't get anything done for the class and I was actually trying to graduate based on merit and not because I was having an affair with my professor.

"Why do you pick up for that woman?" Skyler asked.

I sighed. "Unfortunately she's learning. I have her number muted unless she calls multiple times in a row. I'm always worried that there's a real emergency and end up picking up."

Skyler smirked and shook her head. "You're too nice."

"Maybe," I said, scrunching my face.

"Placement agents are usually paid what percentage of the commitments they are able to garner?" Skyler asked, referring to our worksheet.

"One percent."

"One percent," Skyler repeated, writing down the answer. "*Have* you looked at the tabloids lately, Sophie? I'm not saying you should care. I'm just saying you should probably be aware of what's going on so you don't end up caught off guard."

I sighed. I really did not want to peel back the curtain on that part of my life but I knew Skyler was right.

"Look, I know it's not easy. But take it from someone who's run from something before, you need to know what you're dealing with."

"Fine," I said with a huff as I slid my laptop over and googled my name. I clicked on the first news story that popped up and read the title aloud to Skyler.

Where in the World is Sophie Strong?

"What's it say?"

I rolled my eyes as I read through the article. "It says nonsense. Some people are hypothesizing I left because of the fallout. Others say I'm taking time off to write new songs and will be back. And others theorize

I died in an undisclosed plane flight. I'm surprised my old label didn't release a statement about the last one in order to cash in on a big funeral."

"I'd go to your fake funeral."

"Awe, thanks babe." I smiled at my friend's dry sense of humor. I brushed an errant piece of red hair out of my face as I scrolled down to the bottom of the article where people could write in comments. My features softened as a few obvious fans left notes.

"Sophie! I miss you! Come back to us!"

"I don't believe a word of what they said about her. Sophie Strong is an amazing artist and that's what really matters!"

"Fuck Sophie Strong. She's a backstabbing bitch and I seriously hope she died in a plane crash."

Ah, and there it was. I sighed and closed my computer. "It's all just speculation. No one has said anything about me being here."

"Weird," Skyler said, turning the page to our worksheet over. "I wonder why it's all started up again."

I walked over to sit back down next to my friend and complete my own version of the homework. "Probably because they've run out of peoples' lives to ruin, so they thought they would just revisit their past victims."

"Well, at least your life isn't boring."

I blew the same stray strand of hair out of my face. "I prefer boring over this bullshit."

Skyler shrugged. "If you had boring, you may have never hooked up with the sexy professor."

I pushed my friend gently and Skyler laughed. "Stop calling him that."

"Fine. If you had boring, you may have never hooked up with the sexy businessman."

I rolled my eyes. "Or maybe I would have and we'd be living happily ever."

"Doubtful," Skyler said, fixing me with her lavender gaze. "Take it from someone who's been where you are. You had to go and experience the other side of things before you realized how good of a guy you left behind. Just be thankful he was still waiting for you when you got back."

I leaned forward and gave my friend a hug. I knew some serious shit had happened in Skyler's past that she'd never shared and I wouldn't push her. She knew I was here if she ever needed me. "I love you, babe."

Skyler smiled. "Love you too. Now finish your homework. I'm not going to let you cheat off of me," she said, pushing me back.

"Fine," I said with a smile as I got to work on my own assignment.

I THREW the newspaper down on my coffee table with a bit too much force. I got up and walked to the kitchen, intent on pouring myself a stiff drink. Sophie had elected to spend the evening at her loft and to work on the assignment I'd given to the class. I thought about fighting her at first, but I had to respect her commitment to the course and to her schooling.

So, with the evening free, I'd decided to get caught up on current events and thought reading the newspaper might be a nice escape.

Unfortunately, I'd been wrong.

Even respectable local papers were starting to pick up this "Where in the World is Sophie Strong?" nonsense and it made my stomach churn. I had worried about how long Sophie could go before someone noticed that she was here. Of course her new hair color and ink had done a lot to hide her former pop star self, but I still worried it was only a matter of time.

I poured myself three fingers of brandy and walked over to the window overlooking the city. I took a drink and tried to think of how I could protect her in all of this.

Of course, the real question was how to handle this situation long term. In a few weeks Sophie would graduate and we would be free to see each other out in the open and not hide our relationship. I often attended high-profile dinners and events and I had every intention of showing Sophie off to the world if she would let me.

The Sophie I remembered loved going to parties and would never shy away from the chance to meet new people. She was an extrovert through and through, the exact opposite of me most days and I adored her for it. While I was skilled enough now to get through these events with ease, having Sophie there with me might make them marginally enjoyable.

I knew that she didn't want to hide away. She'd been forced into this situation by people who sought to make money off her innocence and good nature. It made me sick. I took another drink of my brandy and looked out at the lights.

Sophie still hadn't told me exactly what had happened. She'd said that the fact that I believed that she hadn't done half the things the tabloids had reported was enough for her and she didn't want to relive the past. I wasn't going to push her when we'd just gotten back together. But at some point, I wanted to know the name of the fuckers that thought they could mess with her and win.

I wasn't vindictive. I wasn't vengeful. But the idea of someone using Sophie for their own personal gain? I grit my teeth and swirled the liquid around in its crystal tumbler. There was no way I was going to just let that slide. I knew Sophie didn't want me to get involved because she thought it might somehow harm my business, but my business was so beyond that at this point. Besides, some things were more important.

Putting my glass down, I reached into my pocket and pulled out my phone. I knew Sophie wasn't going to just volunteer information about her past life right now—that was fine. Even if she thought she knew who was behind the entire scandal, she may have been wrong. Media types had a way of hiding their footprints and pinning dirty deeds on other people.

But I knew a man who had a particular knack for finding out who the real bottom feeder was. I used him most often when deals went south and people thought they could disappear or avoid service. One call to Gustaf and a process server would be showing up to their hidden doorstep within the hour.

I pressed my thumb on the man's name and placed the phone to my ear. "Gus, been a while. . . . Yeah, when business is booming, I'm not usually in need of your skillset," I said with a chuckle. "I've got a personal matter I'd like you to look into for me. Sophie Strong . . . that's right, the pop singer. Her reputation was all but destroyed about a year ago. . . You guessed it, I want to know who. . . . Let me know when you find something. And send the bill to my personal residence if you don't mind. I'm sure I don't have to tell you where I live." I laughed at the man's response before hanging up the line.

Now I just had to play the waiting game.

EIGHTEEN

Sophie

"CONGRATULATIONS. YOU'VE ALL EARNED A PASSING GRADE FOR THIS seminar," Connor said as the students all smiled, looks of relief on their faces. A murmur of thank you's and a few hands clapping went around the room before the students began to chat amongst themselves and clear out of the room.

Connor began to collect the papers on the desk and I could see him watching me out of the corner of his eye as I did the same. I'd been pretty nervous about my final grade, but we all had to submit our final exam anonymously and I'd managed to do pretty well.

"I gotta get to the Pancake," Skyler said, pulling me in for a kiss to my temple and a hug. "You good to get home yourself?" I nodded before Skyler darted out the door in a rush.

I purposefully got my things together slowly, pretending to look over the exam that I'd pulled out of the pile with my ID number on the top.

I'd been wanting to talk to Connor about all the publicity that had been popping up over the last few days without potentially adding more to it.

Thankfully, the last student cleared out and Connor's deep voice boomed in the classroom. "Did you have a question, Ms. Stronglen?" he asked, leaning against the edge of the desk, crossing his arms over his broad chest.

I looked up at him and my heart clenched. I knew he wasn't going to like what I was about to say. "Connor, have you been watching the news lately?"

Connor furrowed his brow and gave me an interesting look. "Why do you ask?"

"I really want to be with you, Con. And I want to be around you . . . like all the time," I said with a blush to my cheeks. "But for whatever reason things are heating up right now about me and I'm afraid things are going to hit the fan. I don't want to cause problems for you or your company."

"Soph," Connor said. I could tell he was fighting the urge to walk towards me, but we couldn't chance someone coming back into the classroom for some reason. "I'm not worried about that in the slightest."

"Connor, you should be," I said insistently. "The people that did this to me, they're not joking around. If they think looping you into all of this will sell more tabloids, they'll do it and not give a shit. I'd never forgive myself if that happened to you."

Connor's jaw set. "Sophie, I understand that better than you know. And I'm currently working on that issue."

"Connor no!" I said, a look of horror coming across my face. "What did you do?"

"Nothing, yet," he said. "But I'm not going to let you live your life in fear of these people, that's for damn sure."

I chewed my bottom lip. I'd woken up this morning with renewed intention to try and put some distance between me and Connor after Skyler made me read the headlines yesterday, but Connor was, as usual, making things difficult.

"Connor, please don't be stubborn about this. I don't want to hurt you."

"Sophie, what would hurt me more than my face ending up on some foolish tabloid is you walking away from me again."

"I'm not trying to walk away from you, Connor! I'm just trying to protect you so that we can be together later!" I knew I was raising my voice and was thankful that it was a Sunday and the building was dead.

"Soph, if you insist on continuing this discussion, then we'll need to do so somewhere else."

"I'm not insisting on continuing the conversation, Connor. You just need to trust me on this," I huffed.

"Sophie," Connor said. "I trust you and I know what you're trying to do. But if you think I'm going to agree to losing you when I just got you back, you're insane."

The intention I had this morning died at his words and I sighed.

"Look, I have no intention of spending another night away from you. I'm parked in the back of the student lot. Follow me out in ten minutes and we can talk about this somewhere more private," he said, his voice soft and caring.

I opened my mouth to object but Connor gave me a stern look and I closed it before saying, "Fine."

He gave me a smile before gathering the last of his papers and made his way to the door. "Ten minutes," he said looking back at me and I nodded.

Aubrey

I HATED BEING at the university on Sundays but I had two very valid reasons for being here today. The first was that I needed to proof the final exam before it had to be submitted to the registrar's office tomorrow and the second was because I knew Connor was teaching a seminar this weekend.

I'd made sure I dressed to the nines in case we ran into each other. Connor could see just what he was missing. Unfortunately, I'd not come across him and after his warning in the middle of the semester, I wasn't going to actively seek him out.

I grumbled as I walked back to my car at the back of the student parking lot. My feet ached from my heels and I just wanted to go home and soak in my bathtub. Getting in, I pulled down my visor and checked my makeup. What I saw when I lifted the mirror back up made my blood boil. Stupid Sophie Strong was walking past my car, making her own way to the back of the parking lot. I hated her and was seriously disappointed that final exams were graded anonymously.

I watched as she made her way to a silver Lexus, parked in the last row of spots. I furrowed my brow as she got into the passenger seat and I wondered who the woman was slutting it up with now. Of course, it had to be Connor, confirming everything I had thought—he had left me for Sophie.

I quickly searched out my phone from my purse and swiped open the camera. If I could just zoom in enough to capture the photo, I could give it to Lennie to have placed in the tabloids.

"Fuck!" I cursed as Connor pulled down his own visor to block the sun before pulling out of the parking lot quickly. I looked down at my phone and still smiled. It wouldn't implicate Connor, but it'd still be the perfect photo for the paper.

Sophie

"SOPH, I really am done talking about this," Connor said in his deep voice and I put my hands on my hips. "I'm not letting you work remotely at the internship. There is one week left before final exams start up. Nothing's happened so far and nothing is going to happen."

He walked over to me and wrapped his arms around me. I tried to squirm against his firm grip but it was useless. Connor was far too strong and even more motivated to get me to calm down.

"Connor," I said, the last of my will to fight against him giving out.

"Shh," he said comfortingly before placing a kiss to the top of my head.

I gave in. I knew it was a mistake but there was no way I could pull back from him now. For the first time in my life, I felt accepted and loved for who I really was. My conflicting emotions had me shuddering and Connor just held me tightly against him. "I'm not going anywhere," he whispered against my hair. "I won't let you push me away, Soph. I love you."

Tears started falling down my cheeks and Connor moved me over to the couch and just held me while I cried. He rubbed gentle circles against my back as I let all my emotions out. Finally, I pulled back and looked into his cool blue eyes. He smiled and wiped the wetness from my cheeks with his palm.

"I just didn't want you to get hurt," I said finally.

Connor pulled me in and placed a gentle kiss to my lips. "I know. You can't hurt me Sophie because I'm not letting you go ever again."

I looked down and shook my head. "How can you be so smart and yet so stupid? I'm a mess. You should be with someone more put together."

Connor tickled my ribs slightly and I giggled. "Where's the fun in that?"

I rolled my eyes. "You're stupid, but I love you."

Connor's gaze became intense as soon as I said the words. "Tell me again."

"You're stupid?"

He shook me gently. "Soph."

I smiled. "And I love you."

Connor moved forward and pressed his lips against mine for an insistent kiss. He moved me so that my legs were wrapped around him as I straddled him on the sofa. Connor stood and grasped my thighs as he walked us to his bedroom.

Laying me out on the large bed, he climbed on top of me and set out to explore every curve of my body. I sighed into his embrace and opened my mouth as he pushed his tongue against my lips. I swirled my own against his and delighted in the taste of him.

"Con," I breathed out as he pulled back and started pressing kisses against my jawline. My breath hitched as his teeth grated against my neck before he sucked the skin gently. I knew I'd likely have marks I'd need to cover up later, but I couldn't bring myself to care.

"Fuck, Soph. You have no idea how happy you make me," he said as he moved his lips down my body.

"I still say you're stupid," I said. He pulled my top up and over my head and got rid of my bra with fluid movements.

"The only thing I want you saying is my name as you come," he said before he was palming one breast and licking the tip of the other.

I thought I might say some silly retort but Connor's ministrations had me losing my concentration. My hands thread through his hair and I wanted nothing more than to be joined with him again.

My core ached with need and I began to rub my thighs together, trying to relieve some of the pressure. Connor's strong hand moved down to my thighs at my movements, pinning one open. He looked up at me and smiled before working his way down my body, pressing each inch of my skin with gentle kisses before he was looping his fingers into the top of my jeans and pulling them off my body along with my panties.

My sex clenched at the cold air against my heated folds but Connor was on me in a moment. His thin lips were pressing kisses into the side of my thigh, just next to my weeping flower and I wanted him on me in a way I'd never experienced before.

"Connor," I breathed out as his fingers danced against my folds.

He let one finger slip inside and I moaned. "Fuck, Soph. I've never gotten the chance to eat this tight little pussy of yours. Tell me you want it."

"Yes," I breathed out as he picked up his pace and added an extra finger.

"Tell me, Soph. What do you want me to do?"

"Lick me," I said through moans.

"Come on, Soph. You know what I want to hear," he said, letting his lips ghost against my folds.

"I want you to eat my tight little pussy."

"Good girl," Connor said as he replaced fingers with lips and sucked my folds. I moaned and closed my eyes at the sensation. His tongue darted out to circle around my clit and I nearly came right there. He flattened his tongue and licked me from entrance to clit and back down again before his tongue finally began to circle my entrance.

"Oh yes, Connor. Tongue fuck me, please," I nearly begged.

He speared his tongue into my wet heat, tasting the deepest parts of me.

"Yes, Connor!" I exclaimed as his finger came up to my clit. He stayed there, keeping his movements fluid and his rhythm constant and I felt my walls clench before pleasure crashed like waves through my body.

Connor moved in, sucking my clit and circling it with his tongue to draw out my orgasm. "I'm going to fuck you now, Soph. You're mine, you understand me?"

I couldn't respond. All I could do was nod my head as my sex continued to pulse from my release. I cracked an eye open to watch Connor strip his clothing off with a purpose and sighed at how amazing he looked. He pushed my thighs opens with his body and held his cock at my entrance.

Normally he'd tease me into submission, make me beg for his cock but he didn't wait this time. He slid his length into my wet heat. My walls were slick from my release and he moved against me easily. I wrapped my legs around his hips, encouraging him to pump into me faster and harder.

My breasts bounced against him, my hardened peaks dusting against his chest. I felt his cock stiffen before he crashed into me, pushing his body into mine firmly with a roar of my name on his lips.

I MADE my way out of the bathroom, wearing nothing but one of his dress shirts again and he reached for me. "Come here," he said as he pulled me into him. He pressed gentle kisses against my red hair and I sighed into his embrace.

"You're sure about all this, Con?" I asked against his chest. "About me?"

"Soph," he said, brushing my questions aside. "I've always been sure about you. You're the one that took so long."

I just smiled and curled into him further. A year ago I could never have imagined that I'd be here, in love with Connor Driscoll, a few final exams away from graduating from college. Between him and Skyler, I finally felt like I actually belonged somewhere in the world. It was nice, but I hoped it would last. Things in my life always had a way of crashing down around me.

"Hey," Connor said, pulling me away from my thoughts. "I have something I want to give to you." He moved me so that my feet touched the floor gently and he stood before he pulled me into the living room. I rocked back and forth gently, the porcelain tile cold against my feet as I waited for Connor as he pulled something out of a nearby closet.

"I was going to wait until your graduation day, but right now feels right."

I watched as he pulled a guitar case from the closet and my eyes widened. Connor walked over to me and handed it to me.

I looked at him with questioning eyes and he encouraged me. "Go on, open it."

I walked the case over to the nearby sofa and set it down gently. I clicked the locks open and lifted the top. I gasped.

It was my old guitar, completely refurbished and gleaming in the low lights.

"Connor, is this—?" My words melted away as I ran my fingers down the instrument.

"It is. It was your first guitar. Damn thing was so busted but you'd given it to me, thinking I could learn. Of course I never did, but still."

I smiled as I ran my fingers along the varnished wood. I'd found the old Gibson in a pawn shop when I was in middle school and saved up my allowance for months in order to buy it. The thing had been falling apart then but by the time I'd gotten to college, it was almost a lost cause. But it had a special meaning to me since it was my first and I'd never had the heart to sell it.

When Connor had expressed interest in my music, I'd given it to him.

Connor chuckled. "I was never really into learning to play the guitar. I was just into you and your music."

I knew I should say something, but I was so astonished, I didn't know what to say. When he'd pulled the case out, I half expected he bought me some crazy fancy expensive guitar. But he hadn't been so cliché. He was always surprising me.

"Like it?" Connor asked.

I turned around and flashed Connor a wide grin. "I love it," I said as I jumped into his arms. I kissed him for all I was worth and could feel him smile against my lips.

He put me back down on the floor and nodded his head towards the instrument. "Go on. I want to hear you play. Just like old times."

I smiled as I thought back to the times at the loft when I would practice my guitar and Connor would sit and listen while he did his homework or studied. I shook my head. I'd been so stupid back then for not realizing what I had all along.

"I haven't played in over a year," I said to Connor a bit nervously.

"Then it sounds like you're overdue," he said, turning me around and patting my ass. "Go on."

I smiled and walked forward grabbing the guitar. I sat on the floor and strummed my fingers over the strings, tuning each one in turn. Connor took a seat on the couch and watched me. Within a few minutes, chords and words were tumbling from my lips as I sang one of my more famous songs. As the words tumbled from my mouth, I hoped Connor realized I'd written the song about him.

NINETEEN

Aubrey

"ARE YOUR PEOPLE READY?" I ASKED THE VOICE ON THE OTHER SIDE OF the phone.

"We've been ready for weeks, Ms. Knight."

"Good," I said with a satisfied nod. "I'm about to email you a photo and an address. Run the photo in tomorrow morning's papers and then have your reporters waiting at the address around four-thirty. Are we good?"

He was quiet on the other end of the line before he spoke up. "Ms. Knight, this is quite impressive. Too bad you didn't get a good view of her gentleman, but it's still good, nonetheless."

"Yes, well," I said. "Just be sure your people are where they're supposed to be tomorrow and you'll finally have your second payday at this girl's expense. And be sure to get all the exits. I'll not have this opportunity go to waste just because they were able to slip out the back."

If this guy fucked this up I'd be seriously angry. I wasn't even asking for a cut of the inevitable proceeds that were going to result from this. Artists might hate it, but everyone in this industry knew that people made money when they loved you *and* hated you. But, I didn't care about any of that. I just wanted to see two people who had wronged me fall.

"They'll be there."

I hung up the phone and took a hard seat. This would teach Connor Driscoll and his stupid little plaything to embarrass a Knight.

"HERE'S that final report you asked for, Kris," I said as I placed the neatly printed pages on his desk at the end of the day.

"Thanks!" he said with a bright smile. "Ready for finals?"

I made a face before I giggled. "I sure hope so. The good news is at least I know I have a passing grade from Mr. Driscoll's seminar."

"Oh that's right," Kris said. "I forgot you attended his private equity seminar. Did you like it?"

I nodded my head. "It was really interesting," I replied honestly.

"Well, there's less than a half-hour left to the day," Kris said. "Mr. Driscoll usually likes to debrief with the interns before they leave on their last day. His schedule is clear right now. Let me ask him if now is a good time."

"Okay," I said with a nod of my head. Kris left his seat and walked into Connor's office for a few moments before walking back out and letting me know he was available.

"Great!" I said.

"If I don't see you before you leave, it's been great working with you," Kris said.

I turned and reached out to shake his hand. "Thanks for everything, Kris. I hope you stay in touch!"

Kris nodded before returning to his seat and I walked into the office.

"Con?" I said as I walked into his office. I furrowed my brow as I watched him quickly toss a newspaper into the trashcan beneath his desk. He looked up and his features softened as he took in my appearance. Given that today was the last day of my internship, I'd spent a little extra time getting ready. I'd worn an emerald green wrap dress with tasteful jewelry and had thrown my hair up in a high bun.

He smiled at me and motioned to the chair in front of his desk. "Ready to review your internship experience?"

I giggled and sat down where he indicated. "I guess so."

"Well, I usually start off by saying the student has come a long way and grown a lot during the semester before asking them what they enjoyed most about their experience. Unless, of course, the student was a bit of a brat and then I'd ask them what lessons they'd learned." A glint of mischief flashed in his eye before he said, "So, Ms. Stronglen, what lessons did you learn while at Phoenix Development?"

I huffed and narrowed my eyes at him. "Not funny, Connor."

He chuckled. "You were a bit of a brat when you got here, Soph," he teased.

"You're lucky I love you," I said before sticking my tongue out at him.

A loud knock on Connor's office door had him furrowing his brow. "Come in," he said in his booming voice and Kris opened the door. He looked frantic and a bit out of breath.

"Kris, what in Christ's name is the matter?" Connor asked, looking at his assistant with a worried glance.

"I'm sorry to interrupt," he said. "I was heading out and there's an entire party of reporters and photographers waiting at the entrance," he said. "I just wanted to make sure you knew."

My heart began to beat hard in my chest and I looked between Connor and Kris.

"Thank you, Kris. I appreciate you letting me know," Connor said, remaining extremely calm. Kris nodded and excused himself before leaving us alone.

"Connor?" I looked at him, my eyes sad. "What are you keeping from me?"

Connor sighed. He pulled the newspaper out from under his desk and handed it to me. Tears started to well in my eyes as I looked at the photo and the headline.

"Sophie Strong at it again with a Mystery Man!"

Connor's face had been blocked by his visor and I wasn't sure exactly when the photo was taken because it was cropped to show just the two of us, but it was fairly recent.

"Connor, this is what I told you would happen! And now they're after you!"

Connor stood and rounded his desk. "Sophie, stop. This is not a big deal. Come on, we'll sneak out the back. My place is walking distance and no one will be any wiser. I know you carry a headscarf and large sunglasses in that big bag of yours."

I chewed on my lower lip as I thought about what Connor was saying. I really had no other option. "Alright," I said as I tried to brush tears away from my eyes.

"Come on," Connor said as he grabbed my hand and pulled me down the hallway to my cubicle so I could try and disguise myself. We made our way to the stairs at the back of the office and began the long trek down fifteen flights. When we finally reached the bottom, Connor pulled me close to him and cracked the door open slightly. It was one of those fire exit doors that only went one way and I could tell he was checking to make sure we didn't walk into an ambush with no escape.

Hearing no movement or voices on the other side, he opened the door all the way and we stepped outside. As soon as the door closed and my vision cleared, I heard someone shouting "There they are!" from the corner of the building.

"Shit," Connor said as he started to pull me away from the building, but it was too late, we'd already been spotted.

The click of cameras began to flash as lights flooded my vision and people crowded around us.

"Sophie! Sophie Strong!" people shouted trying to shove microphones into our faces. "Do you have anything to say?"

"Where have you been this past year?"

"Would you like to comment on the rumors circulating about your business dealings?"

I started to shake under all the scrutiny and Connor pulled me tighter against him. "Ms. Strong will not be making statements at this time. We'd ask that you kindly clear the area," he said in a booming voice.

Someone pushed in front of the crowd and reached for my scarf, tearing it and my glasses off of my head before he reached for me again. The sound of cameras clicked as I gasped and I looked up at Connor to watch his eyes glaze over with rage.

"Hey!" he yelled, grabbing the offender and placing a punch to his jaw.

"Connor no!" I gasped. I was wrenched away from him as people pulled at me and tried to get photos of the fight that had broken out.

Tears streamed down my face as I realized that everything I'd feared had come true. Connor was getting caught up in my bullshit. He'd likely be sued for assault or worse. Everything he'd worked for had been ruined after only four months of me being in his life.

I pushed my way through the sea of reporters and ran as fast as I could in the opposite direction, refusing to turn around even when I heard Connor's voice calling my name behind me.

TWENTY

Five Years Ago

"YOU'RE COMING TO THE SHOW TONIGHT, RIGHT CON?" SOPHIE ASKED as she hurried around the loft, trying to gather everything she needed for this evening's performance so she could head straight there after classes finished.

"When have I ever missed one of your performances, Soph?" I asked, my lean legs propped up on the coffee table as I lounged on the sofa, reading over some of my class notes.

Sophie took a moment to stick her tongue out at me before she made her way to the door. "Just don't be late," she said as she turned the knob.

"Soph," I called out to her.

"What?" she said in an insistent voice. "Con, I've got to go! I'm going to be late!"

I pointed to the corner of the room. "Guitar," I said with a smirk on my face.

Sophie's eyes widened as she realized she'd almost forgotten the instrument. She scurried over to it and slung the case around her back. "What would I do without you?" she said as she ran back towards the door, stopping to press a kiss to the side of my head.

I closed my eyes briefly as her lips touched my skin, but it was over in a heartbeat. "You'd be incredibly unorganized. And also sad and lonely, obviously," I said with a laugh, regaining my composure.

"Alright, alright," Sophie said with a chuckle as she headed back to the door. "See you later!"

"Bye," I said, raising my hand before the whirlwind of a woman closed the door behind her. Sophie was like a tornado, all fast spiraling energy, but when she was gone, things always felt eerily quiet.

I stretched my arms over my head and let out a yawn. As I brought my hands down, my fingertips danced over the area where Sophie had kissed me. She'd been doing that more often recently and I couldn't help but wonder if she shared the feelings I had for her. I'd wanted to tell Sophie about my true feelings for her since the moment I'd met her sophomore year, but almost two years had gone by and I still couldn't find the courage. Her friendship meant so much to me that every time I thought I might confess, thoughts of being without her filled my head and I'd chicken out.

But tonight was different. We'd just finished our first week of classes for our last semester and I'd vowed I was going to be honest with her. Sophie always played at the Talons, a local coffee shop slash hangout for students at the nearby Tenleytown, every Friday during the semester and I always sat right in front. Sophie wasn't just a talented musician, she was the entire package. She wrote all her own songs and the room always went quiet when she sang, everyone mesmerized by her voice.

After tonight's performance, I was going to tell her how I truly felt. If she didn't return my feelings, so be it. I'd rather know that than spend the rest of my life wondering.

My phone alarm went off and I groaned. I pulled himself off the couch and grabbed my gym bag before heading to afternoon track practice.

♪

"I'D GO with you guys, but I've gotta get to the Talons," I said to a few of my track friends as I pulled on my shirt in the locker room.

"You're always hanging around that redhead. What's the deal, man? She your girl or something?" the one to the right asked.

"Nah, we're just friends," I said, knowing if I lied it would likely get back to Sophie and I didn't want to deal with that. She usually came with me to team parties and someone would be sure to mention it.

"She available then?" the other one asked and I gave him a stern look.

"Not sure." My blue eyes were intense and a bit of a scowl was on my face as I said the words.

My friend threw up his hands with a chuckle. "No worries, man. I get it. But you better make your move sooner or later. Otherwise someone who cares less is going to move in on your territory."

"Yeah," I said, pulling my gym bag over my shoulder. "I plan to. See you guys later." I waved my goodbyes and headed towards the door. The cold air hit me as the automatic doors opened. A flip of my wrist told me that I was on time to catch one of the buses that took students over to Tenleytown and I sighed in relief. If I was late for the start of her number, Sophie would never forgive me. I shook my head. I didn't get it, but Sophie said she always performed better when I was there.

My thoughts were a scrambled mess as I boarded the bus. I'd been going to these shows for over a year now, so I knew exactly how they went. Sophie usually performed last these days because she had been doing the gig the longest. She always sat with me during the other numbers before she finally went on. Both of us usually worked on homework until it was her time to perform. Once she wrapped up the show, we always walked back to her loft together. It wasn't far from the Talons and unless it was raining, it was just nice to get out.

I knew I was going to talk to her on the walk back to the loft, but I was nervous about what I wanted to say. I ran a hand through my unruly black hair and tried to think it through. How do you admit to your best friend of over two years that you've been madly in love with her the entire time? I groaned. I'd thought about this very moment many times before and had various speeches planned, but none of them ever felt right.

I sighed. I was just going to have to speak from my heart. I just hoped I'd find the right words.

The bus pulling into the station startled me out of my thoughts. I'd been sitting in the back so I had to wait for the others to clear out before I could finally depart. Stepping onto the platform, I passed the metro station in front of me and made my way towards the Talons.

"Con!" Sophie called out as she saw me walk through the door. I smiled at her as I made my way over to our usual spot, the table right next to the stage. "Practice go okay?" she asked as I took a seat and put down my bag.

"Yeah. You make it to class on time?" She blushed under my blue gaze and scrunched her face slightly. "So that's a no," I said with a chuckle. "Come on, Soph! It's our last semester. Gotta make this one count!" I said, trying to encourage her to work on some of her less desirable habits.

Sophie ran chronically late. She was never on time for anything, except for the Friday evening shows at the Talons. Her being late was actually how we had met. She'd been running to catch the bus and I had seen her. Her beautiful red hair was loose and flying wildly behind her as she ran. I knew from the moment I saw her that I wanted her.

The bus driver wanted to leave, but it was the last bus of the evening and I knew she would have been stuck finding her own way home in the dark and I just couldn't allow it. So I'd stood with one foot on the bus steps and one foot on the platform until she made it there.

She'd been completely out of breath as she climbed up the steps and the bus driver had given me a pretty nasty look, but I didn't care. We sat in the back together and that was when our connection started. Unfortunately, I found myself squarely within the friend zone within the first week.

It wasn't completely my fault. When we'd first met, Sophie was seeing some guy. By the time she'd broken things off with him, I had found myself squarely within the dreaded zone by default. At first, I wanted to wait until she'd gotten over the breakup to admit my feelings for her. I didn't want to be the guy that tried to pounce while she was vulnerable. But the longer I waited, the more entrenched I got, until I'd found myself unable to pull out from underneath the heavy mantle of friendship.

"Why would I start changing things right at the last minute?" Sophie asked, bringing my attention back to her. "That's just silly."

I shook my head. "You're going to have to be on time when you get a job, Soph."

"Meh. That's a future Sophie problem. Drink?"

I nodded and she jumped up to grab us our usual as the first performer walked onto the stage. I reached down and pulled my laptop out of where I'd stashed it in my gym bag so I could knock out some assignments due next week. Looking up, my eyes connected with a man who was sitting in the corner looking quite out of place.

Talons was a place for college students to hang out, get work done and drink coffee. It was usually full of twenty-somethings in sweatpants and leggings on Macbooks. So an older gentleman sitting in the corner in a full suit stood out to me rather quickly.

"Here you go," Sophie said, placing the hot chocolate in front of me. I smiled and took a sip, forgetting about the stranger in the corner momentarily. We busied ourselves with our work before it was finally Sophie's turn to go on.

"Wish me luck." She grabbed her guitar and a crumpled piece of paper that held her lyrics before stepping onto the stage.

"Good luck," I said with a smile as I turned to face forward, closing my computer.

"Hey guys. Thanks for coming out today and for sticking with me till the end," Sophie said, her lips close to the microphone and her slightly deeper voice soothing. A good number of people stopped their quiet talking and turned their attention to her on stage.

Out of the corner of my eye, I saw that the man in the suit was still

here, paying much closer attention to Sophie than to the other perform-
ers. I furrowed my brow, but Sophie strummed a chord on her guitar and
it pulled my attention back to the front.

She played gentle chords as a backdrop to the introduction to her
song.

"I wrote this song during one of my classes this week," she said in
her mellow voice. A bit of laughter could be heard across the room and
she chuckled. "Anyways, it's about someone really special to me."

My breath hitched slightly. Who was special enough to Sophie to
warrant their own song? Had I somehow missed her meeting someone?
Did I miss my chance to tell her how I felt?

But as soon as she said the name, all my fears melted away.

"It's called Blue Eyes Stopped the Bus."

She started to sing and everyone quieted to listen.

> Baby with your blue eyes
> Looking at me so nice
> Telling me I better come on.
>
> I could see you standing there
> Acting like you didn't care
> 'bout anything but getting me home.
>
> Now you don't know
> The way I feel
> But that doesn't mean
> That this ain't real

When her soothing voice finally reached the chorus, I had half a
mind to run up to the stage and pull Sophie into a searing kiss right in
front of everyone but I contained myself. I'd planned to tell her everything on the walk home and I wanted to stick to my plan.

> Cause your blue eyes stopped the bus
> And then they stopped my heart.

Yeah those blue eyes stopped the bus
And now I don't ever wanna be apart.

When she'd finished, the room sat in stunned silence before everyone finally began to clap. Sophie smiled and stood, taking a quick bow of her head before jumping off the stage and smiling at me. The crowd died down and she put her guitar back in her case. "What'd you think?"

But before I could answer, the man in the suit approached us.

"Ms. Stronglen. My name is Jack Tanner. Would you mind speaking with me for a few minutes? I have an offer I think you might be interested in."

I surveyed the man up and down. He was balding slightly and definitely had a few extra pounds on him. His dark brown eyes matched his dark hair, but I could tell his suit was expensive. I couldn't decide if I trusted this man or not.

"Um, okay," Sophie said with a bit of uncertainty in her voice.

The man gestured to the table a few seats away and she shrugged at me as she followed him. I sat back down and opened my laptop, but positioned it so I could look over the top and keep an eye on the pair. I watched as Sophie listened to what the man was saying. She looked skeptical at first, if a little bit bored. But after a few moments, her expression changed to one of excitement before the man handed her his card. She stood and shook his hand and watched as he exited.

I walked over to where she was standing. "Soph? What did he want?"

"Con!" she said, throwing her arms around my neck and giving me a hug. She pulled back and I could clearly see the excitement in her eyes. "He's from one of the biggest music labels. They want me to record an album and go on tour! I'm gonna be famous!"

TWENTY-ONE

I COULDN'T BELIEVE HOW SCREWED UP THIS EVENING HAD BEEN SO FAR. I was happy for Sophie, of course. But I was also incredibly skeptical about the entire situation. It seemed too good to be true and I worried about my friend.

Instead of being able to confess my love to her on our way home like I had planned, Sophie had spent the entire walk on the phone with her mother. The two women had gushed about the chance to go to Los Angeles and Sophie was already planning out how to put her coursework on hold for the foreseeable future.

I had grimaced when Sophie decided to call her mother. Sophie had grown up without her father and her mother was the worst enabler of them all. I often wondered if the woman had a moral compass other than money. I sincerely doubted it and knew Sophie wasn't going to get sound advice from her mother.

Back at the loft, I was pacing back and forth. It was a bad habit of mine while I was upset. I just couldn't sit still.

"Con, please sit down," Sophie said with pleading eyes. "I don't understand why you're so against this."

I turned to look at her and tried to smile but I couldn't. "I'm not against it, Soph. I just think it's a really big decision and you need to think about it a little bit more."

"What's there to think about?" she asked, looking honestly perplexed.

I was incredulous. "What's there to think about? Soph, the man wants you to drop out of school! You've only one semester left before you graduate. How irresponsible is that?" I walked from one side of the small space and then back to the other.

Sophie rolled her eyes. "Con, I don't need a degree to go on tour or record an album."

"Soph, please don't tell me you're being that short-sighted with all of this?"

That had Sophie angry and I could see her attitude shift before I felt it. "Short-sighted? Connor, we're talking about an album and tour deal. It would be short-sighted to give all that up to finish some stupid business degree."

I grit my teeth. I couldn't believe this was happening. "Why can't they just wait until you're done? What's a few weeks to let you graduate?"

Sophie shrugged her shoulders. "They want the album recorded so they can release it in the summer. I told the guy I already had a good deal of songs written. It'd just be a matter of getting into the studio and getting them worked out, but that's going to take a little bit of time."

I ran my hand through my dark hair, frustrated that I couldn't seem to get my friend to see logic. "Look, Soph. I'm happy for you. Truly, I am. I want you to be happy. But I'm also just worried that this isn't going to end well."

"Of all the people I thought I could count on to support me in this, it was you, Connor!" she yelled.

"I am supporting you, Sophie!" I yelled back. "I'm just trying to make sure you don't make the biggest mistake of your life."

"Biggest mistake of my life? You're not my father, Con. I don't need you trying to babysit me!"

I stopped my pacing and fixed her with my ice-blue gaze. "You're right. I'm not your father. I'm supposed to be your best fucking friend. That was supposed to count for something but I guess even that wasn't enough."

"What the hell is that supposed to mean?" Sophie screamed.

"It means I love you, Sophie!"

The words tumbled out of my mouth and there was no pulling them back. They were words that had been on the tip of my tongue since I'd met her and the thought of losing was pushing me over the edge.

The silence stretched on between us. Sophie sat in stunned silence at my confession.

"For how long?"

"For how long? Since the day I met you!" I sputtered, totally losing my cool. This was absolutely not the way I'd envisioned admitting my feelings to Sophie.

"Well, what the fuck, Connor? Why would you keep something like that from me? And why are you telling me now, of all days?"

"I'd planned to tell you on our walk home, but you had to go and get discovered and ruin everything!" The words were out of my mouth before I had a second to think about what I was saying. I hadn't meant that. I was happy for Sophie. Her music meant everything to her and I wanted to do everything I could to support her. Just the thought of her leaving and so quickly had my heart tied in knots. "Sophie, I didn't mean to—" I started to say but Sophie cut me off.

"No, Connor. I think you've said enough. You should just go. We'll figure this all out," she said, turning away from me.

"Sophie." I tried to approach her but she moved away.

"Just go, Connor. I can't be around you right now. I just need some time to think."

I grit my teeth. I pulled my hand back from the woman I loved. She'd rejected me, that much was clear. My worst fear had come true. I'd confessed my true feelings to her and it had ruined everything. After all we'd been through, in that moment, I felt like nothing more to her than some throwaway item.

"Fine, Sophie. If that's the way it's going to be, then I hope you get everything you want out of this." With those words, I turned on my heel and bounded out of the loft, slamming the door behind me.

I TURNED, his name on my lips just as I heard the door slam. Tears slid down my face as I stood there in silence, the moments stretching on. This was supposed to be something happy. Why did all of my relationships always end with screaming and tears?

My phone rang and I ran to it. "Con?" I answered without looking at the screen.

"Uh, no. Ms. Stronglen, this is Jack Tanner. I've just heard back from my manager. They want you in LA as soon as possible to start recording. We've arranged a flight that leaves tomorrow morning."

My eyes widened. "Tomorrow morning? So soon? I won't have any time to pack or anything."

"You won't need anything, Ms. Stronglen. Accommodations will be arranged for you and we can have your belongings packed up and delivered. Although, I doubt that you will need most of them once you're provided with wardrobe, et cetera. Just bring yourself and your guitar and we'll see you on the West Coast tomorrow, yes?"

"Um, yeah," I managed to stammer out.

"Excellent," Jack said before the line clicked off.

I looked around the loft. I'd be leaving all this behind me tomorrow morning. It was all happening so fast, I didn't know how to process it. Walking over to my desk, I sat down and pulled out a piece of paper.

I took a deep breath, before writing *"Dear Connor."*

TWENTY-TWO

Sophie

I HAD TURNED ON MY PHONE THE MOMENT THE PLANE LANDED AT MY stopover in Denver. I scrolled through my messages and voicemails, but nothing from Connor had come through. I sighed and scrunched my eyes as I let my head fall back into the large cushion of the first class seat the media label had booked for me.

This entire situation felt so strange. I'd always imagined what it would be like when I finally got my chance, but I hadn't expected to be so sad about everything I was leaving behind. I'd barely slept last night and despite my best efforts to fall asleep on the plane, I'd probably only managed thirty minutes total. My dreams had just given my brain another opportunity to play my fight with Connor on repeat and it was making me sick.

I'd known Connor for years and I knew he couldn't get out a straight thought when he was upset. He hadn't meant what he'd said and I knew he certainly didn't mean to hurt me. As soon as I'd had the opportunity to calm down, I'd realized this. But despite trying to reach him all night long, his phone was off.

I found a quiet spot at my next gate in the terminal and took a deep breath. Pulling out my phone, I pressed the first person in my favorited contacts and held my breath. With each ring, I could feel my heartbeat increase before finally—

"Hey. You've reached Connor Driscoll. Sorry I missed your call."

"Damn it, Con!" I shouted aloud, thankful no one was close enough to hear me. I threw the phone down next to me as I felt tears slide down my cheek. I gave myself a moment, before I finally summoned my courage to try again. If he didn't answer this time, then I'd try and figure out something to say to him.

"Hey. You've reached Connor Driscoll. Sorry I missed your call. Leave a message!" his voice repeated after my second try. I pushed down a sob I could feel crawling up my throat and tried to steady my voice.

"Hey, Con. It's me. I think we left things on bad terms and—" I suppressed a sob and tried to continue. "I know you never meant for any of that and neither did I. I don't know. Maybe you went to the loft already. But when you do, just grab the letter I left for you. It'll explain everything and just—well, call me when you get it. If you want to. . . . I guess I'll talk to you later, then. Please, just call me back, Con. I need—"

"If you are satisfied with your message, please hang up. Otherwise, please press 1 to re-record."

"Fuck," I cursed, hanging up the phone. I had rambled and the system timed me out but I knew if I tried to re-record the message, I'd probably just start sobbing. I took a deep breath. There was nothing else I could do now. I needed to remind myself that I was taking the first steps to the rest of my life. I shouldn't be sobbing in a corner by myself at the airport.

I needed coffee and looked around for the nearest Starbucks. I grabbed my bag and tucked my phone into my pocket, but not before making sure the ringer was turned all the way up.

♪

"SOPHIA STRONGLEN," the sign the driver was holding up read. I sighed at the idea of someone telling the entire world what my real name was. I hated the name Sophia, it's why I insisted on being called Sophie. Everyone but my mother obliged.

"Hi, I'm Sophie," I said as I approached the man.

"Sophia?" he asked and I rolled my eyes.

"Yes, but I go by Sophie." He nodded his head and reached for my bag before directing me out of the airport. It was evening now, the flight plus the layover having taken me most of the day, and the lights glowed as the cars zoomed past us. Towering palm trees reached up towards the moon and I sighed as the warm air greeted me.

My eyes widened as we walked closer and closer to a black stretch limo and my jaw almost dropped as the driver opened the door for me. I climbed inside and he closed the door behind me.

"Where are we going?" I shouted to him from the back of the car.

"To the studio and then to your apartment," he shouted back at me.

I startled as my phone rang. I pulled it out of my pocket quickly, hoping it was finally Connor returning my call, but it was Jack Tanner.

"Hi, Mr. Tanner," I said, trying not to sound deflated.

"Ms. Stronglen, I trust you were able to locate the driver per my emailed instructions."

Beep.

I pulled the phone away from my ear momentarily and my heart clenched as I looked at the screen. "Con" was lighting up my phone.

"Yes, yes," I said, trying to hurry up the call.

"Great. I trust you had a good flight."

Beep.

"Yep."

"Great. Well, we're going to see you in just a few minutes here at the studio. After that, the driver will·take you to your new apartment in the City."

Beep.

"Okay great."

"See you soon, then, Ms. Stronglen!"

I pulled the phone down from my ear and tried to swipe up to answer Connor's call.

"Con?"

"Soph?"

I breathed a sigh of relief to hear his voice. "Where have you been? I've been trying to get in touch with you all day."

"Where have I been? Soph, I got your letter. Tell me it isn't true."

I gulped.

"It is," I said softly. I looked out the window and watched the palm trees lining the sides of the highway blur past me.

"Soph." He sounded defeated. "How could you leave without saying goodbye?"

"I'm sorry, Con," I tried to say.

An awkward moment passed between the two of us, neither sure what to say.

I cleared my throat. "You'd really like it out here. It's warm and there's a ton of palm trees. I know how much you hate the cold."

I heard a small sound on the other end of the line before he said, "Sounds nice."

More silence stretched between us.

"Soph, I didn't mean what I said."

"I know, Con. I'm sorry too."

"I really hope this is everything you want it to be."

I smiled. "Thanks, Con."

"I should probably get going," he said.

I winced. I knew Connor was upset. He never lasted on the phone that long normally, but when he was upset? Well, I was lucky I was getting this much out of him. I'd give him time to cool down. He'd come around sooner or later. "Okay. Can you call me tomorrow? I can tell you about everything going on out here."

"Sure, Soph. I'll call you tomorrow night, okay?" He still sounded so sad.

"Okay, Con."

"Night, Soph."

"Night, Con."

The phone call clicked off and I leaned back against the cushion and closed my eyes. He just needed time, that was all. Things would go back to normal between the two of us and then he'd be a part of my life again.

TWENTY-THREE

Sophie

"Ms. Stronglen," Jack Tanner said with a beaming smile, reaching out a hand as I made my way through the large glass doors. "I'm glad you made it safely."

"Thanks," I said, shaking his hand and trying to suppress a yawn.

He smiled. "Not to worry. We won't be keeping you very long. We just wanted to make some introductions and show you the studio you'll be using tomorrow."

"Tomorrow?" I said, a bit startled at how fast things were moving.

"Oh, yes. If we have any hope of getting you on tour this summer, we need to drop a record and fast. At the very least, a single needs to drop within the next week or two. I know you said you had a lot of options, so I'm sure that will be no problem. Besides, we've got the best mixers in the studio ready to help you."

I shook my head, feeling my stomach flutter a bit at everything.

"This way," Jack said, leading me through the sleek lobby and over to a fleet of elevators. He pushed the button and the doors immediately opened. The pair stepped inside and Jack pressed the button for the highest floor. I gulped as I started to think that maybe I was in over my head and I should have stayed back in D.C. after all.

"No," I tried to tell my subconscious. *"You have wanted this your entire life. This is your dream finally coming true!"*

With renewed intention, I stepped out of the elevator and into the sleek lobby. I looked around and instantly felt underdressed in a pair of black leggings and pink sweatshirt with my hair piled on top of my head in a messy bun. I tried to smooth my flyaways back a bit but I knew it was hopeless.

The rubber soles of my sneakers pressed against cream-colored and highly polished marble. In front of me were a few elevated platforms, each lit with a low strip of lighting that made the couches placed atop look as if they were floating. Further back I could see sleek conference rooms encased in glass and up above me lights hung on strings from an interesting array of geometric designs.

"Ms. Stronglen," a woman's voice called out. I turned at the sound of heels clicking against the floor and I looked up into a pair of friendly brown eyes. "I'm Rebecca Murphy. So glad you were able to make it here and on such short notice." She reached forward and I shook her hand. "We're all very excited about you."

I couldn't help but smile at the woman. She wasn't who I thought I might meet. I thought for sure that I would be meeting some stuffy old executive that secretly still listened to his music on records, but not in the hip way. Instead, Rebecca Murphy was an attractive, middle-aged woman, likely in her mid-forties. She wore a perfectly tailored navy skirt suit and her brown hair was tied at the nape of her neck in a tight bun. Bright red lipstick and tasteful makeup made her seem a bit younger than her years and I couldn't help but instantly like her.

"I'm excited, as well," I responded. "Thank you for the opportunity."

Rebecca smiled and gestured for me to sit on one of the nearby couches. Jack excused himself to give us some time to chat but assured me that he would be back to escort me to the waiting limo.

"Sophia Stronglen," Rebecca said with an excited grin. "Tell me, how long have you been writing songs?"

I tucked a flyaway piece of red hair behind my ear and blushed. "Since before I can remember, I guess. Oh, and everyone just calls me Sophie," I added.

Rebecca nodded her head. "I'm sure Jack has scared you to death already with schedules. That's sort of his thing. But with your talent, I'm sure things will be effortless in the studio."

I blushed again. No one had ever been this complimentary of my music. Well, except Connor.

"We've gone ahead and taken care of accommodations for you. And I hate to give you paperwork to review when you should be concentrating on making music, but you know how the lawyers are," Rebecca said with a roll of her eyes and a smile. She reached for a stack of documents I hadn't noticed on the side table. A good deal of little yellow tabs were sticking out of the side and she handed the compendium to me.

"We really want you making music as soon as possible, but this comes first. Take your time reviewing it and let Jack know if you have any questions. As soon as it's all signed, we can get you into the studio and let you do your thing."

I ran my thumb along the edge of the papers and nodded my head. Inside my stomach dropped. How was I supposed to read through all of this by myself? That worry that I was in over my head started up again and I swallowed hard.

Rebecca must have sensed my discomfort because she spoke up again. "I can't tell you how much Jack gushed about you when he called me after listening to you perform. What was the song you sang at that little shop?"

"Blue Eyes," I said, feeling a pang of sadness about Connor being across the country.

Rebecca clapped her hands together. "I love it. And I can't wait to hear it myself. Well, Ms. Sophie, I've kept you here long enough but I just wanted to meet you in person." Rebecca stood and I followed her lead. We shook hands and Jack appeared, ready to lead me back down to the limo.

We walked back through the building's front lobby and up to the car. Jack opened the door and fixed me with a smile. "Ms. Stronglen, as soon as you've reviewed those papers, please call my cell phone. While there's no rush at all, we do have a studio spot reserved for you as early as tomorrow morning and would love for you to be able to start recording." I nodded as I clutched the papers to my chest. "The driver here will take you to your new apartment. If there's anything wrong, please call me. Whatever time."

I nodded my head in agreement, totally overwhelmed by everything that was happening and Jack shut the door. The limo pulled forward, taking me to my new home.

I UNLOCKED the door with the key the front desk attendant had given me. I searched for a light switch on the wall and gasped as soon as the apartment was lit up. Floor to ceiling windows made the outside wall of the apartment so that I could see the glow of the city beneath me. A sleek kitchen with stainless steel appliances and white cabinets topped with grey polished stone was to the right. A stylish couch and table set sat atop large area rugs that covered rich dark wood flooring.

I walked forward and dropped the pile of papers on the glass coffee table before moving further into the apartment to explore. Just past the kitchen was the bedroom, still sporting those gorgeous windows and equally amazing views. A large television was hung on the wall opposite the extremely plush and inviting looking bed. Two doors were on the far wall and I walked through the first and gasped. It opened up to a large walk-in closet that was already filled with clothes. I turned a tag over and shook my head as I realized they were all my size and all very expensive.

I held my breath as I walked into the bathroom and was just as stunned. Gray marble seemed to cover it from floor to ceiling. A beautiful whirlpool sat in the corner next to a long gray vanity. The shower was encased in glass and I wasn't sure what all the knobs and levers could possibly be for.

I turned and caught a glimpse of myself in the mirror and felt completely out of place. I stood there, my bright red hair in a nest on the top of my head totally clashing with my pink sweatshirt and equally plain black leggings. Peeling my clothes off me, I turned this way and that in the mirror as I turned on the shower and waited for the water to warm. Steam filled the room quickly and the mirror fogged, clouding my ability to see clearly.

THE PLACE WAS WELL STOCKED with everything I needed. Freshly laundered towels had been folded in one of the vanity's deep drawers and I dried my hair with one as I walked into the kitchen. The pink satin sleep pants and white camisole hung loose on my lithe frame and I opened the door to the refrigerator to look inside.

I bit my lower lip as I looked over all the options before finally pulling out a few clumps of grapes and a cheeseboard. A quick search through the cabinet revealed boxes of assorted crackers and I sat down on one of the suede and polished wood barstools with my prizes. I sighed as I tried to make sense of even the first paragraph of the contract I was supposed to be evaluating.

THIS AGREEMENT is made by and between SOPHIA STRONGLEN ("Ms. Stronglen") and CHARISMA RECORDS, LLC ("Charisma"), a division of Eternity Music Group, Inc. ("EMG") (individually, a "Party" and collectively, the "Parties") this 22nd day of April, 2015.

I took a bite of cheese and jumped down the page, figuring that the first paragraphs were probably just formality anyways.

NOW THEREFORE, in consideration of the foregoing and the mutual covenants herein contained, and for other good and valuable considera-tion, the receipt and sufficiency of which is hereby expressly acknowl-edged, the Parties agree as follows.

I chewed my lower lip as I became increasingly overwhelmed by the pile of papers in front of me. Pulling out my cell phone, I swiped it open and let my finger hover over Connor's name. Had it been any other time, I would have called him. He was pretty good at this stuff and always gave me good advice. But, I paused. Connor didn't want me out here, that much was clear. If I called him within a few hours of landing and told him I was already having problems, I might get a large lecture plus, he might use it as ammunition to try and get me to come home.

If nothing else, I knew he would try and tell me to send it to him or go see a lawyer and I didn't want to overcomplicate this. I wanted to start recording. I smiled at the thought of getting into a real music studio as soon as tomorrow and had trouble keeping my excitement in check.

I looked over my list of favorites on my phone and winced as I selected the next best option. Considering I had no one else, this would have to do.

"Sophia?" my mother answered.

"Hi, Mom."

"Sophia, it's almost midnight here. What on earth could you possibly be calling about?"

I sighed. "Mom, I'm in LA. The record label gave me this giant contract to read and sign but I don't understand any of it and I don't know what to do. They won't let me start recording music until I've signed it."

"Well, I don't know Sophia. How much are they saying they'll pay you?"

"Um," I tried flipping through the pages before spotting a page that read "Compensation Schedule."

"It says here a minimum of $100,000 a year plus a percentage of royalties and they'll provide travel, accommodations. You get the idea."

"That's a lot of money for just agreeing to sing songs for them, Sophia. Besides, that's all that really matters, dear. The rest is just a waste of ink that lawyers use to justify their high prices. Just sign it and go do your thing tomorrow."

"You really think that's a good idea, mom?" I wasn't sure why I was asking my mother of all people for advice. But right now, I just needed someone to agree with me.

"Sign it, Sophia. Good night." And with that, the line clicked off.

I heaved a heavy breath as I ran my thumb through the pages. I thought back to Ms. Rebecca and how kind she had been. The woman seemed genuine and really excited about me being there. That tipped the scales in my mind and I put my pen on the line next to the first yellow tab and signed my name.

Thirty signatures later, I picked up my phone to call Jack before dragging myself to bed, completely exhausted.

I TRIED to give the appearance that I was completely comfortable in the new clothing I was wearing as I stood in the lobby where I'd met Rebecca Murphy yesterday evening. Unfortunately, I worried that I was doing a pretty bad job of blending in as I stood there, holding the signed documents to my chest.

Most of the wardrobe in my pre-made closet had already been paired together as outfits and as cute as they looked on the hanger, wearing them in real life was an entirely different situation. The flippy skirt dug into my waist awkwardly and when I walked outside in the morning to get into the black sedan waiting for me, the thing I feared the most was a heavy gust of wind. I at least had to admit that I loved the sequined camisole and leather jacket.

"Sophie!" Rebecca's voice called out to me. I turned and watched the woman in a stunning, deep red skirt suit make her way over. "Jack called me last night and told me you'd be in in the morning. We're so glad we can get started!" She reached her hands out for the documents and I handed them over to her gingerly.

"Did you have any questions as you read through everything?" Rebecca asked, handing the documents off to an aide that appeared from somewhere behind her.

I shook my head, while internally repressing the urge to say yes. When I'd awoke in the morning, I contemplated calling Connor before heading to the studio but I'd ultimately decided not to for the same reasons as last night. Still, this was one of the first big decisions I'd made in years without his input.

"Well, I certainly don't want to keep you from more important things," Rebecca said and I smiled. "Follow me. Jack's already waiting at the studio to show you around."

"Okay," I said, trying to find my voice but still failing. I followed Rebecca to the elevators and we descended a few floors.

"I see you found the new wardrobe we left for you," Rebecca commented in the elevator.

I nodded. "Yes, it was very generous."

"Nonsense," Rebecca responded with a flip of her hand. "You're about to be a star. You need to dress the part now."

I nodded as the elevator doors opened. Jack was standing there in his usual gray suit and half smile, waiting for us. "Sophie! Glad to see you this morning. We're all set up for you inside."

I followed Jack down a hallway lined with golden records and posters of other famous stars the label represented. Finally, we stopped in front of one door and Jack gestured that I should enter.

A young woman silently playing the piano connected to headphones jumped up as we walked through and ran over to introduce herself. "Hey, I'm Tara Cecile," she said with a sweet smile. She had a petite build and her skin was a beautiful chocolate with rich brown hair and matching eyes. I instantly liked her as I shook her hand.

I looked around the room. It had everything I could possibly want and more. A grand piano was tucked into the corner and another electric keyboard was placed beside it. A few guitars stood on stands next to some amplifiers and a wooden stool with a microphone was set in front of them.

"Sophie. Nice to meet you," I said, pulling my eyes away from everything.

"Super excited to make some awesome music together, Sophie," Tara said before nodding at Rebecca and Jack.

"Well," Rebecca said as she clapped her hands together. "We'll leave you two to it."

She and Jack turned around to leave before Jack suddenly turned back. "Sophie. We're going to get you set up with a new phone that has your new email address as well as social media accounts under your stage name. If you give me your phone, we can have all of the contacts and information transferred over for you while you're working here."

"Oh," I said, reaching into my pocket. I hesitated but ultimately handed the phone over to Jack. Everyone seemed to be waiting for me.

"Have you thought about your stage name, yet?" Rebecca asked. "If you haven't, that's okay. We were sort of thinking something along the lines of Faith Foster maybe?"

I made a face and Rebecca laughed and waved her hand. "It doesn't have to be that."

"What about 'Sophie Strong?'" Tara suggested.

Rebecca and Jack smiled and looked at me. "Well, what do you think?"

I nodded my head. "Yeah, I like it."

"Are you okay with it being so close to your actual name?" Jack asked.

I nodded my head. "I've got no one to hide from. I'm an open book!"

"Great, then it's settled," Rebecca said with another one of her big smiles. "We'll get all this set up for you and back to you by the end of the day. Have fun!"

Tara smiled and waved as the pair left, closing the door behind them. "Let's make some music together, Sophie!" she said with a pump of her fist.

For the first time the entire day, I didn't feel anxious.

I WATCHED the two women on the surveillance cameras. They were smiling and working riffs out, one on the piano and another on the guitar. I played with the girl's phone in my hand before finally handing it back to Jack. "I hope you're right about this one, Jack," I said before crossing my arms.

"I am," he said, his tone darker than usual.

I raised an eyebrow as I gave him an inquiring look. "You know how much Eternity hates losing money, Jack."

Jack grit his teeth. "I know. Just don't push her too hard, okay. All that pressure has a way of destroying musical creativity."

I sighed. "This is a cutthroat industry, Jack. We're not in the business of subsidizing little girls who play guitar. As long as she makes us money, we're all good."

Jack rolled his eyes. "I know."

"Make sure her phone is taken care of. Leave family but get rid of the rest of it. This girl needs an image change and I don't want anything interfering with that."

"Standard procedure. I get it."

I gave one last glance to the screen and turned on my heel, walking out of the room.

"SOUNDS like you guys made a lot of progress," Jack said, walking back into the studio at the end of the day. I stood up from putting my guitar away and smiled as Jack approached me. The jam session I'd had with Tara had been amazing. Tara was an incredible songwriter and it made me feel slightly guilty that she wasn't on the cover of some album herself.

"Here you go," Jack said, handing me a brand new iPhone.

I took it and grinned as I turned it over in my hand. I only ever had a model three versions behind everyone else. The screen opened as I looked at it and I scrolled through all the new things that had been added. "You've got all your social media apps on there. Anything you want to post just go ahead and submit it like normal. It'll get routed to your publicist first just to make sure it's got a second set of eyes before it's released."

I nodded my head. That made sense and made me feel a bit better about this whole pop star thing. I was thankful I would have people around me guiding me. I pressed the button for messages but it was empty. I frowned before going to my contacts to find that several people were missing. Most importantly, Connor's information was gone.

"Um, Jack. Not all of my contacts are here," I said, starting to panic slightly. I was terrible with numbers. Everyone I knew was in my phone and I didn't have any numbers memorized.

Jack frowned. "Really? That's odd. I'll check with IT and see if they're able to recover your old phone or a backup. But for the meantime, all your calls from your old number are being forwarded so you shouldn't miss anything important."

I breathed a sigh of relief. I'd been really looking forward to my call with Connor tonight. When he called, I could add his number back. Plus, I wanted to tell him about everything going on here. Maybe he'd finally come around and things would go back to normal. I missed him.

"See you tomorrow," Tara said as she closed the keyboard to the piano.

"Sounds good!" I said with a wave to my new friend before I followed Jack down the hallway and back to the waiting black sedan.

THE CLOCK on the nightstand turned to 12:00 a.m. It was officially no longer today and Connor had never called. As the evening had gone on, I had called my mother and asked her to call my old phone number and sure enough it had transferred. So why hadn't Connor called me? He promised that he would and I didn't have any other way to contact him. Connor had never been a social media man. He was barely a phone man.

I sighed and curled into the plush white sheets. How could I be so stupid. He didn't want me out here. He wasn't going to call and be excited to hear about my day. He clearly didn't want to have anything to do with this. Well, message received Connor Driscoll. I guess you never really loved me, after all.

I PRESSED Sophie's name for the tenth time that night only to be told that the number had been disconnected. Setting the phone down on the nightstand, I turned over into my pillow before a single tear streamed down my cheek.

TWENTY-FOUR

Three Years Ago

I POURED OVER THE CONSTRUCTION PLANS FOR THE PROPOSED development again. I'd been working at Phoenix Development for a little over three years now. I'd secured the job when I'd gotten out of college thanks to Professor Philips at the business school. Professor Philips had become a trusted mentor during my senior year. I used to go to him for advice and the man never steered me in the wrong direction.

When I had graduated and started working for Phoenix, I'd put my head down and over these last three years, had risen the ranks faster than anyone could have predicted. But the results spoke for themselves. I'd been able to broker deals quite unlike others and the properties I reno-vated always turned a profit.

But my rise to the top hadn't been without ruffling some feathers.

Many at the business were part of the old guard and believed that the way of the past was the way of the future. Profits for the company were down as a result and the Phoenix name was steadily declining.

I shook my head as I looked over the plans again. I simply couldn't understand why management refused to get on board with what the consumer wanted. Businesses wanted offices they could market and people wanted to live in residences that were updated but also responsible. It wasn't enough to just be the fanciest building on the street anymore. Consumers wanted more and I knew that.

Phoenix's president, George DeSantis, had inherited the company from his father but had never married or had children of his own. He and I had our fair share of disagreements over the years, but George couldn't deny just how profitable I was to the company.

"Well, what do you think?" George asked me. As he leaned forward, the oak and worn leather chair creaked with age, the perfect soundtrack to George's office. I hated coming in here. The office space itself was promising, with a view that stretched out over the city unlike any I'd ever seen. But, the decor looked like it'd last been updated in the 1970s, which was likely accurate.

A heavy oak desk was in the center of the room, the wood full of intricately carved scrolls and designs and showing some serious age. Dark bookcases lined the walls, giving the entire office an overcast look despite the floor to ceiling windows that made up two walls. Various statues and awards lined the bookcases, all of them from decades past. It was everything I was fighting against at Phoenix.

"I don't like it," I said, pushing the plans back to the man on the other side of the desk and folding my arms over my chest.

"What do you mean, 'you don't like it?'" George asked incredulously. "It's our best design yet."

"I'll be lucky if I can sell it for a fraction of the build cost."

"Don't be ridiculous, Connor."

I wasn't being ridiculous. The plans had already taken that award for the evening. "Starting with the most obvious problem, the design of the lobby. A giant crystal chandelier? Honestly, George. Who do you think is going to be looking to buy in this building?"

"Oh, I don't know. All sorts of people and businesses."

"People looking to buy are young. As are the businesses. You've got to know your market and design around them. This will put the company under, for sure."

George leaned back into his chair heavily. His eyes were tired and his stark white hair gave away his age from a distance. His tie had been loosened with the top of his shirt undone and his sleeves had been rolled up. Overall, he just looked tired.

"Maybe I've lost my edge for all this," he said heavily. He turned his chair to look out over the city. "When I inherited this company from my father, I had such big dreams. But I turn eighty next year and honestly, I'm tired."

I quietly listened to the man's confession. There had been rumors circulating around the company that DeSantis was considering retirement. But with no heir to take on the mantle and no ready buyers available, his retirement would mean the end of the company. A lot of good people would lose their jobs. George was a lot of things, but he had a good heart.

"George." The man turned around and he fixed me with an intense gaze. "Do you want to retire?"

George sighed. "Of course. I've wanted to retire for the last twenty years. But how can I?"

"Still no interest?"

"Nothing."

I rubbed my chin with my hand. It was nearing six in the evening and evidence of my dark beard was starting to show. I thought about my next words carefully and then spoke. "I'm willing to make an offer."

"Connor, you've got a great mind and business acumen, that's for sure. But you're still so young. Your time will come."

"I'm serious George. I've got the capital. If no one else is willing to take it on, I will."

I had thought a lot about this and I'd made my decision a long time ago. If I could ever get George to sell me the company, I would buy it. I didn't live a lavish lifestyle. And every penny I'd made on commissions I'd reinvested in other properties around the city. I'd started small at first, renovating smaller homes. But by my second year out of college, I'd purchased and renovated my first commercial project and it had been a huge success.

I knew I could bring Phoenix back from the ashes, like its namesake. I just needed the opportunity to make it happen. Besides, under the right leadership, I was convinced that even the old guard could get with the times. And if they refused, they could always find work elsewhere. But at least they wouldn't be forced out their jobs because the company folded.

"You're serious about this?"

"Yes." My answer was simple but full of conviction.

"Were you hoping for a discount or something?" the old man asked with a chuckle.

I shook my head, my attitude still deadly serious. "No. Whatever price you offered to the public, I'll pay."

George leaned forward and looked me in the eyes. "If you really think you can do it, keep this company running, I'll accept your offer. But if you think you're just going to tear everything down and fire sell the buildings, then you can go to hell. There's a lot of good people out there relying on this place to feed their families."

I had to chuckle at the man. If I were in the same position, I'd probably say the same thing. It's why I'd stuck around Phoenix for as long as I had. I could have easily gone off on my own or accepted the many offers from competitors that paid significantly better. But I believed in this company and its ethics.

"George. I think you know me well enough to know that I would never do that. I am making this offer to ensure those people out there don't lose their jobs. But, I also understand how much this all means to you. I'd be willing to put some restrictions on my actions in the Sale Agreement. I won't agree to hold on to every building in our portfolio, but rest assured, the company will thrive under my leadership."

A more egotistic man might have taken what I said as a slight against his own leadership, but George wasn't that man. He simply stood, grinned and reached his hand across the desk.

I stood as well and shook his hand.

"Have your lawyer call mine. I'm sure you know the number."

I WALKED BACK to my apartment alone that evening. A bit of mist was falling in the cool summer night and dusted the tips of my dark hair. The city was always quiet in the evenings and my walk home had become a time for me to think through my problems.

But tonight, when I should have been feeling excited about the next chapter in my life, I felt more alone than ever. My mind drifted back to my evening walks with Sophie after she played at the Talons. A sad smile graced my features as I tried to put it out of my mind.

Normally, I was successful in pushing down thoughts about Sophie, but tonight the pain was too intense. It'd been a few months since I'd last tried to call her. The result was always the same. The operator would inform me that the number had been disconnected. But, I was holding out hope that maybe one day, that would all change.

I pushed the door open to my apartment building and nodded at the doorman. The elevator appeared quickly and I stepped into the little car and rode it all the way to the top. This building was one of my more successful renovations and I'd kept the top floor to myself. Admittedly it was too much space for just one person. And given how infrequently I was here, I really should have put it on the market and cashed in. But the sales of the units had more than covered the costs of the renovations and some small part of me was hoping that one day, there might be someone else there to share the space with me.

I'd tried dating. It was always a fail. I wasn't the type of man women wanted today. I didn't wear floral printed ties or go to yacht parties. I didn't have a social media presence and I found bars deafening. Given how often I was working, I didn't really have the time to invest in a relationship.

The few hours I did have to myself each day I spent ensuring I kept in shape and working on my own portfolio of properties. Every now and then I'd broker a deal with an agent on the other side who expressed interest in me, but it was only ever just sex. The last woman I'd ever felt a true connection with was Sophie.

And she was very much gone.

And very much all around me all the time.

Her face was on advertisements and her music was on the radio constantly. Even if I wanted to forget her, the world wouldn't let me. It was either trying to send me a very clear message or I was the butt of its biggest joke.

I made my way into my apartment and threw my bag down on the nearby counter. The lights came on as I entered the space but it was still just as lonely there as it ever was. I made my way over to the liquor cabinet and poured myself a drink. Turning, I surveyed the city below me and took a sip of my whiskey. It was extremely bitter.

TWENTY-FIVE

"Sophie! I can't believe it! You're here! How is this even possible?" I asked the woman standing in front of me. She didn't look like her stage self anymore. Instead, she looked like she did when she had left. Her beautiful hair was still red and falling down in waves against her back. Her green eyes glimmered at me and she smiled.

"Don't worry about any of that. I came back to see you and that's all that matters."

I walked forward and pulled her into my arms. I'd been dreaming of getting a chance to make the last evening we'd had together right and now was my opportunity. I wouldn't second-guess my feelings this time. There'd be no delays; there'd be no arguments. She would be mine and that would be it.

I opted not to speak, but instead to show the woman in my arms how I felt about her through action. My lips pressed against hers and I moaned when she readily submitted to me. I pushed my tongue into her mouth to swirl against her own, tasting her for the first time in my entire life. I was like a man who had been starved and was being fed the sweetest of cake. I almost couldn't handle how good it felt.

My hand came up to thread through her hair and I growled as I tilted her head back and claimed her neck. "Connor," she gasped as I sucked her skin roughly into my mouth.

"I've needed you for so long, Sophie," I said between kisses and she sighed.

"I know, Con. But I'm here now."

"And you're going to be mine," I said in a low voice.

Sophie didn't respond. Instead, I could feel her body give in to me and I growled my appreciation. "Come here, beautiful girl. Let me show you everything you've been missing."

I easily lifted Sophie and carried her to my bed. Laying her down, I climbed over her, pulling the flimsy dress off her body on my ascent. As her form was revealed to me, I sighed. I'd dreamed about this moment since I'd first met her and now I was finally living my dream.

The dress peeled off her breasts and I smiled as I realized she was wearing no bra. She looked up at me with a slight smile and I ditched my own shirt and trousers quickly. I pressed my body into hers and heard her sigh. Her soft curves molded against my hard edges and I rocked my firm erection against her.

She gasped and I didn't want to wait any longer to explore every inch of her body. I moved down her form, sucking and licking as I went along. Sophie's delicate fingers thread through my hair and she gasped as my lips latched onto one of her thighs. "Connor please," she begged me and I smirked against her skin.

But as much as I wanted to tease her, I wanted to taste her more. I pulled the small slip of lace back, revealing her glistening sex and groaned. "So fucking wet for me, Sophie. God, I knew you'd be amazing." I didn't give her a chance to respond before I moved forward, flattening my tongue and licking her from entrance to clit.

I worked her to the soundtrack of her moans until she screamed my name, breathing out her release. I couldn't wait any longer. I'd waited years to be joined with this woman and waiting another second was sure to break me. Boxers were pulled down, panties were pushed aside and within moments I was pushing my cock inside of her.

Sophie's head fell back and I grit my teeth as I rocked against her body, thrusting in and out of her at a punishing pace. I wanted to take it slow, but her body gripping my cock felt too good. "Sophie," I groaned her name as her legs wrapped around my trim waist.

"Fuck, Con," she breathed out as I continued my rhythm. I could feel my release threatening to come too soon. I didn't want my time with Sophie to end. I wanted this to last forever.

"Con, just come," Sophie whispered against my ear and I let go, crashing over my edge.

When I'd finally recovered my breathing I pulled out of her and wrapped my arms around her. She turned to look at me and I kissed her. "I love you, Sophie. I don't ever want to be without you."

Sophie just smiled and we fell into a blissful sleep.

I AWOKE the next morning and smiled. I reached across the bed for Sophie, but she wasn't there. I sat up and looked at the empty room and my stomach dropped. The entire thing had been a dream.

I sighed and let myself fall back into the bed. I moved a hand over my eyes and groaned. This wasn't the first time I'd had this sort of dream but this time it had felt so real. Why Sophie continued to plague my thoughts even after all of this time must be the cruelest fate the world could bestow upon me.

The alarm next to me started to ring, signaling it was time to get up and head to the office. I had a rather large closing occurring later in the day and I wanted to get some stuff done before that ate up most of my afternoon. Once again, I'd just have to try and put Sophie out of my mind.

"PLEASURE DOING BUSINESS WITH YOU GENTLEMEN," I said, standing and shaking each board member's hand in turn. The conference room was full of smiles all around as everyone celebrated the successful closing of another Phoenix development.

I had done the math in my head on the way over and when ink dried on this deal, it would net me a little over two million dollars in profits. I'd been working on the project for months, but this deal I'd managed to broker had been the most profitable yet. And the simplest things drove the price up. Mainly, green technologies. It was a great P.R. point for companies, especially those that specialized in drilling for oil, like these folks.

I'd known it all along and from the moment I had taken over Phoenix, I'd implemented a new policy. All new developments would be upgraded to support green technology like solar panels, energy-efficient appliances, and rooftop gardens, if possible. The results spoke for themselves and Phoenix Development was once again a household name.

There had certainly been some disagreements at the start. But people either got on board or they left. It'd been several years since anyone had pitched me a giant crystal chandelier in a lobby, if that was any sort of a gauge.

"We're all going to the restaurant across the street," the man to the right of me said. "Please, join us."

"We already had Nate's secretary call to make sure their bar was fully stocked," another man said with a laugh, joined by a few chuckles around the room.

I had no doubt that this man actually did have his secretary make such a call. I also knew I couldn't refuse the invitation. "Of course," I said with a nod of my head.

We all exited the building lobby and headed across the street to an upscale Italian restaurant. These closings always ended the same way. Handshakes all around followed by heavy meals, heavier alcohol and in my case, waking up to a bedmate in the morning that I didn't remember picking up.

And so it was the same with this deal. Pasta, red wine, darker liquor and large steaks adorned the table as the men all retold stories and jokes they'd told a million times before. By the end of the night, I excused myself and walked to the bar where a leggy brunette was sitting. "Can I buy you a drink?" I asked her and she looked at me with a bit of a raised eyebrow.

"Only if you promise not to have another one," she replied with a bit of a giggle.

"Oh, darling. I promise, I can handle my liquor."

She threw me a saucy grin. "By the looks of it, that's not the only thing you know how to handle."

"Let's say we skip the drink and go right to dessert?"

"I've always had a sweet tooth," she said, before sliding off the chair and following me out of the restaurant.

SEX WITH A STRANGER was what it was. Sure, the first few times you pick up a girl at a bar and manage to bring her home, it's a big rush and a bigger ego boost. But, I started to realize fairly quickly that these random hookups only provided sexual relief for a few days and did nothing to help my emotional state. I was still very much a mess internally.

I'd thought that taking over at Phoenix would give me something to focus on. But I'd been wrong. Once I'd put my plans into motion, the company began working like a well-oiled machine and I was needed less and less each day. I was still the public face of the company and had my fair share of meetings and closings to attend, like this last one. But by this time, they'd become second nature to me and didn't require much, if any, preparation.

I knew what this encounter was, as did the woman. You didn't go home with someone from a restaurant bar after not even exchanging names and expect to spend the rest of your life with them. We were both using one another for temporary release.

Besides drinking, sex had become a bit of a sad escape for me. I wasn't proud of it. I felt like I should be doing more with my life. But it was what it was. My apartment was still too big for just one person. So finding a way to delay going home or numbing the pain when I got there was my constant mission.

The woman was very beautiful, with rich brown hair and high cheekbones. I was sure that someday, she would make some other man very happy. She looped her arms around my neck and tried to kiss me but I pulled my face away and pressed kisses down her neck instead. I didn't want that type of intimacy with anyone, but she didn't know that.

I pulled her zipper down, releasing her from the confines of her black dress easily and she kicked it aside. Her entire outfit was black. Black dress and black lingerie. It would do for tonight. It matched the color of my soul anyways.

I turned her around and pushed her face down against the hotel comforter. She groaned as my fingers moved against her skin before I pulled them back and slapped her ass. She gasped and I hit her again, not hard, but enough to make the skin turn slightly pink.

She turned around to look at me and gave me what, for any other man, would be an intoxicating smile. But for me, I was just going through the motions tonight. I needed a fix and she was my drug of choice.

I didn't bother removing her lingerie or the rest of my own clothing. Keeping a physical barrier between us made me more comfortable. I pulled her panties aside and could see that she was wet for me.

"Oh fuck," the woman moaned as I plunged my fingers in and out of her core. I kept my movements steady and the sounds of her pleasure increased in the small space. She was close and I knew it and I didn't let up. When she finally came, she groaned and collapsed on the bed.

The sound of her grated on me slightly and I decided I wanted to end this. I grabbed the condom I'd left on the nightstand when we'd gotten to the hotel and ripped it. Pushing my pants down enough to free myself, I rolled it onto my length before pumping myself a few times.

I plunged into her core before she'd even had a chance to come down from her high. She gasped at the intrusion but I kept my movements firm and steady. I lost myself in the snapping of my hips and the feel of her body pressing against me. Within minutes, I was pulling her hard against my body as I pulsed out my release.

I let go of my grip on her and she collapsed forward, breathing hard. I ripped off the condom and threw it in the trash. I tucked myself back into my pants and adjusted my clothing. The woman turned over, her brown hair fanning out around the comforter in a mess and she smiled at me. "Clothes on? Kinky."

This girl had no idea what the true meaning of kinky was. She righted her own lingerie and her breathing started to even. Never knowing what to do in these situations, I excused myself and went into the bathroom and closed the door. I looked at myself in the mirror and barely recognized the man I had become. My eyes were bloodshot and try as I might, my hair wouldn't lay flat.

My hands gripped the granite vanity and I looked down into the sink. In many ways, I felt like I was circling my own drain and it had all started the moment Sophie had left. I hated that I was still thinking about her. Even after all this time, I couldn't seem to get her out of my head. She was why I was here.

I shouldn't be at this hotel.

And she shouldn't be in Los Angeles.

I wanted her back in my apartment. I wanted to pull her against me while I ran my hands through her fire-red hair. I wanted to tell her I loved her and hear her say it back.

I ground my teeth as I tried to force these thoughts out of my head. I was still such a mess without her. And she probably didn't even know. Or care. I needed another drink.

How long I stayed in the bathroom, I couldn't say. But by the time I'd opened the door again, the woman was gone and I breathed out a sigh of relief.

Ripping the sheets off the bed, I fell onto the mattress pad and into a fitful night's sleep.

I RUBBED my face as I drove down the road. I was exhausted and knew I probably shouldn't be driving, but at this point, I just wanted to get home. I flipped through the stations and grimaced as the most overplayed song came on the radio.

> Baby with your blue eyes
> Looking at me so nice
> Telling me I better come on.
>
> I could see you standing there
> Acting like you didn't care
> 'bout anything but getting me home.
>
> Now you don't know
> The way I feel
> But that doesn't mean
> That this ain't real
>
> Cause your blue eyes stopped the bus
> And then they stopped my heart.
> Yeah those blue eyes stopped the bus
> And now I don't ever wanna be apart.

Groaning, I turned the radio off and decided more than needing to go home, I needed something to eat. I pulled my silver Lexus into the nearby diner parking lot. This diner was one of my go-to's. There were no booths or tables. Only a row of seats at a breakfast bar. It was as if the place was built for people who had no one.

I grabbed a newspaper from the nearby stand and sat down at the far seat. The waitress came over and set a cup of coffee in front of me. "The usual?" she asked and I nodded my head.

"Sophie Strong tops the charts again!" the headline read and I sighed. Sophie's face was plastered everywhere these days and her songs were all over the radio. She looked nothing like my Sophie from what felt like eons ago. Her beautiful red hair had been bleached to an unnatural shade of blonde and instead of leggings and a sweatshirt, she was always in some glitzy getup.

My eyes raked her body up and down in the photo. She was on stage in nothing but what appeared to be a diamond-encrusted bra and panty set with odd jewelry that traveled up both wrists and calves. Her guitar-slinging days were done, having clearly traded her acoustic roots for something more auto-tuned.

I sighed and turned the page, intent on finding the business section.

"Connor Driscoll?" a familiar voice asked.

I pulled my paper down and smiled as I recognized the man approaching me. He was slight in stature, but then again, almost everyone was compared to my impressive height. He had dark hair that was thinning a bit and was sporting a long sleeve polo shirt with a pair of old jeans.

"Professor Philips!" I said, standing to shake the man's hand.

"Please, call me Ben. Mind if I join you?" he asked, pointing to the seat near me.

"Please," I said, pushing my paper aside.

"Well, you look a little worse for wear," the old professor said with a bit of a laugh. I couldn't help but chuckle. I knew I didn't look great. My suit was wrinkled and my hair was ruffled. Even without my bloodshot eyes, I wasn't securing any modeling contracts this morning. "Rough night?"

"You could say that," I said, taking a sip of my coffee. I'd always felt bad that we had lost touch after I graduated. "I'd reached out to the university to try and get your contact information when I heard you retired, but they refused to give it to me."

"Lawyers and their privacy lawsuits," Ben sighed with a shake of his head. "I'm sorry we fell out of contact, too. But from what I've been reading, you've certainly been keeping yourself busy."

"Yeah," I said, setting my cup down. "This whole industry isn't as glamorous as I thought it might be, though."

Ben shrugged. "I suppose that all depends on you."

"What do you mean?"

"I know all the wheeling and dealing that goes on behind the scenes, Connor. Don't forget, I left the private sector to work at the university because I'd simply had enough of it."

"That's right," I said.

"I'm just saying, there's a difference between playing the game and being a game piece. I know it's hard, but try not to get so caught up in all the extra bullshit that goes on around you."

"Easier said than done."

Ben smiled and thanked the waitress as she set a cup of coffee in front of him. "So, other than business, what's new? Married with kids yet?" he teased.

"Hardly," I said with my own chuckle.

Ben looked down and saw the photo of the newest pop star topping all the charts. "That's your Sophie, isn't it?"

I grimaced. "Yeah."

"You two were inseparable during college. Have you stayed in touch at all?"

I sighed. "No."

Ben furrowed his brow. "I guess your relationship didn't end on a high note, then."

"Well, we never ended up getting together," I admitted, falling back into my easy routine with Ben.

"Oh, Connor. I'm so sorry. I know how you felt about her," he said with a pat on my shoulder.

I shook my head. "It was probably for the best."

Ben smiled and nodded. "There's always one that gets away."

I nodded and tried to smile and Ben caught on that this wasn't a topic to dwell on. "Alright, so nothing to keep you busy aside from work."

"Unfortunately, yes. That's probably why I seem to keep getting myself into trouble, showing up at diners looking like this," he said with a gesture to my overall appearance.

"We all have to let loose sometimes," Ben said. "But have you ever thought about maybe doing something productive with your extra time?"

"Like what? I'm stretched pretty thin, as is. I wouldn't be able to commit to anything that required too much time."

"You know, the college is always looking for successful folks to teach seminar courses and companies to host interns."

"I dunno," I said.

"It's one weekend a semester to teach the course and you get to have someone work at your company for free during the semester."

"Well, when you put it like that."

"Just think about it," Ben said.

"Alright," I said as the waitress set my food down, leaving us to reconnect over an impromptu breakfast.

TWENTY-SIX

Sophie

I STRUMMED MY FINGERS AGAINST MY GUITAR IN FRUSTRATION.

"Maybe a G chord, here?" I said aloud to myself, playing it in time with the rest of the notes I had jotted down and sighed. It was terrible. The entire song was terrible, just like the rest of my creations had been lately. I'd tried bringing them to Tara to see if I could get some help turning them around, but even she wasn't able to assist.

> *"Maybe you should just take a break for a while," Tara suggested as she closed the cover to the keyboard.*
>
> *I sighed and shook my head, my bright blonde hair swaying from side to side. "That's really not an option for me right now. Or ever. You know what the schedule around here is like."*
>
> *"Yeah," Tara said, turning to face me. She gave me a sad look. Tara had been working for this music label for several years. She'd admitted*

to seeing a lot of talented people suffer from burn out and get shuffled out the door with no remorse. It's why she said she never tried to get close to the people she worked with. But despite that, we had become friends over the years we'd worked together.

"I really didn't think it would be like this," I lamented as I put my guitar in the stand before sliding down the wall to sit on the floor.

"No one ever does," Tara said. "This industry is crazy cutthroat. When everyone's constantly looking for the next big thing, it's hard to concentrate on what you've already got."

I nodded my head in commiseration. "Is that why you always stay in the background? I know how talented you are, Tara."

Tara waved her hand at the idea. "No way. No offense, but I see what they put you guys through. The constant tours, interviews, appearances. I really do value the ability to walk down the street and not have people shouting at me or trying to take my photograph. Besides, it's not about that, it's about the music. And I get to work on that here."

My shoulders slumped. Between the two of them in the room, Tara was definitely the smarter one in my eyes. I'd been totally mesmerized by the glitz and glam of everything in LA. when I'd arrived. Too bad I didn't know I basically signed my life over when I signed that contract all those years ago.

Back in my apartment, I shook my head and tried to refocus, but it was no use. I'd been thinking of Connor more and more lately. It still hurt that he had never ever tried to call me like he promised he would. I didn't have a lot of friends in college, but since moving out to LA, I'd lost touch with everyone from my past.

Everything about me changed the day I agreed to become Sophie Strong. My name, my hair, my wardrobe, even my personality. I used to like who I was. Sophia Stronglen was vibrant and had goals. Sure, I was crazy headstrong and could be a bit of a brat at times, but I at least had things driving me.

Sophie Strong was none of those things. I was compliant and submissive to a fault. People around me made all the decisions for me, down to what I wore every day and where I would be. Half the time, I didn't even know my own schedule until things were happening. Then I'd be whisked away in a car or on a private jet to the next big thing, makeup, costume and hair waiting for me.

The first few shows I had played when I was still a breakout artist had been so exhilarating. I thought I'd finally found my true calling and that this would be the job for the rest of my life. Fans were dedicated and kind and the label allowed me a bit more freedom to connect with them in the way I wanted to.

But now, with the entire world watching me, everything was scrutinized. Anything I wanted to post on social media was screened and quite often entire posts I would write were rewritten or just deleted. It didn't matter though. People still found time to write increasingly nasty comments. For every person that called me too skinny, there was another claiming I was too fat. And for every person that said my music was too upbeat, another would be there to claim it made them sad. There was just no winning with people.

The shows started to blur together and for the last few months, I had lost all motivation to even look at my guitar. I pushed my instrument aside and rolled over onto my back. The ceiling fan blades circled overhead, stuck in a predetermined path and even that made me feel sad. I exhaled and realized how ironic it was that I was constantly surrounded by people, but always felt so lonely.

Even if I could call Connor, I knew I had no right now. What was I supposed to say after not speaking to my former best friend for four years? *"Sorry I left and didn't say goodbye right after you confessed that you loved me?"* It didn't matter now. Connor dodged a bullet. No one deserved to be with me and I deserved no one.

My phone chimed and I groaned but reached for it. "Yeah?"

"Sophie, it's Jack and I think you know why I'm calling."

"Yeah."

"Any progress?"

"Sorry, I'm trying, Jack."

"I know, but my hands are tied, Sophie. You're contractually obligated to provide a certain number of publishable titles a year. You're coming up to the end of the year and well, you're basically an entire year behind schedule."

"Thanks for reminding me."

"I hate to say this, Sophie, but unless you can get me something by tomorrow end of day, we're going to have to bring you in for a meeting."

I tried to inhale and exhale as quietly as possible. There was no way I was going to have something ready by tomorrow and Jack knew that. But, like always, this company and its executives excelled at making you elect your predetermined fate. It must be some sick fetish for someone at the top. "Just schedule the meeting, Jack."

"See you tomorrow, Sophie."

I just hung up the phone, not wanting to hear his voice anymore. I rolled over and reached for my guitar. Sitting up on my bed, I began to play a haunting melody and the words tumbled out of my mouth easily.

> Another crack appears
> I'm surprised it's holding together.
> I use it to hide the tears
> A mask that makes me look better
>
> But pieces fall away
> The strain is just too much
> More of me revealed each day
> I'm breaking without your touch
>
> A million cracks, a million scars
> A million reasons you were right
> A million cracks, a million scars
> Forever by myself tonight.

It was the first song I had managed to write in the better part of a year. And I knew there was no way the label would go for it. It wasn't in keeping with Sophie Strong's high pop and impossibly cheery image. No matter. It would just be for me then.

"HI, SOPHIE." Rebecca Murphy greeted me as I walked through the door. I opted not to shake her outstretched hand and I scrunched my face at her perfect brown hair and tailored black suit. The color seemed fitting, considering this was likely my funeral.

Rebecca sat down and gave me an appraising look. It was obvious I was not doing well. My hair was in a piled mess on the top of my head and I was wearing the same tracksuit I'd worn at our last meeting. Even still, I didn't appreciate her look of disdain, considering she was the greatest source of my misery.

"Is there anything you want to discuss, Sophie?"

I gave her a bored stare. "You're the one that insisted on meeting. Seems like you have something to say, not me."

Rebecca cleared her throat, trying to maintain her calm façade. So fucking fake. She'd shown me her true colors and I was still angry at myself I hadn't seen her for what she was at the beginning.

"Yes, well, I think I've got a proposal that will help make things a bit easier."

I didn't respond and just continued to twirl my bleached hair around my finger and chew on a piece of gum. Anything that she suggested wasn't going to be for my benefit. Of that I was sure.

"Your contract is currently with Charisma Records and it requires you to produce twelve publishable songs per year. I know that this schedule has been a bit difficult for you lately and I think I've worked out a deal with one of our affiliates."

I blew a bubble and continued to look at the woman in front of me. I didn't trust Rebecca at all. Despite her calm and charming appearance, she'd proven to me enough that she was only interested in profit margins at the expense of people and their lives.

"What's this got to do with me?"

"It means, Sophie, that your contract is being assigned to another label. They're still part of Eternity Music Group, but you'll have a new team and your production schedule will be a bit more manageable."

"So what? Jack, Tara, everyone that I've known and worked with over the past four years?" I asked in disbelief.

"Unfortunately, yes. That team belongs to Charisma Records. But you'll have a new team of great people."

"So, your solution to me not being able to meet your production schedule is to give me an entirely new group of people to work with? How is that supposed to get me to make music any faster?"

"Well, once the assignment goes through, your production isn't really Charisma's concern anymore."

I bristled. This was absolute bullshit. "Well, I don't agree to it."

Rebecca gave me a sickly sweet smile. "You don't have a say in this, dear."

"What the hell is that supposed to mean?"

Rebecca reached for a stack of papers behind her and my stomach sank with realization. Of course it was the contract she'd pushed in front of me all those years ago. The one I really *really* should have called Connor about, but for some strange reason, had decided to call my gold digger of a mother instead.

"Right here," Rebecca said, flipping to the middle of the contract and pointing to Paragraph 52.

"Assignment. Neither this Agreement nor any rights or obligations hereunder may be assigned either voluntarily or involuntarily, by operation of law or otherwise, by either party without the prior written consent of the other party, provided this shall not preclude Charisma from assigning this Agreement to an affiliate of EMG without the prior written consent of Ms. Stronglen."

I closed my eyes briefly and let the glass-encased conference room slip away for a moment. I should have expected something like this to happen. The label was only going to bankroll my expensive apartment and lifestyle for so long. And without another album ready to drop on the horizon and the accompanying shows, appearances and merchandise sales, I was surprised I lasted as long as I did.

I blinked my eyes back open and looked at Rebecca. "Fine. When can I meet my new team?"

"Tomorrow," Rebecca said, standing up. "We have a car arranged to take you there in the morning."

I stood and nodded before turning and leaving without another word.

THE OFFICE I found myself at the next morning was nothing like Jack's at Charisma Records. These walls were an off yellow and looked like they were in desperate need of a fresh coat of paint. I looked down and realized the carpet tiles were peeling at the edges and I grimaced. The particleboard bookshelves that lined the walls were covered with odd knickknacks and the number of files strewn about the tiny space with no apparent rhyme or reason was disconcerting.

I'd been instructed to sit in one of the chairs that faced the orange oak desk but I couldn't bring myself to do it. The cushion was wearing and I could see the layer of dust on it.

"Sophie Strong?"

I turned at the sound of my name to see a short, balding and heavy-set man making his way towards me. His dress shirt was full of wrinkles and the top button had been undone to accommodate the size of his neck. "Lennie Webb. Nice to meet you." He held his hand out and I shook it gingerly. "Have a seat," he said, gesturing to the chair in question and I tried to fake a smile. As Lennie turned to sit in his own chair, I quickly grabbed a file off his desk and placed it on the cushion so I at least wasn't in direct contact with it.

"Well, Ms. Strong. First off, I'm a huge fan and we're all really excited to be working with you at Tymar Records."

"Great," I said, trying to look excited but I knew I was failing miserably.

"So, I'm not sure how much you were told about us here?"

I shook my head. No one had told me anything. Not even the name of the record label I'd been assigned to.

"Well, we're a subsidiary of Eternity Music Group and we've onboarded quite a few stars from Charisma over the last few years when their schedules got too much."

"So you're a dumping grounds for Charisma?" I asked, the bile heavy in my voice.

Lennie chuckled uncomfortably and put up his hands. "I wouldn't go that far. But yes, we do take on artists who need a less compressed schedule. There are times when we transfer them back to Charisma if they are ready, or to another affiliate within the Eternity family. But let's not worry about that now, Ms. Strong. I want to talk about you and what you need from us."

"Well, a recording studio, obviously. I used to work with someone to help work out chords and lyrics and stuff, so that'd be great to have again."

Lennie looked uncomfortable. "Well, we do things a little differently here, Ms. Strong. We don't actually own any studios. When you're ready to record something, you can go ahead and let me know and we can get a room rented for you."

I scrunched my face. "I don't get it? Where am I supposed to write my songs?"

"Not to worry!" Lennie said. "We've already arranged for a keyboard to be at your apartment when you arrive this afternoon."

I grimaced. All this was going to do was make things that much harder for me. "If you don't mind, Mr. Webb, this is just a lot to take in. Maybe we could finish our meeting later this week?"

"Of course, Ms. Strong. Your car's waiting for you downstairs to take you to your apartment. If there's anything you need in the meantime, just give me a call," he said, reaching to the cardholder at the front of his desk and handing me his card.

"Thanks," I said with a smile that didn't reach my eyes before standing to leave.

I breathed in the cool air when I stepped outside, not having realized how suffocating that place was while I was trapped in that office. A different car than usual was waiting for me out front but the driver had a sign that said, "Ms. Strong."

"I'm Ms. Strong. What happened to Jared?" I asked, referring to my normal driver.

The man in a slightly wrinkled suit just shrugged his shoulders. "I don't know Jared."

I sighed. "Okay, whatever," I said, climbing into the back of an older town car. As we pulled away from the office building, he turned right whereas he should have turned left to go back to my apartment. "Hey, I think you're going the wrong way," I said to the driver but he shook his head.

"No. This is the right way."

I groaned. Today could not get any worse. First, I had to spend the morning with Lennie and now my driver didn't even know his way back to my apartment.

After a few moments of silence, the man finally drove past rows and rows of duplexes. I scrunched my face as we pulled into the driveway of one of the units. "Where the hell are we?" I asked as the man opened my door. I probably should have been worried about my safety, but I was so used to being shuffled from unknown place to unknown place by strangers at this point, that the thought didn't even dawn on me.

"Your apartment," the driver said, as if he didn't understand what the problem was.

I huffed and pulled out my phone. I pressed the button for Jack and placed the device to my ear. He answered on the third ring and I really had to stop myself from screaming at him. "Jack, what the hell? Jared didn't show up to pick me up and now this new driver has brought me—I don't even know where the hell we are—but he's insisting it's my apartment. Can you tell Jared to come get me?"

I heard Jack's sad sigh in the receiver and my stomach dropped. "Sophie. Your contract has been reassigned. That means that all of the accommodations that Charisma was contractually obligated to provide, your apartment, your driver, et cetera, are now being handled by Tymar. I'm sorry you had to find out this way. I thought Lennie would have told you."

I couldn't believe this. "What about all of my stuff?"

Another sigh. "Almost everything in that apartment was provided to you by Charisma, Sophie. We've had your personal belongings delivered to your new apartment. I wish you the best, Sophie. Truly."

Before I could curse at the man, he hung up, leaving me standing there in front of a home I didn't recognize with yet another stranger.

I grit my teeth. "Do you have a key or something?" The driver just shrugged his shoulders and I let out a strangled cry of frustration. "Just go. I'll figure it out," I said, stomping forward. The building was plain and looked like every other one on the block. Concrete steps led up to a small porch and the structure was made of grey vinyl siding. The whole thing looked cheap.

I tried the worn brass knob on the builder's grade door and it opened. A set of stairs led up to a kitchen and a dark hallway led to a bedroom on the main floor. I opted to walk upstairs and grimaced as I looked at the cheap carpet, plastic floor and outdated white appliances. I made my way downstairs and hoped I might find something better but I was disappointed. A queen-size bed without a frame was pushed against the wall of the space and a few boxes with my belongings were on the other side.

My guitar had clearly fallen over and the case had opened so that the instrument was lying face down. I slid to the floor and grasped my head in my hands as my entire world crumbled around me.

TWENTY-SEVEN

LENNIE

"Look, Ms. Strong. I know we have a relaxed schedule here, but you need to give us something to work with. We paid quite a large sum of money to Charisma because we believed in you! You don't have anything you can give to us?"

Sophie shook her head, looking more washed up than ever. This was the third meeting in three months and they were all the same. I asked if she'd managed to write anything and she'd just shake her head and say no.

"Are we done here?" she asked in a bored tone.

I sighed, trying to keep the façade up. "I guess so. Just keep trying, Ms. Strong. I know you're an extremely talented young lady. You just need to find your muse again!"

"Whatever," Sophie said with a huff as she left my office.

A few minutes passed before my business partner walked into the office. Isaac Jacobs sat down in the dust encrusted chair. I hated Isaac but I couldn't deny we worked well together. His grey suit was freshly pressed and his hair was combed back in a style that said he thought he was better than everyone. He crossed his legs and fixed me with an interesting smile after handing me a drink.

"So, what do you think?" Isaac asked, swirling his own drink in his hand.

I shook my head. "She's got nothing left. I thought maybe of all the has-beens she would have pulled through, but she's just as chewed up as the rest of them."

"So, the usual?" Isaac asked and I nodded.

"Yeah. Go ahead and start the rumor mill. Let our preferred people know where she's going to be and make sure the driver knows to drop her off at the scheduled locations where the photographers are waiting so they can get their photos."

"This is my favorite part," Isaac said with a smirk.

I shook my head. "I don't understand why torpedoing peoples career is a hobby for you."

"Oh, it's more than a hobby. I've made it a living thanks to you, Lennie," he said, raising his glass before taking a drink.

I momentarily felt bad for what I was about to put this girl through. Her only faults were being young and stupid, and at her age, I was the same. Then I thought about how much money it cost me to buy her and all the money to put her up in an apartment and those feelings instantly faded. This was how this industry was. If you couldn't stay famous, you became infamous.

"You know me," I said, stretching my hands wide before placing them behind my head and leaning back. "I'm just in this for the money."

"Think we'll make it back on this one?"

I scoffed. "I know Charisma tried to charge us more for her, but let's be honest. Sophie Strong has been number one on the charts for the last three years. The entire world is going to watch her fall and they're going to eat it up. This is going to make us very rich men."

I leaned forward and picked up my glass. "To Tymar Records!"

"Take your money and run," Isaac said before we clinked our glasses together.

"Ms. Strong! Sophie!" the reporters shouted as I tried to get out of the car. "Is it true that you stole your songs from Tara Cecile?"

The cameras flashing at me were disorienting and I blinked as I tried to make sense of the scene in front of me. The driver told me we were just heading to a meeting with Lennie and some executive about me going on tour, but somehow there were a million reporters blocking me from going anywhere.

"What? No, that's ridiculous," I replied. Why would someone think that I stole Tara's songs? How would anyone know about Tara anyways?

"Ms. Strong, over here!" another journalist waved frantically to get my attention. "What about the rumors that you were trying to seduce label executives to get special treatment at Charisma? Any comment?"

"What?" I couldn't believe what I was hearing. Seduce who? What the hell is this?

Trying to go anywhere with the throng of paparazzi in front of me was impossible and I climbed back into the safety of the car. The cameras still flashed through the tinted windows and I put my head down so I could avoid being seen. "Just go!" I yelled at the driver.

"But your meeting?" he asked.

"We'll have to reschedule it I guess, or something. I don't know. Just get me out of here!" I nearly screamed. The car zoomed off, leaving the hoots and hollers of the reporters behind.

♪

I CRASHED into my bed as soon as I was back to my place. Lennie had called to let me know that the meeting had been cancelled since I didn't show up and the executive no longer wished to work with me. I was so passed feeling anything about everything at this point that the news didn't even phase me.

I flipped on the small television that I had bought for myself and was affronted with a video of this afternoon. The newscaster was speaking over the sound of the recording.

"We turn now to the press conference with Ms. Tara Cecile and Mr. Jack Tanner of Charisma Records regarding the Sophie Strong revelations."

I watched in horror as the woman I considered to be my friend walked up to a podium in front of flashing cameras, followed closely behind my old manager, Jack. Tara looked calm and composed in a professional grey suit dress, something I had never seen her wear in all our years working together.

She cleared her throat and began to tell the biggest lie I had ever heard.

"Good afternoon. It's under very sad circumstances that we're here today, but I cannot keep my silence any longer. I am here to confirm that over the past three years, Sophie Strong has stolen the songs that I wrote. I am an employee with Charisma Records and was assigned to assist Ms. Strong with her recordings. However, I had left my own journal with songs in the studio by accident after one of our first sessions. All of the songs you've heard Ms. Strong claim to write were actually written by me."

"Ms. Cecile! Why didn't you come forward sooner with this information? Why wait until now?" a reported barked.

"Thank you for your question. Unfortunately, Ms. Strong threatened to get me fired if I said anything so I kept quiet. I knew it wasn't right and now that she's no longer with the group, I finally feel safe to say something."

"Are you thinking of suing Ms. Strong for copyright infringement?"
"I haven't made any decisions at this time."

The reporters all tried shouting more questions at her but she stepped out of the way to allow Jack to take the podium. Sitting across from the television, I was in absolute disbelief.

"I think we can all agree that Ms. Cecile has been very brave today. Unfortunately, the startling confessions don't end just with her. I am here to confirm the rumors that Ms. Strong did approach several executives to offer her advances in exchange for preferred treatment with Charisma. Of course, this is strictly against our high ethics and policies at Charisma and as soon as someone was brave enough to step forward and report it, Ms. Strong's contract was terminated."

"Are you trying to say that Ms. Strong offered to trade sexual favors in exchange for preferred treatment?"

"I was trying to be diplomatic, but yes. That is correct."

I turned off the television. I'd heard enough of their lies. I curled up on the bed and looked over at my guitar. It had a layer of dust on the case, just like everything else in the boxes I'd never bothered unpacking.

My phone rang and I looked at it but turned it off when I saw it was my mother. I did not have the energy to deal with that woman right now. I wished I could cry, I wished I could feel something, but I just laid there, totally numb to the entire situation. I knew any normal person would be sobbing their eyes out right now. There was no coming back from this. Whoever decided to spread this rumor had done it to make money off of my misfortune and they did so knowing I would never be a pop idol again.

My phone rang again and I sighed but picked up this time. "Yeah."

"Sophie, I've just seen the news. I know none of that is true. We have a good relationship with Charisma. Just hold tight. We'll get all this sorted for you. I already have my best person on it," Lennie's voice came through from the other side.

"Okay," I replied simply before hanging up the call.

I didn't know who to trust anymore. It didn't make sense for Lennie to sell me out. They had just bought my contract. But then again, they certainly stood to gain from selling me out to the paparazzi. I pursed my lips into a thin line. I had no other option than to trust him at this point. My entire career had been placed into his hands. At the very least, he hadn't shown me any real reason not to trust him. Through it all, he'd been kind and understanding when I continually failed to produce music. Maybe he was serious about helping me through this.

"SOPHIE, did you manage to avoid the crowd out front?" Lennie asked, getting up from his desk.

I managed a nod and sat down at the chair in front of his desk, no longer caring about the dust and clutter. "What the heck happened?" I felt silly even asking, but I just couldn't wrap my head around it.

"Look, Sophie. You're a sweet girl. But before we talk any further about sorting out this mess, I need to know for sure. Was any of what they said true?"

I shook my head vehemently. "No, of course not! I wrote all of my songs, I promise!" I winced, realizing how bad it looked that I'd been unable to produce anything over the last three months now that I was no longer with Charisma. I wished I had some real proof, but I wrote all of my songs the same way: sitting on the floor of whatever space I happened to be in with my guitar and jotting down lyrics and chords.

The music had a mind of its own. Secretly, I never really considered myself a songwriter as much as some receiver for music that came to me unexpectedly. I never had a method for writing songs, which was why the last year had been so hard for me.

"Do you have any way to prove this?" Lennie asked, picking up on exactly my worry.

I looked down and wrung my hands slightly. "Not really." How could I be so stupid and throw away my notes after the songs were written and entered into the computer? At least I would have had some physical evidence that I worked on the songs.

"Well," Lennie rubbed the back of his neck and looked uncomfortable. "Maybe just keep thinking about that one and see what you can come up with. In the meantime, what about the second rumor?"

I threw up my hands. "Mr. Webb, I swear. I would never. That's just not the kind of girl I am."

Lennie nodded, his bald head glinting in the harsh fluorescent lights. "I know. I believe you, Sophie. Gosh, this is really not a good situation, is it?"

I bit my lower lip. I knew I should want to cry, but just like last night, the tears wouldn't come. "What can I do? I want to clear my name. I want to get back to the music. I don't want any of this."

I watched as Lennie paused in thought before he pressed a button on his receiver. "Isaac, why don't you come in here and we can all strategize."

The door to Lennie's office opened and I had to stifle a groan at seeing Isaac. I certainly wasn't guilty of trying to come on to anyone at Charisma, but Isaac was guilty of that behavior with me. I had turned him down politely at first and then his advances got more persistent.

There was nothing I could do in this position, especially now. I knew I wasn't making Tymar any money so I had no leverage. Besides, the only person to tell was Lennie and he'd been Isaac's business partner for years. I was powerless and I knew it. The best I could do was just try and avoid him.

"Sophie," Isaac said with a smarmy smile before sitting in the chair next to me. He was wearing a dark navy sports coat atop grey trousers and his dark brown hair was greased back like always. I tried not to breathe in too hard, given how overwhelming his cologne was. I shifted to the right in my chair, trying to put as much distance between us as possible.

"Hi Isaac," I responded curtly.

"Isaac, I'm sure you've seen the news reports. Sophie has guaranteed me that none of the rumors are true. Do you have any suggestions on how we might go about clearing her name?"

Isaac placed a thin finger to his lip and tapped several times, apparently contemplating Lennie's question. "Well, the easiest way to discount

Tara's song stealing story is to produce a killer hit. We could record the entire song writing process from start to finish. It doesn't definitively prove that you didn't steal your original songs, but it would certainly put the seed of doubt in people's minds."

"Sophie?" Lennie turned to face me, giving me a pitiful look. "What do you think?"

"I'm not sure," I hesitated. "I've just been having a really hard time writing lately." I snapped my head to the side as Isaac let out a strangled laugh. "I'm sorry, is this funny to you?"

"Actually, yes," Isaac said, turning his gaze on me and I tried not to shiver in disgust as his eyes raked my body up and down. "You've been accused of stealing songs and then we ask you to write your own to prove that you can and you say you can't. It doesn't look good for you, Sophie. Please understand it from our perspective."

"Well, maybe if I didn't have to deal with all of this shit I could focus on writing," I snapped, anger starting to well up inside of me. It was an odd feeling considering I hadn't felt much of anything over the last year. It would have been a welcome relief to feel something if it hadn't been Isaac who was sitting next to me.

Isaac leaned forward. "Oh, is that so? So then what was your excuse for the last twelve months?"

"Fuck you! You don't know what I've been through," I said and Lennie jumped in to try and calm the waters.

"Guys, guys. Please," he said in a desperate voice. "None of this is helping. We are supposed to be on the same team." He turned to look at Isaac. "We both believe you Sophie," he said before turning back to me. "Isaac, please let's try and keep it constructive?"

Isaac leaned back and the chair squeaked in protest. "I was just saying what we were all thinking. Someone had to."

"Stop it, Isaac," Lennie said in a firm voice. "Let's move on. What should we do about the Jack issue?"

"That one's easy," Isaac said, standing up and walking towards the small liquor cabinet in the corner of Lennie's office. He leaned down and grabbed a bottle of whiskey and poured himself three fingers. He swirled the drink in his hand before turning back around and taking a sip.

"You've always get the good stuff, Lennie," he said and I rolled my eyes.

"Isaac," Lennie said, starting to get angry himself, which was something I had never seen before.

"Alright, alright. The Jack-problem is fairly easy. We set Sophie up with someone else and we announce that they've been in a serious relationship for the last year."

I couldn't believe what I was hearing. "So, your solution to people telling lies about me is to lie more? Lennie," I said, turning back with pleading eyes. "Please tell me you can't agree with this?"

The older man frowned and looked uncomfortable. "I don't know, Sophie. It could help take the pressure off for a little while."

"This is insane. Who would even agree to go feed the public a lie like that, anyways?" Isaac took another sip of his drink and smiled. I looked at him in absolute horror and shook my head fervently. "No. No way. Not happening."

"Oh, come on, Sophie. Multiple women have assured me that I'm quite the gentleman. Besides, I know you and this industry better than anyone. As long as you were committed to making it believable, we could make this work."

"First of all, you don't know a damn thing about me," I snarled, finally finding my voice. "And second, I'm not going to go out there and publicly humiliate myself over some stupid rumor. My dignity is worth more than any of this."

"Sophie," Lennie said, trying to calm me down. "Maybe you should at least consider his proposal?"

Isaac smiled into his glass again, looking entirely too pleased with the situation. "It wouldn't take much, Sophie. We just would have to make a few public appearances, stay at a few hotels overnight so the paparazzi could see us together, that sort of thing."

My lip curled in disgust at his words. Was this all just some elaborate scheme to try and get me alone in a hotel room? Was this guy really that sick? "Please, tell me you're joking." My gaze snapped to Lennie and I gave him a frantic look. "Is this just some joke you two are trying to pull to lighten the mood or something?"

Lennie and Isaac looked at one another before looking at me. Lennie spread his hands and shrugged his shoulders. "I'm sorry, Sophie. But it's not. I don't really see any other way around this."

"As much as it would disappoint me," Isaac said, swirling his liquor again. "If I'm truly so disgusting to you, we could try and arrange to set you up with someone else. But there would be a cost to it. Not everyone's willing to give you their services for free, like I am," he said over the lid of his glass.

"Why are you okay with this?" I demanded of Lennie. He had seemed so nice and this was his business partner. He couldn't possibly be okay with Isaac trying to take advantage of the situation and me this way, could he?

"Isaac, give us a minute," Lennie said.

Isaac shrugged and downed the rest of his drink before placing it on the little table. As he walked by me, he let a single finger brush through my hair and I shuddered as he closed the door on us.

"First, I know Isaac comes off really strong, but believe me when I say that he's actually a really nice guy and he means well. I know he would be the perfect gentleman and wouldn't make you do anything you didn't want to do."

I tried to swallow what he was saying but I just couldn't. He was making me sound like some high end call girl.

"Second, Isaac's right. There's really no better option. Sure, maybe if we had more money, we could hire someone to take his place instead. But that's another person to pay off and keep quiet and that's risky. Isaac's trustworthy and has a vested interest in making this work."

My mouth went dry at his words. He really was on board with this. I couldn't believe how badly I had misjudged him. I shook my head, finally realizing how naive I had been from day one.

I stood up and Lennie followed me with his eyes. "This is just a lot to take in right now, Lennie," I said. "I think I just need to go home and think about it. Maybe we can meet tomorrow and continue the conversation?"

"Of course," Lennie replied, having gotten used to me abruptly ending meetings. "We'll see you tomorrow. Come by when you're ready to talk."

I gave him a curt nod before storming out of his office. I blew past Isaac who was waiting outside. He reached for me but I quickened my step and just narrowly missed his grasp. "See you tomorrow, Sophie," he called after me but I just kept running.

TWENTY-EIGHT

Isaac

"So, what do you think?" I asked Lennie as I poured myself another drink. I sat down in the chair where Sophie had been, still warm.

Lennie rocked back in his chair and put his hands behind his head. A wicked grin broke out across his face. "Don't you think it was a little soon to pull the good-cop bad-cop act with her?"

I rolled my eyes. "Not at all. That girl's washed up. Look, I know Becca's doing what she's doing at Charisma so they have a reason for transferring the girl away that makes them look like angels. Sophie had potential, but that's gone now."

"So, how do you think she'll handle this? Britney style bender or do you think she'll agree to your proposal?"

"Damn I hope she chooses the second. I'd like to have some fun with her before she's totally useless to us."

"I've seen the way you treat your women, Isaac. If she chooses you, she'll be more useless than if she goes on a full out bender."

I chuckled into my glass. "Your words wound me. I had something a little more refined in mind for this girl than the usual treatment."

"Oh yeah, like what?"

"There's nothing better for popularity than a well-timed sex tape. I'm happy to lend my services in such a valiant effort."

Lennie rolled his eyes and shook his head. "How're you gonna convince this girl to get in bed with you? She hates your guts."

"Who said anything about convince?" I let my tone turn dark.

We laughed and Lennie cleared his throat. "But, in all reality. Just make sure you've got a plan ready to deal with whatever happens. Personally, my money is on a bender," Lennie said, sliding a one-hundred-dollar bill across the desk.

"I'll take that wager," I said, reaching for my own wallet and placing my own on top of Lennie's.

"Watch her close," Lennie said as I got up to leave.

"I always do," I said with a glint in my eye.

Sophie

LOS ANGELES HAD BECOME a prison for me. I spent most of my time between the four walls of my depressing bedroom and now I couldn't hope to leave even if I wanted to. The adrenaline from my conversation with Lennie and Isaac was starting to wear off and my mind was a cluttered mess.

Lennie had always seemed like he was on my side. Isaac had always been a self-possessed asshole but I never had to deal with him too much. The fact that Lennie was on board with Isaac's plan made me feel genuinely panicked. I had absolutely no bargaining power in this situation.

Unless...

I looked over at my guitar case, still leaned up against the wall. It had a layer of dust on it and I walked over to it. I brushed off the dust and laid it on the floor. The locks were stiff, reminding me of how long it had been since I'd even tried to play something. Lifting the instrument out of its coffin, I leaned against the bed and cradled it in my lap.

My fingers moved over the strings with ease and I fell into a trance as I began to tune each one in turn. I flipped on my phone's audio recording app and took a deep breath. I closed my eyes and opened myself up to the melody that I knew was already inside me. It had just needed to find its way out.

Within minutes, I started to sing.

> Making deals with the devil
> It's an interesting thing
> Thought I could be an angel
> But I ain't got no wings.
>
> He asked for my soul
> But that's already gone
> I said "Take what you need"
> He said "You'll be my pawn."
>
> And now I'm dancing with the devil
> Round and round in circles
> But even he can't own something
> This wild and free

The lyrics and melody came to me easily and as soon as I set my guitar down, I knew I'd done what I couldn't get myself to do in over a year. More than that, I knew that this song would top the charts if it were ever released.

I stopped the recording on my phone and carefully returned my guitar to its own prison. Closing the case, I made my decision. Lennie and Isaac would never hear that song. And there would be no meeting tomorrow. This town would be my prison no longer.

Los Angeles could say whatever it wanted about Sophie Strong as far as I was concerned. I was leaving her behind.

TWENTY-NINE

Sophie

Present Day

"Sophie! Sophie Strong!" people shouted trying to shove microphones into my and Connor's faces. "Do you have anything to say?"

"Where have you been this past year?"

"Would you like to comment on the rumors circulating about your business dealings?"

I started to shake under all the scrutiny and Connor pulled me tighter against him. "Ms. Strong will not be making statements at this time. We'd ask that you kindly clear the area," he said in a booming voice.

Someone pushed in front of the crowd and reached for my scarf, tearing it and my glasses off of my head before he reached out again for me. The sound of cameras clicked and I looked up to see Connor enraged.

"Hey!" he yelled, grabbing the offender and placing a punch to his jaw.

"Connor no!" I gasped. I was wrenched away from him as people pulled at me and tried to get photos of the fight that had broken out.

Tears streamed down my face as I realized that everything I'd feared had come true. Connor was getting caught up in my bullshit. He'd likely be sued for assault or worse. Everything he'd worked for had been ruined after only four months of me being in his life.

I pushed my way through the sea of reporters and ran as fast as I could in the opposite direction, refusing to turn around even when I heard Connor's voice calling my name behind me.

"Sophie!"

His voice sounded desperate, but I wouldn't let myself turn around. I continued to run. I was good at that now. I'd already destroyed my own career. I wasn't going to bring Connor's down too.

A nearby metro station was up around the corner and I put my head down and sprinted to it. The escalators made their sad, squeaking noises as they helped carry me into the dark, underground beneath the city. I didn't need to take anything with me this time.

My guitar, my belongings.

None of it mattered now.

I had one goal in mind.

After that, I would disappear again and this time, no one would find me.

When I finally made my way to the bottom, I allowed myself to get lost in the crowd, closing in close to the person in front of me so that I could pass through the turn table without swiping a metro card. The train came quickly and I breathed a sigh of relief as I took a seat at the back of the last train, tucked into a tiny pair of orange cushioned seats, hidden by a darkened glass panel that people had tried to carve their names into.

The train lurched out of the station and in the dark corner, I felt a single tear fall down my cheek.

♪

"Now arriving Ronald Reagan International Airport," the train operator said over the loudspeaker. I lifted my head and brushed the few stray tears out of my eyes. As soon as the train had made its way out of the tunnels, Skyler had called me.

"Sophie, I just heard what happened. Are you okay? Where are you?"

"I'm fine, Sky," I responded.

"Tell me where you are. I'm coming to get you."

"Don't worry about it."

"Sophie stop. I'm really worried about you. Please, just tell me where you are."

"NOW ARRIVING AT CRYSTAL CITY," the announcement blared over the loudspeaker and I winced.

Skyler was quiet for a minute before she spoke. "Soph, why are you going to the airport? Where are you going?"

I cursed under my breath. Damn Skyler for knowing this city so fucking well. "Don't worry about it, Skyler. I just need to make something right and then everything can go back to normal."

"Sophie so help me I will call in a bomb threat if you don't tell me where you're going. And orange jumpsuits really aren't my thing. So I'm going to need you to be honest with me or else."

I hesitated but relented. "I'm going back to LA."

Skyler gasped. "What? Why?"

"I just need to make something right. I can't have everyone following me and I've roped Con into all of this now. I just need to do this. Please don't tell him, okay?" I begged.

"I don't know about this, Sophie."

"I love you, Sky. You've been the best friend I've ever had. I really don't deserve you." With that, I hung up the line.

I stepped out onto the platform and looked at my phone. It'd been almost an hour since I'd run from Connor but he hadn't tried calling me. He probably saw what being with me would truly be like and decided to run the other way. It was better this way. I could at least fix this for him. I owed him that much. Then he could finally be free of me.

I made my way into the airport and approached the ticket counter. "I need a ticket to Los Angeles. The first one available."

The older woman behind the counter smiled and nodded her head. "It's pretty late in the day so we might be able to get you to Denver, but you may be stuck with an overnight layover."

I sighed. I wanted to get out there as soon as possible, but if that was the best I could do, I would make it work.

"We've got a flight leaving for Denver in an hour that I can fit you on. It'll be an overnight layover there and then the next leg departs at seven. That'll put you in LA by nine-thirty."

"Okay," I said, not having any other choice. I handed over my license and a credit card and shook my head when the agent asked if I would be carrying any bags with me.

"Travel light, I see!"

"Something like that," I murmured as I took back my cards and the ticket the agent handed me.

We exchanged pleasantries and I made my way through security easily. The airport was fairly empty at this hour. Not many people were flying out of the city at six in the evening. I found myself a corner chair and curled into it, waiting the few minutes before the agent boarded the flight.

I WALKED out of the police department and looked down at my watch. It was already after seven in the evening. The cops had shown up given the raucous and I'd been asked to come down to the station to give a state-

ment. I knew if I refused, they would just bring me in anyways and I much preferred going there of my own choosing.

Ultimately, the district attorney had indicated he wasn't going to prosecute as this was a clear case of self-defense when the photographer attacked Sophie and then me. But the entire ordeal had eaten up precious time and had prevented me from even calling Sophie. I hailed a cab and directed it to the loft while I pressed her name and placed my phone to my ear.

"The person you are trying to reach has a voicemail box that is not set up yet," the voice on the other end of the line said.

"Damnit Soph!" I cursed aloud and the driver raised an eyebrow slightly. "Can we go any faster? It's kind of an emergency."

The driver nodded, but kept his same speed and I sighed as I tried calling Sophie again.

When we finally arrived at the loft, I threw the guy a few bills that more than covered the fare and sprinted up the stairs. I banged on her door but she didn't answer. "Soph! It's me! It's Connor! Please, open up!"

I tried to peer through the curtains that were slightly pulled back from the window to see if she was inside. It looked dark and a pit in my stomach formed.

"Professor Driscoll?" a woman who looked vaguely familiar called out to me from the parking lot. I looked down and recognized her from class. She had bright silver hair and intense lavender eyes and a good deal of ink on her body. She'd been the girl Sophie sat next to during my seminar.

"Skyler, right?" I asked as I bounded down the stairs to speak with her.

"Yeah."

"Do you know where Sophie is?" I knew I sounded frantic and Skyler gave me an interesting look. "Please." I looked desperate and anxious and I hoped she could tell that those were two emotions I was not used to feeling.

"She's at the airport."

"She's what? Where is she going?" I exclaimed.

"LA. She said she had something she needed to handle there."

I ran my hands through my dark locks and tried not to scream. "Why didn't you try and stop her?"

"I did. I threatened to call in a bomb threat if she didn't tell me where she was going."

"Oh," I said a bit sheepishly. "Sorry. I'm just a little out of it right now. I need to get to her."

"What happened?" Skyler asked. "I saw the news. How did they find out she was here?"

"Who knows," I said, rubbing my brow and trying to think of my next move.

"Look." Skyler gave me an intense stare and I met her gaze. "I know I haven't known Soph as long as you have, but I do know she's got a good heart. She thinks her life is an inconvenience to you." I opened my mouth to say something and Skyler put up her hand to stop me. "We both know that's bullshit. And that you're the only one that can convince her of that."

"Thanks," I said and the girl nodded.

"So, what are you going to do?"

My phone rang and I pulled it out of my pocket quickly. "One second, I have to take this. It could be about Sophie," I said as I answered the call. "Gus, please tell me you've got something, man."

"I could use a little more time to do some more digging, but I saw the news and figured this information might be useful to you right now," my private investigator said from the other side of the phone.

"You have no idea," I said.

Skyler motioned for me to follow her as she walked up the stairs to Sophie's apartment and used a key to let us both in. She sat at the break-fast bar while she watched me pace back and forth as I spoke on the phone.

"Alright, tell me something good," I said.

"Sophie originally signed a contract with Charisma Records, a subsidiary of Eternity Music Group. She worked with them for a little over four years before her contract was finally assigned to another subsidiary of Eternity, Tymar Records.

"I got a hold of the original contract she signed and I'm emailing it to you now. But let's just say that it wasn't the most favorable of terms. Terribly one-sided and complex and if the dates of when she arrived in LA and when she signed this contract are correct, it was the same day. There's no way she, let alone a lawyer, could have gone through this entire contract in one day."

"Shit," I said under my breath.

"Yeah. But it gets worse. All those rumors about her stealing songs and coming onto music execs is bullshit."

"I knew that, but how do we prove it?"

"Tymar is owned and operated by a Lennie Webb and Isaac Jacobs. They've owned a number of companies that are formed as Eternity subsidiaries right before Charisma offloads a contract to them. They were pretty clever about using registered agents and they like to hide their names, but I found them. These two fuckers seem to have a special knack for torpedoing celebrity careers and have been associated with a number of entities that were created just before Charisma offloaded to them."

"Jesus Christ," I said.

"Yeah. So, while I don't have any concrete evidence that the rumors were fabricated by them yet, we do have pretty good circumstantial evidence and a pattern of behavior to point to."

"Do you have these guys' contact info?" I asked.

"On its way to you now."

"Thanks, man. Keep on it. Anything else you find, let me know as soon as possible. Don't worry about waking me. I'll be up."

"Sounds good, boss," Gus said before hanging up the phone.

I pulled the phone from my ear and phoned Kris. "Kris, sorry for calling you after hours but I need a big favor. Can you book me a private flight to LA as soon as possible? I need to be there no later than tomorrow morning. . . . And I also need you to form an LLC. Name is MMS LLC and make me 100% owner but make sure my name isn't easily found. . . . You're a life saver, thanks man."

I put the phone down to see Skyler smiling at me. She had her arms crossed in front of her and was grinning like a Cheshire cat. "It sounds like you've got a kickass plan to save our stupid Sophie."

I nodded and looked around the room to see if there was anything I needed to bring with me. I looked in the corner to see Sophie's guitar leaning against the wall and her laptop on the nearby desk. I walked over and grabbed both, slinging the guitar onto my back before turning back to look at Skyler.

"Willing to give your professor a ride to the airport? You look like you drive faster than the cabbie."

Skyler grinned and uncrossed her arms. "Driving fast is sort of my thing." I rolled my eyes but smiled nonetheless.

"OVER HERE ACTUALLY," I said, pointing to the private airfield next to the airport.

"Fancy," she said.

"I don't normally see the need to put an entire jet into the sky for just one person—green development company image and all that—but tonight I think the extra pollution is warranted."

"I'll plant some trees for you next time I go for a hike," Skyler said with a laugh. I thanked her as I got out of the car. "Bring her back to me, Connor!" Skyler called out after me as I closed the door and ran forward, guitar still slung across my back.

Within thirty minutes, I was in the air reading the contract Gus had emailed me on Sophie's laptop. Gus had been spot on with his evaluation. This contract was the most unilateral thing I had ever seen.

But people who valued money over everything else often left themselves vulnerable. Their greed blinded them in ways others, like myself, could exploit.

I pulled open an email and began drafting:

Mr. Webb,

I am writing to you regarding your ownership rights of the Sophie Strong record label. I understand that recent events have made owning this contract a difficulty for anyone, but I specialize in these situations. Call it an expensive hobby of mine.

I'm very interested in purchasing her contract and am willing to offer up to $2 million cash on hand to make this happen. I will be in Los Angeles tomorrow morning and would be happy to sit down to discuss the details further with you. However, I think lawyers are overpriced and would be happy to make it a quick close situation.

Looking forward to hearing from you.

Sincerely yours,

C.D.

I spent the next hour reading through the important points of Sophie's contract before an email popped into my inbox. I smiled to myself. Too easy.

Thank you very much for your email and your generous offer. My colleague and I would be happy to discuss the details further. Please meet us at the address below tomorrow morning at nine. We look forward to working with you.

Lennie

I chuckled. These bastards were all the same. Greedy, materialistic and so self-centered they couldn't spot a trap a mile away when money was on the table. I would delight in taking these idiots down and giving Sophie back everything that had been stolen from her.

I moved to pull back up the PDF window but accidentally clicked the photo reel. I smiled to myself as I realized that this must have been her old computer, since all the photos were from when we were in college. I shook my head at how bad my hair was back then as I scrolled through each photo. No wonder Sophie hadn't been into me back then. If one good thing came out of all of this, it was an update to my wardrobe.

I clicked right to the next photo but a video came on instead. It was Sophie, sitting on the floor of the loft, holding the same guitar I had in the seat next to me. Her fingers danced on the strings.

"Okay, I just wrote this so it might not be all the way worked out yet

but. Wait, why am I talking to myself?" the former Sophie said with a roll of her eyes before she started to sing.

> Cause your blue eyes stopped the bus
> And then they stopped my heart.
> Yeah those blue eyes stopped the bus
> And now I don't ever wanna be apart.

I froze. This was the song that had made her famous. The one Tara whatever-her-name-was had claimed Sophie had stolen from her. I shook my head and couldn't believe what good luck I was having this evening. It must be Lady Karma, trying to make up for how royally she had screwed me earlier. I quickly emailed the video to myself, wanting to make sure I had a copy at the ready in case I needed it.

I looked at my watch. I'd land in LA in about four hours, which meant four more hours to study this contract before I paid back everything these assholes had coming to them.

THIRTY

Sophie

THE FAN BLADES CIRCLED OVER ME AS I LAID OUT ON THE BED. I'D bought a change of clothes and checked into the hotel attached to the airport for my overnight layover. The bits of metal and plastic made their slow circle over my head. At this point, I couldn't remember how many different ceiling fans I'd looked up at over these past five years.

My life had constantly been on the move, never in the same place for more than a few days until I was off to the next. I'd always thought I was on the straight and narrow. The biggest joke was that I was attached to some fucked up gear that seemed to delight in swinging me around and around in an endless cycle of disappointment.

Just when I thought I might have found some semblance of normalcy, I was right back where I started. The paparazzi chasing me and Connor yesterday had shown me that I was never going to be able to escape this life. I thought I left Sophie Strong behind in LA but I'd been wrong. I could dye my hair back to its original color, tattoo my body and wear what I used to wear, but none of that mattered. I was a changed person, made by and for music executives that only cared about the money I made them.

For a brief moment, I thought I could see a life with Connor. He wanted me, that much was obvious. And try as I did to resist him, I just couldn't. And now I'd dragged him into all this mess. But that ended now. I was going to go back to LA and fix the mess I'd made. I'd find some way to clear his name, even if it meant I had to step back into the world I hated.

I crawled under the covers, having finally cooled off from my long shower and my mind drifted to Connor. It was sad to think about how I would never see him again, but it was for the best. He needed to be free of me, even if it would be the hardest thing I'd ever done.

But as much as my mind knew what needed to be done, my body didn't agree. Just the thought of Connor had me heating up and I couldn't stop my hand from sliding down my body to between my legs. I thought about the last time we'd been apart. It was when he was on his business trip to California. He'd made me admit some of my darkest fantasies to him over the phone and when he'd returned, he'd more than delivered. My finger began to circle my clit as my brain forced me to relive the memory.

"Let yourself into my place. There's something waiting for you on the bed. Strip naked and put it on and wait for me like the good girl you are."

I read the text over and over, my arousal growing with each word. I knew I shouldn't be so giddy to see Connor. He'd only been gone for two weeks. Considering I'd gone the better part of five years without seeing or even talking to him, the fact that I barely lasted two weeks should have chimed warning bells in my brain. But I was too excited about finally getting to see him again. Logic had no place in my brain right now.

The doorman gave me the key to Connor's apartment when I walked in per his instructions. I thanked him as I took the little bit of metal and waited for the elevator. As the car brought me higher and higher, my own arousal began to soar with the anticipation of what he might have planned.

I'd confessed so many things to him over these past two weeks. For some reason, it was a lot easier to admit to things over the phone or via text message than it was in person. And admit I did. I'd been sexually repressed for five years during my time as Sophie Strong. My only companion during that time had run on batteries and even that got old after a while.

But, there was no way to connect with someone when you were constantly on the road, in meetings or in the studio. Building a relationship took time. You had to get to know the person. I didn't have time for people. Or rather, I wasn't allowed time for people. So I was always alone.

But I already knew Connor. Or at least, I thought I did. I was quickly discovering that this Connor was very different than the one I had left behind. This Connor was strong, confident and dominating. He didn't always give me what I wanted, but he always gave me what I needed. But he only took as much control as I released to him. I knew I was falling into a dangerous place with this man. But when you're tumbling downhill in an avalanche, there's not much you can do. You just have to wait and try and dig yourself out when you finally reach the bottom.

The bell of the elevator pulled me out of my thoughts and I stepped out into the penthouse lobby and walked forward to Connor's door. It seemed rather silly to have a lobby for just one apartment, but I'd seen sillier designs in my travels.

Unlocking the door, I laid the key on the counter and kicked off my shoes. I hadn't worried about what to wear when I got Connor's text. It was clear that he wasn't going to see it anyways. Stepping into the bedroom, I looked at the perfectly made bed. There on the plush white comforter was a small slip of satin.

I picked up the piece of fabric and turned it in my hands, realizing it was an eye mask. I couldn't help the smile that started to spread on my lips. My phone chimed and I pulled it out of my back pocket and swiped up to read the new message.

"Naked. Face down on the bed. Mask on. Now."

I chewed my lower lip as I blushed. Placing the fabric down on the bed, I made my way into the bathroom and turned on the shower. I rid myself of my clothing and jumped into the spray to rinse off for just a minute before toweling off. The white bedspread looked so perfect. I wanted to make sure I was worthy of it. Internally I laughed, knowing as soon as Connor got there, the thing would be drenched with my arousal even before we started.

Making my way back to the bed, I pulled the piece of fabric over my eyes and laid down on the bed as he instructed. Naked, face down, mask on. As I waited, the loss of my sight increased my other senses. I strained my ears to try and hear any indication that Connor was finally back.

The time passed but I had no way of knowing how long I'd been waiting. I felt utterly exposed and equally strung out the longer I waited. For a single moment, I worried that maybe Connor had forgotten about me and then I heard the door open.

I nearly groaned from that sound alone and my arousal peaked. I rubbed my legs together as I heard the click of his dress shoes against the porcelain tile. I wanted so badly to thread my fingers between my legs, but I knew he wouldn't be pleased. So I waited as the wetness between my thighs increased.

He said nothing as he walked around the bed. The click of his shoes was so close, I knew he could just reach out and touch me. With my eyesight blinded, the scent of his cologne was overpowering and I sucked a deep breath down. I'd missed the way he smelled.

I gasped as something soft touched my wrist. I couldn't quite make out what it was at first. Whatever it was wrapped its way around my wrist and it dawned on me—it was a fur-lined leather cuff. The smallest tug pulled my left arm away from my body but I stayed still.

The click of Connor's shoes told me that he was coming to the other side of the bed. My suspicions were confirmed when another soft cuff caressed my skin and I nearly sighed as he secured it. I pulled slightly against the cuffs and realized my arms were very much immobilized now.

A deep chuckle echoed across the room somewhere to the right of me. I wished so badly that I could see him right now. He probably looked stunning and I wasn't used to being denied. "Connor," I said in a breathy voice.

A single finger danced across my skin. It moved from the cuff on my right wrist and down my forearm before slipping into the crook of my elbow. I was moaning just from that small touch and I couldn't believe it. "Connor." His name slipped from my lips again but he didn't respond. That sinful finger just trailed its scorching path further and I had to bury my head into the soft comforter.

One fingertip. That's all it took to make me come undone. I was complete putty in his hands. How Connor did it, I didn't know.

Further down it traveled, now over the swell of my ass. It stopped to play against the bottom of one cheek, tracing the crease there. It inched so close to my center and I was sure the spot beneath me on the bed was quite drenched by now. Just as it got close to my prize, it pulled away and I groaned.

"Connor."

Still no response.

My legs were pressed together and that finger fell into the crease between the two, making its way down towards my ankles. It sent shivers up my spine and I wanted nothing more than to grind my pussy against something and just come already.

The touch moved down to my right foot. It caressed my instep gently and I let out a moan I didn't know I was holding back as heat pooled low in my belly.

"Please," I begged.

Still no answer.

My right ankle was pulled to the side and I gasped as the cool air hit my partially exposed core. Another soft cuff wrapped around my ankle and a slight tug told me it was firmly in place. Those sinful footsteps echoed across the room again. My left ankle was wrapped and secured like its pair and I moaned, knowing I was now completely exposed.

I bit my lip, still waiting, totally under his spell and at his mercy. The

IVY WILD

bed depressed slightly between my legs and a single finger made its way up my slit. I cried out at the feeling as shivers wracked my body.

"So wet for me, Sophie," he said, his voice deep and full of hidden promises.

"Connor."

Another swipe of his finger before the sensation was gone again.

"I missed this wet little cunt of yours."

"Fuck."

"In time."

I moaned and the bed lifted as he stepped off. Something warm started to move against the instep of my foot and I was breathing heavily at this point. I just needed him to stroke my clit. Just once. I knew I'd come as soon as he touched me there.

But his tongue danced across the instep of my left foot. I tried to squirm, but the cuffs held me firmly in place. I couldn't do anything but lie there and take whatever this man decided to give me.

Finally, he started making his way north. His progress was slow but steady. He lavished kisses to each part of me, exploring the curve of my legs and the swell of my ass. Just as I finally thought I might get some relief, he pulled back.

I could feel his body over mine, caging me beneath his hulking frame.

"You want to come, don't you?" he husked in my ear.

It was more of a statement than a question, but I answered.

"God, yes."

"Beg me for it." His finger darted out and caressed the swell of my breast pressed down against the comforter.

I whimpered as his touch became more insistent.

"Beg for what you want, Sophie." His voice was intense and I shuddered.

"Please, touch me, Connor."

His finger brushed the nape of my neck, sending more shivers coursing through my body.

"Touch you where?"

"My pussy."

238

"So you can what?"

"Fuck, Connor."

"So you can what?"

"Come."

He leaned in closer and I could feel his hot breath against my ear. *"All together."*

My brain was a scrambled mess so how I said the next words, I didn't know. *"Please touch my pussy so I can come."*

"Good. Girl."

His body pulled away from me as the bed shifted. A single finger slipped between my thighs and began to circle my clit.

"So wet."

"So close," I moaned.

Two fingers entered me while his thumb stayed on my clit and after a few pulses, I was crashing over the edge. My breath hitched as my muscles drew up and a garbled moan of his name fell from my lips. I couldn't move and my body struggled against the restraints as waves of pleasure crashed through me. His movements slowed but only enough to match the pulsing of my walls as he worked me down slowly so I didn't crash.

When my breathing evened, I felt him pull his fingers out of me gently. A popping sound had me wondering if he had just licked them clean, only to be confirmed when he said, *"Delicious."*

I heard a zipper drop somewhere behind me and felt myself getting aroused again at the thought of what might be next. My ankle restraints were loosened slightly and a hand came down to caress my ass. The touch was warm as he cupped my curves.

"Pop that ass up for me so I can fuck your tight cunt."

I gasped but pulled my legs up as far as the restraints would allow. My wrists were still firmly in place and I writhed as Connor's hand made its way up and down my ass cheek.

"This wet pussy is mine," he said as his fingers played with my folds.

I moaned at his words. His. I was his. I wanted to be his.

"Say it."

"Yours."

"What."

"My pussy."

"Sophie."

"My pussy is fucking yours, Connor Driscoll. Please fuck it as hard as you want."

"Fuck yes," he cursed. His cock slammed into me and I screamed at the intrusion. He slipped in easily, all the way to the hilt. Connor was large and my walls rippled around his length before he started to move.

"You're mine, Sophie," Connor grunted as he continued to thrust in and out of me. With each movement, the tips of my breasts danced against the comforter and I could feel my walls tightening around his length as his cock pressed into me over and over again.

"Connor."

His rhythm was steady and fierce. Everything I wanted from a man. He continued to pound into me, slapping my ass as I gasped his name each time his cock pressed inside of me.

"I'm going to come," I breathed out between thrusts.

Connor didn't stop his pace.

"Do it, Sophie. Grip my thick cock with your tight little cunt."

"Fuck." The words were coupled with my second orgasm of the night before I collapsed.

The feeling of my walls gripping his cock like a vice was too much. With a roar of my name, Connor pulled my hips hard against him and let himself go inside of me.

"Connor," I breathed out as I came, thinking back on the memory. It was nothing like being with him. No orgasm I'd given myself had ever compared to the ones that Connor lavished on me.

I curled in on myself in the bed, pulling the covers close around me as the heat of my orgasm faded. I knew I shouldn't be reliving these memories. I needed to put Connor behind me and remembering how completely he fucked me wasn't going to help. I grit my teeth as tears began to flow down my cheeks.

Before I couldn't cry.

Now I couldn't stop.

♪

THE ALARM RANG in my ear and I rolled over to shut it off. I'd barely slept all night, my mind just constantly turning over what I was about to do, likely trying to make sense of it.

Pressing my feet to the floor, I reached over and grabbed the receiver on the hotel phone. I'd turned my cell phone off before boarding the plane last night and hadn't turned it on since. I knew as soon as I did, I'd have a million calls from Skyler and—

—I didn't want to think about whether Connor had called or not.

I looked up at the ceiling and steeled my resolve. This was going to be the hardest call I might have to make in a while. Touching the numbers, I pressed the receiver to my ear and waited.

"Lennie Webb."

"Mr. Webb, it's Sophie. Sophie Strong."

There was a pause on the other end of the line before his voice came back. "Sophie! My gosh. Are you okay? Where are you?"

"I'm coming back to LA, Mr. Webb."

"You mean you're not here now?"

"Something like that. Look, I was scared before. But I'm willing to do whatever I need to now to get my name cleared. I've got a song ready and," I swallowed hard. "If Isaac's offer is still on the table, I'll take it."

There was some shuffling on the other end of the line before Lennie spoke again. "Sophie. This is all very sudden."

"Please, Mr. Webb." I closed my eyes. I needed this man to agree. If I released my new song, it would help clear the stolen song nonsense. And if I agreed to admit to a relationship with Isaac, it would hopefully take the spotlight off of Connor and put it on him. He'd be free of me.

"Sophie. I've got something in the works right now. I tell you what. Why don't you come by my office in the afternoon and we can talk about everything. Sound good?"

I winced. I didn't want to wait until the afternoon. Besides, I had nowhere to go and couldn't risk being seen all over LA. Intent on just getting to his office when I got there and waiting if I had to, I agreed. "Okay, Mr. Webb. I'll see you later today. And," I choked back a sob. "Thank you for helping me."

"Don't mention it, Sophie. See you later."

The call ended and tears streamed down my face as I put the receiver back in its cradle. Slapping my face with both hands, I pulled my sweat-shirt and leggings on and wiped the tears from my eyes. I needed to get on my flight so I could get this over with. The sooner everything started, the sooner it would be over.

The airport was quiet on a Saturday morning and I ducked into a small shop on my way to my gate and bought a scarf and a pair of sunglasses. I secured the scarf around my neck and put the sunglasses in my hair, knowing I would need them as soon as I touched down in LAX.

I opted to walk along the long corridors rather than ride the little trams stationed every so often to help busy people get places faster. I wasn't busy and I did not want to get to my destination faster. These were my last moments as Sophia Stronglen. As soon as the wheels touched tarmac in California, I'd be Sophie Strong again.

How I hated wearing that mask.

It was so heavy now.

Connor

SIX HOURS of flight time and a three hour time difference meant that I landed in LA just before midnight. I had a car take me to a hotel within walking distance of Webb's office and was thankful for the time difference and the few hours of sleep I could manage.

I tried Sophie's phone as soon as we'd landed, but it was still off. I tried it again before I went to sleep and still nothing. Curse that woman and her lack of phone etiquette. When I had her back safe in my arms, I was going to talk to her about that.

No more running.

No more hanging up phones.

No more turning them off.

She needed to understand that she was mine now and that was never going to change.

I wanted her.

Every part of her.

I didn't care what fucked up history Sophie had. I didn't even care about our five years apart at this point. I just cared about her. She was the one. I'd always known that. But she was just too damn stubborn to see it herself. Well, that was going to change.

I loved her.

I'd said it before and I knew it to be true. Loving Sophie was like a universal truth. As sure as apples fell from trees, I would always love Sophie.

I'd poured over her record deal on the six-hour flight. It certainly wasn't enough time to read the entire thing, but I got the gist of it and there were certain provisions I knew I could use to my benefit in my upcoming negotiations with Webb. If what Gus said was true, it was unlikely that this man or his partner ever paid much mind to the contracts they siphoned off from Charisma or other Eternity Group affiliates. Which meant there was room to take advantage.

I had just really wished that Gus had been able to get his hands on the assignment agreement between Charisma and Tymar. Sophie would probably be pissed at him, but I'd given Gus permission to hack into her email. Sophie always used the same password for everything, including her internship email. It hadn't been a hack job as much as just a plug and play job for Gus.

I told him I didn't want to know about anything that wasn't record label related. Besides, Gus was the most trustworthy guy I knew. Still, Sophie would be pissed. It was sort of ironic that we had to go to all that effort originally when her computer was now sitting right next to me. But the advanced information had given Gus the ability to dig into Charisma and Tymar, which was what was making this entire trip possible.

I wanted nothing more than to burst into Webb's office tomorrow and plant a fist right to his jaw for everything he had put Sophie through. But sometimes, the best victories were won on paper.

Where Sophie might be in the city was a mystery, but I sincerely hoped she would show up at Webb's office. It was either there or Charisma. It didn't make sense for her to go anywhere else given what Skyler said she had on her mind.

My stomach dropped at the thought of her alone in the city some-where. My fingers fisted in the sheets as my heartbeat increased and I tried to take calming breaths to cool my temper. Sophie was a smart girl. I trusted her to be okay. But I hated that she was by herself again. Why she insisted on always going it alone, I just couldn't understand.

That was a lie. I did understand. I had a difficult childhood, as had Sophie. My relationship with my parents was strained, to the point where they no longer talked. I had learned to rely on only myself from an early age.

I knew Sophie never knew her father and that her mother was basi-cally useless. Perhaps that's why we had gotten along so well. In some ways, we were very much the same person.

But I'd always found comfort in relying on her. I hadn't realized it until she left, but I'd come to rely on her for so much. It was why I'd been such a wreck when she'd disappeared.

I shook my head to free the bad memories. Those times were over. That me was gone. This me knew what I wanted and would get it. And that was Sophie.

My cock twitched at just the thought of her. I rolled onto my back on the hotel bed and let my mind drift to my woman. My need for her was overwhelming and as soon as I had her back in my arms and I knew she was safe, I would fuck any doubt she had about whether we should be together right out of her mind.

My boxers tented at the thought and I released myself from their confines and began to stroke myself. I closed my eyes as I thought back to the last time I had her in my apartment. I knew Sophie loved being restrained. The cuffs were a particular favorite of hers but as much as I loved having her completely under my control, there were times when I loved the feeling of her moving freely against me.

Her fingers danced across the soft leather, following the curves on the sofa as she looked up at me, her green eyes flashing like emeralds in the low light of the evening. The corner of her lip twisted into a slow smile and I wasted no time in taking a seat and reaching out for her hand.

I was already in just my briefs and I'd stripped her down to that fabulous lacy red bra set she was so fond of. One of these days I was going to snap that thong in half but I'd try and hold myself back today.

"Come here," I said, leading her to me. I guided her so that she was straddling me, the small of her back pressing against the curve of the sofa. "Have you ever been on one of these?" I asked, referring to the curved lounge.

She shook her head and bit her lip. I grinned and thrust my hardened manhood against her panty covered core easily and she gasped. She looked down at my feet on the floor and smiled as she looked back into my blue eyes.

"Just take me already, Connor," she said, wrapping her arms around my shoulders.

I didn't need a second invitation. I pulled her against me, smashing my lips against hers. I bit down hard on her lower lip, the one she enjoyed chewing so much and she gasped. I used the opportunity to push my tongue into her mouth and she responded, swirling her own against mine.

She groaned as my hands caressed her beautiful curves. Pulling back, I breathed out, "I need this off you," before I unclasped her bra and tossed it to the side. My hands closed over her breasts as soon as they were free. I pushed her back slightly so that she was draped against the curve of the couch and I moved in to tongue her hardened peaks.

Sophie gasped at the sensation as I circled each tip with my tongue before sucking them into my mouth gently. I palmed each in turn before my hands slid lower. My thumb toyed with the slip of lace and I so wanted to tear the thing in two but I held back again. Instead, I pushed the fabric aside and pressed my fingers against her heated core.

"So fucking wet, Soph."

I began to thumb her clit and she moaned at the feeling. My fingers slid around her folds easily given how slick she was and all I wanted to do—all I needed to do—was shove my thick cock into her weeping core and fuck her until she came.

My own boxers were pushed down and I released my hardened cock. Pushing her panties aside, I let my tip gather moisture from her folds all while I held her draped over the curve of the sofa.

She looked absolutely stunning like this, spread out for me. Waiting for my cock.

"Tell me you want this cock," I said to her as I continued to move my erection over her folds, not entering her.

"Fuck, Connor. Please," she moaned.

"Sophie," I chided, but I was barely holding on myself.

"Fuck me with that thick cock of yours, Connor."

"Sophie," I groaned as I slipped my member into her tight cunt. Her walls rippled around me and I pushed my thumb against her clit as I began to move. I leaned back myself, using the other curve of the sofa as leverage as I thrust up into her.

Her tits bounced deliciously in time with each of my thrusts and her lips stayed parted as she moaned my name. My rhythm was firm and steady and within minutes, she was breaking around me. I absolutely loved watching her come. She'd go rigid for a moment before letting out the most erotic moan I'd ever heard, usually garbled up with my own name, which only made me harder.

Her walls clenched me hard and I grit my teeth at how fucking amazing it felt. I pulled her forward and she collapsed against me, but I didn't care. I supported her weight as I thrust into her from below and she continued to moan my name in ecstasy as her walls pulsed their release.

"Sophie!" I groaned her name as I spilled my release inside of her before wrapping my arms around her, holding her tight to my body.

"Fuck." I cursed and came, my seed spilling onto my stomach as I breathed out my release. It took me several deep breaths to calm myself down before I was finally able to get up and get into the shower and clean myself off.

As the steam surrounded me, I leaned my head against the tile and closed my eyes. I needed Sophie back with me. Maybe she thought she was doing me some big favor by running from me. But she didn't know how much of a fucking mess I was without her.

"No more running, Sophie."

Tomorrow I would find her.

And then she would be mine.

THIRTY-ONE

Sophie

THE WHEELS OF THE PLANE BOUNCED AS THEY TOUCHED DOWN ON THE tarmac, jolting me awake. I was surprised that I had fallen asleep at all, given how anxious this entire situation had made me. Rubbing the sleep from my eyes, I waited as everyone in front of me disembarked the plane.

I thought back to the last time I'd been flown out to Los Angeles and how different this trip was. Charisma had flown me first class and there had been a limo driver waiting to bring me to their fancy studio. Afterwards, I'd gone to my luxury apartment and made the worst decision of my life—signing that damn contract.

Maybe I would have signed it anyways if I had taken more time with it, but at least I would have understood what I was getting myself into. I could have planned better. Instead, everything was just thrown at me on a need to know basis. And any hope of sitting down and trying to make sense of the stupid thing was off the table, given how busy they kept me.

I shook the wayward thoughts out of my head and tried to steel my resolve. Crawling back to Lennie and Isaac was not going to be easy. I really thought I could make it on my own back on the east coast. It was just sad that I'd been so wrong.

The airport didn't seem nearly as glitzy as the last time I'd walked through it. Everything was like that nowadays. I yawned and glanced down at my watch. It was only nine and Lennie had said he couldn't meet with me until the afternoon.

Spotting a coffee stand in the distance, I decided that I could spare the few minutes to get myself something to eat. My stomach growled its agreement, reminding me that I hadn't eaten anything but airplane pretzels for the last twelve hours.

Waiting in line, I tried to think through what I might say to Lennie and Isaac when I arrived, but I couldn't shake the bad feelings swimming in my gut. Instincts were telling me that I needed to run as far away from these men as I possibly could. But I had listened to those instincts six months ago and not only had I not solved my own problems, but I'd caused problems for someone else.

No. I wasn't going to think about Connor right now. If I did, I knew I'd never be able to go through with what I needed to do.

The feeling of someone looking at me pulled me out of my mind and back into the present. It was a barista and the girl turned around as soon as I looked at her. With her back facing me and her hair up in a hat, I couldn't quite make out who it was, but she seemed so familiar.

Finally, it was my turn and I approached the counter. "Good morning, what can we get started for you today?" the hostess behind the register asked.

"I'll have a skim latte," I said, going with my usual.

"Great. Anything to eat?"

I peered into the glass case and pointed to a butter croissant in the window. "I'll have two of those," I said. I needed to carbo-load my emotions into submission for this afternoon.

The hostess nodded. "Tara, can I get two butter croissants, please?"

As soon as the hostess said her name, the girl named Tara turned around and locked eyes with me.

"Tara?" My eyes widened in shock as my previous friend and current accuser turned to look at me.

"On it," Tara responded to the hostess, turning away from me.

"If you could just step to the left, we'll have that right out for you shortly," the hostess said and I nodded.

I watched Tara as she busied herself with orders. She was different than I remembered her. Tara had always had an upbeat personality, but she was more subdued now. Her eyes looked sunken in, like she was constantly tired. They were missing the light and laughter I was used to seeing there.

Tara walked over to where I was standing with my order. "Marie, I'm going to take my fifteen," Tara called over to the hostess, who nodded her agreement. She pushed the food and drink into my hands and whispered under her breath, "Follow me."

I knew this was another person I should be running away from right now, but I followed her, my feet moving of their own volition. I'd never understood why Tara did what she did. Now I might get the chance to ask her. That was worth whatever the consequences might be. Besides, things couldn't get any worse than they already were.

I followed Tara into a private lounge area. I looked around the little room and was thankful no one was here. A few rows of airport chairs lined the space atop Berber carpet and the words "Quiet Area" were painted on the glass door. As soon as the door closed behind us, Tara turned around to me with worry on her face. "Sophie, what are you doing here?"

Surprise at her question was an understatement. "What am I doing here? That's all you have to say to me?" My attitude flared.

"Sophie, I'm trying to help you!" Tara said, the desperation coming through in her voice.

"Help me? What, like the way you helped ruin my career?"

"I had no choice!" Tara bit back.

That knocked me off-kilter for a second. I clenched my teeth and narrowed my eyes. "We all have a choice, Tara. Sometimes, they're not easy. But we still have a choice."

"Oh yeah? Then tell me why you're back? Did you choose to come back, hm?" Her hand was on her aproned hip and I knew she was goading me.

Tara had a point. I didn't really feel like I had a choice in this. Sure, I could run away to some other part of the country, or another country entirely, and try and start over. But that might cause major problems for Connor and I didn't want to do that to him. So I was doing the only thing I could do. But was that really a choice?

"What happened, Tara? You owe me that."

Tara clenched her teeth.

"Look, I'll tell you what I'm doing here, but only after you tell me why," I said, trying to bargain.

Tara's eyes softened and she nodded her head. Falling back into one of the leather sling chairs behind her she let out a dramatic sigh. I sat down opposite her but didn't say anything.

"Charisma moved me from working with other artists to you only when you arrived."

My jaw clenched. If this woman was about to say that she claimed I had stolen her songs just to save her job, I wanted even less to do with her now than ever before. But I stayed quiet and let Tara continued.

"My brother. He's got a pretty good record deal with Charisma. He's really good. Not as good as you and he hasn't quite blown up yet, but the money he makes helps care for our dad." I could see the tears welling up in Tara's eyes, but she brushed them aside. "My dad—he was in a bad accident about ten years ago. He requires constant care and without my brother's paycheck, we couldn't afford it."

Tara looked at me with pleading eyes. "What I did to you, Sophie. I'm so sorry. I really am. But they told me they would terminate my brother's contract if I didn't do it."

I pinched the bridge of my nose and closed my eyes. This was all so much. I was having trouble processing it. It made sense, because me and Tara had gotten along so well. I'd never been able to understand why

Tara had betrayed me this way. But, I also didn't know whether I should trust her.

"Why are you working here now?" I asked Tara, as she opened her eyes again and took a steadying breath.

Tara's lips quirked and she shook her head. "They fired me as soon as everything was over. You weren't around anymore and they hadn't found their next victim, so I was let go." Tara turned her gaze on me. "Why did you leave, Sophie? I thought you liked working with me?"

I blinked in surprise before I leaned forward in the chair. "What do you mean? I never chose to leave. Is that what they told you?"

Tara's eyes widened. "But they told me that—" Her words faded as realization settled over her features. "They told me that you'd decided to go with a different record label. They said you didn't like your team anymore—me in particular—and that was why you weren't producing music." Tara shook her head. "And then they said it was no loss anyways because you had been coming onto a few different music executives and there had been complaints with human resources." She put her head in her hands and her cap fell to the floor as her hair spilled out. Tears ran down her face as she sobbed. "Sophie, I'm so sorry. I don't know why I believed them."

"Shh, it's okay," I said. I'd never realized just how young Tara was and I couldn't hold it against her. I'd believed everything Charisma had told me when I arrived, too.

"No, it's *not* okay. I helped them ruin your life. That's not okay!" she cried into her hands.

I moved over to the seat next to Tara and put my arm around her. Tara let me pull her into a hug.

I held her as she cried, telling her that it was okay and that she shouldn't blame herself. Tara settled enough to pull away from my embrace. "I don't understand why you're being so nice to me."

I looked up at the ceiling and tried to find the right words. "I think I just realized that we were both victims of things we didn't understand. I'm not saying that what you did, lying about my songs, was right. But, I guess I understand why you did it now."

Tara swiped tears away from her eyes and nodded her head. "I don't deserve it, but thank you."

I gave her another hug and we separated. "So, why are you here, Sophie?" Tara asked.

"I'm just trying to make right some of the problems I caused myself, I guess."

Tara looked at me seriously. "Sophie, what are you thinking of doing? These people are no joke and I—" she hesitated. "I know things that you probably don't know. You need to be careful."

I furrowed my brow. Was she talking about Lennie? He seemed totally harmless. Isaac, maybe. "I have to do this," I said, renewing my intention.

"Will you just tell me what it is you're planning to do?" Tara asked. "It was part of our agreement, after all."

I gave her a small smile and nodded. "I didn't leave Charisma by choice. I was forced to go to Tymar when Charisma assigned my contract over to them. Anyways, my manager Lennie said that he had a plan for dealing with the rumors."

Tara narrowed her eyes. "I don't trust it, Sophie. I've heard his name before."

"Who's? Lennie's?"

"Lennie Webb?"

My eyes widened as I nodded her agreement. "What have you heard?"

Tara looked nervous. "I just know what my brother told me and he said he'd only heard rumors. But, apparently Lennie is referred to as 'the Fixer' around Charisma. He takes over as manager for people who Charisma doesn't want anymore." Tara inhaled deeply. "Sophie, I'm so sorry. I had no idea they sent you to him."

I considered what she was saying. It was a lot to take in and I wasn't sure I fully understood the implications. "So what if he's called the Fixer? I mean, that's not a bad thing, right? I'm going to him because I need him to help me fix this image problem."

Tara shook her head slowly. "No, Sophie. He's the Fixer in the bad way."

"What do you mean?"

"I mean, he's the Fixer for Charisma. Not for you. He makes problems—for *Charisma*—go away." I chewed my bottom lip but Tara continued. "He also reports directly to the top."

"What do you mean, the top?"

Tara looked around the room as if wanting to make sure no one was close enough to hear. "Like the head honcho for Eternity."

I shook my head. "What are you saying?"

Tara sighed and leaned in close. "I'm saying, he reports directly to Xavier Payne."

"Who?"

Tara put her head in her hands. "You seriously don't know who that is?"

"Should I?"

"Um, yeah. Kind of."

"Well, who is he then?"

"He's the owner of Eternity Music Group—and God only knows what else. He's a very powerful man, Sophie. And from what I've heard, he skirts the line between legal and illegal. He's never been accused of anything formally, but I've heard things." She shook her head. "We really shouldn't be talking about him."

Tara looked like a woman afraid of conjuring up a ghost just by saying its name, but I nodded my head. Tara had already given me a lot of information and I didn't want to push her any further. "So then, what do you think I should do? I have a meeting with Lennie this afternoon."

"You shouldn't go," Tara responded immediately.

I shook my head, wisps of red hair waving back and forth. "That's not an option. I told you, I have my reasons for needing to fix this."

Tara sucked her top lip into her mouth and looked like she was trying to come up with a plan. Finally, she threw up her hands. "I don't know, Sophie. I just wouldn't go anywhere near that man. And I certainly wouldn't volunteer to work with him again. It seems like you finally got yourself free of all this. What could be so important that you'd have to drag yourself back in?"

"Sometimes we do crazy things for the people we love," I said, more to myself than to Tara.

"Yeah," Tara said in quiet agreement. "Look, Sophie, I have to go. But, I really don't want this to be the last time we see one another." She looked earnest and I nodded my head.

"Here," I said, pulling her arm towards me and snagging a marker from her apron. I scrawled my new phone number across her arm and handed her back the sharpie. "Text me when you get a chance. We'll figure everything out."

Tara nodded and stood. "Okay." She moved in and we embraced before she made her way to the glass door. Turning back briefly she said, "Just be careful. And don't trust anyone associated with Webb, Sophie. I mean it."

I dipped my head in understanding and Tara closed the door behind me. I sank back into the seat and let out a heavy breath. Tara had been blackmailed into telling those lies? What about Jack? Was it the same with him? And Lennie couldn't be trusted? He was Charisma's fixer? And some guy named Payne was behind the entire thing?

I closed my eyes as the questions swam around my brain. It was all too much. And it called into question everything I had come out here to do. Or had it? I still needed to get the attention back on me and away from Connor. And as far as I could tell, the only option for doing that right now was agreeing to Isaac's proposal—as sickening as it was.

THIRTY-TWO

LENNIE

"MR. PAYNE, SO GOOD TO HEAR FROM YOU," I SAID INTO THE OFFICE PHONE as I patted my forehead with a handkerchief. Speaking with Xavier Payne always made me nervous and therefore sweaty. Isaac sat across from me in the office, trying to look calm but I knew even he was anxious around Payne.

"This better be worth my time, Webb," the deep voice echoed across the small office.

"Of course, Sir," I replied frantically. "We received an offer to purchase Sophie Strong's contract late last night."

"From whom?"

"Some unknown investor. But he's coming here this morning to discuss the terms of the deal."

"Remind me who Sophie Strong is again," the deep voice commanded.

"Right. She's that little girl from D.C. Her biggest hit was Blue Eyes. Charisma transferred her over to us last year."

"Oh, that's right. You two really made a mess of her career, didn't you?"

I looked at Isaac and gulped. "I'm sorry, Sir. What do you mean?"

"That girl had potential, is what I mean. She hit a lull, sure, but she might have bounced back."

I saw Isaac grit his teeth and I knew instantly what he was thinking. That was easy for the legendary Xavier Payne to say now. His instructions were that when an artist's profit margin ceased to be positive, they needed to stem the bleeding. And Payne's instructions were always followed.

"Well, Sir," I said, looking at Isaac frantically for support. "She wasn't making the group money any longer and for quite some time."

"Yes, well. What's done is done. So what was the reason for you bothering me?" The voice was agitated.

"Right, okay, well you see, Sir. Sophie also contacted us yesterday. She wants to work with us again. If she hadn't turned up, we would have just sold the contract for as much of a profit as possible. But now that she's indicated she might be willing to return, we needed your approval as to what to do."

Payne's dark chuckle on the other side of the line had me patting my forehead again. "You two really are idiots sometimes, aren't you?"

"Yes, Sir," I immediately responded and Isaac shot me an annoyed glance.

"You've had your fun ruining this girl's life. I know you both get your rocks off by dragging these things out—especially you Isaac—but enough's enough. Any more of this and you risk ruining Charisma's reputation for discovering this girl in the first place."

"Understood, Sir," I said as Isaac pursed his lips.

"Charisma still holds the rights to her past songs, correct?"

"That's correct, Sir."

"Good. Then sell her for what you can and be done with it."

"Yes, Sir."

"There better not be any more problems. Otherwise, you'll both see your positions and your profits dry up fast. Understood?"

I gulped. Payne's threats weren't anything to be trifled with. "Yes, Sir. No problems. We'll get it taken care of."

THIRTY-THREE

"I'LL NEED TWO COPIES OF EACH DOCUMENT PRINTED," I SAID, HANDING a USB drive to the hotel receptionist.

"Okay, Sir," the young blonde said, taking the little device. "Give me just one moment." She walked it into the back room and after a few minutes, appeared with four sets of documents. Handing the pages and the drive back to me, I thumbed through each page to make sure they were all in order and nodded my thanks.

"Your car is waiting just outside," the woman said and I nodded a thank you again.

I had woken up early this morning to knock out a draft of the documents I knew I was going to need. The benefit to still being on east coast time was that I had a head start on the day. And today would be an extremely important day.

If everything went according to plan, I'd free Sophie from the confines of her repressive contract and have her on a plane back to D.C. with me by dusk. I'd given strict instructions to Gus that the moment she turned her phone back on, he was to grab her location and call me immediately. So far though, my phone had remained silent.

Entering the car, I confirmed the address with the driver before we pulled away from the hotel. I looked out the window as we drove the streets. I'd studied and played out what I was going to say to Webb countless times this morning, there was no more I could do at this point. The best I could do was to relax and center myself.

I watched the tall palm trees flash by. Los Angeles was so very different from really anywhere on the east coast. It just had a feel to it that was entirely unique and almost seemingly at odds. The famous laid back California vibe to me seemed like a façade. There was a much darker undercurrent running through this city that I couldn't quite put my finger on.

People said that about D.C. But to me, D.C. was at least open about its faults. People came into the city for four or eight years, depending on who they were attached to and then they left. Each one of them thought they were more important than the next and they weren't shy to say so.

But, in LA everyone was smiles and good spirits on top. But I had no doubt in my mind that those same people would turn around and stab you in the back the moment you let your guard down, as they had done to Sophie. This area chewed people up and spit people out, all while throwing a Shaka hand signal.

"You sure this is the place?" the driver asked as he pulled up to the old building. I pulled out the map on my phone and verified that it was, indeed, the right address.

"Looks like it," I said. "I'll ring you when I need you to come back." I tapped a button on my phone and carefully slipped it back into my pocket. The driver nodded and I exited the car.

I looked up at the building in front of him and shook my head. Sophie always did have a way of getting herself into interesting situations. And this topped the charts.

The brick façade of the two-story building was crumbling in places and a half-finished paint job wrapped around one corner of the building but not the other. Large holes where banners or signs had previously been hung dotted the brick and the windows all had bars on them. A chain-link metal fence circled the entire building in the rear and the parking lot to the left had a few cars that looked abandoned, one of which was missing tires. The hum of overtaxed air conditioners reigned down from the roof of the building, providing an odd soundtrack to an even odder situation.

"Good morning!"

The door with flaking paint opened and out walked a boisterous looking gentleman with an equally over the top voice. His dark hair was missing on all but the sides and he clearly had not visited the gym in several decades. His tie was loose around his neck, which was odd, given it was so early in the day, but perhaps it was because the buttons on his collar simply couldn't keep up with the strain.

He bounded down the steps and reached his hand out. My back stiffened. I did not like this man, at all. He had the feeling of a conman written all over him. Too loud, too happy and too excited about everything.

"So glad to finally meet you," the man said, offering me his hand. I shook it but kept an impassive mask on. "I'm sorry, I don't believe I caught your name from your email."

Clearly fishing for information. I straightened my tie. "I don't believe I provided it. Let's talk inside, Mr. Webb."

"Of course, of course," the man said, almost bowing before turning and running back up the stairs to open the door. I walked through and had to work on keeping my mask in place as I walked inside. The lobby was just as run down as the exterior, but it smelled of mold and old newspapers.

"Right this way," Webb said, leading me down the hall to a back office.

As soon as I stepped inside, I knew where the old newspaper smell was coming from. The room was a cluttered mess and dust clung to every surface possible. Another man was sitting in one of the chairs facing the old oak desk and he stood.

"Isaac Jacobs," he said, offering me his hand.

"Nice to meet you, Mr. Jacobs," I replied, once again, not giving my name. I needed to tread lightly with this pair. While I had no real proof, it was obvious from Gus' information that they were involved in Sophie's tumult. Whether they recognized me from the brief coverage Sophie and I had gotten in D.C. or not, I didn't know. I had something prepared if they did, but I'd prefer not to play that card unless I had to. Negotiating with them as if I were just some interested investor would make this morning a hell of a lot easier.

"Please, have a seat," Webb said, gesturing to one of the decrepit chairs.

I winced but sat regardless. Leaning back, I let Webb start the negotiations.

"Well, I can't tell you how surprised we were when we received your email yesterday. Do you mind telling us a little bit about yourself? Why you're interested in signing on with our Sophie?"

This man-made me sick.

"Simple really," I said. "I've made quite a bit of money in real estate and I'm looking to expand into a different market. I'm single and I heard Hollywood parties were some of the best in the world. Owning a successful pop star could do a lot to elevate my image."

"Right, right. Well, I'm sure you understand that Sophie has hit a bit of a rough spot lately. But we really do believe she'll pull it around. In fact, we're meeting with her today about just that."

I raised an eyebrow. That was news to me. I didn't want Sophie anywhere near these two. But it also gave me information on her eventual whereabouts.

"I believe that as well. Hence my interest in the girl."

Webb nodded. "Shall we discuss terms then?"

I nodded. "But before we do so, how is that you acquired Ms. Strong's contract from Charisma?"

Webb rubbed his jaw and looked first at Isaac and then at me. "Charisma had just found out about the claims that are now public. They were looking to offload her before those broke."

"Is that so," I said, wondering how much I could walk Webb into a corner.

"We of course, don't believe any of it to be true," Isaac chimed in, giving his partner an intense glance. "We believe that Sophie was wrongly accused. We're hoping those rumors will be cleared up in no time."

"Of course, of course," Webb said, jumping onto his partner's wagon. "We were very lucky to be in a position to pick up Sophie when Charisma was unfairly looking to move on."

"So then why sell to me? If you believe in Sophie so much, why offer to offload her again?"

Webb looked uncomfortable under my intense blue gaze. "Well, we all have a price, I suppose. And your offer was just too good to not seriously consider it."

"So then, you think I've overestimated what her contract is worth?" I chuckled internally. These two were too easy.

Web spread his hands wide in front of him. "No, no. Of course not. What I meant to say is that, perhaps Sophie would do better with a fresh start."

"Alright," I said, satisfied that I'd pushed the man sufficiently off-balance. "Let's talk terms. By what device did you acquire Sophie?"

"Device?" Webb looked confused and I wondered if he was being slick or if he really was just an idiot.

"Did Sophie re-sign with you? Or did Charisma assign her contract to you?"

"Oh," Webb said, catching on. "It was an assignment."

I nodded. "Then I will need to take a look at that agreement, if you don't mind. I need to know exactly what I'm offering to purchase."

"Of course," Webb said, reaching into his desk. He rummaged through a few drawers before nervously walking to a rusted cabinet in the corner of the office. "I think I actually put it over here," he said.

"Take your time," I said calmly. The calmer he was, the more I knew I could push Webb. The man clearly wanted to get rid of Sophie's contract. His nervous attitude and Isaac piping up to try and smooth over the situation was proof enough. I wasn't exactly sure what their motivation was for suddenly wanting to be done with Sophie. Perhaps, they realized she was more of a handful than they expected when she ran out on them to D.C. It was difficult to say.

"Here it is!" Webb said, pulling a document from the bottom of an unorganized stack on top of the old cabinet. He shuffled his way back over to me and handed him the papers.

I flipped it over in my hand and had to suppress my surprise at how little there was to the document. The entire thing was two pages. Compared to the monstrosity Charisma had tricked Sophie into signing, it was almost laughable. A page of recitals, two agreement points and a second page of signatures. I studied it carefully, my eyes narrowing in on the last sentence of the agreement:

Charisma Records assigns its entire interest in the Agreement to Tymar Holdings, LLC excepting any songs produced by Ms. Stronglen as of the date of execution.

"Says here you don't own any of her songs," I said, pointing to the last line of the first page.

"Oh? Is that so?" Webb asked, reaching out for the document. I handed it to him and watched his face morph. It was obvious he was hoping I wouldn't notice. "Oh, that's right. Unfortunately, Charisma does still own her current catalog. But anything else she produces and any revenue from tours etc., we own."

"So she can go on tour but she can't play any of her old songs?"

Isaac chimed in when Webb looked lost for words. "Presumably, if Sophie were to go on tour, she would be playing a new album. If she wished to play any past songs, her owner would simply have to negotiate a license deal with Charisma. It's fairly standard practice and they are quite reasonable."

I grit my teeth. The way that man said "her owner" made me want to punch him right in the jaw. "That's unfortunately going to affect the price. Her current catalog is undoubtedly very popular and I haven't heard that she has anything in the works."

Webb looked disappointed but nodded his head. He handed me back the document, and I flipped it over to the second page to look at the signatures.

Charisma Records, LLC: by Rebecca Murphy, Managing Member.
    Seen and acknowledged by Eternity Music Group, Inc.: by Xavier Payne, President.

I looked at the scrawl of a signature beneath Eternity Music Group's block. The name sounded so familiar, but for the life of me, I couldn't place it. I put it out of my mind for now. I needed to handle this situation and then I could worry about Charisma and Eternity.

"Well, gentlemen," I said, putting the paper back on the desk. "I've got to tell you, I'm pretty disappointed that you don't own her current catalog. It sort of brings the entire deal into question for me."

"Surely there must be something we can do to convince you otherwise," Webb said. "Like I said, Sophie is due to make an appearance here today. Perhaps we could arrange a private meeting between you and her?"

The way Webb said "private meeting" also made me feel sick. And angry. There was an implication there that I didn't like. And if I had my way, Sophie would never have to be in the same room with these fuckers ever again.

"I'm not saying that I'm not still interested, but my original offer was intended to include her entire catalog."

"We understand," Webb said, nodding at Isaac. The man next to me stayed silent, however. "Would you like to make another offer for us to consider now that you have more information? We'd be happy to entertain it."

I rubbed my jaw and let the silence stretch out around us. I wanted to see just how far I could push this man. "Alright," I finally said and Webb breathed a sigh of relief. "A million two," I said. "And that's being generous. I'm only getting half the rights, so roughly half the offer, plus a little something extra as a show of good faith."

Webb looked over at Isaac, who nodded his head quickly. "Deal!" he said, standing up to shake my hand.

"Glad to hear it."

"Shall we have a drink?" Webb asked, rubbing his hands together.

"I'd like to get the paperwork out of the way first, if you don't mind,"

I said, reaching into my briefcase to pull out one of the documents I'd asked the hotel receptionist to print. I had had a feeling that Tymar had inherited Sophie's contract through an assignment and I'd drafted an equally simple form in the morning before arriving. Pulling a pen out of my suit pocket, I wrote in $1.2 million on the blank line.

I slid the two pages across the desk and Webb grabbed the papers greedily. "Looks good to me," he said, running his eyes over the words far quicker than anyone could possibly read.

"Then all that's left is for signatures," I said.

Webb reached out and grabbed a pen. Flipping to the second page he paused briefly. "You've got a line for Sophie to sign?"

"Most contracts require the subject to consent."

"Oh, right right," Webb said. He scribbled his name across the page under "Tymar."

"Excellent," I said, signing my own name on the line. "All we need is Sophie's signature and it will be official. She's coming here this afternoon you said?"

"Yes, I can have her get here earlier though, if you'd like?" Webb still looked nervous.

"No need," I said. "I have no doubts she'll agree. As soon as she sees the team and accommodations I'll be providing her, I'm positive there will be no question in her mind."

Webb nodded.

"Now that the paperwork is taken care of," I said, tri-folding the document and tucking it into my jacket pocket, leaning back in my chair, "let's have that drink."

Webb jumped up and poured drinks for all three of us. I took the lead, engaging Webb in banter and small talk until Isaac finally excused himself. Within the hour, Webb was having his third whiskey and I felt like he was finally sufficiently loose-lipped.

"I've got to ask you something, Lennie, and please be honest. What's the real situation with Sophie?" Webb smiled but I pressed on. This was where the true meeting began.

"What do you mean?" Webb asked with a sly look on his face.

"Oh, come on," I said, relaxing my stance just a bit. "Number one artist suddenly accused of stealing songs and harassing employees? Around the time that she's failing to produce songs? I'm her new owner now. Do me a solid and tell me what really happened." I hesitated before finally adding. "You two had something to do with it, yes?"

I could tell Webb was toying with whether or not to say anything. I knew I had him in a good spot. He really had nothing to lose at this point. I just hoped all the groundwork I'd laid was enough.

"Yeah, we did," he said, holding his drink up and taking a sip.

"So, what's the real story?" I asked, pretending to take a sip myself, the liquor just touching my lips.

Webb leaned across the desk as if motioning him to get closer and I had to hold my breath at the stench that was rolling off him. "She's crazy depressed. Can't write for shit right now." He laughed and I had to suppress my rage at the man for being so heartless to my woman.

"So why start the rumors?"

Webb shook his head. "Money, man. You can sell locations and pictures to the pap. They get their pictures and you get money. I'm telling you, having an artist that everyone hates is sometimes better than one everybody loves. 'Cause I ain't gotta do shit to protect her reputation, ya know what I'm sayin'?"

"So it was you and Isaac that started those rumors? She didn't steal songs or harass anyone?"

Webb laughed, spittle flying everywhere. "Of course not! Have you ever met the girl? She's just some little pansy. She couldn't hurt a fly."

Bingo. I had him right where I wanted him. "That's really disappointing to hear, Mr. Webb," my demeanor shifting entirely. "You really should have disclosed that fact to me before we signed the documents."

"It's too late now," Webb said, clearly trying to keep the upper hand.

"For you, it is." I pulled out my phone and showed him the screen. Webb's face went white as he realized the device had been recording the entire conversation. "You see, I always record my business transactions. Promises are so often made and then broken during these times. It's just good to have a record, don't you think so?"

Webb tried to reach for the phone, but I pulled it back. "It wouldn't matter anyways, Mr. Webb. This phone backs up to my personal servers instantly. I've got as many copies as I wish of this entire transaction, ready to distribute on command."

Webb leaned back into his seat, the adrenaline in his blood sobering him quickly. "What do you want?"

I reached into my briefcase and pulled out the second document I'd had printed. I slid it in front of Webb and smiled as the man read it. "You planned this!"

I shook my head. "No. But I always like to come prepared."

"You want me to amend the sales price to one hundred dollars? Are you out of your mind?" Webb was nearly foaming at the mouth. "No way in hell I'm signing this!"

"That's a shame," I said, my face impassive. "I thought you'd like to at least make some money."

"What nonsense are you spouting?"

"Simple," I said with a wry smile, reaching down for the final document in my briefcase. "You see, in Sophie's original contract with Charisma, Charisma warranted that they would do everything in their power to enhance her image with the media. When you inherited her contract, you took on that responsibility." I shoved the massive document in front of Webb with the relevant section tabbed. "Putting aside the fact that your admission makes you guilty of defamation, which last I checked, is still a crime in twenty-four states and I know a few overzealous prosecutors who would love to make an example of you, you've breached your contract. Any judge would rule in Sophie's favor and the entire agreement would go up in smoke." I leaned back, ready to strike the final blow. "But, if you'd like me to just go public with this information instead, I'd be happy to ruin the image of both Tymar, Charisma and, what was it, Eternity? I'm sure Mr. Payne will be pleased to know you were the cause of all this."

I thought I'd throw the name of the head honcho in for added effect. I didn't expect Webb to go deathly white and throw up his hands in defeat. "Alright. You win. I'll sign."

Payne was someone I was going to have to ask Gus about. But I could worry about that later. Right now, I'd just wrenched back a piece of Sophie's future. I needed to find her. Hold her in my arms and tell her that everything was going to be okay. That I wouldn't stop until I'd righted all the wrongs these people had done to her.

Webb scrawled his name across the paper and shoved it back in my direction. With a small smile, I signed my own name to the paper before I placed the document into my jacket next to the first. I reached for my wallet and pulled out a crisp $100 bill. Handing it out to Webb, I chuckled and said, "Pleasure doing business with you, Lennie."

At that moment, a noise behind me grabbed my attention and I turned around to see Sophie, standing there, tears in her eyes.

THIRTY-FOUR

Sophie

TARA'S WORDS RANG IN MY EARS THE ENTIRE TIME I SAT IN THE BACK OF the cab. The scenery flashed by me but my mind was preoccupied with trying to make sense of everything my . . . was she still my friend? . . . had just told me.

I wanted to believe what Tara had said. I wanted to believe that she'd been tricked into a horrible situation just the same as I had. The fact that she was no longer working for Charisma was showing. If Tara had really been some insider, planted to set me up, she would likely still be working there.

I groaned in frustration and the cab driver looked at me in the rearview mirror. "Everything okay, Miss?"

"Just fine," I lied through gritted teeth.

"Is this your first time in Los Angeles?" the driver asked in a thick accent.

"Unfortunately, no."

The man chuckled. I could see in his dark brown eyes that he'd meant no harm by his response. He was just trying to make small talk. "This town can be very difficult, is true."

"That's the understatement of the century," I muttered under my breath.

"Why you come to Los Angeles, huh?"

I tapped my foot. I didn't want to be impolite but I wanted to try and think about everything going on in my head right now. "To fix something," I finally said. It was the most honest answer I could give at the moment.

"Ahh," he said, shaking his head. "You should never come to Los Angeles to fix something. Los Angeles is for running away from your problems. Not for fixing them."

I let out a small chuckle. Except for me, it had always been the opposite. I'd come here to try and live out my dream and had ended up running away from the many problems it had created.

"Why'd you come to LA then?" I asked, finding myself being pulled into the conversation.

"Are you trying to know what I run from?" he teased.

I shrugged. "Maybe? I don't know."

"I came to Los Angeles to make money," he admitted honestly. "That's the only other reason to come here."

The corner of my mouth lifted and I shook my head. At least he was being honest.

"Yeah, well, I hope those aren't the only reasons. Cause I really did come back to fix something."

The car slowed down as the driver pulled the cab in front of my destination. The cabbie turned around and leaned over the seat. He fixed me with an intense gaze. "I like you, Miss. So I'm gonna tell you something. If someone in that building," he said, pointing to the run-down office in front of us, "tells you they can fix your problems, you run away 'cause they lie. Nobody does nothing around here for someone else unless there's money. Like you and me. I drive you here, but only 'cause you pay me, yes? You understand?"

I looked at the driver. He was older than I had originally thought. His tanned skin hid the many wrinkles that I could see in the light and the headrest had blocked my view of his greying hair. I nodded my understanding and handed him some cash. "I understand. And thank you."

The driver held up the cash and said, "this is all the thanks I need. Good luck, Miss."

I closed the door behind me and the cab zoomed off, leaving me standing in front of a building I'd hoped I'd never have to look at again.

The place was the same. Faded. Just like my dreams. But I steeled my resolve and walked up the concrete steps to the plain glass door. The words of Tara, confirmed by the cab driver of all people, rang in my ears.

"Just be careful. And don't trust anyone associated with Webb, Sophie. I mean it."

I was going to be careful and I wasn't going to trust Webb or anyone around him. But I still needed to do this. For Connor. I owed him that much. And because, for what it was worth, I loved him.

With renewed intention, I pushed open the glass door and was immediately confronted with the one person I'd dreaded seeing again.

"Sophie," Isaac's face lit up as I walked in the door. "So glad to see you back."

He was sitting in one of the small reception area's waiting chairs. A styled suit hung on his lithe frame and he was reading a magazine with calm confidence. I knew plenty of girls would find Isaac attractive, but there was something disgusting about him that no amount of cologne or perfect hair could cover-up.

"Hi Isaac," I said, choking back my revulsion. If this plan was going to work, I knew we'd be working together closely and I need to somehow move past my aversion to him. As I looked at him and considered the offer he'd made all those months ago, the words of the cabbie sounded in my head. I wondered what Isaac was really after in all of this. He wasn't just volunteering to put himself out there for nothing. There had to be something in it for him.

"Come to see Lennie?" he asked, putting the newspaper down and uncrossing his legs. His eyes raked my body up and down but I refused to quiver under his gaze.

"Yes," I said simply.

"After all this time, you've come back to us." He got up and moved across the room to where I was standing. I tried to move back but a row of chairs caged me in. His finger slid down my cheek and I looked at him with daggers in my eyes. "Did you miss me, Sophie? You can admit it. Thinking about the offer I made you keep you up at night, is that it?"

I thought I might hurl up the contents of my breakfast at his words. "Not quite," I said as I turned my head away from him.

Isaac chuckled and moved back to his seat across the little lobby. "Well, Lennie's in a meeting now. I guess you'll just have to wait out here with me," he said, patting the seat next to him.

I rolled my eyes and sat down in a chair on the opposite wall. "I'm good here, thanks."

Isaac shook his head and made a tisking sound. "One of these days, Sophie. One of these days." He didn't finish the words, but the implication was there and it made me sick to my stomach. I tried to distract myself by looking around the room but I could feel Isaac's eyes on me.

The office building was quite small and voices carried easily. I heard a conversation coming from Lennie's office that had my brow furrowing. "Who is Lennie meeting with on a Saturday morning?"

A smug smile rested on Isaac's lips as he looked at me. "Wish I could help you darling, but not even I know his name. Some investor here to talk about your contract."

"What?" I exclaimed, leaping up out of my chair.

"It's a shame really. I'll still pitch my problem-solving skills to him when he and Lennie conclude their business and I hope he accepts. You're about to be under new ownership, little miss."

"The fuck I am," I said, my temper flaring. I did not need to be assigned to some new prick. I wasn't just some piece of meat to be tossed around or bartered off. Of course Lennie and Isaac planned to sell my contract. Tara had been right. They weren't to be trusted. And anyone who thought they could buy me like some commodity to trade at the open market could go right to hell.

I ran down the hall. I knew Isaac jumped up to try and stop me but I was a few steps ahead of him. I burst through the door to Lennie's office and froze.

There was Connor, looking as smug as ever, handing over a $100 bill, the words "Pleasure doing business with you, Lennie," on his lips.

"Connor?"

I couldn't believe what I was seeing. This had to be some sort of a nightmare. Why was he here? With Lennie? Holding out money and looking as smug as ever?

None of this made sense.

Until Lennie spoke.

"Ms. Sophie. I expected you a little later today, but I suppose now is as good a time as any. I'd like you to meet your new owner."

"New owner?" Tears streamed down my face as the last person in the world I ever thought would betray me stood there, looking stupefied.

Anger began to replace the hurt I was feeling at the situation. He was the entire reason that I was here. I'd flown across the entire country for him! To do right by him so that he could finally be free of me.

Suddenly, I started to call into question everything that had happened between the two of us. How did Connor know Lennie? Was this all some ruse to pull me back into the spotlight? Was Connor in on it?

Did he lie when he said he loved me?

My mind began mixing my exhaustion with my nerves, hurt and confusion.

Connor Driscoll could go to fucking hell as far as I was concerned. I was so done with all of them.

"No one fucking owns me," I spat as I turned on my heel and ran out the door. I blew past Isaac, shoving him into the paper thin walls as he tried to reach for me before bursting through the front door.

I could hear Connor's voice behind me, calling my name, just like he had yesterday when I'd run from him. But this time, I wasn't running away from a situation. I was running away from him. From his betrayal.

"Sophie!" Connor jumped up out of his seat as soon as I bolted from him again. "Sophie!" he bellowed as he chased me down the front steps of the building.

I could feel Connor hot on my heels. I needed to get away. I needed to think. And I needed to not think. I just didn't want to be here, in this fucking city anymore. And I didn't want to talk to Connor. Nothing he could say would make this right.

I needed to get lost in a crowd somehow. Bolting up the street in front of me, I powered up the sidewalk towards one of the busier streets. I regretted not having exercised more, because Connor was gaining on me. I just needed to push a little bit more and then I'd be lost in a sea of people and he'd never find me.

"Sophie, stop!" His deep voice was frantic and tugged at my confidence. Maybe there was some explanation? Maybe all of this was a mistake?

Then the words of the cab driver rang in my ears.

"Nobody does nothing around here for someone else unless there's money."

I shook my head and pressed on, breaking into the crowd of people.

"Move!" I heard Connor yelling at people as he pushed them aside, following close on my heel. "Sophie!"

I put my head down and closed my eyes. I ran as fast as I could to try and pull away from him. Finally, I felt the bodies around me dissipate and I thought I finally had done it.

I opened my eyes—

—and knew I was fucked.

The last sound I heard was the screeching of breaks as a bus careened towards me, before my world went black.

THIRTY-FIVE

I WATCHED IN HORROR AS SOPHIE RAN HEADFIRST INTO A BUSY intersection. Onlookers gasped as a large bus came careening towards her. I tried to yell her name, scream at her to get out of the way.

But everything felt like it was moving in slow motion.

As if the world was laughing at me.

Making me watch a scene that would haunt my dreams forever at the slowest possible speed, yet not allow me to do anything to stop it.

The bus started to swerve as it tried to break. When it finally stopped, Sophie was on the ground and people were looking around to see if anyone might step in to help.

I rushed forward and knelt beside her. I gathered her in my arms and breathed a sigh of relief. The bus had stopped in time, but just barely. Sophie had collapsed from the pure shock of the situation, but she hadn't been harmed.

"Sophie." Her name was a whisper on my lips and she blinked her eyes open at me.

"Connor." Her voice was hoarse but my name on her lips had never sounded sweeter.

I curled her into my arms and lifted her as I stood. "You always were such a pain," I said with a sigh of relief into her hair, but she didn't respond.

The bus driver opened his door and looked at me frantically. "Is she okay? I didn't hit her," he panted.

I shook my head. "No. You didn't. She's okay. Just shocked."

The driver's face turned angry. "Well, what the fuck, man? What the hell was she doing in the middle of the intersection? She could have killed herself or someone else."

I just nodded curtly at the man and walked Sophie back onto the sidewalk. People stared at us, some of them holding up their phones and taking videos. I sighed, knowing this might make the evening news and not in the good way. A few others clapped and I just kept my back straight, holding her tight against me as I walked her back to the quieter streets.

Kneeling gently, I fished out my phone and called my driver. "You got my location from the GPS? Good. Make it fast."

Sophie started to stir and I tucked a few strands of her bright red hair behind her ear. "It's okay. You're okay."

"No, no," she murmured as her eyes began to blink open. "Can't trust . . . " Her words were jumbled.

"Shh, just rest," I said, trying to keep her calm while we waited for the car. "Everything's okay."

"No, no it's not. It never is," Sophie muttered. Her eyes blinked open and a flicker of recognition was there. Within seconds, I went from holding her tightly in my arms to being slammed into the brick wall I was leaning against.

My breath left me as I stumbled back in surprise as Sophie jumped up. "No. Fuck you, Connor! You'll never get to hold me like that again. You don't deserve it, you fucking two-timing prick."

I grit my teeth and stood up. "Sophie. You don't understand the situation."

"Like hell I do," Sophie yelled. "I completely understand the situation."

She turned on her heel to run but I was faster this time. I had my hand around her wrist and within seconds, had her turned around so that I was hugging her body tight to my own. She struggled against me. "Get off me, Connor!"

"No. You're going to calm down and listen to reason. I'll not have you running off and getting yourself hurt or worse this time." Just then, the black sedan rounded the corner and I breathed a sigh of relief. "The car's here. We can talk about this at the hotel."

"Like hell I'm going anywhere with you," she spat, trying to dig her heel into my shoe. I grit my jaw but didn't let her go.

"Stop it, Sophie."

My tone was dark and commanding, leaving no room for argument. I felt her body respond. Enough so I knew she would cooperate, even if she would give me attitude about it.

The driver pulled up and exited the towncar. "Sir, is there a problem?"

"No problem," I replied, my expression hardening. "She just had a bit of a scare."

"Understatement," Sophie bit back.

I moved in close to her ear. My breath was hot against her neck and she tried to pull away. "I'm going to let you go now. I need you to get into the car and not cause a scene. I will explain everything back at the hotel. Do you trust me?"

"I thought I did," Sophie snapped.

I sighed but I loosened my grip on her nonetheless. Sophie wrenched herself free and looked at me with daggers in her eyes. "Fuck you, Connor," she said, before getting into the car. She slid all the way over in the back seat, pressing herself as far against the door as possible. I sat next to her and closed the door. The driver made his own way back to his seat and looked at Sophie through the rearview mirror.

"Ma'am, no offense to Mr. Driscoll, but I need to confirm that you are willing to drive back to the hotel. I'm not in the business of kidnapping."

I resisted the urge to give the driver a dirty look. I knew the man was only doing his job and should be applauded for having such good character. But I also was not interested in chasing Sophie all over Los Angeles at the moment.

Sophie turned her head to look at me. Her eyes burned with hostility. "It's fine," she finally snapped before looking back out the window. My mouth twitched as I tried to hide my relief and the car pulled away from the awful place.

The ride was silent. Sophie refused to speak to me and refused to even look at me. I didn't try and force it on her. I always knew when a fight with Sophie was coming on. I'd known it when I was in college and I sensed it just the same now. Her temper was like a raging inferno. It burned bright and hot but only for a short while. Mainly because she incinerated everything around her.

But I had learned. I never tried to stop her fires. Sure, sometimes I'd get caught up in them, but for the most part, I waited and listened to try and understand what was really getting her upset. I was serotinous in a way, only releasing my true potential when the outer layer was burned away by fire. I'd give her the space she clearly wanted, but I wasn't letting her out of my sight.

If I was being honest, I worried that if I did let her leave, I would never see her again. I was unwilling to entertain that thought. Especially when this entire situation was a misunderstanding. The documents tucked securely against my chest would clear everything up, even if it was only half the battle.

As soon as the car pulled up to the hotel,

Sophie

Connor had his hand firmly around mine. He didn't seem to care that I gave him a look dripping with disdain or that my hand was balled up into a little fist.

"Come on," Connor directed me, tugging gently on my hand when he opened the door. I followed him begrudgingly. His hand moved to the small of my back as he walked me through the hotel lobby, his blue eyes darting from left to right as he surveyed the space. He was on edge. I could tell.

I guess I sort of understood why. If I had watched Connor almost die in the middle of an intersection, I would have been shaken too. Except, given the circumstances, I was having a hard time feeling sorry for him.

This was the first time I had ever been inside the InterContinental. When I stayed in Los Angeles, which was rarely, I was always at my own apartment. The building's exterior was an impressive tower of curved glass reaching up towards the sky, but the lobby was truly breathtaking.

Large palms dotted our approach and inside the lobby, curved wood covered the walls. The entire place felt refreshing and modern. Of course Connor would choose to stay in a place like this.

His movements stilled and I realized we had already made it to the elevators. Connor touched the keypad, apparently entering his room floor to get the assigned elevator. As we made our way up the floors and finally down the hallways, his hand never left the small of my back, even as I tried to pull away from it ever so slightly.

"Here," Connor said, as I almost walked past the room. I huffed and he opened the door, stepping aside so that I could walk past him with a flip of my hair. I was trying my best to irritate him, but nothing seemed to shake his calm exterior.

I stepped inside the well-appointed room and sucked my bottom lip into my mouth in irritation. To the left was a glass-encased bathroom, complete with a white porcelain full-length soaking tub. Wood paneling created a seamless appearance where the television was mounted, across from which was a comfortable looking king size bed.

I tried to stifle a yawn. I was angry, yes. But I was also incredibly tired. Over the last twenty-four hours, I had barely slept. It was really adrenaline that was keeping me going at this point.

I pursed my lips and turned around to face Connor. The man I thought I had loved. The man that had betrayed me. I rolled my eyes as he calmly removed his suit jacket, placing it over the back of a nearby chair. He turned around to look at me and fixed me with that ice-blue gaze of his. "What, Connor?" I finally snarled.

Connor's expression remained calm and impassive, which only served to piss me off more. "Are you sure you're not injured?" he asked. He looked like he wanted to approach me but I took a step back.

"No. Not physically anyway."

Connor looked relieved but I held my ground. I crossed my arms in front of my chest and began to tap my foot. "If that's all you brought me here to ask, then I guess I'll be going then."

"You're not going anywhere." His voice was deep and foreboding and it sent a shiver down my spine. I hated that I responded to him this way. This was the man that betrayed me. I didn't know what the situation was between him and Webb but I didn't want anything to do with either of them. They could all fuck right off as far as I was concerned.

"Who are you to tell me what to do?" I bit back.

"Sophie. I know you're upset, but there's an explanation, I promise."

"Oh really? Because I would love to know how first, you even fucking know Webb and second, what the fuck you're doing here."

Connor went to open his mouth but I cut him off.

"What possible explanation could you give to me for sitting in that man's office, shaking that man's hand, and handing that man cash? Hmm?"

Connor crossed his arms over his chest but stayed quiet.

"What? No fucking answer, Connor?" I pointed my finger at him. "I'll tell you what I think. I think that I came out here to help clear your name at the cost of my own and you were fucking backstabbing me the entire time. That's what I think!"

"What the hell, Sophie? You really think I would do something like that to you?"

"I didn't think so, no. But then I saw you shaking hands with that man!" I was yelling now and Connor's own temper was starting to flare.

"I'm here for you, Sophie! I've always just been here for you! Look around and realize when people are trying to help you!"

"You trying to help is the reason we are in this mess. I was fine with disappearing. And then you had to come back into my life and make me fall in love with you all over again. I thought I'd finally gotten over you, Connor!"

Connor groaned in frustration, his head tipping back as he closed his eyes. "Only you could turn falling in love with someone into a point of attack and I don't want to hear it, Sophie. You came back to D.C. You came to my company. You had to know what that would do to me. You can't put your pieces on the chessboard and then be upset when you're forced to play!"

"I'm not trying to play anything, Connor! I'm just trying to fucking make it through this fucked up life. I'm not even thirty and my fucking dreams are toast."

"Bullshit," Connor said.

"Yeah, what would you know? You didn't want me to come out here in the first place, anyways."

"And was I so wrong in the end?"

"Fuck you, Connor!"

I walked off and looked out the window at the city below me. I hated it. I hated everything about this place and just being here made me angry. Los Angeles had stolen everything from me.

"Why did you come back here, Sophie?" Connor finally asked, breaking the awkward silence.

I didn't turn around. I'd rather look at the city that had betrayed me than the man. "I came back to try and do right by you."

"And what exactly did that entail?"

"Not that it's any of your concern, but I was going to agree to announce a public relationship with Isaac to try and make people question the harassment charges since they so clearly didn't believe me."

"Fuckin'a, Sophie. You really think that was going to *fix* the problem?"

I whirled around, my eyes dripping with contempt. "That's what you have to say to me about all of this? How about, 'thanks Sophie for caring about my business and my reputation.' I'm trying to do right by you, Connor."

Connor took a step forward, but I had nowhere to go but press my back up against the glass window. "When are you going to understand that I don't need you to protect me from your life?" He took another step. "That I want to be with you. And if that means punching paparazzi that try and attack you on the regular, then so be it." He took another step and he was right in front of me now. His hands rested on either side of me, caging me with his body. "I want it all with you, Soph. The good, the bad and the ugly."

"Don't you dare kiss me, Connor." My words were like ice.

"I'm not going to kiss you, Sophie. I'm going to explain. And then," his eyes stayed fixed on me and I fought the shiver that they sent down my spine, "we'll see what happens. Now, come here," he said. He pushed his hands off the window and turned around to walk to the little desk. I stayed planted and watched as he pulled out three documents and laid them out on the wood. He turned around and looked at me. "Come here, Sophie."

I clenched my jaw but pushed off the glass myself. I took several steps forward but stayed on the other side of the desk, the computer chair serving as the Berlin Wall to this Cold War.

Connor turned to face me but I kept my eyes down and on the pages. I didn't know what any of them were. I'd had enough with stupid slips of white paper messing up my life. I knew that I at least owed Connor the chance to explain, but I wasn't going to go out of my way to make it easy on him.

"After you ran from me, I was asked to go to the police station and answer a few questions about what happened. I would never have let you out of my sight let alone fly to a different state if it didn't mean I'd risk being arrested."

I gulped. I wanted to ask whether he was okay and whether he'd have to deal with a lawsuit or worse, but I kept quiet and let him continue.

"It was a pretty clear case of defense of another, so no charges. I drove to your apartment but you weren't there. Skyler told me where you were headed, but she didn't know why."

"Traitor," I murmured under my breath but Connor shook his head.

"You're wrong. She's a true friend, Sophie. Don't be cross with her. She did right by you."

I crossed my arms and huffed, but let Connor continue.

"When you wouldn't tell me what happened at Charisma, I had my guy do some digging."

My eyebrows shot up my face. That was news to me. "Do some digging? What, you hired a private investigator to spy on me?"

"I know you're angry. With everything you've dealt with, another invasion of privacy is difficult. But for me, the end justified the means. It had to be done, Sophie. I needed to know what we were dealing with."

I scoffed and shook my head. "Whatever, Connor."

"For example," Connor continued, ignoring my outburst, "were you aware that Lennie and Isaac actually work for Charisma? They didn't buy your contract, Sophie. Charisma uses them to soft exit stars they no longer have use for while maintaining their image."

"Soft exit my ass," I said, rolling my eyes.

"Yes, well, apparently they've been a bit more heavy-handed lately. Lennie and Isaac were the ones that planted the rumors about you."

I twisted my lips. I didn't know whether I could believe him. It jived with what Tara was telling me, but how could they be so nice to me while at the same time playing me so badly? "Why should I believe you?"

Connor didn't respond. Instead, he pulled out his phone and placed it on the desk beside the papers. A few touches to the screen and a conversation started to fill the small space. I recognized the voices immediately. It was Connor and Webb talking to one another.

I listened quietly with my eyes closed, trying to make sense of what was going on.

"I've got to ask you something, Lennie, and please be honest. What's the real situation with Sophie?"

"What do you mean?"

"Oh, come on. Number one artist suddenly accused of stealing songs and harassing employees? Around the time that she's failing to produce songs? I'm her new owner now. Do me a solid and tell me what really happened. You two had something to do with it, yes?"

I grit my teeth at hearing Connor say that he was my new owner, but this conversation was too important to interrupt, so I stayed quiet. I'd deal with that later.

"Yeah, we did."

"So, what's the real story?"

"She's crazy depressed. Can't write for shit right now."

"So why start the rumors?"

"Money, man. You can sell locations and pictures to the pap. They get their pictures and you get money. I'm telling you, having an artist that everyone hates is sometimes better than one everybody loves."

Connor touched his finger to the device and the sounds stopped. Silence filled the room as silent tears ran down my cheeks.

"Do you believe me now?" he finally asked me.

"So I was played. But if these guys were such shit, why were you in on it, Connor?" I turned my tear-filled eyes to him. "Why would you let them do something like that to me?"

Connor looked at me and I couldn't look away. "Sophie, I came out here to save you from them."

I shook my head. I couldn't make sense of that. "How? How can I believe you?" The tears were falling in greater numbers now and I looked down, not wanting him to see me breaking.

"I emailed that shit bag and made him an offer to purchase your contract, Sophie. I wanted you away from them for good."

"So you paid them off? You let them make money off of my suffering? That's almost worse, Connor."

Connor didn't respond. Instead, he just pressed his finger to the phone again and let the recording play.

"So it was you and Isaac that started those rumors? She didn't steal songs or harass anyone?"

"Of course not! Have you ever met the girl? She's just some little pansy. She couldn't hurt a fly."

"That's really disappointing to hear, Mr. Webb. You really should have disclosed that fact to me before we signed the documents."

"It's too late now."

"For you, it is. You see, I always record my business transactions. Promises are so often made and then broken during these times. It's just good to have a record, don't you think so?"

I heard scuffling as if the device had been moved quickly and then Connor's voice, still calm and in control, started back up.

"It wouldn't matter anyway, Mr. Webb. This phone backs up to my personal servers instantly. I've got as many copies as I wish of this entire transaction, ready to distribute on command."

"What do you want?"

The sound of more paper shuffling filled the room before Webb's voice was all but screaming into the device.

"You planned this!"

"No. But I always like to come prepared."

"You want me to amend the sale's price to one hundred dollars? Are you out of your mind? No way in hell I'm signing this!"

Connor reached out and stopped the recording again. He turned to me, his gaze heartfelt and sincere. "That's what you saw when you walked in, Sophie. Me handing that piece of shit a one hundred dollar bill for your contract rights."

I gulped as Connor shifted two of the papers forward. "Here's the original, with a sales price of $1.2 million. Which, to be clear, I would have gladly paid, and more, to get you away from those men. I had a wire ready for up to $2.5 million."

I blinked my eyes and shook my head. I couldn't believe what I was seeing, but as I reached out and flipped the document to the second page, there was Webb's signature.

"But," a small smile graced Connor's lips. "I do hate seeing the bad guys win. So," he pulled down the second document, "Here's the amendment. Dropping the price down to one hundred dollars."

Again, I flipped it over and saw Webb's signature. I couldn't believe what Connor had pulled off. He had conned a conman into giving away everything.

He used the sleeves of his shirt to wipe the tears off my face. "You signed for MMS LLC. Who is that?"

"It's a limited liability company I had created. I didn't want Webb and Jacobs to have my name in advance."

I nodded with a sniffle. "What's it stand for?"

Connor's eyes flickered with—something—but I wasn't sure what. But before I could get a good look, he was back to his calm, impassive mask. "I'll tell you when the time is right. Incidentally, Lennie and Isaac's entity Tymar stands for 'Take Your Money and Run.' I thought you should know."

"Okay, so what? You own me now? Is that it?" I knew I shouldn't be upset at him. Everything he had done for me was—incredible. But still, the idea that I was somehow still owned by someone or some entity, I just couldn't stomach it anymore.

Connor reached out and pulled down the third paper. "Only until you sign your name here," he said, pointing to the signature line on the document.

As I read the words on the page, my eyes widened. It was written in simple enough terms that even I could understand it.

Assignment of Membership Interest.

As of the Effective Date, Connor Driscoll does hereby transfer all of his membership interest in MMS LLC to Sophia Stronglen.

Connor's signature graced the bottom of the page.

"Agreed and accepted by Sophia Stronglen." There was a blank for me to sign next to those words.

I looked up at him, my tears running down my face again, but this time I couldn't be bothered to hold them in. "Connor, why?"

Connor didn't hold himself back any longer. He invaded my space and pulled me close against his body. I allowed it and he breathed a sigh of relief as he pressed his lips into my hair and kissed my head softly. "Because I love you. Because I've always loved you. Because I always will love you."

I began to shake as I sobbed and Connor just held me tightly, not letting me go as I vented all my emotions. When I finally calmed, I looked up at him. I knew my green eyes were ringed with red from my tears, but he still looked at me as if I was beautiful.

"I thought you hated my dream."

A slight smile lifted Connor's lips as he pulled me back against him. He pressed another soft kiss against my hair. "I never hated your dream. I just hated you being away from me. I'm selfish that way. I want you all for myself."

"I don't want to stop singing," I said, my voice muffled against his vest.

"I know," he said softly before pulling away slightly. I stood there as he walked to a nearby closet and opened the door. My body shivered at the loss of him. "Which is why I brought this with me."

I gasped as he pulled my guitar out of the closet and I ran forward. "Connor, I—" I didn't know what to say but Connor was there to fill in the words for me.

"Start with signing the documents, Soph. Then we go after Charisma and Eternity and whoever else ever thought it was a good idea to fuck with you."

I put my guitar down and looked up at the man just moments ago I wanted to murder. How quickly things changed in my life. "Why Charisma? Why Eternity? I know they did wrong, but, I just want to be done with them."

Connor sighed. It was an odd expression for him. "Unfortunately, that's not an option. Charisma retained the rights to your current catalog.

When you sign those documents, you'll own the right to your future songs and any concerts you play, but not your past songs."

"Bastards," I said with a shake of my head.

"They'll pay for what they've done, Soph. I swear it."

I looked into his blue eyes. They were full of conviction and for the first time in a long time, I finally felt at ease. "I trust you."

THIRTY-SIX

I COULDN'T STOP MYSELF FROM MOVING FORWARD. I COULDN'T STOP myself from pulling her into me. And I couldn't stop myself from pressing my lips to hers.

When she didn't resist it, but instead opened her mouth to allow me in further, I groaned and knew this was the woman I wanted to spend the rest of my life with. My time with Sophie this past semester had been everything I knew it could have been and more. It only cemented in my mind how much I wanted Sophie—how much we were meant for one another.

"Sophie, I need you," I breathed out and she nodded.

"I need you too, Connor. I'm sorry," she said but I stopped her from saying anymore when I smashed my lips back down over hers. I didn't want her apologizing. I didn't need that from her. I just needed her in my arms. I needed my cock buried into her warm heat. I needed to know that she was well and truly mine.

"Fuck, Con," she breathed out as she arched her head back. My tongue grazed over her neck, my teeth nipping at the sensitive skin before I soothed the area. My hand was on her collarbone first, charting a path for my lips to follow. Her breathing increased as her panties began to soak through before I had even ventured further south than her shoulders.

Sophie reached down, unclasping my belt and pushing my pants down to my ankles quickly. The need to be joined with her was animalistic and I didn't want to wait until we were both completely rid of our clothing. Softer times could wait. I needed to fuck her—hard.

She dropped to her knees as soon as my cock was free and wrapped her plump lips around me. I was rock solid already and she moved against my length, coating me in her saliva before circling my crown with her tongue.

"Fuck, Soph," I groaned as my fingers thread through her hair. She moaned her response and my fingers tightened against the back of her head. I began to guide her movements, pushing her on and off my cock, fucking her face with a slow, intense rhythm.

A swift tug released her hair from its messy bun as it tumbled down to her shoulders. My fingers twisted into her red mane and I pulled her off my cock with a smile. "Don't think I'm going to let you ruin the ending."

Sophie licked her lips and stayed quiet, instead chewing her lower lip and looking up as she kneeled in front of me.

I was down on the ground with her in an instant, turning her around. Her leggings and panties were pulled down roughly, exposing her backside and slit. A rough hand landed on one ass cheek, then the other before my fingers speared into her center.

"Fuck, Connor!" she screamed as my fingers worked her, spreading her wider while I thumbed her clit.

"Take off your shirt," I instructed and she complied, pulling everything up and over her head, including her bra and tossing it to the side.

As soon as her breasts were free, I reached forward, fisting one in my hand before tweaking her nipple.

"Ah!" she moaned and I could feel the intensity inside of her building.

I knew she was close but I didn't want her coming just yet. "Don't come," I said, my tone leaving no room for question.

"Connor, please," she begged, but I wasn't on her schedule.

I withdrew my hand from her core with a gasp of her own and shoved my fingers into her mouth. "Lick that beautiful pussy juice off my fingers, Soph. Then I'm going to fuck you into next week."

Sophie's tongue wrapped around each digit in her mouth. I watched as she tasted herself on my fingers before closing her eyes and taking a deep breath.

My fingers withdrew with a pop of her lips and before she had the chance to contemplate what was happening, I had sheathed myself with one swift snap of my hips.

"Fuck!" she yelled.

My movements started instantly, giving her no time to adjust. My large cock moved in and out of her and with each thrust of my hips, I knew she was climbing higher and higher. The sound of our coupling filled the small room and filled me up just the same.

Her arms gave out as her body collapsed to the floor but I didn't stop my movements. She was barely holding on at this point. "Connor, please," she begged again.

"Scream. My. Name." I instructed her, in time with each thrust.

"Fuck, Connor!" Sophie let go as the orgasm overtook her.

"So. Fucking. Tight." I was nearing my limit. Her walls pulsed around me like a vice and I was gritting my teeth as my balls drew up. "You're fucking mine, Sophie," I grunted as I finally let myself fall over that edge.

My body collapsed as I spilled my seed into her, snapping my hips the last few times so that I could truly fill her up with everything I had. When I was finally spent, I rolled to the ground, pulling Sophie with me. Reaching up, I grabbed the edge of the duvet and with a swift tug, it was floating gently onto us from its resting place on the bed.

Sophie's soft curves molded against my hard edges as my fingertips trailed against her skin gently beneath the blanket. Neither of us said anything, but we didn't need to. Our breathing began to even out and I kept her tight against my body. I was never, ever letting her go.

THIRTY-SEVEN

LENNIE

"You do realize that this is one fuck up too many, right Webb?"

"I know, Sir. I'm very sorry, Sir." My voice was shaky on the speaker.

"Well, what the fuck happened?"

"Oh, right, well. Unfortunately, that investor, you see, he got some information on us that could have really tarnished Charisma and Eternity's reputation. I thought it would have been more prudent to agree to his demands."

Payne's voice was eerily calm. "To what end?"

"Well," I swallowed hard. "We signed over our portion of Strong's contract."

"For how much?"

Silence.

"One hundred dollars," was my tentative response.

I could almost hear Payne smile on the phone. And then he laughed. The sound filled my small office and I stayed silent. Payne was an intense man. I had never *ever* heard him laugh. Aside from public functions where Payne put on the most impressive of masks, I'd never even seen Payne smile. This did not bode well for me or Isaac.

Finally, the laughter subsided and Payne's voice returned to its eerie calm. "You do realize the reason for which I keep you and Isaac around, don't you Webb?" His voice was like ice in contrast to just moments ago.

"I do, Sir. Yes, Sir."

"You're supposed to be the Fixer, Webb. Tell me, just what did this unnamed man have on us that could so tarnish our reputation?"

"Well, you see, Sir. We, uh, the rumors about Sophie. Well, I—we—admitted to starting them." I was fumbling over my words and I knew it. I also knew that if Payne was angry before, he'd be livid now.

Only two things seemed to matter to Payne. The first being his reputation and the second being money. Interfering with his goals on either was dealt with swiftly. Unfortunately, I had tested the strength of both chains.

Sweat rolled down my face as I tried to wipe it off with my handkerchief. I wondered whether Payne had any reach in Mexico. It wouldn't be hard for me to cross the border this evening. Being on the run wasn't my favorite pastime, but I'd done it before and come out on top. Perhaps, my luck would hold true this time.

I tried to crane my neck to see where Isaac might be. Isaac should be here on this call and instead he was god only knows where. It was all Isaac's idea to start those rumors in the first place. I had nothing to do with it, as far as my memory was concerned.

"Is there anything else you'd like to admit to, Webb? Might as well lay it all out on the table now. You know I'll find out sooner or later if you're hiding something from me." His words were dark and full of promise—just not the good kind.

I gulped. "He knows that Charisma holds the rights to Strong's catalog."

"Well, Webb, at least you got $100 out of this whole thing. Because that's the last cash you'll ever see from any of my endeavors."

I knew what that meant. This was the way Payne fired people. Well, this was the way he fired people over the phone. Generally, someone else followed up on the unspoken threats at a later, undisclosed time.

"Put Isaac on the line," Payne instructed.

"Isaac's not here," I replied nervously.

"He probably tried to get a head start. Perhaps he was the smarter of you two, after all."

I gulped. I glanced around my office frantically, wondering if Payne already had eyes on me somehow. Of course Payne knew where I worked, but when you work for someone like Xavier Payne, you always have to expect the time to come when the relationship fails and an exit strategy is needed.

I jumped up from my chair and clumsily climbed onto my desk. It'd been several decades since I'd had to do this and I'd clearly been a lot thinner, if not a bit taller, back then. The desk creaked under my weight as I reached up to remove a ceiling tile directly above where I sat. My hand reached around, searching out the bag that I had verified was there just a few days ago.

"If you're looking for that grey bag you stashed in the ceiling, Webb, I'm happy to let you know my cleaning crew picked it up. They didn't think it was smart to have so much cash just lying around for anyone to find. Rest assured, I've got it safe here. When you come to my office tomorrow, you'll leave with it."

I nearly fell off the desk at Payne's words. I had no doubt Payne wasn't intending for me to leave *with* the bag, but rather *in* it.

"Uh, yes, of course, Sir," I said, trying to reformulate a plan in my head.

"Incidentally, who was it that got you caught up with this man in the first place? I need a name."

I sat down heavily on the desk as it continued to groan its protest. As soon as the man had left, I had someone look into him. His name was Connor Driscoll and he'd been seen with Sophie in the media debacle that had been set up in D.C. I wondered absently whether Payne had planted the Aubrey girl on purpose. But there was no harm in holding the information back from him. It she was his girl, then I'd get points for owning up to it, and if she wasn't, maybe she'd take some of the heat away from me, enough so that I could figure out a way to get the fuck out of Los Angeles.

"Her name's Aubrey Knight. Her father is Bob Knight, the congressman."

"Alright, Webb. You know the drill. Tomorrow morning, at my office. If I don't see you here before ten, well, you know the consequences."

"Yes, Sir," I said. "I'll be there." The call ended and I jumped off the desk and bolted for the door. I didn't care if I had to sneak through a hole in the fence. By morning, I would not be in this country.

Aubrey

"UNKNOWN" flashed on my screen and I debated whether or not to pick up. Usually unlisted numbers were my father calling from work and I really just did not want to talk to him right now. On the other hand, I really did not want to deal with the lecture that inevitably followed anytime I failed to live up to one of my parents' inane expectations.

"Yes?" I answered sharply.

"Ms. Knight. This is Xavier Payne."

That was definitely not who I expected on the line. I tried to recover my shock with a clear of my throat. "Excuse me. Uh, Mr. Payne, what can I do for you?"

"It's my understanding that you've had some recent dealings with a former associate of mine. A Leonard Webb?"

"Uh, briefly, yes." I decided that less was likely better in this situation. I didn't know much about Payne, but what I did know hadn't instilled any confidence that he had a hidden, softer side.

"Elaborate, please," Payne added.

I hesitated. I really did not want to and I wasn't sure how much Payne already knew. There was no way he didn't know something. And if I had my guesses, he knew more than he would ever let on.

"I had heard that Mr. Webb was looking for the whereabouts of Ms. Strong. I learned that she was in D.C. and simply provided him that information."

"Why?"

"Excuse me?"

"Well, Ms. Knight. I've never known a person to do something out of the goodness of their own heart. At least not for a stranger. I know that Webb didn't pay you. So then, why did you go to the effort of helping him?"

I swallowed hard. Just as I suspected, Payne knew more than he was letting on.

"Well." I tried to think about what to say and measured each word. "Her no longer being in D.C. would have been more convenient for me."

"What's your relationship with Connor Driscoll?" he asked bluntly.

"My relationship?" I replied, a bit surprised by such a personal question.

"Did I stutter, Ms. Knight?" His tone was dark and I shivered.

"No. I'm just not sure how to answer the question."

"Honestly, of course." His voice sounded amused, but I knew it was at my expense.

"He was a friend, until recently," I replied vaguely.

"What happened?"

I huffed. I knew I shouldn't test this man, but I really was at my limit. "I'm not comfortable speaking about my personal relationships with a stranger, Mr. Payne. Please understand."

Payne chuckled. "No offense intended, Ms. Knight. I understand."

Silence filled the space between us before finally Payne spoke again. "Well, Ms. Knight. That's all, for now." Those last words sent a shiver down my spine. The line went dead and I pulled the phone down and stared at the device. The screen seemed to flicker until I realized that was just my hand shaking.

I tried to take deep breaths and steady my nerves. I'd survived a phone call with Xavier Payne, for now.

Payne

"THAT BAD?" Rebecca asked as she walked into my office. I was sitting with my back to her, looking out over Los Angeles from my elevated vantage point. I turned around to face her. My amber eyes fixated on her as she took a seat in front of me. Rebecca looked stunning in her navy tailored skirt suit. Her brown hair was tied back in a tight knot and her matching brown eyes held hints of promise. She was a few years past her prime and I had no attraction to her as a person, but physically, I enjoyed her company. It had been quite some time since any woman excited me mentally. It was a shame really. Even a woman as smart and accomplished as Rebecca hadn't done it for me. She'd certainly tried her hardest, but I lived by a set of rules that no woman had yet to satisfy.

"You've had your finger on the pulse of the dynamic duo more than me lately. What are your thoughts?"

"Honestly?" she asked, raising her eyebrow. I nodded and her features shifted. "They've gone rogue. What they did with the Strong girl wasn't protocol. Everyone knew it and they did it without getting permission. That sort of stunt is only used for the worst of cases. Where artists are too valuable or too far gone. For Christ's sake, the only thing worse they could have done was release a sex tape."

My eyebrows shifted. "I'm sure that was their next plan."

"No doubt. But they left us all scrambling to try and make their story work or risk us looking like we were caught off guard."

"Which would have raised suspicions."

"Exactly. We ended up having to threaten a young girl with her brother's career to get her to cooperate. It's not the way I like to do business, Payne. You know that."

I sighed. "Yeah, I know."

"I would have fired them a few years ago, but they know a lot and replacing them would have proven difficult."

"Agreed. Although, next time a bit of a heads up would have been appreciated. You are supposed to be my eyes on the ground in this industry."

Rebecca nodded. "It's hard to tell when exactly people are really going to go rogue. This was their first bad screw up." She lifted a slender eyebrow. "I'm guessing that things have continued to go downhill if you're involved? What am I missing here?"

"It seems that they involved an outsider. Not only that, but that involved *another* outsider. Some man named Connor Driscoll. Big shot developer in D.C. from what I've been told. Apparently, I even bought a building from the man a few years back. Small world."

"I'll say. Is he a threat?"

"Hard to know," I said, rubbing my jaw slightly. "I think she's his woman and he's just defending what's his. I can respect that."

"The girl wasn't in a relationship when we picked her up and she didn't have any while she was with us. She really had no one."

"Yeah. I think he's a ghost from her past."

Rebecca's forehead creased. "That's frustrating. We followed standard protocol. Tried to distance her."

"It happens."

I knew I was being unusually reasonable today and I could tell it was putting Rebecca on edge.

"So how's he involved?"

I gave her an interesting smile. "Apparently, he conned our conman. Got him talking, which isn't too hard these days as far as Webb's concerned. Got the whole thing on record. The deal for her contract dropped from $1.2 to $100 within the span of a few minutes." I looked thoughtful again. "If I didn't personally have a stake in this situation, I would have said I was impressed."

"No kidding. Although, Lennie has become somewhat of an idiot lately."

"Well, that's taken care of."

Rebecca studied my face. "You have varying levels of 'taking care of.' Which is this?"

"His own cowardice will have him running south of the border by midnight. The problem will take care of itself. Which, incidentally, is my favorite type of solution." Rebecca dared a smile. I knew that she understood that in some ways, she was responsible for Webb and Jacobs' actions as their ultimate overseer.

"And Isaac?"

"Difficult to say at the moment. He may turn up or he may not. Once I have better details, I'll deal with it."

She nodded her head in understanding. "Out of the two, I'd say Isaac has a bit more potential. I'm not too displeased at cutting Webb loose. But Isaac," she paused, measuring what she wanted to say. "He's impulsive and an ass, but he has the drive."

My face was unreadable. "I'll deal with him."

"Understood," Rebecca responded, raising her hands in the air as a white flag. "So, what do you need me to do?"

"At the moment, nothing. But be prepared for some trouble in the future. Don't end up like Webb. Don't let this man play games or pull one over on you."

A smirk formed on her thin lips as they curved up into a smile. "Oh, if this man does come knocking, he clearly doesn't know what he's dealing with."

"It's not a game, Becca," I said, my voice louder and more stern. Her features quieted and I looked at her with my intense amber eyes. "I don't want problems, you get me?"

She shivered. "Yeah, I get you."

Rebecca and I would never have worked as a couple. What was more, I knew she wasn't capable of giving me what I needed. She loved power and the feel of being in control. But so did I. Personality-wise, we clashed.

But physically, we meshed and well. The bedroom was the one area in which Rebecca allowed herself to give over her control and I was all too happy to take it. It'd been quite some time since the last time I'd called her in for a personal meeting. Usually, my calls were quick and over the phone. But whenever there was a particularly bad problem, I would call her personally and instruct her to come to my office.

She knew what these meetings meant. Something had gone seriously wrong and that I needed the type of release not too many women were willing to give to me.

I had exacting tastes. I lived by a set of rules and I expected others to follow them, especially the women with whom I had relationships. My reputation was of utmost importance to me. As a result, I trusted very few people as a policy. The number dwindled to the single digits when it came to women.

"Was there . . . anything else you needed, Sir?"

I raised an eyebrow at her honorific.

"Conference room B. Ten minutes. Go." My voice was dark and she shivered but stood immediately.

"Yes, Sir."

I watched her leave my office, following my commands perfectly. It was too bad Rebecca didn't live up to my requirements, otherwise she would have been perfect.

Oh, well.

She would have to do.

For now.

THIRTY-EIGHT

Sophie

SOMETHING WAS SHAKING ME AWAKE. I GRUMBLED MY COMPLAINTS, trying to curl into myself to go back to sleep.

"Soph. Come on. We need to get up." We had fallen asleep on the floor, the duvet curled around us like a nest. By the time we had come out of our sex induced nap, daylight was gone and the room was dark. "The jets on standby ready to take us back to D.C. and you need to back there so you can concentrate on final exams," he said, kneeling down and scooping me up with the covers.

He carried me into the bathroom, my eyes starting to flicker open with each step he took. When he made it into the glass enclosure, I was conscious enough and he placed me gently on the floor.

I sucked in a breath at the cold tile beneath my feet. I pulled the blanket further around myself as Connor leaned over and turned the knobs to begin filling up the tub. Once he got the temperature right, he turned around and smiled. He pulled me into his frame and wrapped his hands around me in the duvet and leaned against the vanity.

I sighed as he pressed a soft kiss to my temple. "I'll get you warmed up in no time," he said with a bit of a smirk.

I smiled. "I have no doubts." I pressed my lips to his and closed my eyes. I felt like I was living some sort of dream. Last night at this hour I was in an airport hotel in Denver, thinking about how to avoid sleeping with Isaac. Not even twenty-four hours later, I was in a gorgeous hotel suite, with a man completely devoted to me wrapped around my body.

"Con," I said, looking up into his cool blue gaze.

"Yeah?" His response was soft and caring.

"You really sure about all this? About me?"

"Don't be silly, Sophie. Of course I am. You don't ever have to ask me that again. The answer is never going to change."

"It's just . . . a lot. *I'm* a lot."

Connor grinned. "I know. You always were such a pain." His features were light and I knew he was teasing me.

"I'm serious, Con," I said, stamping my foot lightly into the cold tile.

"So am I." He squeezed me tighter and I sighed.

Steam started to fill the space around us and I breathed it in. It, combined with the feel of Connor's strong arms around me, helped calm me down. "So, what's the plan for Charisma? If I know you," I said with a light tap to his shoulder. "You're not going to let this go."

"You do know me," he said with a soft kiss to my lips.

"I can write more music, Con." For the first time in a long time, I actually believed that to be true. It was as if a fog had lifted from my mind and the music was finally flowing to me once again.

"I know that. You're incredibly talented, Soph, and I never doubted you for a second. But, they've stolen things from you and I'm going to get them back."

I couldn't stop the smile that crossed my features. I pressed my forehead into Connor's chest and closed my eyes. "I don't get it. I don't deserve you. Not even a little bit. Why are you so devoted to me? I'm nothing."

Connor's fingers fisted in the blanket at my words. "You're not nothing, Soph. You're everything to me. And I'll spend the rest of my life trying to convince you of that if I have to. But I hope one day you can see what I see."

"You never were very smart," I said with a giggle.

Connor chuckled. "I manage somehow."

He pulled away from me briefly to turn off the water. He tested it and nodded his head. "Come on, I'll help you," he said, pulling the duvet away from my body.

I shivered as the blanket left me but even more so from the way Connor's eyes raked across my naked form. "Don't be shy, Soph. You've always been perfect."

I brushed aside his comment and I watched him give me a look. But for now, he let me sink into the water before getting into the large soaking tub himself, tucking me between his legs and against his frame.

I sighed into his embrace as his hands came around my body. He moved them gently against my skin. The warm water and his movements helped the shivers from the cold subside, but within minutes, they returned for a very different reason. I didn't understand how Connor could get me going so easily. It was as if he had found an "on" switch on my body that I didn't know even existed.

He didn't say anything, but I didn't need words at the moment. His hand slipped between my legs as his lips fell into the crook of my neck. I chewed my lower lip, trying to repress the moans that were crawling up my throat. His teeth nipped at my neck slightly before he pulled back to whisper in my ear. "Let go, Sophie. Just relax. I'll take care of you." My sex clenched at his words and I released my lip. "Good girl," he whispered with heated breath before sucking the lobe of my ear into his mouth.

I gasped as he released it and moved back down my neck. His fingers were circling me lower now, stirring me up as my breathing increased.

"Connor," I breathed out, but his rhythm didn't stop. Instead, his fingers moved from my folds to enter my channel and I gasped. His thumb stayed outside, rubbing slow circles around my clit, driving me closer and closer to an edge I knew, mainly from Connor's skilled fingers.

"Just relax." His voice was deep in my ear again and I tried to follow his direction. A hand came up to caress my stiffened peak as the other one made its slow consistent rhythm against my core.

"Connor." His name was a jumbled mess on my lips as his fingers and lips played me like some sort of instrument. "I'm gonna—"

"Do it, Sophie. Come for me."

"Fuck!" I cursed as I let myself fall over that cliff. My walls squeezed his fingers and he timed his thrusts with my pulses to draw out my pleasure.

Connor let me come down slowly, but he was by no means done with me. His cock was rock hard for me by this point and I could feel it against my back. Connor wrapped a heavily muscled arm around my middle and lifted me easily, the water supporting his efforts. Even with the water, I was slick with arousal and he pulled me back, slipping into me easily.

"Fuck," I breathed out as he entered me. My walls pulsed, still sensitive from my release, not to mention how he'd made me come just a few hours before. He started to move, emptying and filling me with each thrust of his hips up into my body. His fingers dug into my thighs as he gripped me, holding me steady as he snapped into me over and over and over again.

One hand came up to cup my breast and I keened as he tweaked one of my nipples. My body was so sensitive, I could feel everything he was giving to me and it was incredible. "Connor," I breathed out.

He grunted his response, increasing the pace of his thrusts until he was nearing his own end. "Sophie, you're fucking mine," he roared out as he came inside me, his cock pulsing its own end as he filled my pussy with his seed.

"I LIKE THESE," Sophie said, referring to the thick bath towels as she used one to wring the water from her red locks.

I smiled and came up behind her, planting a kiss on her neck. "I'm glad. You feel better?"

"Yeah," she admitted. "I guess a series of orgasms will do that to a girl."

"I'd say more experiments may be needed," I said with a chuckle before pressing another kiss to her neck. She smiled and I turned her around, still holding tight to my body. "You ready to go back to the city?"

Sophie frowned. "I thought we were staying here? Taking care of the whole Charisma thing?"

"No," I said with a shake of my head. "You've got final exams to take. Or did you already forget about that little detail?"

Sophie twisted her lips in silent protest. "I don't want to have to come back here," she admitted. "I just want to get everything over with and out of the way so I can just live my life."

I closed my eyes at her words and pulled her close. I rested my chin on her head and sighed. "I know, Soph. I know. But this is important. I need you to finish your degree. If you don't want to do it for yourself, do it for me."

Sophie pulled back and looked up at me. I could tell she wanted to fight, but my intense look told her she wasn't likely to succeed. "It's not that I don't want to graduate. In some ways, I'm afraid of going back there as much as I'm afraid to stay here." She sighed and let herself fall into my embrace even more. "I'm confused. I don't feel like I belong anywhere."

I loosened my grip enough to tilt her chin up so she was looking directly into my eyes. "You belong right here, Soph. With me. Don't you ever forget that." I pressed my lips against hers and she sighed.

I pulled back and she nodded. "Thank you, Con."

"I love you, Soph. Everything is going to be okay."

She burrowed into my chest and I felt her relax as she took a deep breath. "So, how do you plan on handling Charisma?"

"Right now, I just want you to focus on getting through finals. These last few days have been extremely difficult for you and I want you in a good place so you can do well."

"Fine," she said, a bit of her brattiness coming out. "There's no use fighting with you."

I smirked. "Now you're getting it."

Sophie pulled back and rolled her eyes. I gave her an interesting look, before saying, "Don't tempt me, Sophie. When you act like that, I really do want to take you over my knee." Sophie bit her lower lip and gave me a half-lidded smile. I smirked as I took in her expression. "Naughty girl," I said, my fingers on her chin. "Don't worry. There's plenty of that for you in your future. Right now, we've got to get to the airport."

Sophie's eyes widened. "We're leaving now?"

I nodded. "Jet's on standby. And you need to get back and get settled. So, yes, now."

IT HADN'T TAKEN us long to gather our belongings from the hotel. Within the hour, a black Navigator was driving us to the airport for our flight.

"You never struck me as the splurgy type," Sophie commented.

I raised an eyebrow as I continued scrolling through my emails, trying to ensure there was nothing important that I missed. "How so?"

Sophie shrugged. "I've known you a while and seen how you spend money—or rather don't spend money."

"I spend money when I need to."

Sophie laughed. "Yes, in a world where most people are spending it based on wants. I'm just surprised that you booked yourself a private flight, that's all."

I turned and looked at her. "Getting to you as quickly as possible was an absolute necessity."

Sophie shivered under my gaze. "Well, mission accomplished."

"Indeed," I said, turning back to my phone. I noticed an email from an address I didn't recognize.

From: Skyler Jackson
To: Connor Driscoll
Subject: What the fuck
Message: I've been trying to call Sophie for the better part of two days now and you haven't told me whether she's okay. Seriously losing my shit right now. Got your email from your company website, by the way, in case you thought I was a creeper.

I winced. I'd completely forgotten about Skyler when I'd gotten Sophie back safely. She had this way of making the world and all my responsibilities in it fade away. I handed the phone to Sophie, who read the message with genuine horror.

"Oh shit," she said, fumbling in her purse for her phone. "I'd completely forgotten that it was still off."

As soon as the device was powered on, a call from Skyler lit up her phone and Sophie answered.

"Sky?" she answered. Skyler spoke loud enough on the other end that I could just make out what she was saying.

"Sophie, oh my god. Are you okay? Is Connor with you?"

"Yes, I'm fine. He's here."

"Well, punch him in the kidney for me, would you?"

"Um," Sophie turned and looked at me and shook her head. "I don't think that's a good idea."

I chuckled internally.

"I've been worried sick about you."

"I know, I'm sorry!"

"Ugh, whatever. I'm just glad you're safe. You can tell me all about it when you get back."

"Okay. And Sky?"

"Yeah, Soph?"

"Thanks. Connor told me what you did. Just—thanks."

"I got you, baby. Love you. Get your ass back here. Finals start on Monday."

Sophie laughed. "Yeah, we're heading back now. I'll see you soon."

"Hey, Soph, before you go, can you hand me to Connor?"

"Um," Sophie drew her eyebrows together at her friend's request. "I guess." Sophie turned and handed the phone to me. "She wants to talk to you."

I frowned but put the phone to my ear. "This is Connor."

Skyler dropped her voice low, to almost a whisper so I had to push the phone into my ear to hear her.

"I'm telling you because I don't know what sort of state she's in right now. But the media frenzy hasn't calmed down out here. Papers are still publishing the photos and I've seen the press hanging out around the college, waiting for her to show up."

I tried to keep my face impassive. I knew that if I showed any sign of there being a problem, Sophie might refuse to go back to D.C. And she could be difficult, to say the least.

"Thanks for letting me know. I'll handle it." The call ended and I handed her back the phone.

"What did she want?"

I looked at her, my expression unreadable. I debated hiding the fact about the press from her. However, considering that the last time I hid my plans from Sophie she'd almost gotten run over by a bus, I opted for the open lines of communication plan. "Things are still a little heated in the city."

Sophie narrowed her eyes. "What do you mean by 'heated?'"

I remained calm, but Sophie could obviously tell there was some-thing underneath my impassive mask. "It's only been a day, Sophie. The press is just lingering, that's all. It will be handled."

Sophie scoffed. "Handled? How the hell does something like that get handled? Connor, if there's a problem still in D.C.—If all this is going to cause you trouble then—"

I turned my head and held her emerald gaze. "You said you trusted me." It was a statement as much as it was a question.

Sophie hesitated. She was slipping into her old habits and she had vowed to try harder for me. I needed to remind her of that. "I do."

I nodded. "Then trust that it will be handled."

Sophie turned and slumped back into the leather seat. "Fine," she said, crossing her arms. "I feel like a shit friend for not calling her sooner."

I understood what Sophie was feeling as well. I really should have been more in control of this entire situation. "She's a good friend. I'm sure she's already forgiven you."

"Yeah," Sophie said with a sigh as we pulled up to the airport.

THIRTY-NINE

Sophie

"IT FEELS LIKE A LIFETIME AGO THAT I WAS ON ONE OF THESE THINGS," I remarked, looking around at the interior furnishings. The seats were a cream colored leather against a stylish carpet. A sofa ran most of the length of the opposite wall and further back was the lavatory and a small kitchenette. I ran my finger against the stitching on the chair next to me. "*Embraer Legacy 500.*"

Connor was sitting in a plush leather seat across from me. We'd taken off about thirty minutes ago and the bumpiness through the clouds had finally evened out. He had his leg crossed over his other knee and he looked completely at ease. In his dark navy suit, he looked like a model paid to sell the plane.

"You've never really talked to me about what your life was like during those times, Soph."

I twisted my lips. I knew he was right. I'd been keeping a lot of what happened to me bottled up. I also knew that doing so made it difficult to move past everything. But it was just so hard to relive such an awful past.

"If you don't want to talk about it, I get it," Connor said, his gaze soft and comforting. "But, it may be helpful at some point to let it all out and let go," he added, reflecting my own thinking on the matter.

"I know you're right. But, you also know I've never been good at sharing my feelings."

"That I do know. But, you also know I've always been a good listener."

I looked at him and smiled. His eyes followed me as I moved to sit on the sofa across from him. Connor stood himself, sitting next to me and wrapping an arm around me. I breathed in his scent and let myself fall into him.

There was a question that had been nagging at me for years. When I'd gotten back to the city and seen Connor that first night, I'd wanted to ask him then. It had lingered in the back of my mind for so long now, but if he really wanted me to be honest, I needed an answer from him. I didn't look up at him. Instead, I just burrowed further into his jacket. "Why didn't you call me?"

"What was that?" Connor asked.

I pulled my head up slightly. "All those years ago, why didn't you call me? I waited for you to call that night."

Connor's forehead furrowed as he scrutinized me. "I did call you. I called you repeatedly. For months. It was always the same. Your number had been disconnected."

I closed my eyes. My world started to swim around me. "That doesn't make sense. They forwarded my number."

Connor raised an eyebrow. "Who's they?"

"Jack," I said softly.

"Jack, as in the man who allowed Tara to get up and lie about you stealing songs? Jack, as in the man who falsely accused you of sexually harassing employees?"

Everything was starting to fall into place. I didn't want to believe it.

The extent of how badly I had been played was finally starting to sink in and tears began to stream down my cheeks.

"Shh," Connor said, pulling me close to him again, wiping my tears away from my face.

I hiccupped as I started spilling all of the secrets I had held to myself for years. "The first day . . . they took my phone. They said they forwarded my calls. I didn't have your number anymore."

Connor wrapped a strong hand around my head and pulled me tightly to him.

"Sophie, it's okay," he whispered against my hair.

"No! It's not okay. They stole everything from me. Including you! We could have been together all those years. I never wanted to be apart from you, Connor. I thought you hated me for leaving." My voice was muffled by his jacket and my sobs.

"I could never hate you, Sophie," he said, running his fingers through my hair calmingly. "Not even for a second."

"Oh god, you must have thought I'd completely abandoned you when I didn't call."

"It's okay. All of that is in the past now."

He said it, but I couldn't stop my tears in the present.

I HATED SEEING her cry and the fact that the actions of that company and those that worked for it had made her shed tears even once made me want to do some seriously bad shit.

Everything she was telling me made sense. Sophie could never remember my phone number and if they had taken her old phone away, she would have had no way to call me. The revelation hit me like a ton of bricks. I'd always thought that she had decided to move on, that she had started a new life and that there was no place for me in it.

I let her cry out her feelings, holding her firm against my body, still running my fingers through her hair. I didn't need her to tell me anything else about her experience with Charisma. If within the first day they had taken her phone and wiped everyone from her life except those who made their cut, then I knew exactly what type of people we were dealing with.

Her breathing evened against me and I looked down to see that she had cried herself to sleep. I adjusted our positions so that I was propped against the wall, feet on the sofa and she was tucked against me.

I grit my teeth. I kicked myself for not having more initiative when I was younger. I should have known something was up. But instead I let my insecurities guide my actions. I should have flown out there, tracked her down somehow. But by the time I had the confidence, the money and the know-how to do something like that, I firmly believed that she truly didn't want anything to do with me anymore.

My time apart from Sophie had taught me a lot about myself. I'd had time to grow into the man I was today. In many ways, I thought I'd learned most of life's lessons. But this was an incredibly difficult pill to swallow.

I would never doubt myself again.

I'd almost lost her and as much as I tried to tell myself through the years that I'd accepted that, I always knew it was a lie.

Sophie moaned in her sleep gently as I ran my hands through her bright red hair. I'd cut down everyone that had made her suffer.

She was mine and I'd protect her.

Nothing would ever change that.

"WHERE ARE WE?" I asked, blinking my eyes open as I tried to make sense of my surroundings. I was in a leather seat, but it was different than the ones on the plane.

"We're heading to my apartment," Connor said. "I wanted to let you sleep."

"Oh," I said, rubbing my eyes with the sleeves of my pink sweatshirt and sitting up. My head had been against Connor's lap with my feet on the seat in the back of the large black SUV. I smiled at him groggily. "Thanks. I guess I didn't realize how tired I was."

"It's been a tough couple of days," he said softly, almost as if to himself.

Connor turned his head to look out the window as the lights passed by us on the highway.

"I have stuff I need from the loft," I said.

"I'll have someone sent to go get it. I want you to rest."

I shook my head. "I want to see Skyler."

"You can see her tomorrow," Connor said.

I huffed. "Connor!"

He turned to face me. The blinking lights from the highway flashed across his face, his features hard under the soft glow. He leaned in and I shivered, his hot breath against my neck. "Sophie, I am taking you back to my apartment so I can fuck the last forty-eight hours out of my system. I will take you over and over and over again. I want to see you dripping with arousal on my bed and I want to hear you screaming my name as you come. My bed tonight, loft tomorrow. Understood?"

I bit my bottom lip and my sex clenched at Connor's words. Did he know how much his words turned me on? Did he know how absolutely drenched I was just from listening to him say such filthy things in my ear? "Okay," was all I could muster in response.

"Good girl," Connor said, pulling back with a nod.

I sat in anticipation the entire ride to his building. My mind was filled with all the filthy things he might do to me. I rubbed my thighs together to try and relieve the pressure, but it was no good. I must have been sitting in a puddle by this time considering how absolutely drenched I was.

The interior of the car was dark and I gasped lightly as I felt Connor's fingertips against my leg. His touch was light and sensual. I could feel it through my leggings and I wanted so much more. Slowly, those sinful fingers of his trailed higher and higher still, until they were dipping between my legs.

My head fell back against the headrest and I spread my legs. Connor smirked, probably at how easily I gave into him. But the things he did to me were so thrilling, I never really had a choice.

I was about to let out a moan but he leaned over. "Don't you dare make a sound," he whispered into my ear and I shuddered. "Wouldn't want the driver to know I'm about to finger fuck this tight little cunt of yours, hm?"

I mouthed the word "fuck," as Connor's fingers moved higher, slipping into my leggings and pushing them down slightly. I clenched my teeth, trying to stop the moans of pleasure that were crawling up my throat as his strong hand moved down to cup my sex, slipping my panties aside with practiced ease. When a finger slipped into my warm heat, I groaned and tried to cover it by clearing my throat.

Connor leaned over and his breath was hot against my ear. "Naughty girl. I'll have to punish you later."

I closed my eyes and a second finger slipped into my heat as his thumb began to work my clit.

I wanted to moan.

I wanted to scream his name.

But I couldn't.

All I could do was sit there and try and stay as quiet as possible while he worked me to heights I was becoming more and more familiar with.

His voice was in my ear again. "Don't come."

My mouth hung open. I was so close! How could he do this to me? My hips bucked up in protest but the car slowed and Connor's hand withdrew quickly as the driver exited the car. He turned and looked at me, fixing me with those intense blue eyes as I breathed heavily. His tongue darted out as he pulled his drenched fingers into his mouth and licked them clean. "Delicious," he said. "I can't wait to taste it from the source."

Then his door opened as the driver opened mine. I smiled at the oblivious man and hoped that I'd be able to support my weight. My feet touched the ground, but I hadn't needed to worry, because Connor was there within an instant. His strong arm wrapped around my middle and he pressed a sensual kiss to my neck. "Come on. I've got plans for you, naughty girl," he said as he led me away from the car and towards the building.

I was chewing my lip as we entered the elevator and he smirked. I could tell he had something planned for me.

The doors opened to the fourteenth floor and within seconds, he was leading me into his apartment. Shoes were kicked off and he wasted no time in getting me into the bedroom. I stood in front of him, waiting for his direction and he sighed as he ran his fingers through my red hair. "You're perfect, Sophie," he said in a heated whisper.

I shuddered. I was still riding so close to a high and Connor was pushing me to the edge with everything he did.

"But that doesn't mean you haven't been bad," he said with a cock of an eyebrow. I looked at him intensely as I continued to chew my bottom lip. "And I know just what to do with bad girls." His eyes darted to the floor before looking back at me. "Kneel."

My eyes widened but I complied. His hand gripped my chin and his thumb danced against my lower lip, pulling it from my teeth. "By the end of the night, your voice will be raw and that little cunt of yours will be stuffed so full of my come that you'll be leaking well into the week." My sex clenched at his words. Fuck, he was hot.

His hand left my chin and grasped my wrists. He tugged and I found myself laid out across the curve of the black leather sofa. "Stay just like this," he said as he walked away.

I wanted to protest, but I knew it would do me no good. Connor was in complete control now and I just needed to trust him, submit and take everything he chose to give to me.

Within a minute, he returned with a few lengths of nylon cord. I knew immediately what Connor had planned. I had told him about a very specific fantasy of mine months ago when he was in California. I'd wondered when he might make this happen for me. I was beyond aroused at this point and I closed my eyes. It was getting harder and harder not to come, but Connor must have already known that.

Connor kneeled in front of me and the slightest of smiles graced his lips. His fingers were gentle but firm against the skin of my wrists as he began to wrap small lengths of nylon around and around, cinching my hands together tighter all while creating a beautiful design up my wrists.

"You know you can stop this at any time. Red and yellow, yes?" His voice was low and I knew he was just checking in with me. I nodded my head in agreement, not trusting my voice at the moment. The cord wrapped further and further up my wrists until finally Connor looped it to the leg of the sofa and tucked the ends away. He stood suddenly and made his way around my body. My core tightened in anticipation of what was to come. I was so on edge, but still he was making me wait.

"Con, please," I begged but my pleas did nothing. A finger looped lightly around the waistband of my leggings and I shivered. But Connor never did what I was expecting these days. I thought he might peel my leggings off but his hand moved a bit left then a bit right, driving me mad with the smallest touches, before leaving my body completely.

I whimpered at the loss of contact and Connor chuckled. "Impatient, aren't we?" I twisted my hips this way and that, hoping I could spur him into action but his control was unshakeable.

Connor kneeled down next to me. I was draped over his recliner, ass up and waiting for him. He leaned in close and his breath was a whisper against my ear. "I'm going to make you come so hard you'll never think about running away from me again."

I sucked in a breath before his hand began to rub against my ass, stroking it gently as I moaned beneath him. "You've been real naughty, Sophie."

Another moan.

"Do you know what happens to naughty girls?"

I bit my lip. Connor was toying with me and I wasn't sure how much longer I could take it. "No."

"They get punished."

I toyed with the words on my tongue, but they slipped out before I could stop myself. "Then punish me till I come, Con."

His hand pulled back and the smack pressed hard against my back-side. "Fuck!" I screamed. It didn't hurt. Instead, it sent shockwaves of pleasure coursing through my body.

Connor's hand came down on me again, softer this time and I knew I was gone. His control over my mind, body and soul was ironclad and I just needed to be joined with him. "Please, Con. *Please* fuck me."

"Fuck," Connor breathed out at my words. I knew I had pushed him to his breaking point and his control snapped.

My leggings were pulled down hastily and his cock was out of his trousers within seconds. He rubbed his hardened length as his fingers worked my pussy all to the soundtrack of my moans. "I'm going to fuck you now, Sophie. Scream my name when you come. I want to hear it."

And with that, he sheathed himself inside of me and I felt myself crash into an ocean of bliss as he rode me hard, fast and at a punishing pace.

FORTY

I LOVED THAT SOPHIE SO WILLINGLY GAVE ME CONTROL IN THE BEDROOM. I'd had a lot of time to self-reflect through all those years she'd been gone. I understood that my need for control stemmed from feeling so out of control for so much of it and a large part of that was centered around Sophie leaving me. But her coming back to me and submitting to me so completely? The sense of complete and utter satisfaction it gave me wasn't something that I could easily describe. But that's love—something that can be felt so deeply but simultaneously inexplicable.

I thread my fingers through Sophie's beautiful red hair. Her breathing was even as her head rested against my chest. Her body was curled up next to me in my big bed and I wished we could stay like this forever. The world outside had been nothing but cruel to us, but at least in here, we could find some semblance of comfort with one another.

Sophie was adamant about going back to the loft and I understood her desire. All of her belongings were there and since she had finally relented to my request that she finish her exams, she did need to study. But the media frenzy had not died down yet and I did not want Sophie exposed to any of that. She was still a little shaky after everything that had happened and if I could shield her from the worst of it, I damn well would.

I promised that I would go back to the loft and get all of her belongings, but I was finding it hard to pull myself away from her at the moment. Sophie stirred and I looked down at her. She opened her eyes briefly and looked up into mine.

"Hey," she said sleepily.

"Hey gorgeous," I responded with a kiss to the top of her head.

"Sorry, fell asleep."

I shook my head. "I don't mind. I was just trying to find the will power to pull myself away and head to the loft."

Sophie's face turned into a bit of a pout. "I really think I should go with you."

"Soph." My features were hard and Sophie relented.

"Fine."

"Good girl," I said with another kiss to the top of her head. It took every shred of will power I had to pull myself away from her and out of the bed, all while she watched me with those clear green eyes of hers.

"What?" I asked as I pulled on a pair of jeans.

Sophie shook her head. "I guess I just don't get why you love me so much."

I abandoned buttoning my jeans and quickly made my way to her side. Sitting down, I pulled her into a careful embrace, wrapping my strong arms around her. "Sophie, I'd willingly spend the rest of my life trying to show you just how worthy of love you are."

I felt her sigh against me and I let her go slightly. A few tears glistened in her eyes as she looked up at me and I brushed them aside with my thumb. "How many times have I run from you or caused you problems, but still you come after me and fix everything. Why?"

I smiled softly. "Because I love you."

"You shouldn't."

"There you go being silly again," I replied, pulling her back into another deep embrace. When I finally felt her relax again, I let her go gently and tucked her back into the bed. "I'll be back, okay? I'm going to grab your stuff and come right back."

She nodded. I cupped her face and leaned forward, touching my lips to hers. "I love you, Soph. That's all there is to it. Try not to think too much about it."

She laughed softly. "Okay."

I finished dressing and within a few minutes, was on the road heading towards the loft. In the silence of the car, I had some time to turn over everything that had just happened to us over the last few days. Sophie leaving had only gone to show me that there was no way I could possibly be without her again. Watching her run the opposite direction from me with me unable to do anything to stop her from leaving damn near broke my heart.

But I also knew that as much as Sophie didn't want to admit it, her music and her career was actually really important to her. I wanted to do whatever I could to support that dream of hers that I could. And that meant getting her catalog of songs back into her own hands. I just hadn't completely figured out how to get that done yet.

Ringing blared through the car speakers, startling me as I pulled into the loft's parking lot. I looked at my dashboard to see Gus' name appear.

"Got anything?" I asked my private investigator.

"Yeah," Gus gruffed in response. "But I'm not sure you're going to like it."

I pulled into a parking spot and turned off the car and switched the call to my phone. I didn't want to chance a passerby overhearing any of my conversation.

"Go ahead."

"Xavier Payne. As you know, he's the owner of Charisma Records but that's not all. He operates out of New York but his investments are diversified throughout the country and overseas as well. It's pretty impressive that you were able to find out that he was in charge of Charisma. His name is nowhere on any of the corporate documents. This guy's intense, man."

I sucked in a slow breath at the information Gus was imparting to me. Gus was one of the most intense guys I had ever met. If he was passing that title on to someone else, well, it didn't bode well for getting Sophie's catalog back.

"Is there anything else?"

Gus made a sound on the other side of the phone before saying, "Yeah. Apparently you sold a building to him."

"I what?" I was in disbelief. I was very careful about who I did business with. My company's reputation was of utmost importance and legal always did a thorough search of anyone who proposed to purchase one of my developments.

"About three years ago. The building over on 11th street."

I tried to remember the deal. Three years ago would have been a little bit before the time that I really got my act together to try and turn things around with myself. Perhaps I'd been a little too careless at that time.

"Is the guy into anything underground? Illegal?"

"Not from what I can see, but that doesn't mean anything."

"Yeah, I hear you. Let me know if you find anything else."

"I'll tell you that that's unlikely, but you know I will."

The phone clicked off and I closed my eyes and rested my head on the seat. Perhaps I'd been a bit overzealous thinking I could just go after Charisma and get Sophie's catalog back. My straightforward attitude had always worked out well for me previously, but this might be a different sort of challenge than what I was used to. I shook my head and refocused on my goal. It didn't matter who was standing in my way. I'd figure out some way to get Sophie's life back for her.

Stepping out of the car, I climbed the stairs up to Sophie's door. Sliding the key into the lock, I pushed the door open and startled as a woman was sitting inside on the couch.

"Jesus, Skyler. You could have warned me you were going to be here," I said as I lowered my hand from my chest.

Skyler looked a bit annoyed. "Right. Like you could have told me that you'd found Sophie and that you guys were safe sooner than you did."

I sighed. I deserved that, but being scolded, and by one of my own students no less, was not something I enjoyed. "Yeah well, I told you. We just sort of got caught up in everything."

Skyler's face turned up into a smile and I shook my head at her teasing. "Anyways, stuff for Sophie is on the counter," she said with a nod of her head towards the little kitchen.

The relief was evident on my face as I turned to look at the pile. "Thanks."

"So you gonna tell me exactly what happened out there?" Skyler asked with a quirk of her eyebrow.

I considered the woman in front of me for a moment. She had been through some things in life, that was for sure. And she was fiercely loyal to Sophie, that was also clear. She cared for her friend a great deal and I figured I owed her an explanation of what was going on, since she was the one that helped get us back together.

"Well, I ended up conning the conman out of part of the rights to Sophie's career," I admitted.

"Um, what?" Skyler asked, her eyes widening.

"Yeah. The dirtbags she was working for were the ones that spread all the rumors about her in the first place."

"Holy shit."

"Yeah. It's a long story, but what matters is that I managed to close a deal that bought back all the rights to her career except for her catalog. Unfortunately, that's still owned by some guy named Xavier Payne."

The blood drained out of Skyler's face at the mention of the name. "What did you just say?"

"Her catalog of songs is still owned by a man named Xavier Payne. Well, technically it's still owned by Charisma Records, but that entity is controlled by him."

"So what are you planning to do about it?"

I narrowed my eyes. Something seemed off with the girl all the sudden. Like she was shaken. "Who said I was planning to do anything?"

Skyler crossed her arms and gave me a look. "Seriously, Driscoll? Who are you trying to fool?"

A small smile lifted the corner of my lips. "Am I really that easy of a read?"

"For most people, no. But reading people is sort of my thing."

"Right," I said as I walked over to the pile of Sophie's belongings.

Skyler hesitated. "But, in all seriousness, what are you planning to do?"

Now I knew something was up. I'd only met Skyler a couple of times, but uncertainty was never an emotion she had displayed before. I turned to face her and crossed my arms. "What are you not telling me?"

She fixed me with an intense stare. "Look, I don't like to talk about that man at all."

"You know him?" I asked with raised eyebrows.

"Sort of. I'll tell you what I know but just leave it at that, okay? I don't want any questions about . . . me."

My blue gaze was intense but Skyler didn't flinch under it. "Skyler," I started to say but she held up a hand.

"I will help Sophie however I can. Just please, respect that I've had shit happen in my life that I'd prefer to remain buried."

My jaw clenched but I nodded my head. "Fine."

Skyler returned the gesture and motioned for me to sit on the sofa. She took a deep breath and told me everything she knew.

I GATHERED TOGETHER ALL of Sophie's belongings and made my way to the door. "Thanks, Skyler," I said, my eyes kind and warm.

"It's no problem. Just remember, his biggest weakness is his reputation. He would never do anything to jeopardize the careful image he's crafted for himself. Attack him there and you just might have a shot."

I nodded my understanding, tucking the box of belongings under one arm.

"I understand."

"What is Sophie going to do about finals?" Skyler asked.

"I'm going to make a few calls to the registrar. See if we can't figure out some sort of remote arrangement for her considering all the media hype that is still going on."

"Good." She looked at me as I started to walk out the door. "I'm glad she has you."

I turned back and smiled at the woman. "Same goes for you, Skyler."

♪

I COULD HEAR music filtering into the lobby before I reached my apartment door. I smiled as I pushed the key into the lock and turned it. The chords grew louder and I could hear Sophie humming bits of melody to herself before stopping to jot it down. I stood there in the foyer for a second, just letting the sounds of her songwriting wash over me. I closed my eyes and sighed.

I'd listened to this sort of thing all through college at the loft. I'd be working on an assignment or playing a game and Sophie would always be on the floor with her guitar or in the corner on the small electric keyboard figuring out her next greatest hit. The sounds, disjointed as they were, were extraordinarily calming. They brought me back to a happier time and it gave me hope for our future.

Slipping out of my shoes, I adjusted the box and walked quietly into the living room, trying not to disturb her. As expected, Sophie was sitting on the floor in a pair of my boxers and a white tee, my refurbished guitar cradled between her crisscrossed legs. I turned and looked at her before she finally noticed me.

"Con!" she said with a smile, placing the guitar down carefully before leaping up.

I pushed the box of her books onto the countertop and turned to face her, wrapping my arms around her as she jumped towards me. I kissed her chastely on the lips before pulling back. "You should be asleep."

"Couldn't sleep. Slept on the plane. Besides, this was the first time in a long time that I got the urge to really write something." Her smile was genuine and my chest expanded a bit thinking that I might have had some small part to play in it.

"I'm glad. Don't let me stop you," I said, giving her another kiss before unwrapping her arms and pushing her back towards the guitar.

Sophie giggled and turned around, making her way to the box. "Was Sky mad?"

I thought about whether to share everything Skyler had told me but opted against it. I wouldn't keep anything from her, but at the same time, I didn't want to distract her right before final exams.

"No," I finally responded. "She just said to make sure you came and saw her when everything dies down."

Sophie huffed. "This really sucks. I really hate feeling like I'm imprisoned here."

I lifted an eyebrow. "First off, you're not imprisoned. You're lying low while the media frenzy dies down. And secondly, you've got nowhere to be, because you need to study for finals."

Sophie scrunched her face. "Ugh."

"Soph," I said, my tone deep.

She rolled her eyes. "I know, I know. Always the taskmaster."

I chuckled and shook my head. "It's for your own good."

"You always used to say that," she responded with a shake of her red hair.

"Because it was always true," I responded, crossing my arms. "Still is."

Sophie just stuck her tongue out at me and I laughed. I loved that she was feeling this carefree, especially after everything that had happened to her. Sophie might have claimed that she had been beaten down, but she had a resilience to her that was unrivaled.

I watched as she looked through the belongings in the box. "Thanks for grabbing these, by the way. I still have no clue how I'm going to take finals with everything that's happened."

"We'll get that sorted. I'll get a remote exam arrangement worked out for you."

"Isn't that something I should handle?"

I looked at her with narrowed eyes. "You study. I'll sort out the logistics."

"A man with a plan. Don't I love it?" Sophie said with a sly smile.

I just smiled and shook my head. "What were you writing?"

"Just something new," Sophie responded a bit bashfully.

"Play it for me?"

She chewed her lip as she looked down at the floor. I noticed the shift in her attitude immediately and I jumped to give her an out. "Or later, that's fine."

She looked up and smiled at me. "Thanks. It's not ready yet."

I nodded my head. "You really should get some sleep, Sophie."

Sophie leaned against the counter and looked me up and down. "There's something I've been wondering."

"Oh?" I asked, moving to the other side of the kitchen to grab myself a glass of water.

"You bought everything in my name?"

I placed my glass on the stone. "Well, technically a company I owned bought it and then O transferred my ownership shares to you. But, the end result is the same. Why do you ask?"

"MMS? What does that mean?"

My gaze was unflinching. "Bed, Sophie."

Sophie crossed her arms. "Now I know you're hiding something. You're dodging the question."

"I'll answer it later."

"When's later?"

"After bed."

Sophie huffed. "Connor, don't you think I should know the name of my own company?"

"It's not really important right now."

"So, it's going to be important later?"

"Sophie." My tone told her that I wasn't going to put up with her line of questioning anymore.

"Fine," she said with a huff. "But this conversation isn't over."

I raised an eyebrow. "Noted. Now, bed."

"Seriously, Connor, I'm not tired."

I fixed her with a knowing gaze. "Who said we would be sleeping?"

FORTY-ONE

Sophie

"CHEERS," CONNOR SAID AS HE TOUCHED HIS CHAMPAGNE GLASS TO mine. "Here's to finally finishing your degree."

"Assuming I didn't flunk an exam," I replied with a half giggle.

"Not funny, Soph. You're extremely smart and capable. I'm sure you did fine."

I laughed and took a drink of my champagne. Connor had been truly incredible in getting the university to agree to proctor my exams in one of the conference rooms on the first floor of his condo complex. When I'd finished my last one and come back upstairs, he'd had an entire dinner set out for us.

I put my glass down and took a bite of my pancakes. "I can't believe you got the Friendly Pancake to cater," I said with a laugh before pushing a bite of blueberry pancakes into my mouth.

"I thought about getting a chef, but then realized nothing but this would do."

"Damn straight," I said with a smile. "I'm glad you finally joined me on the dark side," I said, waving my fork at his chocolate chip pancakes.

He smiled. "I can make an exception for special occasions."

I giggled and speared a piece of his dinner before holding it out for him to eat. He fixed me with those intense blue eyes but indulged me nonetheless.

"So, finals over. Now I just need to figure out what to do with the rest of my life."

Connor shook his head. "Sophie, you already have that figured out."

"I do?" I asked, shaking my head before taking another swig of champagne.

"I'm not going to let you give up on your dream, Soph." There was so much conviction in Connor's voice. It made my heart clench a bit, but it also made me sad. I knew that Connor would do everything within his power for me, but it wouldn't be fair to do that to him, especially when the chances of me coming out alive from everything that had happened were slim to none.

"Con. I'm a big girl. I know when I've been beat. It's okay," I said, touching my hand to his across the table. "What you've done for me already is amazing and I don't know how I'll ever be able to repay you."

Connor grit his teeth. I could tell he really didn't want to have this conversation with me over our celebration dinner, but I wasn't giving him much of an option.

"Soph, I know everything that happened to you was really painful, but you have to know that none of that was your fault." I looked down at my pancakes, moving the pieces back and forth on the plate with my fork. "You just had the bad luck of being surrounded by dicks. And I'm not going to let anyone take advantage of you anymore or again."

"Con," I replied quietly. "I just," I sighed. How could I possibly tell him everything I had learned from Tara when I'd run into her at the airport. "Those people—Webb, Isaac, Charisma. They don't operate like a normal business. There's something else going on."

Connor narrowed his eyes. "What do you mean, Soph?"

My eyes stayed fixed on the plate in front of me. "I'm just saying, I don't think they play fair."

Connor shook his head. "Sophie, what aren't you telling me?"

I sighed and looked up into his clear blue eyes. "I ran into Tara when I was at the airport."

Connor's brow furrowed as he tried to place the name. "Tara? Wasn't she—?"

"Yeah," I said with a nod of my head. "She was the one that accused me of stealing her songs."

"Soph, I don't know what she had to say, but I'm not sure you should trust her."

My red hair swayed as I shook my head. "She was working at a Starbucks in the airport, Con. Charisma fired her."

"Why? I thought she was complicit with them?"

I shrugged. "She was forced to say what she said."

Connor's shoulders stiffened. "And you believed her?"

"She wouldn't have lied, not about what she was saying."

"Well, what was she saying?" Connor asked.

My lips pursed. "Her brother. He's apparently got a contract with Charisma. If she didn't cooperate, they'd both be terminated. Their father is ill. Without their paychecks, there'd be no way they could care for him."

Connor closed his eyes. "Sophie, in my line of work, I've heard a number of sob stories, and I hate to say that this is one that is used pretty frequently. A sick parent is always an easy excuse that pulls at the heartstrings."

I looked at Connor with wide eyes. "No. Con, please believe me when I say I know she wasn't lying."

"How can you know something like that."

If I was being honest, I understood why Connor was skeptical. I had been at first too. But there was something about Tara that day and the way she told me what she had—I just knew it was the truth. "I can't explain it, Con. You'll just have to trust me on this one."

Connor grit his teeth and put up his hands. "I'm not saying I don't trust you. You know I do. Just," he paused as I scrunched my face at him, "let me do a little more digging before we decide to just chuck it all."

"I just don't want you getting hurt, Con."

"Soph, that's supposed to be my line. You're mixing up our roles here," he responded with a wink.

"I never really was one to go by the rules," I said, taking another bite of my pancakes as my mouth lifted into a Cheshire-like grin.

"No, Miss Stronglen, you certainly were not," Connor said as he saluted me with his champagne flute before taking a hefty swig.

"Con, just promise me you're not going to do anything stupid."

"Sophie, I told you, you don't have to worry."

"Con, please," I said, the begging showing through in my eyes.

Connor's face softened and he nodded his head. "I promise."

My spirits lifted upon hearing his words and I got to work finishing the rest of my meal.

"Best damn dinner. What's for dessert?" I asked as I pushed my plate forward.

Connor stood, wiping his mouth discreetly on his napkin before circling the small table to my side. "Well you, of course."

Connor lifted me from my place at the table as I giggled. It'd been over two weeks since I'd even had the energy to engage in anything sexual with Connor and I was wondering when he might break.

True to my word, I took studying for my final exams seriously and that had me staying up well into the evenings most nights, even past when Connor had gone to sleep. I had to give Connor credit, he had given me space while I prepared and I was more than surprised that he had managed to make it through an entire dinner before whisking me away to his bedroom.

I giggled as he tossed me onto the bed. "God, the things I've wanted to do to you these past weeks," Connor breathed out as he looked down at me, sprawled out on his bed.

I pulled myself up and onto my knees, bringing myself to the side of the bed. Connor was on me in an instant, pressing his lips against mine as he pulled me flush against his body. I was only wearing a pull on jersey-knit dress. The thing was flimsy and easy to remove and with one swift movement, he had it up and off my body.

He pulled back slightly and I blushed under his gaze. Connor growled as I giggled and pulled at the belt to his jeans. "It's only fair," I said as I tugged on the leather strip, pulling it out of its loops.

Connor fisted his tee in his hands as he pulled it up and over his body. I sat back and watched as each row of sculpted abs followed by his beautiful tattoo was revealed and I sighed. "Maybe those egg white omelets are worth it after all," I muttered.

I caught Connor's eyes as I sucked two of my fingers into my mouth before letting them trail down my body to start rubbing against my clit. If I knew Connor, I knew he had initially planned this reunion to be slow, sensual and seductive, but I had other plans. Right now I wanted to fuck and he seemed entirely on board with that.

He pushed his jeans down and off his body as he watched me continue to work myself ever higher and higher. "Connor, baby," I moaned as I let my head fall back as I continued pressing my fingers over my pussy.

He didn't respond. Climbing onto the bed, he didn't even have to direct me before I was crawling towards him, working my hands over his boxer-clad cock.

"Fuck, Sophie. I missed you," he breathed out and I smiled. I loved driving Connor to a point where he lost control of himself. He was always so calm, so cool, so collected. The only time I was ever able to tip those scales was when we were in the bedroom.

"Missed this more than you know," I said as I pushed down on his shoulders so that he was sitting against the cushioned headboard. It was rare for Connor to give me the space to explore his body and I was going to take advantage of it. I began to trace the outline of the phoenix tattoo spread across his chest, dipping between his hardened pectoral muscles. At the same time, my hand moved down his body to grasp his cock.

He groaned and let his eyes close briefly as I began to pump him slowly, all while my tongue traveled to meet my hand. By the time my lips pressed against his lower abs, he'd opened his eyes back up so he could watch me. My lips opened and wrapped around his impressive cock, all while keeping my gaze locked with his own. His fingers thread through my flaming red hair as I began to work him up and down, circling the crown of his erection in time with my rhythm.

Wrapping my hair in his hand, he pulled me up off his cock and pressed his thumb into my lips. I sucked on it immediately, all while giving him the most wanton look. A glance down showed him that I had been toying with myself the entire time and I smiled as he looked back into my eyes.

"Come here, you dirty girl," he said, laying down fully on the bed. He pulled his thumb from my lips and encouraged me to move forward.

"Con, what are you—?" I began to ask but he interrupted me.

"Sit that perfect pussy of yours on my face, Soph. I'm going to suck that clit until you scream my name."

"Fuck," I breathed out as I felt Connor's strong grip wrap around my thighs and pull me forward, centering me over his mouth. His tongue against my folds had me gripping the large headboard for support and when he reached up to toy with my hardened peaks, I was sure it would only take me minutes to come.

His movements were skillful and he alternated between swirling my entrance, licking my folds and sucking my clit. His rhythm had me riding his face within minutes, and before long, I was screaming his name, just like he had promised I would.

Climbing off the bed, he positioned me on the edge, legs off to one side with my tits up in the air. My eyes were closed as I breathed out my release. He pushed his cock into me deeply and I groaned as my fingers fisted into the sheets. His strong hands gripped the small of my waist as he thrust into my body over and over and over again. His pace was punishing and I writhed under his touch.

I felt Connor's thick length withdraw before I was being pulled off the bed. His movements had an animalistic need to them and I was completely at his mercy. "Con," I breathed out, as he draped my legs over the side of the bed and pressed my breasts into the comforter.

I could feel his strong grip on the back of my neck and I gasped as his hard cock stretched my walls again. Connor's length moved in and out of me in this position and with every stroke, he hit that spot inside of me just right. Connor knew this was the position that could make me come and I knew he wasn't going to stop until I did.

I allowed myself to get lost in his rhythm, the pounding of his body against mine lulling me into a sense of calm as my lower muscles tightened in anticipation of what was to come. His hands slapping my ass was all I needed before his name tumbled from my lips once again.

Connor let himself go as soon as I clamped down on him. His body fell atop of mine as we rode out our waves of pleasure together and he pressed gentle kisses into my neck as our breathing finally started to even.

For the first time in two weeks, my lust was finally sated and he pulled out of me gently. Lifting me from the bed, he cradled me in his arms as I thread my hands around his neck. "Come on, let's get you cleaned up," he said, walking me into the bathroom.

"You'll only just get me dirty again," I murmured against his skin.

Connor chuckled. "That's a promise."

FORTY-TWO

"It all checks out," Gus said over the phone.

"Really?"

After Sophie had revealed her conversation with Tara, I had instructed Gus to do a little investigating to see whether what the girl had said was really the truth. At this point, any information I had that I could use as leverage with Charisma and Eternity when that time came would be needed. I'd really doubted that the girl's sob story was true, but as with everything with this industry, I'd been wrong.

"Yeah. Her brother's been signed with Charisma for a few years now and they actually do have an elderly father who is residing in a nearby nursing home. Not cheap."

"Damn."

"You didn't think it was legit?"

I raised my eyebrows at Gus' forward question. "I guess your skepticism has rubbed off on me."

Gus let out a short chuckle. "When you work in this industry, nothing really surprises you anymore."

"I can only imagine," I said. "Well, thanks for checking everything out. Do you have her contact information?"

"Yeah, I'll send it to you," Gus said and I nodded. "Thanks."

I put down the phone and a knock sounded on my door. The oak slid open and Sophie poked her head in. "Hey."

Her bright red hair was piled on the top of her head in a messy bun and she was sporting one of my shirts as an oversized dress. Simply put, she looked stunning.

"Hey," I said, pushing the phone aside and gesturing for her to come into the room.

She smiled at me and obliged. I shook my head as I watched Sophie walk into the room holding a spatula. "What are you doing?" I asked with a chuckle as she put the utensil on my desk and straddled me in my chair. My hands gripped the curve of her ass and she gasped as I pulled her tighter to my lap.

"Making us breakfast, what else?"

I moved in to place gentle kisses against Sophie's neck and she breathed out a contented sigh while stretching her head back. "Are you trying to get me to burn everything?"

"Maybe," I said with a smirk. "I guess it depends on what you're more in the mood for. Breakfast," I said placing another kiss to her neck, "or *breakfast*," I said with a bit more emphasis on the word before sucking a bit of her neck into my mouth. Sophie moaned as my hands moved up her body and I began to harden beneath her.

"Con, babe," she said between labored breaths.

"Hm?" I hummed my response as I continued to move my lips against her neck.

"Seriously, the stuff's gonna . . ." But before Sophie had the chance to finish her sentence, the kitchen smoke detector blared, startling us both out of our activities. "Shit!" Sophie exclaimed with a laugh as she tumbled off my lap and grabbed her spatula, running back into the kitchen.

I just chuckled at the entire scene before standing and calmly walking into the kitchen.

"Look what you made me do!" Sophie huffed as I strode into the space. She held up a frying pan with something in the center charred beyond belief.

"What was that supposed to be?"

Sophie twisted her lips. "It was *supposed* to be your breakfast." She narrowed her eyes and held the spatula up. "And you better behave otherwise it might still be your breakfast."

My eyebrows raised at her teasing challenge and I stepped closer to her. "Oh, is that so?"

Sophie bit her lip and smiled. "No, not really. Not even I'm that cruel."

I chuckled. "Good to know."

Sophie pushed my shirt a little higher on her shoulders since it was dangerously close to slipping off given our previous activities before walking the pan over to the garbage and attempting to scrape off the mess.

"Who were you talking to on the phone?" she asked nonchalantly.

"No one important," I replied, trying to dodge the question. I walked over to the refrigerator and grabbed two eggs, intent on making an omelet.

"Con," Sophie said, letting her foot go from the trashcan lever and turning to face me. "I'm really not one to hover, but I just have a bad feeling that you're poking your head where it doesn't belong."

I was about to open my mouth to respond but Sophie's ringtone distracted us both from our premature argument. Sophie rounded the counter and smiled as she saw the name.

"Hey Sky! . . . Yeah, finished my last exam a few days ago. . . I know, I'm sorry, I'm a terrible friend. . . . I've just been trying to lie low with everything." Sophie turned and gave me an interesting look. "I don't know. I'd have to ask my warden," she said with a giggle.

"Ask your warden what?" I said, opting to play along with the ruse rather than get angry. The fantasy of being Sophie's warden would be rather fun to act out.

"Sky wants to get together."

I shrugged. "She's welcome here anytime, you know that."

Sophie frowned. "Con, no offense, but I'm really sick of being cooped up here."

I sighed. We had had this conversation before. "Sophie, I'm just not certain it's safe for you to go out yet."

"Give me a minute, Sky," Sophie said as she pulled the phone away from her ear and pressed mute so we could argue in private.

"Con, I know you're just trying to protect me, but it was Webb and Jacobs that orchestrated the whole media frenzy to begin with. Without anyone to pay for photographs, there's no reason for anyone to give a shit about me. I really think everything has blown over by now."

I inhaled a deep breath. Sophie's explanation sounded reasonable and I understood how difficult it must be for her to be separated from her friends and her home during this time. "Okay, but keep your cell on and if *anything* seems slightly suspicious, I want you to call me immediately."

Sophie grinned. "Deal."

"TAKE CARE OF MY WOMAN," I said to Skyler as Sophie climbed into her old hatchback that looked extremely out of place at my complex's garage.

"You got it, boss," Skyler said with a mock salute. "I promise we'll only get into reasonable amounts of trouble."

"That's all any man could ask," I said with a wave as Sophie blew me a kiss and Skyler peeled out of the garage.

As I waited for the elevator to take me back to my apartment, I opened my phone and tapped the email from Gus.

"Tara's contact information below," was all the message said followed by a phone number, email and address. I waited until I was back in the privacy of my home office before I pressed the girl's number.

"Hello?" a tentative voice responded after a few rings.

"Tara Cecile?"

"Yeah, this is her. Who is this?"

"My name's Connor, I'm a friend of Sophie's."

There was silence on the end of the line before the girl finally spoke again. "Okay, what do you want?"

"Tara, Sophie told me everything that happened. She told me about your brother and your father and what Charisma made you do."

The girl was silent, but that was okay. Silence was better than her hanging up on me.

"I've got a plan to fix everything, but I'm going to need your help."

"I don't think I can help you," the girl responded quietly.

I closed my eyes and leaned back in my chair. "Just hear me out. I know Charisma threatened to terminate your brother's contract if you didn't do what they asked."

"Or if I came forward after. I'm sorry, but if Sophie told you everything, then you know why we need that money."

"I completely understand, but what if I told you I was willing to cover the costs of your father's care while your brother moved to a different label? I just need your help, Tara."

There was silence on the line again as the girl considered my offer.

"You seem like a nice man and all, and I'm glad Sophie has someone who wants to fight so hard for her, but there's no way I could go public against Charisma." Her voice became hushed as she added, "There's more going on there than you might think. You really should stay away."

"I'm aware of what's going on," I lied. I had some inkling, but the full extent of Charisma and Eternity's dealings was still a mystery to me. "Which is why this is so important. And I would never ask you to go public. It would just be as simple as securing your word so I could let them know you were willing to talk."

More silence, this time longer. I could feel I was losing her, but I'd put almost all my chips on the table. This was the last one I was able to play.

"Tara, if Sophie's friendship meant as much to you as I know it did to her, you'd agree to help her."

Tara sighed audibly through the line. "I'm sorry. I guess I didn't deserve her friendship, because I just can't."

The line clicked dead.

"Fuck," I cursed, throwing my head back in my chair and covering my eyes with my hands. I really had hoped that Tara would have gotten on board with doing the right thing, especially since I offered to secure her family financially if there was any fall out. Was this Payne guy really as scary as everyone was making him out to be? That was the second person who knew him personally to warn me off.

I grit my teeth. I had made a promise to Sophie that I would get her catalog back and I'd meant it. I wasn't going to just run scared because some bully intimidated people into submission. That's what got us here in the first place and the only way to beat a bully was to punch back.

I just needed to figure out some form of leverage to use against this guy. If what Skyler told me was true, he cared more about his reputation than anything. I had experience exploiting that trait in business deals and I knew I could work the same angle here. But, I still needed something that could threaten Payne's reputation.

The recording of Webb wouldn't be enough and I knew that. While it'd been sufficient to scare a man as anxious as Webb into submission, the media would question it and Charisma could easily claim it was altered. I knew I needed something more.

I thought that might be Tara, but that appeared to be out of the question now. I wouldn't push the girl. She was scared and I could respect her choice, even if I disagreed with it. I stood and began pacing the room, trying to think of what I could possibly do to disprove one of the rumors Webb and Jacobs had started.

Sophie had piled her schoolbooks high at the end of finals in the corner of my office, stacking her laptop on top and my pacing made the pile start to sway and shake.

"Shit!" I exclaimed, lunging for the computer as the stack began to tip. I caught it just in time as the other books crashed around me. I sat on the floor and breathed in a heavy breath before placing the laptop carefully on the nearby bookshelf.

And then it dawned on me.

Sophie's laptop.

The last time I had looked at it, I'd found the video of her writing the song that made her the most famous. The one that Tara had declared to the world at the press conference that Sophie had stolen from her own journal.

I stood and rushed over to my computer. I remembered I had emailed it to myself that night I flew to LA to deal with Webb and Jacobs. I found the email relatively quickly and I double-clicked the video to bring it onto my screen.

A younger, but just as vibrant Sophie was sitting on the floor of the loft, guitar in her lap, fumbling with the computer screen to tilt it just right. When she finally had it adjusted, she pulled back and strummed a chord or two.

"Okay, I just wrote this so it might not be all the way worked out yet but. Wait, why am I talking to myself?" the former Sophie said with a roll of her eyes before she started to sing.

She was perfect.

It was perfect.

And it was exactly what I needed to get this entire mess sorted.

FORTY-THREE

Rebecca

I BIT MY NAILS IN CONTEMPLATION AS I READ AND REREAD THE EMAIL.

To: Charisma Records
From: MMS, LLC
Subject: Meeting
Ms. Murphy,

Allow me to introduce myself. I am the investor who purchased Sophie Strong's concert and image rights from an affiliated entity of Charisma and Eternity Music Group. As such, I have a vested interest in the reputation of my client. I have uncovered some interesting information regarding the accusations levied against her and I think it warrants a meeting. I am prepared to go to the press with this information, but prefer to handle things at the lowest level, first. Please send your avoid dates so we can get a meeting set.

It wasn't signed but I knew it was from Connor Driscoll, Sophie's meddlesome ghost from the past. I continued to chew my nails as I tried to decide what I needed to do.

The thought of informing Payne crossed my mind. I didn't want him thinking I was incompetent or that I'd go running to him any time there was an issue, but whoever this guy was, he had already proven himself clever once before.

"Be prepared for some trouble in the future. Don't end up like Webb. Don't let this man play games or pull one over on you."

Payne's words from our last meeting rang in my ears and it gave me my answer.

Hitting the forward button on the email, I hit the letter "x" and his name populated.

"We should talk," was all I wrote in the body of the email before hitting send.

His response was almost immediate.

"Come upstairs."

I stood and smoothed the fabric to my lavender suit slowly. I took a deep breath, steeled my nerves and then exited my office. Each step in my perfect leather stilettos was measured as I made my way to the floor above me.

I was under no delusions. I may have slept with Payne on a few occasions, but even I was not safe from having my world ripped from me. In some ways, I was responsible for this entire situation. Webb and Jacobs reported to me and had pulled their antics under my watch. While Payne was generally reasonable with me, which in and of itself was quite the feat, I could easily understand him placing this blame squarely on my shoulders.

And if that happened, there would be consequences.

There were always consequences when someone fucked up.

I only hoped that I could salvage the situation enough to count this as a close call and remind myself to never get too complacent ever again.

"Come," Payne said at the tap on his door. I opened the door and his eyes raked my body up and down. "Sit," he said, directing me to the seat in front of his desk with a nod of his head.

I made my way to his desk and did as I was told, waiting for him to start the conversation.

Payne cleared his throat and narrowed his eyes at me. He looked at his laptop and began to read the email in question out loud.

"Allow me to introduce myself. I am the investor who purchased Sophie Strong's concert and image rights from an affiliated entity of Charisma and Eternity Music Group. As such, I have a vested interest in the reputation of my client. I have uncovered some interesting information regarding the accusations levied against her and I think it warrants a meeting. I am prepared to go to the press with this information, but prefer to handle things at the lowest level, first."

He turned his eyes back to me, who was sitting unflinching in my chair. "What do you think he has?"

I let out a repressed breath. "Jack or Tara. Those are the only two people who had any information that might put us at risk."

Payne raised an eyebrow. "Jack Tanner is a long-standing scout with Eternity. He knows the consequences of talking out. But I'm was not against confirming. Go ahead and have Jack looked into, but for the record, my money's not on him."

"Tara then?"

"It is a shame that we had to convince her to speak out against Sophie. She resisted, but her brother's contract had been the perfect leverage. It would surprise me if Tara put something like that at risk, especially given what I know of her home situation." He paused. "But women have a way of doing the most illogical things sometimes." He hesitated again. "We've still got her brother signed with us?"

"That's right," I replied with a nod, keeping my face impassive.

"And there's been no indication that she's had any contact with this Driscoll?"

"Also correct."

Payne rubbed his chin and leaned back in his chair. "Terminate his contract anyways."

My eyes widened slightly as I nodded my head.

"I can tell that you disagree with the decision. But this move is calcu-lated. If Tara did have contact with Driscoll, then it will come out as soon as her brother is informed that his contract is terminated. And if it turns out that she wasn't involved, well, her brother has never made us as much money as I had hoped for." He narrowed his eyes at me. "You think that you're equipped to handle this meeting by yourself?"

I swallowed, trying to hide my nerves. "Yes," I said confidently. "If that's your preference, I'd be happy to handle it."

Payne considered me for a moment and I tried not to shake under his gaze.

"No, I don't think I'll have you handling it," he said abruptly. I stayed quiet and let him continue. "I think I'd rather like to meet the man who has managed to bring two very successful companies of mine to their knees."

My eyes widened. It'd been quite some time since Xavier had shown interest in just about anything. He was always so rigid, so controlled, it was surprising. And to admit that this man might actually be affecting him or something he controlled—well, it wasn't the Xavier I knew.

"I understand," I responded simply, realizing I better not push my luck. I waited with bated breath to see whether Payne would inform me that my contract had been terminated—or worse—but he did neither of those things. He just smiled at me and said, "That's all. You're excused."

I nearly stumbled in surprise as I stood, said "thank you," and exited his office without any further conversation. When I was back downstairs in the safety of my own space, I locked the door, kicked off my shoes and leaned against the solid oak, thankful that I had an office that was actually private, rather than some glass prison.

I took deep breaths as I calmed my heart rate. I hadn't realized that I had been so nervous through our entire meeting. But then again, Payne had that effect on, not just me, but on everyone. I was just glad that I had managed to survive this fuck up. It wouldn't happen again, that was for damn sure.

My breathing back in check, I slipped my shoes back on and strode back to my desk. I had a phone call to make and another artist's heart to break.

FORTY-FOUR

Sophie

"So you've been writing again?" Skyler asked as she took a bite into her burger—well, veggie burger. Skyler had driven us to the outskirts of the town to grab fast food at her favorite "burger" joint, which actually turned out to be a vegan spot. I took a bite of my own plant-based meal and had to admit, the thing tasted damn good. I shoved a few fries into my mouth before nodding with a full mouth.

"Yeah."

"Just yeah?" Skyler responded, jabbing me lightly with her elbow. "That's awesome!" she exclaimed, taking a sip of her "milk" shake.

I smiled and looked out over the scenic overlook. The gently rolling hills below were really gorgeous and I had to give it to Sky. When she'd pulled us off the highway onto what looked like barely a dirt road, I'd been skeptical. But as we sat eating our meal, sitting on a picnic table overlooking the world below us, I finally felt a bit of normalcy return to my life.

"When things with Connor resolved, I dunno, the music just started flowing again."

Skyler nodded her head and smiled. "That's awesome, babe. I'm so happy for you two. He seems really great. I'm totally glad I helped you seduce him."

I nearly snorted my drink as I laughed at Sky's words. "I almost forgot about that. God, it seems like a lifetime ago, doesn't it?"

"Maybe not a lifetime," Skyler said, looking a bit pensive, "but yeah, it does feel like longer than four months."

I took another bite of my burger before I placed it down and leaned back on my hands.

"What's eating you?" Skyler asked. I gave her a look like it was nothing but Skyler insisted. "Come on, you can't hide things from me. What gives?"

I twisted my face but complied. "I just feel like Connor has done so much for me and I'm worried my life is totally going to fuck things up for him."

Skyler shook her head as she put a few fries in her mouth. "What do you mean?"

"I mean, already he's done so much to pull me out from the shit storm my life became. He's really resourceful and super capable. But I'm worried he's about to go too far and is going to get stuck himself."

Skyler narrowed her eyes. "Don't follow."

"Apparently my catalog is still owned by Charisma, or their parent company or something. I don't know, Connor explained it to me but it's all that crazy corporate stuff."

"Okay, so what does that mean?"

"It means, that knowing Connor, he's going to try and get it back."

"So, why are you worried about him? He proved himself capable before. Who's to say he isn't able to do this too?"

I sighed. "When I was back in LA the last time, I ran into my old song coach."

"Wait? The girl that accused you of stealing her shit? That old song coach?"

I tried not to catch Skyler's gaze but I knew the woman had nailed it. "Yeah," I responded a bit sheepishly. "I know what you're going to say, but—" I started but Skyler cut me off.

"Sophie, look I get your desire to want to trust people. I think deep down, it's because you're a really good person, but you can't honestly think that this girl has your best interests at heart."

I shrugged. "I don't see what she really has to gain from it? She just told me that it would be better if I stayed away from Charisma. And I can't help but keep hearing her words as I think about Connor and what he might be walking into."

"What has he said he's going to do?" Skyler asked.

"Nothing yet. But you and I both know that that's unlikely to stay the same for very long."

We stayed quiet, both of us trying to figure out a solution to this rather unsolvable problem. Finally, Skyler piped up. "I just think you need to be honest with him. Tell him why you're worried and if you really don't want him going after your catalog, you should tell him that."

A sad smile lifted my lips. "That's the really fucked up thing, though. Because if there is some chance that Connor might be able to get my songs back . . . does it make me a bad person that I want that to happen? Even though it might put him and his company at risk?"

Skyler rubbed my back comfortingly. "No, babe. It doesn't make you a bad person to want your songs back. If you asked me whether you were a bad person for wanting your songs back and you didn't care what happened to Connor in order to make that happen, well, then I might have a different answer," she said with another jab of her shoulder and I couldn't help but smile. "But obviously, that's not what's going on here. You worked hard on those songs and bad people are profiting from your hard work. It's only natural that you would want that to stop."

I gave my friend a look of gratitude before grabbing the last bite of my burger and shoving it into my mouth. I smiled at the knowing look Skyler was giving me.

"They're good aren't they?"

I had to nod as I savored every last bite. "Fucking delicious," I finally said through a partially full mouth.

Skyler laughed. "See, told you!" She sucked down the rest of her cookies and cream float as I took a drag on my own. The sun was just starting to set and I turned to my friend and wrapped my arms around her.

"Thanks, Sky," I said a bit sheepishly as my friend hugged me back.

"For what?"

We parted and I looked out at the sunset. "For just being here. For being willing to take a chance on me when the rest of the world wouldn't. When everything went to shit I never thought I'd be able to trust anyone ever again. But you really proved me wrong. So, thanks, I guess."

Skyler shook her head. "You don't need to thank me for being a friend, doll. You've given me a lot in return, too. I'm glad I've got you in my life."

FORTY-FIVE

To: MMS, LLC
From: Charisma Records
Subject: Re: Meeting
Dear Sir,

We have received your request for a meeting and are happy to accommodate you on May 1st at 2 p.m. The meeting will be held at Charisma's office in downtown Los Angeles. Please confirm receipt of this correspondence and your ability to attend at the time and place indicated.

I SAT BACK IN MY CHAIR AND SMILED. THAT WAS A BIT EASIER THAN I had expected. Although, the timeframe was cutting it fairly close to Sophie's graduation, that being the third, but I would make it work.

I reached for my keyboard in order to respond but my phone rang,

353

momentarily distracting me. I lifted it to look at the screen and saw a number I didn't recognize. "Connor Driscoll," I said in a firm voice.

"Um, hi, Mr. Driscoll, this is Tara."

My back went rigid as I realized it was Tara Cecile calling me back. I only hoped that she had good news ahead of this meeting.

"Tara. Good to hear from you. What can I do for you?"

The girl seemed nervous and despite the entire width of the country between us, I could feel her anxious energy through the phone. "I was wondering—hoping—that what we had discussed before was still available."

I furrowed my brow as I tried to make sense of the girl's words. "Do you mean my offer to provide care for your father while your brother finds a different label?"

"Yes," she said sheepishly.

"Of course, Tara. I'm a man of my word. If you're willing to help clear Sophie's name, then if your brother's contract is canceled, I'll be sure to assist while he finds something else."

"Yeah, right. Well, they already did that."

"Who already did what?"

"Charisma. They terminated his contract."

My stomach dropped. Did this have something to do with my conversation with Tara? But how could they have known about that? She didn't work for them anymore and last time I checked, it wasn't legal for music companies to wiretap people's phones.

"I'm so sorry to hear that, Tara. Do you and your brother have somewhere safe to stay?"

There was a bit of quiet on the other end of the line before Tara finally spoke. "They've given us a week to vacate his apartment."

I squeezed my eyes shut. I truly could not believe what I was hearing. While I didn't have any direct evidence, I had a feeling that my previous email had something to do with this call. The timing was too suspect for it to be anything else. I wasn't the type of man to create a problem for someone and then leave them to their own devices.

"Tara, I know it's a long-distance but I'd happily put you and your brother up in one of my rental units here in the city. If you'd like, we can have your father transferred out here as well so that you can be near to him."

"Um, can I think about that for a day?"

"Of course."

There was silence on the phone before I spoke up. "I've got a meeting scheduled for May 1st with Charisma. If I came to LA a day or two before, do you think you'd be up to speak about everything that happened with me in person?"

I could hear Tara gulp on the other end of the line and I added, "Please be assured, I'm not going to share anything with Charisma unless you allow me to. And of course, I would not ask you to attend the meeting."

I could hear Tara breathe a sigh of relief before she agreed. "Yes, okay. There's a small diner just outside of the airport. You can't miss it. I can meet you there when I get off my shift at five the day before your meeting."

"Okay, that sounds great, Tara," I said kindly.

"Um," the girl hesitated. "Is Sophie going to be there?"

"No," I said immediately. "Sophie won't be coming to this meeting."

"Oh," Tara said, but I couldn't quite suss out whether the girl was happy or sad about that. "Okay, well I'll see you in a few days," she said before the line went dead.

I put the phone down and realized that I had paced myself clear across the room.

"What meeting is Sophie not going to?"

I startled before turning around to find Sophie, red hair high on her head, in a pair of denim shorts with her arms crossed over her loose lace top.

"You're home," I said, trying to recover as I ran my hand through my thick black hair.

Sophie took another step into the room but didn't uncross her arms. "What. Meeting. Connor?" she asked, emphasizing each word.

"Sophie, I really don't want you to worry about it. I want you to focus on enjoying yourself before graduation."

Sophie's lips twisted and I could tell we were about to have it out about the Charisma matter.

"Connor, please do not tell me you've scheduled a meeting with Charisma over my songs." I leaned against my desk and crossed my own arms.

"Sophie, I told you I was going to handle this for you. Yes, I am in the process of scheduling a meeting with Charisma and everything is going to be okay."

Sophie looked up in agitation. "I don't even have words to describe how angry I am about this right now, Con."

She fixed me with those clear green eyes of hers and I held her gaze. "Quite frankly, Sophie, I don't care how angry you are. I'm doing this, end of story."

"What the fuck, Connor? Why can you not just drop this? Don't you get that I don't want to drag you down any more than you've already been? It's just not worth it."

I couldn't resist the impulse to walk forward and grab her. She stepped back but I wrapped her in my arms and pressed my lips against her hair. She finally calmed and I spoke in a low, soothing voice. "If I've told you once, I've told you a million times, Sophie. You haven't dragged me down at all. Now please, stop saying things like that."

She breathed out a heavy sigh and I loosened my grip slightly so that she could look up at me. "Why is this so important to you?"

"It's important to me because, deep down, I know it's important to you. Those are your songs. You wrote them. They should always be your songs. I'm not letting some thug profit off my woman's hard work."

"Oh, so I'm your woman now?" Sophie asked with a sly smile.

My mouth tightened, as did my grip on her. "Absolutely. And if I had it my way, that would be a permanent arrangement."

Sophie's breath caught in her throat. "A permanent arrangement? What do you—?" she stumbled over her words, not sure what to make of what I had said.

I squeezed her tighter. "It's what I've always wanted, Soph. And I know it's what you wanted too."

Sophie shook her head as tears started to fall down her eyes. "What do you mean? All I've done is mess things up."

I pulled back and Sophie steadied herself as she watched me walk to my desk and pull out the top drawer. I lifted the false leather bottom and grabbed a simple, plain white envelope. Walking it back to Sophie, I handed it to her.

"Do you remember this?" I asked.

She shook her head. She didn't reach for it but I took her hand and put it in hers.

"Read it."

♪

Sophie

I LOOKED up at him but the only thing showing in his eyes was reassurance. I took a deep breath and opened the letter. The piece of old notepaper crinkled in my hands as I unfolded it.

It was in my handwriting, written in red ink. I'd always loved the color red and insisted on doing all of my journaling and songwriting in the color. I ran my hands over the words as I started to realize this was the note I had left for Connor the night I left for LA. The ink had been smeared with water droplets here and there and deep down I knew it was evidence of Connor's tears, shed alone in an empty loft.

Con—

I'm sorry I had to leave like this, but this is my dream! I know you just want what's best for me and I love you for that.

I've known about how you've felt about me for some time now. I wish you would have admitted your feelings to me. I wish I would have admitted my feelings to you.

I love you, Connor Driscoll. I might have been too stupid to realize it, but now that I have to leave you, I know that it's true.

Maybe this is for the best. Maybe I would have never realized it if I didn't have to leave. I know this isn't easy for you. Trust me, it's not easy

for me either. But I know we'll be together again soon. As soon as I get
settled, I want you to come visit me. And then we can figure out us.
  —*Soph*

I looked up from the letter, tears streaming down my face, to find Connor on one knee in front of me.

"Connor, no, what are you doing?" I asked, stumbling over my words upon seeing Connor kneeling in front of me.

"Sophie." Connor took my hands in his and looked up at me with his clear blue eyes. "I love you. I've always loved you. I don't care how complicated your life might be. None of that matters as long as I get to be in it."

"Con, what are you doing?" I repeated, not able to believe what I was sure was about to happen.

Connor smiled. "I'm proposing," he paused, "a deal."

"What?" I exclaimed.

"I want to prove to you that I am more than capable of being your partner in your world, that you don't have to worry about me or what effect your life might have on mine."

"Okay," I said quietly.

"So, here's the deal," Connor said. "When I win back your song rights, we get married."

"Connor."

"I'm serious about this, Sophie. I want you to be mine. Let me get back what belongs to you so we can start a new life together."

I bit my lip as I considered Connor's offer. I still felt incredibly torn about the prospect of getting Connor caught up in my mess. "If I said no?"

Connor chuckled. "Then I still get back your songs and after that, I work on convincing you to marry me."

"Fine," I said, a smile at the corner of my lips giving away how happy I truly was. "You've convinced me."

Connor stood to his full height and wrapped me in his arms. He pressed his lips to mine and I allowed myself to be pulled into his dominating kiss. His hands roamed my body and I moaned my response. I could feel his impressive length begin to harden and press against my body and I groaned.

"Fuck, Con. Why do you always make me want you?"

His lips pulled away from mine long enough to respond, "The feeling's mutual, Soph."

With that, he tugged my top up and over my head so that all I was wearing was a pair of cut off denim shorts. His lips tugged against my earlobe as his hands came up to cup my breasts. My breath shuddered and my body responded to his actions, my nipples puckering against his palms instantly.

Connor pulled back and looked at me. My lips were puffy from his attention and I was breathing heavily. "I'm going to bend you over my desk and fuck you until you can't walk tomorrow, Soph. Do you understand?"

I nodded my head and he kissed my forehead. "Good girl. Now, stand back and strip out of those shorts for me," he said with a sly smile.

I bit my lower lip but complied, taking two steps back and pushing the denim over the swell of my hips. I started to remove my thong but Connor shook his head. "Leave that on." My eyes widened but I complied, standing back up, completely bared to him except for a small slip of fabric covering my sex.

I longed to reach out and touch him, but he was standing just out of reach, his eyes roaming my body like he was some sort of predator. His own hands moved down his body before he unbuttoned his pants and pushed them down far enough so he could free his cock. He smirked at the look of complete longing on my face as he pulled it out and began to stroke it slowly.

"Tell me how much you want this cock, Sophie."

"Fuck, Connor. Please let me suck your cock."

"More," he demanded.

I bit my lip. "I want to wrap my lips around your thick shaft and run my tongue up and down your length."

Connor closed his eyes as he continued to stroke himself to my words. "Okay," he finally said and I rushed toward him, grabbing his cock out of his hands and wrapping my lips around him quickly.

Connor moaned as I got down on my knees in front of him, sucking him for all I was worth. My lips moved deeper and deeper on his length and he groaned. "Fuck, Soph," he said. He thread his fingers through my hair.

"Sophie, stop," he said as he guided me off his cock with the hand he had in my hair. I looked up at him and licked my lips like I was hungry for more. "Face the desk and bend over," Connor instructed and I stood with a smile and did as I was told.

Connor took a moment to tuck himself back into his boxer briefs before walking calmly over to where I was standing. My ass was on display, a single bit of lace dipping between each cheek. Connor reached out with his finger and trailed the black slip of material with the faintest of touches. My breath hitched as I squirmed against the desk and Connor smiled.

When his finger reached the bottom of the material, he pushed it aside so that my sex was exposed, but didn't touch me. He stepped back and left me standing there, exposed and wanting. "Con," I moaned, but he didn't respond. My body squirmed in anticipation and I couldn't see him.

I gasped as I felt his fingers trail up my legs, closer and closer to where I needed him. I had no doubts that I had already left a puddle below where I was standing. I was fully prepared for Connor to tease me, pull back and deny me everything that I wanted, but I nearly keened as I felt his fingers enter me in one swift motion.

His fingers curled against a spot deep within me expertly and he began to work me up the side of a cliff face I had become intimately familiar with. "Con, yes," I breathed out as I climbed higher and higher.

Just when I thought I might come, his fingers withdrew but were replaced with his tongue. The feeling of his mouth sucking my clit had me crashing into an even greater pleasure as I screamed my release and pulsed against his tongue.

Standing, he pulled his cock back out of his boxers and stroked himself a few times. "Grip the edge of the wood, Soph."

I complied and I could feel Connor move the tip of his cock against my drenched slit. "Fuck, Connor, please fuck me."

"Oh, Sophie. I am going to fuck this tight little cunt of yours so hard and so rough, just you wait," he replied, his voice gravelly with need.

He allowed the tip of his cock to slide into me just slightly and I moaned, trying to push myself back to take him in further. A hand came down to slap my ass as he chuckled and said, "Naughty, impatient girl. You will be fucked soon enough."

He pulled out and I nearly whined my frustration. But just as I was about to turn around and tell him that he better fuck me already, he sheathed himself completely. I moaned and my body arched off the desk slightly.

"Keep that grip on the desk, Soph," he said, leaning over me and putting my hands back on the edge of the wood. His breath was hot against my ear. "This tight cunt of yours is mine now."

"Fuck," I breathed out as his words sent tingles straight to my core. Connor pulled back and began to slide in and out of me. His movements were not gentle and with each thrust, I moaned at the feeling of him moving inside of me. Connor wrapped a hand around my neck, using it as leverage to rock against me harder.

I was always impressed at Connor's stamina and he didn't disappoint me. He continued thrusting in and out of me until my fingers ached from holding onto the edge of the desk.

His movements began to falter as he breathed out that he was about to come. "Yes, come inside me, Con!"

With a roar of my name, Connor came, pouring himself into me as he pulsed his release. The two of us stood there, each trying to catch our breath until Connor finally pulled out of me. He pushed himself back into his boxers before grabbing a few tissues and wiping my sex clean.

"Come on," he said, tossing the tissues into the trash and helping me stand. "I'll start the shower," he said, kissing my temple as I smiled up at him, still hazy from my orgasm.

FORTY-SIX

Sophie

IT WAS A WEIRD FEELING FOR ME AS I LOOKED OVER AT THE MAN I MIGHT be marrying soon, rinsing off his body under the spray. I'd meant everything I'd written in that original letter. I really had wanted us to end up together. But when Connor and I had lost touch, I had forced those dreams under the rug.

And when he'd shown up back in my life, I'd felt too guilty about screwing up his to realize how much I really wanted to be with him. Long story short, I knew I was a whirlwind, but I couldn't help loving Connor the way I did.

I was glad Connor had forced his way back into my life. And I was glad he had convinced me to accept his deal. I didn't know whether I would ever have had the courage to take things any further.

"Hey," Connor said, wrapping me in his arms. "I know that look. What's on your mind?"

I smiled and leaned against his warm skin. "Nothing."

"I know that's not true," Connor said softly.

"I'm just glad you decided I was worth it, that's all."

Connor squeezed me tighter. "One of these days, I'm going to convince you just how worth it you truly are, Sophie. I can't stand that you say things like that about yourself."

I sighed. "Don't worry about that now," I said as I finished rinsing off myself before stepping out of the shower. Connor followed suit and grabbed a towel, wrapping it around me and drying me off. I smiled at how caring he was. I really didn't deserve him. "So what's the plan?" I asked as I sat on the edge of the tub as Connor dried himself off. He raised his eyebrow and I gave him a face. "Come on, Con. I know how you operate. You've always got a plan."

Connor chuckled. "Guilty. I'll be heading to LA to handle the negotiations with Charisma."

"Come again?" I asked with a bit of an attitude.

"I said, I'll be heading to LA to handle the negotiations with Charisma," Connor replied in a flat tone.

"Okay, so when do *we* leave?" I asked, putting emphasis on the "we."

"*I'll* be leaving in three days," Connor responded, wrapping the towel around his hips and giving me a firm stare.

Connor must have known that he looked utterly sexy, water droplets meandering their way down his body, with a white towel wrapped low on his hips. I reminded myself that this was too important of an issue to let him distract me.

"You better make sure you book a ticket for two, otherwise I'll head out there myself." Connor was about to say something but I stopped him. "And you know I'll do it, Con."

Connor gave me an appraising look before nodding his head. "Fine. I couldn't stop you from coming anyway, given that you're a part-owner," he said with a wink.

"I'm glad you've seen reason," I said, standing to follow Connor out into the bedroom. "Okay, so we go there. But what's the actual plan?"

Connor let his towel drop and I bit my lip. He turned and caught me gazing at him and he shook his head. "Please, Sophie. Do try and stay focused."

I laughed and threw a pillow at him. He batted it away easily before walking into his closet. When he came out, he was sporting a pair of track pants and a white tee that hugged his form perfectly.

"Are you just going to stay in a towel all day?" Connor said with a raised eyebrow.

I stuck my tongue out at him in a teasing way before dropping my towel and heading into the closet myself, but not before saying, "Please, Connor. Do try and stay focused."

He slapped my ass lightly as I walked into the large walk-in and I giggled.

"I actually got in touch with Tara," Connor said, his voice a little louder so it would carry into the closet.

I paused as I put on my clothes. "Oh? I didn't know you knew her."

"I didn't, Soph. I had a private investigator do some digging on what you told me about her. It all checks out and she's agreed to help us."

I pulled my own white tee over my head and slipped on a pair of panties and cotton shorts. "Uh, she agreed to help?" That didn't seem right to me. Last I talked to Tara, she wouldn't risk causing trouble for her brother or risk their finances considering their father's health. Plus, there was the added fact that Tara seemed deathly scared of this Payne guy. I walked out of the closet and leaned against the doorframe, crossing my arms.

"Yes, she agreed. But a few things happened that caused that change."

I shook my head, the few tendrils of escaped red hair waving back and forth. "What do you mean? Is she okay?"

"She's fine," Connor said as he took a seat on the bed. "But Charisma terminated her brother's contract."

"That's terrible!" I exclaimed. "Her father. He's in a nursing home."

Connor held up his hand. "I'm aware. And everything is going to be taken care of until they get back on their feet."

Realization dawned on my features and I wasn't sure how I felt about what Connor was telling me. "I can't tell if this means you're paying her off."

Connor shrugged his shoulders. "If it means succeeding at my ultimate goal of helping you reclaim what is yours, then yes, that's what I'm doing."

"I can't tell if that's sexy or not," I said with a hint of a smile.

"Yes, it is sexy," Connor said firmly. "Now come here so I can hold you."

FORTY-SEVEN

SOPHIE GRIPPED MY ARM TIGHTLY AS WE WALKED INTO THE SMALL coffee shop. The decor was eclectic, to say the least. Large wingback chairs of varying sizes and colors were placed next to small tables with no sense of rhyme or reason. Larger booths and tables ran along the corners of the shop for those who wanted a bit more privacy.

"This place is a mess," I breathed out as I took in the scenery. The lack of order offended my senses quite intimately.

We had landed at the airport just a few hours before and checked into our hotel, opting to stay at the airport rather than venture into the city. Sophie said she was more than okay with that. If the only time she had to go into the city was for our one meeting, she said she'd be glad for it.

"I think she's over there," Sophie said, pointing to her friend who was sitting in one of the more private booths towards the back of the shop. I turned to look where she was pointing. A man was sitting next to her, slightly older with the same deep chocolate complexion and soft features. I figured that must be Tara's brother.

"She doesn't look like she could do much harm to anyone," I said, considering the girl, who was looking down at her phone. I'd never actually seen Tara before and for some reason, I expected her to be older, perhaps a bit fiercer, than the timid looking girl across the shop. But, as I thought about it, I realized, timid personalities are usually the ones preyed on by people like Xavier Payne.

"Let's get something to drink and then go sit down," I said to Sophie and she nodded.

We approached the counter and I ordered myself a black coffee while Sophie ordered herself a skim latte. As we waited for the barista to prepare our order, I watched as Sophie looked over her friend with a bit of sadness.

While I didn't know her, she looked a little worse for wear. Her hair had been pulled back into a tight ponytail and she looked sad as she scrolled idly through her phone. Sophie must have been staring too long because Tara looked up and caught her eye. Tara's eyes widened in surprise and I winced. I had not told Tara that Sophie would be in attendance. In fact, I had said the opposite. I hoped that it wouldn't spook her.

Tara gave a small wave, which Sophie returned before holding up one finger, indicating we would be over in just a minute. I breathed a sigh of relief that Tara didn't bolt out of the coffee shop upon seeing Sophie.

"Ready?" I asked, handing Sophie her drink.

"I think so," Sophie responded, following me over to Tara's table.

"Hi Tara," Sophie said as she slid into the booth first.

"Hey," Tara said softly before turning to look at me. "I didn't know you were going to be here."

I took the turn to respond. "She insisted," I said simply. "It's nice to finally meet you, Tara," I said, my hand outstretched.

Tara shook it gingerly before tucking herself back into the smallest space possible.

"And I don't believe we've met," I said, reaching my hand across the table to the man sitting next to her.

"I'm Kevin, Tara's older brother," he said, shaking my hand. "Nice to meet you."

"I'm Sophie," Sophie said with a wave at Kevin and he nodded back.

"Are you doing okay, Tara?" Sophie asked, concern for her friend written across her features.

The girl looked up at her. "Yeah, I'm okay. I should be asking you the same question. You shouldn't have come back, Sophie."

"I'll be fine, Tara. You don't need to worry about me," Sophie said, wrapping her arm around mine a bit tighter.

Tara turned to me. "Did you tell her?"

I nodded my head. "We're all very sorry about your contract, Kevin."

Sophie nodded in agreement, trying to reach out across the table to Tara and offer the girl some small semblance of comfort. "I know this must be really hard for your family."

Tara just shrugged. "It's clear I'm not in control of this situation at all. The best thing I can do is try and align myself with the side that is in the right."

"And we very much appreciate that," I said, stepping in to try and get the conversation steered in a direction that would be profitable. I could tell that Tara was emotional and I wanted to be sure that I got everything I could from her just in case she decided to cut the meeting short. While I was surprised that her brother had decided to come, I was actually relieved by his presence. The man seemed to have a calmness about him whereas Tara seemed all nerves. Hopefully him being here would help our time be more productive.

"You probably know that we have our meeting with Charisma and Xavier Pay—" but I couldn't finish my sentence before Tara held up her hand to her mouth to shush me.

"Please, do not say his name aloud."

I furrowed his brow. Every time I mentioned Payne, the rumors and fear surrounding his name seemed to increase tenfold. Of course I knew organized crime existed, but I'd also had Gus look into Payne's background and the man was cleaner than a whistle. If he was involved with something less than reputable, things like that usually left some evidence, if not always a smoking gun.

"Alright. We have a meeting tomorrow with Sophie's former label executives. Is there anything you can do to help us prepare?" I rephrased.

"I think I may be able to help on that front," Kevin said, chiming in. "I was on contract with Charisma for the past decade. I've learned a lot about how they do business and about how the top leadership operates."

"I'm not sure how much Tara has told you, but we are hoping to buy back Sophie's catalog of songs tomorrow. We managed to claw back her concert and image rights, but Charisma still owns her music. I have no idea whether they're even considering a sale, but they at least did agree to meet."

"Yeah, I did hear some of that. And the rumors going around was that you pulled a number on Webb and Jacobs."

My mouth lifted into a slight smile. "Well, it was a bit more complicated than that. They weren't the most sophisticated of adversaries."

"Well, here's what I can tell you," Kevin said leaning in, his voice hushed. "Payne doesn't like people messing up his image. If he thinks you have anything that might cause him issues, he'll meet with you."

I thought about what Kevin was saying. "I have heard that about him before. Do you know why he's like this? I haven't been able to find out much about him or his line of work."

"That doesn't surprise me. No one knows much about him. I think the person he's probably the closest to is that Rebecca Murphy."

Sophie's eyes widened as I looked at her. "She's the one that's in charge at Charisma."

"What sort of relationship does he have with her?"

Kevin shrugged. "No one really knows. But the pair have known each other for a very long time. She's just about the only person that is allowed to go into his office."

"So then, his main office is here in the city?"

Kevin shrugged again. "As far as any of us know. He's got the entire top floor of the building. But, it's not like we were given reports on when he was and wasn't here."

"Yeah, I get that," I said, trying to fit this information into what he already knew about Payne. "So then, for tomorrow, you think threatening going public is our best bet?"

"Depends on what sort of information you've got, but yeah. If he thinks that what you could put out there could actually be harmful, then you'll get his attention. How much that's actually worth is hard to know though."

I nodded. "How do you know all this? Like you said, hardly anyone knows anything about him."

A bit of a sly smile showed on Kevin's face and he cocked his head to the side. "Uh, let's just say that I was pretty close to Ms. Murphy myself on occasion and she liked to complain about things that bothered her after we, uh . . . " His words trailed off but I understood the insinuation.

He put up a hand and smiled. "Understood." Sophie rolled her eyes and Tara was blushing like mad.

"So, what is it you think you have on them?" Kevin asked.

I studied the man's face, still unsure about whether I should divulge everything. It's not that I didn't trust the siblings, but if Payne was truly some shadow that lurked on the wall like people claimed he was, keeping something like this a secret was always the better option.

"It's not much, but I think it will prove Sophie's ownership rights," I said, purposefully keeping my answer vague. "I know you and I spoke originally about being able to tell Charisma that you might recant your statement." I knew I had to tread lightly here. "Is that still something you're okay with me saying?"

Tara looked first at me, then at Sophie and then over to her brother. Kevin nodded and the girl turned back to me. "Yes. The only reason I wasn't willing before was because I was trying to protect Kevin."

Kevin interrupted. "And if I had known what Charisma had asked her to do from the start, I would have told her to hell with this label. We're both very sorry for all the trouble that our actions have caused."

Sophie caught Tara's eyes and smiled. "As I said to Tara the last time we saw one another, all is forgiven. I know they put you guys in a tough situation."

"About that," I said. "Please let me know where your father is receiving care. I'll work on having those bills sent to me while you work on getting back on your feet, which is actually another thing I wanted to discuss with you after all this is over."

Kevin nodded. "Thank you. I can't tell you how much we really appreciate what you are doing. And just so you know, feel free to let slip at tomorrow's meeting that I'm also willing to speak out about their deceptive business practices. I was fed a contract pretty similar to Sophie's. Thankfully they opted to just terminate me rather than pass me on, so I don't think I'll have the same issues that Sophie has had."

"We really appreciate that offer. And just to be safe, go ahead and email me your contract," I said, reaching for my wallet so I could pull out a business card and hand it to Kevin. "I'd like to have legal take a look at it."

"Thanks," Kevin said, placing the card into his back pocket.

I looked down at my coffee cup to see that it was empty. I looked briefly between Tara and Sophie and realized that the pair would likely benefit from a little alone time. "Kevin and I are going to get another round of drinks for everyone," I said, catching eyes with Kevin.

"Oh, right," Kevin said, sliding out of the booth to follow me back up to the counter.

I ordered and turned back to face him as we waited. "I really do appreciate all you and your sister are doing to help," I said. "I'm serious about having legal look at that contract. I'd like to see what restrictions you're under or what ownership rights Charisma retained."

"It's no worries," Kevin said. "But I don't follow. Why do you want to know that?"

"Well, I may be a real estate man, but fate seems to have hit me with two to three extremely talented artists who are all potentially free agents. It'd be foolish to just throw that away."

Kevin smiled as he began to understand what I was proposing. "Well, I hope for my sake that I really am a free agent, then," Kevin said, grabbing the drinks that were placed on the counter for us.

"I've got a lawyer who specializes in random assignments," Connor said with a chuckle, thinking of the attorney he was about to hand this off to. "She'll let us know whether the light is green."

♪

Sophie

"I'M REALLY glad I get to see you again, Tara," I said, trying to make some conversation with my old friend.

"I didn't know you would be here," Tara admitted. "Connor said you weren't coming."

I let out a puff of air and crossed my arms. "Yeah, well, that was royally stupid of him to assume," I said.

Tara smiled softly before her lips turned back into a frown. "I'm scared for you, Sophie. I don't think you should go tomorrow."

"What do you mean?"

Tara sighed. "I don't know. I've just . . . heard things about him that scare me."

"Like what sort of things?" If I could get any information on Payne besides "he's a scary mofo," that would be a win.

"Like, I heard that Webb and Jacobs are still missing."

I shook my head. "Tara, those guys were such scumbags. I guarantee you that they both ran when Connor got one on them."

Tara shrugged. "I dunno, Soph. I just have a bad feeling about the whole thing."

I reached my hand across the table and grabbed Tara's. She looked at me with wide eyes and I smiled. "Everything's going to be fine and I'll be fine. I promise, okay? You don't have to worry."

Tara nodded her head. "I really hope you're right, Soph."

"Cheer up!" I said, squeezing my friend's hand before releasing it. "Look, the guys are back with more drinks," I said and Tara smiled, but it didn't reach her eyes.

FORTY-EIGHT

Sophie

As soon as we got back to the hotel, I pulled my red hair out of its high bun and shook it out. Massaging my scalp, I tried to ease the headache I could feel building in my mind.

"You okay?" Connor asked as he slipped off his shoes and hung up his brown leather jacket.

"Yeah," I said, letting myself fall dramatically onto the bed. "It's just a lot to process, you know? If you had asked me five years ago when all this started whether I thought I'd be here, fighting to win back the songs that I wrote, well," I threw my arm over my face, "you know how the saying goes."

"That I do," Connor said, walking over to the bed and sitting next to me. He laid beside me and pulled me close. "But hey, I don't want you to worry about anything. If what everyone says about Payne is true, I've got something that I know will win your music back."

I moved my hand aside and looked up at him. "What did you find, Mr. Driscoll?"

Connor chuckled and moved in to kiss me. He moved his lips against mine slightly before pulling back and brushing a stray piece of hair behind my ear. "I like it when you call me that," he said with a bit of a wink.

I couldn't help but smile. "I bet you do. But seriously, what do you have? Don't you think I should know?"

"I'll tell you everything, Soph. But first, I'd like to help you relax a bit." His fingers brushed against my jawline before traveling down my neck to my shoulder.

I let out a long exhale as his movements caused shivers to move through my body. "Oh yeah, well what did you have in mind?"

"That's for me to know and you to experience," Connor said as his fingers began to move further down my body. He worked his way down the curves of my side, his fingers moving easily over my silk blouse before moving further down to the swell of my hips.

His hand slipped down to my knee before making its way up my thigh to dip below my skirt. I gasped as his fingers traveled higher and higher and Connor didn't wait. He leaned his head down and captured my lips as his fingers brushed over the slip of lace covering my warm heat.

He pushed his tongue into my mouth, a little sign to me that he wanted control. There would be no asking and no permission needed. He pulled back briefly. "Tonight I'll have you the way I want you. And in less than twenty-four hours, I'll have you again, but this time you'll be wearing my ring on my finger."

I moaned into Connor's mouth as his tongue danced with mine. I loved it when Connor's dominant streak showed through. Of course I loved his more sensitive side, but when his possessive nature came out to play, it was all-consuming. It was also exactly what I needed right now. I just needed to be surrounded by him, to forget about how nervous I was for tomorrow, and let Connor take the lead.

His finger brushed against my core again and I gasped as Connor pulled his lips away from mine. "That's right, baby. Get nice and wet for me. I want your juices dripping off my cock by the time I'm finished with you."

"Fuck," I breathed out at Connor's filthy words. Oh yes, the intense Connor was paying me a visit and the thought of that only got me that much more turned on.

"I think we can do without this," Connor said as he pulled his fingers back from my core and slowly pulled down the zipper to my skirt. When he reached the bottom, it unhooked and the material fell away from my body, leaving me in nothing but a silk blouse and a pair of panties. "Perfection," he said, as his fingers glided along my exposed thighs.

I opened my legs, trying to encourage Connor to put pressure on the one spot where I really needed him to be, but he just laughed softly and gave me a knowing look. "Impatient girl, as always. But no, you'll be waiting for a little while longer." As he said those words, his fingertips brushed over my center so lightly that I almost couldn't tell if he had touched me. Even still, just the small amount of contact had my nipples puckering against my bra and a moan escaping my mouth.

Connor sat up and began to move slowly to unbutton my blouse. Starting at the bottom, the material began to fall away from me with each button he slipped through.

"Connor," I breathed as my body began to squirm in anticipation.

"Don't make me get the bindings, Sophie," Connor chided. "Stay still."

"What? You have bindings with you?" I gasped.

Connor chuckled. "Stay still," he repeated.

I tried to still my movements, but Connor was driving me crazy with his agonizing pace. The last of the buttons slipped through and the blouse opened. Bra straps were slipped down my shoulders and before I knew what was happening, Connor had pulled my bra down, exposing me fully, but still keeping the garment on me.

"God, I love seeing you like this, Soph," Connor murmured under his breath.

"Like what?" I breathed out, secretly hoping Connor would say something filthy to me again.

"Exposed. Wanting. Wet. Your body is so beautiful. If I had it my way, you'd never be allowed to wear clothes again. You'd walk around naked in my apartment and I'd bend you over every surface and fuck that beautiful pussy of yours whenever and however I liked."

"Fuck," I breathed out, feeling more than on edge at the images Connor was causing to float around in my head.

"You like that, don't you?"

"Like what?" I asked, my words turning into a moan as Connor began to trail the pads of his fingers against my stomach.

"The idea of me taking you whenever I wanted? Being completely at my mercy? Just my little plaything? There to be fucked by this big cock," he said, grabbing my hand and pressing it against the raging erection he was sporting through his jeans.

"Yes, Con," I said as my fingers tried to wrap around his thick length through his jeans. But he pushed me away.

"Not yet. Right now, I'm going to play with this body of yours. Take everything I want from it. Only then will I allow you to have my cock, understand?"

I tried to respond, but my mouth had gone dry. But Connor wanted an answer. "Understand, Sophie?" he asked as he leaned down and whispered the words against my ear.

"Yes," I moaned as his fingers returned to my body, higher this time. His movements danced around my hardened peaks and I thought I might beg for him to touch me, but I knew that would only cause him to go slower. I knew the only thing I could do was to sit and take exactly what he wanted to give me at his own speed.

"Stand for me, beautiful girl," he whispered against my ear.

His words confused me. I'd been so caught up in his movements. "What?" I asked.

"Stand, Sophie," he ordered.

I complied, stumbling to my feet, turning around to face where he leaned back on the bed. "Take off the blouse," he directed. "But keep the bra on," he said with a sly smile.

I bit my bottom lip as I let the blouse slide off my body before throwing it onto the back of the nearby oversized chair. I felt totally exposed, despite the fact that I still had on a lace thong. It was something about my bra being pulled down and my breasts tumbling over the tops that felt so—dirty. But I loved it.

The look of lust Connor was giving me was unlike anything I had ever seen. His hand was on his erection, kneading it through his jeans as he watched me. "Turn around," he husked and I complied, twirling on my toes to expose my backside to him. "Bend over," he instructed and I could feel my wetness begin to slide down my thighs.

Connor stood and moved behind me, his fingers trailing against my behind lightly. "You're such a good girl, Sophie. Perfect, truly," he said, before pulling back and sitting back down on the bed. He removed his jeans before giving me another command. "Turn around again," he instructed and I complied.

I watched him with rapt attention as he moved his hand against his erection. He still hadn't freed it from the confines of his boxers and I wanted nothing more than to fall to my knees and take it in my mouth, until I could feel it press against the back of my throat. "Connor," I breathed out as I watched him work his length through the material.

"Touch yourself, Sophie," he instructed me and I moaned as my legs quaked. I brought my hands up and ghosted them over my hardened nipples. Just the small amount of pressure from even my own hands was driving me to higher and higher heights. I let one hand slip down over my panties and press against my clit. I let my head fall back as shivers coursed their way through my body. Even without Connor touching me, I felt ready to come. Him, sitting there on the bed, stroking his own cock to my touching myself was beyond erotic.

Just as I thought I might crest over the edge, I heard the word "Stop," coming from Connor's lips.

"Wha—?" I was beyond strung out. I absolutely needed this release and he seemed to delight in denying me.

"You only come by my hand," Connor said, as he stood and wrapped his hand around the back of my neck before he pulled me against his body for a deep kiss. His lips moved against mine as he pressed his hot erection against my abdomen.

When he pulled back, I was gasping for breath and begging him for release.

"Soon," was all he said before he took my hand and led me to the oversized chair in the nearby corner. He sat down on it, his legs spread wide and pulled me down between them, my back to his front.

With a graceful move of his fingers, he unclasped my bra and pushed it off my arms, so that I was completely bare except for my panties. His mouth began to move against my neck, pressing heated kisses to the skin there before pulling back to whisper filthy things in my ear.

"Spread your legs so I can slip my fingers into that tight little cunt of yours, Sophie," he breathed and I moaned.

I did as I was told and I was rewarded when his hands came up to cup my breasts. His thumbs danced against the undersides as my nipples puckered harder. "Please touch me, Connor," I let slip from my lips.

"I am touching you, Sophie," he responded, his thumbs dancing against my nipples momentarily before returning back to move against the bottom of my breasts.

"No, please, Connor," I moaned.

"You want me to touch that perfect pussy of yours, hm?" he husked against my ear. I nodded vigorously. "Stir up that wet little cunt of yours and dip my fingers inside until you scream, is that it?"

"Yes, please," I breathed out.

"Soon," he said, teasing me still and I groaned. His fingers finally came up to tweak my nipples and I gasped at the sensations that ran through my body before settling in my core. I felt like I was going to explode over the edge just from this.

I could feel Connor's thick erection pushing into my back and I tried to move against it, grinding my ass cheeks against him in the hopes of speeding things up.

"Naughty girl," he said with an extra hard pinch to my peaks and I gasped as my sex clenched at the sensation. "You get this cock when I say so and not before." One hand left my breasts to cup my jaw and he pulled me back so his mouth was right against my ear. "You understand me?"

"Yes," I said instantly.

"Say it for me," he ordered.

"I get your cock only when you say so."

"That's right. You'll get fucked when I want to fuck you and not before. Say it."

"I'll get fucked when you want to fuck me and not before."

"Good girl," Connor said with a kiss to my neck before releasing my jaw and returning his hand to my other breast.

I didn't know how long he sat there, toying with my nipples, driving me to higher and higher heights. But after what felt like an eternity of soaking the chair beneath me, he finally moved one hand down my body and towards my sex.

"Yes," I breathed out before he'd even reached the destination, the anticipation for what was to come too great.

Connor chuckled against my skin before pressing a kiss to my neck. Carefully, he pulled back the lace, pushing it to one side, my lower lips falling free. "You're soaking wet for me, hm Sophie?" he asked as his fingers hovered over my sex, still not touching me.

"Yes!" I moaned as my body writhed against his, his one hand still kneading each breast in turn.

"You love being exposed like this, don't you? Cunt out and dripping wet?"

"Yes!"

"I wonder what I should do to this gorgeous pussy," Connor mused, his fingers dancing around the wetness of my vulva.

"Please, Connor. I can't take anymore," I begged.

"Oh, that's not true, Sophie. You'll take everything I give you and more. Cause you're my dirty little slut."

"Fuck," I moaned at his words as my sex clenched.

"Say it."

I hesitated but Connor kissed my neck and whispered "It's okay, Sophie. I love you. Say it for me."

"I'm your dirty little slut."

"Yes, Sophie," he said, sliding his fingers against my lower lips in reward.

My body arched at just the small touch as he began to stir up my wet cunt. He held me still against his body with his other arm, my breast spilling between his fingers as his arm clamped me to his form.

"My dirty little slut, you love it when I play with your cunt, hm?"

"Yes!"

His fingers moved inside me slightly, rimming my entrance as his thumb began to stroke my clit. "Connor, I'm going to come," I moaned and his fingers pulled out of me.

"Not yet, baby. I want you coming on my cock," he said as I gasped. With a swift movement, Connor turned me around and freed his erection from the confines of his boxers. I moved my knees forward and sank down, taking his cock inside of me. My walls clenched and it only took Connor a few pumps of his hips for me to career over the edge, having been denied for so long.

"Fuck me, Connor!" I screamed as I let go, my orgasm ripping through my body in a way I had never experienced before.

"That's it, Sophie. My darling little slut, pulse that tight pussy of yours all over my cock," he said through gritted teeth as he continued to pound into me.

I collapsed against him as the waves of pleasure continued to crash through me, my strength completely giving out. Wrapping his arms around me, Connor stood, still staying inside of me before switching our positions. He laid me against the chair face up so he could thrust into me from his knees below. He pressed his thumb to my clit to draw out my orgasm as my breasts bounced in time with each of his thrusts.

Within minutes, he was following me over the edge, releasing everything he had into my body.

FORTY-NINE

Sophie

I PULLED THE CHOPSTICKS APART AND PLUCKED THE FIRST BITE OF SUSHI into my mouth as quickly as possible. I was absolutely ravenous following what could only be classified as a marathon sex session with Connor and I could not wait any longer.

"I see someone's hungry," Connor said lightheartedly as he sat down next to me on the sofa and pulled apart his own chopsticks. We had made ourselves a makeshift dining table using the ottoman and I was about to sit my ass on the floor just to be closer to the food.

"Starved," I said with my mouth full of rice and vegetables.

Connor smiled and shook his head before taking a bite of his own.

"This is good," I said, grabbing another piece of the many rolls we had ordered with my bits of wood.

"I'm glad you like it," Connor said, taking a sip of water.

We ate in relative silence for a while, both of us hungry enough to quell our lust for conversation at the moment. Finally, when I felt myself starting to slow down hunger wise, I leaned back against the couch and shot Connor a lazy smile. "Thanks for earlier," I said. "I guess I really needed that."

Connor gave me a sideways grin and nodded his head. "Truly, the pleasure was all mine. I love having sessions like that with you."

"Sessions, huh?" I said with a teasing smile.

"I'm not sure what else you would call it," Connor replied simply.

I thought about his words and had to agree. Saying that what they had done was "having sex" or "fucking" or "making love" just didn't fairly capture the essence of our encounter.

"And in less than twenty-four hours, you'll be the future Mrs. Driscoll, and just you wait," he said giving me a knowing smirk.

"Speaking of that," I said, trying not to get turned on at the insinuation in his voice, "we were going to talk about our plan for tomorrow. What sort of stuff you had to bring to the table."

Connor put his chopsticks down and leaned back on the sofa. He turned to face me, resting his head against his hand. "It's not what I have to bring to the table," Connor said. "It's actually something you had all along."

"What do you mean?" I asked, confused by his words.

Connor got up from the sofa and made his way over to the desk huddled in the corner of the room. He grabbed his laptop and brought it back to where I was sitting. Clearing a spot for the computer, he placed it on the ottoman and clicked through a few menus before pulling up a video.

My eyes widened as I saw myself, sitting on the floor of the loft, several years younger, my guitar in my lap.

"Okay, I just wrote this so it might not be all the way worked out yet but. Wait, why am I talking to myself?" the younger version of myself said to the screen.

"Connor, how did you get this?" I breathed out, not believing what I was seeing.

"I found it on your computer the night I flew to LA to meet with

Webb and Jacobs. I was trying to find something I could use against them and I stumbled on this."

I shook my head in disbelief. "I thought for sure I had deleted this. I never recorded myself after I made this video," I admitted. "I couldn't stand watching myself on tape."

Connor chuckled. "That's pretty ironic considering you went on to become a famous pop icon."

"Yeah, well, my life is pretty much the definition of irony at this point," I huffed with twisted lips.

Connor just smiled softly and wrapped a strong arm around me. I allowed myself to sink into his warm embrace, the smell of his sandalwood cologne washing over me as I closed my eyes and listened to the song I had written about Connor all those years ago, the one that had made me famous. I'd never gotten the chance to tell him that it was about him. At first, I didn't know how he would react and then it just felt like the time had passed to say something.

But here, in this moment, with his arm wrapped around me as I relaxed in his embrace, all those worries fell by the wayside.

"You know, I wrote this song about you," I said in a small voice.

Connor's arm squeezed me tighter and he pressed a gentle kiss to my hair. "I know."

"When did you figure it out?" I said, not lifting my head from where it was resting against his chest.

"I had an idea the first time you sang it at the coffee shop. But I think the first time I knew for sure was when I heard it on the radio," he replied, a bit of sadness coating his words.

"Oh," I replied, feeling a twinge of guilt rise up within myself. "Sorry—" I began to say but Connor shook his head.

"None of that matters now, Sophie. What matters is that you are here with me. That's all that's ever going to matter. For a while I thought I could do this whole life thing without you, but now I know how foolish I was being. I was just existing then. You coming back into my life has changed everything, Sophie. All for the better."

"I love you," I said softly against his chest. Connor lifted my chin so that I was staring into his clear blue gaze. The smallest amount of moisture had accumulated at the ends of my eyes and he wiped each away in turn.

"Don't cry," he said softly. "There's no reason for tears. I love you and that's never going to change," he said before pressing a soft kiss to my lips.

We basked in the moment for as long as we could before reality set in about preparing for tomorrow's meeting. "So, this video is a pretty big deal. But do you have anything else?"

"Well," Connor said, adjusting us so that we were once again facing one another on the couch. "I think with being able to tell him that Tara is willing to publicly recant her statement and Kevin is happy to go public with their way of business, that might be enough to get him to sign things over."

I rubbed my eyes as the tiredness from the day was beginning to set in. "Do you think he's going to try and price gouge you or something? I mean, my songs can't be worth very much right now. Everyone still hates me."

"That will pass, Sophie. Don't worry," Connor said reassuringly. "But yes, I do expect there to be some bargaining involved price-wise. Please do not think it has anything to do with your worth. I just hate the idea of this man making any more of a profit off of you more than he already has."

I yawned, trying to cover it with the back of my hand. "I'm not offended. I agree with that."

"Okay," Connor said, standing to his full height. "Bed. I need you at your best tomorrow. We're going in as a united front on this. You are my partner, after all and the stakes are extremely high."

I gave him a bit of an annoyed look but didn't try to fight him given how tired I was feeling. "Fine," I said, allowing myself to be pulled up and off the sofa and into his arms. "Speaking of that, you never told me what the letters meant."

"Hm?" Connor said, as he began to walk me over to the bed.

"MMS, LLC? The name of the company you gave to me," I said with a laugh.

"Oh," Connor said, realizing what I meant. "I thought you might have figured it out by now."

"Figured what out?"

"That it stood for 'Marry Me Sophie,'" he said, pressing another kiss to my temple.

My eyes widened at his words. "You—you knew—"

"Knew long before I asked you that I wanted to marry you? Yes. I've known for a long time that I wanted to make you mine, Sophie. And there was no way in hell I was going to throw away this second chance fate had given me," he said against my hair as he pulled me in close to his body. He pressed another light kiss to the top of my head before saying, "Now get some sleep. I'm going to stay up just a bit and get things organized. Tomorrow will be over before you know it and then we've got the rest of our lives to make up for lost time."

I WATCHED the rise and fall of Sophie's chest as she finally fell asleep. It had taken her some time and I could see her toss and turn as she tried to get comfortable for a bit before her breathing finally evened. I understood exactly how she felt. As much as I tried to play it off, I was nervous about tomorrow's meeting.

Despite my best efforts, the most I'd been able to find out about Payne was rumor and hearsay. The only thing that was concrete was the building he'd bought from me a few years ago. I only hoped that the information I had to lay on the table was enough to spur Payne into action.

I'd meant what I'd said to Sophie. If I could get out of there without paying a dime, that would be my goal. I had the money sitting in an account ready to be wired at a moment's notice but I hated the idea of someone making profit off of Sophie's suffering.

I sat at the small desk, the only light in the room the small lamp next to me. I shut it off and leaned back with a sigh, taking a sip of bourbon

I'd ordered from the downstairs bar. Looking out the window at the city lights, I tried to calm my own nerves. I understood why Sophie didn't like this city. There was an edge to it, but everyone denied it. I was fine with tough tactics, hell, I was more than able to dish them out. But I was always honest with my intentions. This place was anything but honest.

FIFTY

Connor

"Shit, I forgot my purse!" Sophie cursed as she climbed out of the sedan parked in front of the hotel.

"It's alright," I said calmly, "we've got plenty of time," I said, looking down at my watch. I knew Sophie's nerves were alight this morning so I'd been sure to leave additional time for us to get to the meeting location and feel organized before our allotted timeframe.

"Okay. I'll just run upstairs and grab it," Sophie said, stepping out of the sedan.

"I'll go with you. Please hold the car," I said, turning to the driver.

"No, it's fine," Sophie called out, already making her way towards the revolving doors of the hotel lobby. "I'll be right back," she said before disappearing behind the rotating glass.

My brows furrowed as my lips thinned. I did not like the idea of leaving Sophie alone in this town, not after what had happened here last time. I took a deep breath, trying to calm my own nerves and reminded myself that Sophie was perfectly capable of grabbing a missing item by herself.

I looked down at my phone, scrolling through my emails as I sat in the backseat of the sedan, waiting for Sophie to come back out.

"Sir?" the driver said in a tone that had me instantly worried. I turned to face where the man was pointing and looked in horror as two men in indistinguishable black suits with black shades led Sophie to a sedan parked to the left of the lobby.

She was being held firmly on either side by each of the men and she looked like she was trying to struggle against them, but they held her firmly so that she didn't make a scene.

"Sophie!" I yelled as I vaulted out of the car, but it was no good. By the time I reached the car, Sophie and her captors were inside and the only thing I could do was bang on the hood as it zoomed past me.

I sprinted back to my own sedan and wrenched open the front passenger door. "Follow that car," I bellowed at the driver before slamming the door shut.

"Sir," the driver hesitated and I grabbed him by the scruff of his jacket. "You saw those two men kidnap my woman. Follow the damn car," I said, releasing my hold on the man roughly.

The driver seemed to finally understand the severity of the situation and shifted the car into drive before speeding off after the other unmarked black sedan.

♪

Sophie

"JUST WHAT THE fuck do you think you guys are doing?" I cursed at the unknown men. Everything had been fine as I walked through the lobby of the hotel with my purse, but just as I exited the hotel, two large men had grabbed me on either side and firmly led me to a car parked just beyond the hotel portico.

Now one of the assholes was driving while the other still had his grip on my arm sitting next to me in the backseat. I thought about trying to struggle, but I had no way of knowing who these men were or if they meant to do me harm. I wasn't even sure if they had weapons on them, but I figured they must. The best thing I could hope for was to try and get away as soon as they got to the second location.

"Who sent you?" I asked, trying to see if I could at least get some information out of the men, but they stayed completely silent. I tried to wrench my arm away from the man's iron grip, but his fingers only wrapped around my slender arm harder and I yelped in pain. I was certain that was going to leave a bruise.

The thought briefly flashed across my mind that these guys were somehow related to Payne or even Webb and Jacobs and my stomach began to do somersaults. I tried to crane my neck around despite the man's death grip to see if Connor was anywhere close. I had heard him screaming my name and saw him punch the hood of the car as I had been driven off. I hoped he hadn't broken his hand in the process.

I managed to catch a glimpse of another black sedan following close behind us with two men in the front seats. But as I tried to crane my neck further back, the brute next to me pulled on my arm again, forcing me to look forward. "That hurts," I huffed at him, frustrated that I couldn't tell whether it was Connor in the car or not. I closed my eyes and tried to calm myself down. I would be no good at helping myself out of this situation if I was a bundle of nerves. I knew that Connor would do everything in his power to rescue me and I needed to do everything in mine to make his job easier.

After about fifteen minutes, I could tell they were in the downtown business district. The car pulled up to an underground garage door and I looked around as much as possible to try and get my bearings. If I managed to get to a phone, I wanted to be able to give as much identifying information as possible. Of course the jackasses had stolen my purse off me as soon as they got their hands on me. I'd seen the first guy throw it on the seat beside him when they got into the car. If I was just able to get my hands on it, I could try and call 911.

The car slipped into the darkness of the garage and I tried to prepare myself for whatever might be waiting on the other side.

♪

Connor

I WATCHED in horror as the car they were following disappeared behind a locked garage door.

"I'm sorry, Sir. This is as far as I can take you," the driver said.

I leapt out of the car and sprinted up the stairs of the building. It was an extremely modern looking building, but I couldn't be bothered with the decor. I ran straight to the reception desk and careened to a halt. "There's a garage attached to this building. Where does it let out inside?" My breathing was heavy and the woman's eyes widened as she looked at him.

"Sir, is there something the matter?"

"The garage? Where does it let out?" I demanded of her.

"Guests can select any floor they wish to go to from the garage levels. Is there someone you're looking for? Perhaps I can assist?" she asked with a wary glance.

I looked around, trying to figure out exactly where I was. The building had at least twenty-five floors, of that I was sure. There was no way I could search every one. By the time I did, Sophie could be moved to another location or worse.

"What's the address here? Is there a list of tenants?"

"Yes, our directory is right over there," she said, pointing at a lit case on the other side of the lobby.

I ran over to it and scanned the names to see if I recognized anything. My eyes landed on one name in particular before I glanced up at the top at the building's address. "The fuck?" I breathed out as I put the pieces together.

"Eternity Music Group" was emblazoned across the top, stating it was located on floors twenty through twenty-five, with the lobby located on the twenty-fourth floor.

"Shit," I cursed, suddenly realizing just what had happened. "Fucking Payne," I muttered through grit teeth. I ran over to the elevators and pressed the call button only to hear a chime to my right. I made my way into the little car and pressed "24."

"If that bastard hurts her, I swear to God I'll kill him."

FIFTY-ONE

Sophie

My eyes darted around the garage as I tried to think of a way to make an escape. Unfortunately, both men had an iron grip on each arm again and I was coming up short on escape plans. I did notice that the driver had grabbed my purse, which I thought was odd. Why would kidnappers need to ensure I had my lipstick? Even worse, I thought for sure they would have wanted to get rid of my phone so the police couldn't track my movements.

The elevator arrived as soon as one of the men pressed the button for it and I thought this might be my chance. Whatever sicko was waiting on the other side of the little car was certainly someone I did not want to meet.

"Owe!" I screamed suddenly and one of the men startled enough to loosen his grip on my arm. I wrenched myself free from the other and ran like the blazes out of the small glass enclosure for the elevators. But it was all for nothing. The garage was a maze and there were absolutely no signs or exits as far as I could see.

The men caught up with me easily and without a word, once again grasped me around each arm, perhaps a little tighter this time, and led me back to the glass enclosure. As the elevator doors opened and the men walked me into them, my hopes of getting out of this situation began to close, as did the doors in front of me.

I saw the man that was holding my purse press his finger to a small glass screen before pressing the button for the twenty-fifth floor.

"Fancy," I muttered under my breath, but the man said nothing. Soft jazz music played in the elevator as it whisked me to my doom. Another dose of irony for my over the top life.

The doors opened but my feet rooted to the spot. I didn't know what I was about to walk in to and frankly, I didn't want to know. But my captors had other ideas because when they realized that I was resisting them, they all but lifted me out of the car and set my heels on the polished marble floor with a click. The doors closed behind me and as soon as I heard the metal press together, the brutes released their grips on my arms. I turned around and tried pressing the call button but nothing happened.

"I'm afraid that only works if you have the right transmitter," a deep voice said from somewhere behind me.

I turned around, keeping my back to the elevator doors as I continued to try and keep my finger on the button. The only thing I could hope was that the elevator gods would sense my panic and grant me this one wish.

A tall and stunningly handsome but slightly older man appeared from behind a large marble column. I tried to take stock of my surroundings, but the place seemed so vast. My back continued to press against the gold metal elevator doors and beneath my stilettos was polished white marble that extended as far as I could see.

The man who must have orchestrated this entire fiasco was standing in front of me, leaning nonchalantly against a pure white marble column. His silver brown hair was slicked back against his head and his face, despite being clean-shaven, was showing signs of a five o'clock shadow, despite the fact that it was morning. He was wearing a navy blue suit and oddly enough, an orange floral necktie.

He caught me looking down at the fabric and his smile was slick, lifting the corner of one side of his mouth in a stunningly handsome grin. "You don't like it? Eh, I dunno. The girl at the shop told me it was the style of today. Maybe she was yankin' my chain. What do you think, boys?"

"Looks good," the brute to my left said with a grunt.

I turned and gave him a death glare. "So you do fucking talk."

The man directly in front of me chuckled. "I'm sorry. They don't usually have much to say. Less around women. Pretty girls make them nervous."

"Who the hell are you supposed to be?" I spat at the man, my back still pressed firmly against the elevator doors.

"Oh, I'm sorry sweetheart. I thought you knew. I'm Xavier Payne."

My eyes widened at his announcement. *This* was Xavier Payne? Eau de'crime boss was rolling off him in waves, but he was also not what I had expected at all. But then again, every description I had been given of Payne had differed, so I wasn't sure exactly what I expected.

"Why did you kidnap me?" I asked him with a wary glance.

Payne pushed off the column and stood up straight, taking another step forward so I could see him clearly in the light. "Certainly didn't mean to frighten you, Ms. Stronglen. We had a meeting and I know you don't live in the city anymore. I just wanted to make sure you didn't get lost making your way here, that's all."

I narrowed my eyes at his bullshit. "That's very kind of you," I said, trying to keep my demeanor calm. It was clear that this man wanted to separate me from Connor, for what reason I wasn't sure. But the one thing I couldn't do was get flustered and lose my cool. I had a temper to me, that was for sure, but for now, I really needed to keep it in check. "Alright, so now that I'm here, should we proceed with the meeting?"

"Of course," Payne said, taking another step forward before placing a hand in the small of my back and leading me gently through the massive space. I looked around as we walked, trying to keep my distance from this man but also not make my disdain for him too obvious. It seemed like the entire floor was his. I had no doubt that he had living quarters here along with his office, it was just too large with too many doors not to.

He led me down a marble-lined hallway, my heels echoing in the space with each step. He stopped in front of a door, turned the golden handle to open it for me before gesturing that I should enter. I took small steps forward, wanting to make sure Payne was following me inside and didn't have some crazy plan to lock me up. But he followed behind me without hesitation and I felt a bit more at ease.

He closed the door behind us and circled around me to sit at the large oak desk that was prominently displayed in the center of the room. "Please," he said, gesturing to one of the leather tufted chairs in front of his desk. I took a seat as did Payne in his grander version.

"I have to admit, Mr. Payne," I started up, dancing my finger along the oak of his desk. "This is a bit uncouth."

"What do you mean?" Payne responded, his eyes flashing with a bit of curiosity.

"Well, the meeting was scheduled with my business partner, Connor Driscoll. I'm not sure I appreciate him being cut out of our correspondence without explanation."

Payne held up a hand. "Not to worry, Ms. Stronglen. Your partner is just downstairs in our corporate lobby." He turned to look at his wristwatch, the diamonds on the device catching the overhead lights. "By my estimation, we've still got fifteen minutes before our formal meeting is scheduled to start. I thought you and I could have a chat about a few things first."

I shrugged and leaned back in my chair, crossing my legs. I was glad I had opted for the more conservative black dress for today's meeting. I had picked it out specifically. More than ever, I'd wanted my clothing to convey that I wasn't just some little girl anymore that they could manipulate. Things had changed, I had changed, and I was a woman who would demand their respect.

"I'm not sure what we would need to discuss in private," I said with mock curiosity.

Payne leaned forward across the desk. "You're a smart woman, Ms.

Stronglen. Sharp as a tack and as clever as a fox. Obviously, I wanted to have a discussion with you, and just you, in order to make you a proposal that might not be in the best interests of Mr. Driscoll."

That caught me a bit off guard. Payne wanted to make me an offer? Something that would benefit me but not Connor? What could that possibly be?

"Okay, I'll give. I'm intrigued. But I will have to remind you, that I'm highly skeptical about your offer. I don't see how a deal could benefit me while simultaneously harming Connor. Our relationship isn't quite like that." The words slipped from my mouth and I instantly wondered if I'd said too much.

"Oh, I'm very much aware of your relationship with Mr. Driscoll, Ms. Stronglen," Payne said, confirming my suspicions that I had indeed, opened a can of worms. "I'd say that you've done quite a good job about keeping your potential nuptials out of the news." I tried not to show my surprise but obviously failed considering Payne's slight smirk. "Surprised I know?"

"A bit," I admitted sheepishly.

"That's alright, Ms. Stronglen. You see, much of my business is information. It pays to know things before the other man."

"Or woman," I corrected him.

He grinned and bowed his head. "Or woman."

"Alright then, Mr. Payne. I'll hear your proposal."

Payne smiled and folded his hands in his lap as he leaned back in his chair. "You were a very successful contract for us for quite some time, Ms. Stronglen. I'll admit, things were not handled correctly towards the end and for that, I do apologize."

I kept quiet and resisted the urge to ask whether Webb and Jacobs were still alive.

"But despite the harm that's been done, I don't think it's permanent." He looked at me, clearly trying to gauge my reaction.

I tried to look as impassive as possible. "So, what's your point, Mr. Payne?"

The corner of his mouth quipped into a small smile. "My point, Ms. Stronglen, is that I would like you to come back and work for me. But this time, not for Charisma. I'll be handling your contract personally. And you can have your lawyers look at it and take all the time you need to consider it before signing. No one will rush you. But what I can guarantee you is a minimum seven-figure salary, full upscale accommodations in the city and fame unlike you've known before."

I studied Payne's face for a few moments before I responded. "What's the catch?"

"Very good, Ms. Stronglen," Payne said with a chuckle. "As I said, sharp as a tack. The catch is that you'll need to terminate your relationship with Mr. Driscoll—and permanently. You're a highly sought after and coveted pop idol, Ms. Stronglen. I can undo the damage those two idiots did to your image, but if we want people to start falling for you again, you'll need to be available."

"Why should I trust you? Your company and employees put me through absolute hell over the past few years. What makes you think I would want to be owned by you again?"

"I have no doubts that you wouldn't want to be owned by anyone, Ms. Stronglen," Payne said. "And I understand your concerns. As a show of good faith, I'd be willing to release all of your songs back to you. No ownership over anything. Just a new partnership."

I could see the gears in the man's brain turning. I couldn't tell whether he actually thought this scheme of his would work or whether this was some sort of sick game he liked to play with people.

I knew my answer before Payne had even finished his proposal. But at the same time, I didn't want to seem like I wasn't at least considering both sides before I gave him an answer.

"It's a generous offer, Mr. Payne, truly," I said with a bit of a smile. "It's definitely tempting. But of course, you designed it to be that way."

Payne leaned back and shrugged. "You don't catch many flies without some honey. Isn't that how the saying goes?"

"Something like that," I said with a small giggle. "But unfortunately, I'm going to have to decline," I said with a shake of my head.

"You're saying that your relationship with this Driscoll character is worth more than seven figures a year plus everything else I'm offering? Even your own catalog of songs?"

"Quite frankly, Mr. Payne, I could care less about my songs. I can always write more. But, I can't write another Connor Driscoll into existence. If the price I have to pay for being with him is to continue with my name smeared and lose my old songs, then so be it. I'd rather be a nobody than a sellout."

"Well, Ms. Stronglen. I guess that concludes our private meeting. It seems we'll proceed with the joint meeting," he turned to look at his watch, "and we're just on time."

I stood and nodded my head, before following him out of his office and back into the large foyer.

FIFTY-TWO

"I'M SORRY, SIR, BUT YOU'LL JUST HAVE TO WAIT. MR. PAYNE WILL SEE you shortly."

"No, you don't understand," I growled at the receptionist. I understood that she was just doing her job but now was not the time to stonewall me. I was about to completely lose my temper.

The phone rang and she held up a finger to me. "Just one moment, please." She answered the phone and I ground my teeth in frustration. "Yes, Mr. Payne," she said and I whipped my head back around to look at her. She met my eyes and nodded. "I'll let him know. I'm sure he'll be relieved."

The slightly older woman turned her graying hair and brown eyes onto me. "Mr. Payne and Ms. Stronglen will be meeting you in Conference Room 3. I can lead you there," she said, getting up from her seat and walking around the large desk to where I was standing. "If you'll follow me," she said, before swiping a card next to the frosted glass doors that had blocked my access for the last fifteen minutes. She held one open and I straightened my jacket and smoothed my hair back against my temples before striding forward.

"Thank you," I said to her curtly as I walked through the doors.

She led me through a maze of conference rooms before finally opening the door to one all the way to the back. As the large oak door swung forward, I could see Sophie leaning against a side table, looking calm and perfectly safe.

"Sophie," I said, striding through the door to pull her into my arms. I didn't care that another man was in the room or that the receptionist was still hanging out in the doorway. All that I cared about was the fact that she was safe. As I held her against my body, my fear and anxiety about the entire morning melted away and my breathing began to even. I pulled back and looked at her. "Are you okay?"

"I'm fine," she said as I brushed a stray piece of hair behind her ear. "A little frazzled but fine, nonetheless."

"Thank god," I said, moving my hand down to grasp hers before turning around to look at the man across the room. He was currently saying a few words to the receptionist and I leaned towards Sophie. "Is that him?"

"Yeah," Sophie whispered back. "He's not what I expected."

But that was all she could say before the door closed. I had to restrain my urge to walk over to the man and land a punch squarely on his jaw. But, as much as I would like to do that, I knew that would derail the negotiations pretty quickly and Sophie and I didn't fly all the way across the country for nothing. Perhaps when the ink had dried on paper, then I might think about giving the man what he deserved.

"You must be Connor Driscoll," Payne said, striding forward with an outstretched hand.

My back stiffened but I walked forward and shook the man's hand, nonetheless. "I don't think my partner and I had quite the same expectations about this meeting as yourself, Mr. Payne," I said in a dark tone.

Payne chuckled lightly before gesturing to the two cushioned seats separated by a small end table near where they were standing. "I did apologize to Ms. Stronglen about the mix-up. But I'm glad we got it sorted now," he said, brushing off my comment. "Please, sit," he said, taking a seat opposite them.

I looked around the conference room. It was floor to ceiling windows on three walls, giving stunning views of the city around us. If it had been any other office, I might have been impressed. But I knew how Charisma had the type of money it did to be able to afford such accommodations. And that left me somewhere between angry and disgusted.

"So, I understand you've come here to negotiate the release of Ms. Stronglen's catalog, correct?" Payne asked, crossing his legs and leaning back in his chair.

"That's correct," I said with reservation in my voice. The man in front of me was catching me off guard. He was nothing like I expected and even less like what the rumors made him out to be. I walked into this meeting prepared to deal with someone who was cold, heartless, callous. Instead, I found a man that while calculating, seemed friendly and likable. How could so many people get it so wrong, I wondered.

Unless they hadn't gotten it wrong. Unless Payne was putting on an act to throw me off my game. Considering everything I'd heard about the man, I thought the latter was more likely. Which was fine, I had prepared for all contingencies.

"Well, I don't think we'll need to have too much discussion about that," Payne began. I leaned forward in my seat, ready to pull the thumb drive out of my pocket with Sophie's video out to show the man just what he was dealing with. "Because I've already decided to release the catalog back to Sophie."

Sophie and I looked at one another, both of our masks breaking upon hearing Payne's announcement.

"We can draft up the contract with some sort of nominal consideration. What was it you paid for her concert rights? A hundred dollars? We could do something like that."

I wracked my brain, trying to find some reason why Payne would agree to do this. But I was coming up empty. In all the scenarios I played out over the last weeks, I hadn't prepared for one where Payne willingly turned the rights over, for damn near nothing, without even a fight.

"Oh, but of course I'd have to ask you both to sign a confidentiality agreement," Payne said nonchalantly.

My eyebrow raised and I finally began to put the pieces together. "So, I'm guessing you're more than aware of the meetings we've had recently."

"Yes," Payne said, fixing me with an interesting stare, almost as if he was trying to size me up. "It became pretty apparent pretty quickly that you were not going to go away and the longer you hung around, the more problems you were likely to cause for me. I've already lost two employees and an artist as a result of your actions." His tone wasn't threatening, but the words were. "I need to stem the bleeding, as the saying goes."

I looked at Sophie, who nodded. "We're agreeable to signing a confidentiality agreement. I have no doubt you'd want your lawyers to do the drafting, but we may have some comments to the final version."

"I'm agreeable to that."

"Can you have your receptionist type up a memorandum of today's meeting we can all sign now, to at least memorialize our intentions?" I asked. You didn't get to where I was, as young as I was, without learning a thing or two. I'd had too many parties deny agreeing to terms after everything had been hashed out in person. Getting something in writing quickly was always a safe bet.

"Of course," Payne said, reaching over to the office phone and dialing a three-digit code. "Bridgett, could you pull together a memorandum of understanding quickly? . . . We'll go ahead and fill in the specifics, thank you dear."

Payne hung up the phone and nodded back to me.

"I'd like to know," I said carefully, "how you found out about our intentions."

A sly smile lifted the corner of Payne's mouth. "We both have private investigators, Mr. Driscoll. It just so happens that I have more than one."

That definitely wasn't something I liked hearing. The idea that someone had a leg up on Gus was a scary thought. "Why do what you do? What's your motivation?" It wasn't important for me to know for the deal, but I did genuinely want to understand this man for some reason.

Payne smiled. "Haven't you ever wanted to do something just for the thrill of it, Mr. Driscoll? Build a brand, add to your image? I find fascination in the new. I find that it keeps my mind from . . . wandering," he said, choosing his words carefully.

"I can't say that I know what you mean, Mr. Payne," I responded in a flat tone.

"Oh, I don't think that's so true," Payne said, tapping his fingers against the armrest of his chair. "I don't buy buildings from just anyone, Mr. Driscoll. If I didn't think you had the same drive, the same motivation, then I'd never have agreed to do business with you."

The idea that I shared something in common with this man was unsettling.

We sat silently, staring one another down until the receptionist broke the tension with a knock to the door. She bustled in and handed the mostly blank page to her boss, who nodded his thanks. Payne leaned forward and turned the document over to me. "I'll let you do the honors," he said as I took the document.

There were a few numbered blanks and I grabbed a pen and began outlining our agreement.

1. Charisma Records, LLC ("Charisma") agrees to sell and MMS, LLC agrees to buy all 'Sophie Strong' songs owned by Charisma or an affiliated entity for the total price of $100, cash in hand paid.

2. As further consideration for the purchase, the parties agree to execute a confidentiality agreement.

3. Both the Purchase and Sale Agreement and Confidentiality Agreement shall be memorialized in separate agreements, which both parties agree to work in good faith to draft and execute promptly, but in no event later than one week from today.

I looked over my writing and nodded, handing it back to Payne after getting Sophie's nod of approval. I watched as Payne's eyes darted from one side of the page to the other and could sense Sophie's nerves increasing as she waited for him to sign the paper.

While this was not the final settlement agreement, Payne signing this document signified an end to a period of her life that, undoubtedly made her stronger, but she would nonetheless like to put behind her.

"Looks fine," Payne said, scribbling his name on the page before handing it back to me who signed it along with Sophie.

"Bridgett," Payne said, turning to the older receptionist who had stayed in the room near the door. "Would you be a dear and make a copy of this?"

"Of course," she said, taking the page from Payne's hand and exiting the space quickly. Within a couple seconds, she was back with a copy in her hand. "Thank you, Bridgett. That will be all."

She smiled and left the room, closing us inside again. Payne reached forward, handing me the original. I looked it over one last time to ensure it was the same document we had all signed before folding it and tucking it into my suit pocket.

"We'll get you the final versions of the agreements in a day or so," Payne said, standing up and buttoning his suit jacket.

Sophie and I stood as well.

"It's been a pleasure doing business with you, Mr. Driscoll," Payne said, reaching an outstretched hand. I shook it, not breaking eye contact.

"Lay a hand on my woman again and I promise you, I'll drag your reputation through the deepest filth, even if I have to destroy my own to do it," I threatened in a low voice.

Payne's eyes locked with mine. "I don't doubt that, Mr. Driscoll. Not to worry. I stand by my word." I released my grip and he turned to Sophie.

"Ms. Stronglen, it's been an absolute pleasure. I wish you all the best in your future endeavors."

Sophie shook his hand lightly and nodded curtly, opting not to say anything.

Bridgett appeared to escort us back to the lobby and to the first floor where the driver from this morning was waiting for us.

Payne

I WATCHED the receptionist lead the pair out of my office and as soon as the door closed I sank back into my chair. I hated losing a good thing and Sophie Strong was a good thing. It was a shame that people had fucked things up so royally where she was concerned. Even still, in some ways, I felt like I owed it to the girl to give her her life back.

I knew I could have drawn the entire thing out. Make them lay all their cards on the table. I also knew Driscoll was willing to pay serious money to get those rights back. But I didn't need the man's money. Plus, a long drawn out negotiation would have only hindered my chances at securing that confidentiality agreement, which was crucial.

I had wondered if Sophie would go for my original offer. I seriously hoped she would. Because the alternative was me giving up on her completely. Her coming back to Charisma willingly was essential to be able to ensure my and the company's reputation wasn't further damaged. Driscoll's resourcefulness put me at risk.

No, violence or accompanying threats would not solve this particular problem. I hated giving in, but in the list of my priorities, my image won out and the only way to ensure it wouldn't be tarnished from this mess was to give them what they wanted. I had had my own reconnaissance done on Connor and it was clear that the man had information that, if he decided to go public, would damage me irreparably.

Plus, as much as Driscoll clearly hated me, for which I could understand, I respected him, a lot. What I'd said about doing business with him wasn't a lie. Driscoll might never admit it given our newly formed history, but buying the development I did had helped put him on the map. I liked the man and his work ethic. I wanted to support people like himself. People who had come from nothing to build something better for themselves.

I ran a thick hand through my hair and considered the phone sitting next to me. Thoughts of the little brat Aubrey crossed my mind. My dealings with her were far from over. Her antics had cost me money and I always got even. A small smile tugged at the corner of my lips. Teaching her a lesson would be—enjoyable—but that could wait. I pressed my fingers to the phone, dialing a three-digit extension.

"Yes?" Rebecca's voice responded on the other end.

"Come upstairs," I said simply before hanging up the call. This afternoon had been tiresome and I needed a release to wipe it from my mind.

SOPHIE COLLAPSED AS SOON as she and I crossed the threshold of the hotel room. "Sophie!" I exclaimed as I caught her in my arms.

"I'm fine," she said. "I think my nerves finally caught up with me is all," she said with a small smile.

I picked her up and gently laid her on the bed. I pulled her close to me, wrapping my strong arms around her as tears began to stream down her cheeks. "It's alright," I said softly, holding her. "Everything's okay now."

Sophie allowed herself to shed a few tears as I held her against my form. "I can't believe you did it," she managed to say after a few moments.

"What are you talking about, Sophie? Whatever you said to him before I got there clearly laid the groundwork. My mind was already completely made up by the time I got involved. I don't know what you did, but it worked. You're incredible, baby."

"Don't be silly," Sophie said, wiping the tears away from her eyes.

"I'm not," I said, tilting her chin so she was looking up at me. "Not many women could handle being kidnapped and come out winning on the other side, Sophie. You don't give yourself enough credit."

"Yeah, well, I guess I learned from the best, then," she said as she curled into my body.

I chuckled. "I've never been kidnapped, so I'm not sure I should be getting any credit."

Sophie shook her head. "Your strength got me through, Con. Through this entire thing. Without you, I . . ." The words died on her lips.

"I love you, Sophie," I said simply in response. I moved slightly and pulled a small velvet box from my pocket before holding it in front of her. "I know we had a deal, Sophie. But, I hope you know you can still say no." I opened the box to reveal a beautiful emerald set around a halo of small diamonds on a golden band. "But, I hope you don't."

Sophie's breath hitched as she saw the ring. I was not a nervous man. Few things made me anxious anymore. But as I stood there, waiting for her response, I'd never felt so nervous in my life.

"I could never say no to you, Con. Especially not now," she said.

Waves of relief, happiness and love crashed through me at her words. Years of being apart from her, years of pining after her, all of it vanished.

I smiled and lifted the ring from its setting before slipping it over her finger. She held it up to look at it and I brought her hand back to kiss it. "You make me a better man, Sophie," I said, pressing a kiss to her hair before tilting her chin to face me again. "And today you made me the luckiest."

FIFTY-THREE

Sophie

"SERIOUSLY, STOP DOING THAT," SKYLER WHISPERED WITH A JAB OF HER elbow. I startled and pulled my hand away from the wedding band I was spinning around my finger.

"Bad habit," I replied sheepishly in a hushed voice. I tried to pay attention to the commencement speaker who was talking about chasing your dreams, but the speech had me alternating between feelings of sadness and excitement, considering the state of my own.

My marriage to Connor hadn't been announced, but a few tabloids had managed to snag some pictures of us during random errands and it was all but official that Connor and I had secretly gotten hitched according to the magazines.

And they weren't wrong. As soon as we landed back in D.C., we'd had a private ceremony at Connor's apartment. Skyler had been the only one in attendance. Of course as soon as the news broke, my mother had left several irate messages followed by one saying she wouldn't have been able to make it anyways given her cruise schedule, but that was nothing new.

As much as Connor was trying to keep me away from the media, their attention on me had an unintended consequence. Questions started buzzing about whether the sexual harassment claims could really be true if I had been in a secret relationship with my old flame all this time. Even more so, because no one had followed through with a lawsuit against me. And when it came to celebrities doing wrong, there was always a lawsuit.

The speech finished and everyone stood to applaud but I stayed seated, completely lost in thought. Payne had been true to his word and had sent over the documents to be signed by Connor and me within a day of our meeting. The lawyers made a few minor changes to justify their high cost, but no substantive edits were required and the agreement had been inked just before my graduation ceremony.

It was surreal knowing that I owned my entire persona as a pop idol now, or at least what was left of it. I also knew that I couldn't have done it without Connor's help. I still didn't know what I did to deserve him in my life, but he was insistent that I did.

The long wait to hand out certificates began and I leaned over and placed my head on my friend's shoulder as they waited for our turn. "What are you going to do after this, Sky?" I asked. The last few weeks had been such a whirlwind. Except for the one day Skyler managed to steal me away for vegan fare and sunsets, I hadn't been able to spend much time with my friend.

"Not sure yet," Skyler admitted. "But when I figure that out, you'll be the first to know."

"I could use a marketing coordinator for the new label," I said. Over the last couple of weeks, Connor and I had been in touch with Tara and Kevin. It turned out that Kevin being terminated from Charisma was just about the best thing to happen to him because not only did it terminate all of the company's rights over his material, but it left him free to pursue a different label or even his own without any waiting period.

Finding myself as an equally free agent, the four of us had begun talks about starting a new label ourselves under a different model for artists. We were still working out the kinks, but I thought the idea had a lot of potential and could really help ensure emerging artists weren't taken advantage of.

"I appreciate the offer," Skyler said. "Let me think about it and I'll get back to you. I'm not usually a 'work with friends' type person."

"Maybe that's why you've never found your dream job," I said in a teasing voice. "Follow your dreams, Skyler!" I said, repeating the words of the commencement address.

"Dreams are bullshit," Skyler said with a laugh. "Take it from the girl whose dreams decided to punch her in the mouth."

"Maybe those were the wrong dreams," I said with a yawn. "This coming from a girl whose dreams pretty much kicked her in the teeth."

Skyler laughed. "You and I should probably take some self-defense classes then."

"Hm, I think I'm done taking classes for a while," I replied, sitting up straight and stretching. "Oh look, this is us!" I said as the entire row stood to be shuffled to the front of the auditorium to collect our diplomas.

"Please take me away from this place," I said as I ran towards Connor and wrapped my arms around his neck.

He laughed as he picked me up gently to kiss me before placing my feet back on the floor. "It was important for you to go to your graduation, Soph. Especially since the school said that they were increasing security to prevent any paparazzi just for you."

"They shouldn't have. It would have been the best revenge to make those photographers sit and watch people get handed slips of paper for over two hours."

Connor chuckled. "Always so quick-witted, Mrs. Driscoll."

"Mr. Driscoll," I said with a smile as I thread my arm through his. "Take me home, please? I've got a song brewing in my mind that I really want to write down."

"Oh yeah?" Connor asked as he led me towards where he was parked. "What about?"

"Dreams that end up punching you in the face."

Connor raised an eyebrow in amusement.

"And the heroes that catch you when you fall," I added.

"Sounds like the next billboard topper to me," he said with a genuine smile.

"Yeah," I said, looking at Connor as we reached the car. His blue eyes turned to catch my emerald ones and I smiled. "I love you, Con."

Connor pressed a kiss to my red hair before wrapping his arms around me. His whisper was soft and loving against my skin. "I love you too."

The End

Want even more Untamed Romance? Stay in the loop!

Subscribe to the Newsletter:
https://ivywildromance.com/#subscribenew

Join my Reading Group
https://geni.us/ivywildreaders

Stalk me on:
Tiktok: tiktok.com/@ivywildauthor
Facebook: facebook.com/ivywildromance
Instagram: instagram.com/ivywildauthor
Twitter: twitter.com/ivywildauthor

Books by IVY WILD

The Kings of Capital

The Estate

A billionaire romance

Infamous

A second-chance romance

Brightly Burning Bridges

An enemies-to-lovers bully romance

Beautiful Surrender

An enemies-to-lovers BDSM romance

Standalone

My Fiancé's Bodyguard

A forbidden, mafia romance

Novella

In Bed with the Enemy

A steamy, enemies-to-lovers romance

You are beautiful

Printed in Poland
by Amazon Fulfillment
Poland Sp. z o.o., Wrocław

11711569R00239